# The Blind Man &
# the Beauty

## and Other Stories

# Arturo Loria

# The Blind Man &
# the Beauty
## and Other Stories

## Translated by David Tabbat

The Sheep Meadow Press
Riverdale-on-Hudson, New York

All inquiries and permission requests should be addressed to:

> The Sheep Meadow Press
> 5247 Independence Avenue
> Riverdale-on-Hudson, New York 10471

Distributed by the University Press of New England.
Cover: Honoré Daumier, *Parade de Saltimbanques.*
Designed and typeset by SM.

Printed on acid-free paper in the United States. This book meets
the guidelines for permanence and durability of the Committee
on Production Guidelines for Book Longevity of the Council on
Library Resources.


Library of Congress Cataloging-in-Publication Data

Loria, Arturo.
  [Selections. English. 2004]
  The blind man and the beauty and other stories / by Arturo
Loria.
      p. cm.
  ISBN 1-931357-10-2 (alk. paper)
  1.  Loria, Arturo--Translations into English.  I. Title.
PQ4827.O745 A25 2004
853'.914--dc22
                                                    2003026775


*We are grateful to the New York State Council on the Arts, a state agency,
for thier support.*

# Contents

# Acknowledgements

The publisher is especially grateful to Tobia Milla Moss, the Roman, for introducing him to the work of Arturo Loria, and for his numerous suggestions and insights related to the editing and production of this book.

— SM

# Introduction: Allegories of Dislocation

A sense of dislocation from identifiable times and spaces fills many of Arturo Loria's stories: they take place in unnamed cities and cross landscapes dotted with untitled landmarks; they contain sparce signs of epoch or era, though they clearly span several centuries; they are populated with figures called simply "the waiter," "the knife-grinder," "the blind man," "the beauty." But despite such refusals of name and place and date, Loria nevertheless locates his shopkeepers and corpse bearers, his traveling performers and aging coquettes, his jealous goats and captive hawks quite firmly. Whether in attitudes of isolation or self-delusion, traps of ruinous desire or defeated ambition, the significant locations in Loria's fictional world are emotional. As physical boundaries and external markers prove insubstantial in these stories, seemingly useless as bearers of meaning, psychic ones become vivid, impermeable, defining.

Loria composed most of the stories included in this collection between 1928 and 1932 ("The Goat" is a later piece, written in 1952), and in the context of the post-World-War-I era, during Mussolini's ascent and the consolidation of fascist power, the apparent distance between the world of Loria's fiction and the world of its composition is, at first, somewhat startling. With echoes of Boccaccio and Cervantes, Kafka, Poe, and Hawthorne, Loria's stories emerge from a deep literary past, revealing a diverse world, detached from political upheaval and marks of the modern. But it is precisely in the seeming archaism of Loria's stories that their timeliness becomes clear. Given the obsessive attachment of fascist culture to technological modernity, Loria's adherence to older aesthetic modes, his excavation of unspecified pasts, and his insistent portrayal of a multiethnic world largely unmarked by national boundaries become forms of refusal.[1] In the context of the fascist cults of youth, strength, and vigorous masculinity, Loria writes of aging men, filled with shame and fear, isolated from their families, outcast from their communities. As policing ethnic and religious boundaries becomes the obsession of the political culture, Loria writes of the artificiality and arbitrariness of such boundaries. Throughout these fictional studies in shame, self-loathing, and fear turned outward, Loria reverses the obsessions of fascist Italy's dominant culture and ultimately offers glimpses of its deepest pathologies.

Born in 1902 to a large, half-Catholic, half-Jewish family, Loria's understanding of the problem of boundaries and classifications was nuanced and personal. Loria was baptized twice into the Catholic church. In 1939, the year following the passage of Mussolini's exclusionary racial laws, he was confirmed in Pisa, after which he learned for the first time that he had also been baptized as an infant. Living in two faiths simultaneously, Loria writes of his religion as something that resists the categories demanded by others:

> I think if someone were suddenly to ask me the question, "What religion do you profess?" I would not know how to reply, whether out of love for the truth, or from a crafty calculation as how best to please the person who asked.... So I would have to answer, "I have the religion of believing that some day I will have (and die in) one" — a response not foreseen in any questionnaire with little spaces to be filled in. If I were rich, I would place a faceless herm in my garden and inscribe upon it my faith in the "Unknown God."[2]

For Loria, no question of religion can be asked with neutrality and no response given with honesty, since the question both presupposes and overdetermines any reply. And indeed, despite Loria's temptation to profess the "Unknown God," many of his critics (perhaps following the example of the state) seemed insistent on reading his work for evidence of "the Semitic mark."[3] Amid the critical acclaim that met his first three collections of stories, his reviewers remained preoccupied with locating in his writing what Luigi Baldacci strangely describes as the "permanent patina of dust that the caravan has brought along with it."[4] Both acclaimed and exoticized, Loria's stories rarely invoke anti-Semitism overtly, but in their detailed anatomies of the anxieties of individual and collective identity, of exotic fascination and xenophobic scapegoating, of isolation and the dissolution of social institutions, they can be seen forming a lyrical and sharply drawn response to its deep roots and long history.

Loria's fiction first appeared in 1926 in the journal *Solaria*, edited by Alberto Carocci, and for the next few years, he was affiliated with the influential group of Florentine writers and artists – including Eugenio Montale and Marino Marini – who converged around the magazine. His early stories were widely praised, and *Solaria* published his first short story collection in 1928. Four years later, with three collections published, Loria won the Premio Fracchia awarded by *L'Italia letteraria*. Loria was well-reviewed by Italy's leading writers; he could count Italo Svevo and Emilio Cecchi, as well as Montale, among his admirers. Fatefully, there is also a photo of Loria at table with Roberto Longhi, paragon of Italian prose, stylistic beauty, and complexity. Nevertheless, Loria seemed to end his literary career as swiftly and decisively as he began it; his last collection, *La scuola di ballo*, came out in 1932, after which he published only sporadically. Whether Loria's failure to continue his earlier successes is attributable to the increasingly dangerous position of being both well-known and Jewish in Italy, to the war itself, to the tremendous personal losses he endured throughout the 1940s, or to all of these things, the startling brevity of Loria's career remains a particularly vexing problem in his peculiar biography.

The affinity that Loria expresses in his early stories for itinerant, isolated, and marginalized characters suggests much about his own rather solitary life and habits. Partially disabled by a case of polio in his infancy, Loria walked with a limp all his life. He fell in love with a Polish painter named Polia in France in 1929, and the two of them lived and traveled together until her untimely death four years later. Loria never married after Polia's death, remaining for the rest of his life with his family, in a separate apartment in their large villa outside of Florence. In 1933, Montale wrote of Loria's seeming distance and isolation, even in the midst of his circle of friends and colleagues:

> Once lunch is over, he gets into his Hispano Suiza and sets off for some unknown destination. Here we have the only mysterious side of his life. When I meet Arturo at the house of common friends, I am not re-assured that I know the "rest" of him, the part that remains in the shadows and is denied me.
>
> And when you get right down to it: where does Loria find the betrayed hearts, the furious husbands, the lovers, the madmen, the rascals, the beggars, the café owners, the pimps for his novellas? And around him, where does he find the faithful people who "know how to listen to him"? In his heart, there is a constant need to let himself go, a hankering after goodness, a vein of generous optimism that needs to gush forth, to break down every barrier. I look around me and all I see are people worried about the European

> crisis, job seniority, and bimetallism.
>
> Well then, who sees Loria? Who listens to him when he speaks?… In a word, Loria, in love with life, is condemned, like all true artists, to live only in function of his art.[5]

Taking the perspectives of outcasts and wanderers, Loria's stories privilege the solitary figure, whose isolation comes into relief against corrupted and crumbling social structures. In "The Blind Man and the Beauty," his itinerant characters evoke the picaresque tradition of Cervantes, as they initially move haplessly through a series of farcical episodes only to die in a startling eruption of gruesome violence. The one story in the collection that is clearly set in a specific place – "The Blind Man and the Beauty" literally opens with a sign-post, marking the spot between Carpi and Mantua where the eponymous characters were burned alive for murders they did not commit – it is also the story of a collective crime. The two aging performers are invited to portray a king and queen who disguise themselves as beggars in a play staged by a traveling theater troupe, and their exuberant performance makes them the favorites of the crowd. But the lines between fantasy, fiction, and reality quickly dissolve as a murder, first staged within the play, is committed by one of the players at the end of the story. With the discovery of the crime, it is the blind man and the Beauty – first outcast, then applauded, then scapegoated – on whom the town directs its vengeance in a bloody outburst of irrational violence. Rather than expiating this crime, the inscribed cross that stands at the opening of the story serves as a reminder of the town's collective madness and culpability, a sign which might also be read as a warning addressed to Loria's own nation.

The shifting lines between fascination, desire, and hate structure and poison relationships throughout Loria's fiction, and in two stories, he focuses in particular on the complex desire to cross racial and ethnic boundaries in search of an "exotic" experience that converts all too easily into disavowal and aggression. In "The Sirens," the thwarted longings of two women emerge in a merciless sketch of their self-delusion and mutual parasitism, as they seek what they imagine as a scandalous thrill in an evening at the "Negro Dance Hall." The sketch opens with one of the women standing naked before a mirror as she towels herself off after a bath, but rather than a moment of self-examination, the scene exposes the woman's elaborate efforts to *not* see her reflection – to catch only fleeting glances of her body in disconnected parts, so that she can remain blind to her aging face, her veined feet, her sagging skin. Edmea's strained refusal to see in the opening scene becomes emblematic of the life that emerges in the rest of the story, as she and her companion pursue a desperate charade of pleasure and sociability. The women move from a showy dinner at a restaurant they cannot afford to the dance hall in order to "try everything in the world," as Edmea says. But the desire for "exotic" experience that leads them to the "Negro Dance Hall" ultimately reveals nothing to them of the people they gaze upon as curiosities, instead exposing only a hollowness in the women themselves, an empty terror at the sense of their own defeated lives.

In "The Arabian Café," Loria offers an even more sustained examination of a peculiarly European fascination with spectacles of other races, of the sexualization of difference, and of the paranoia that often lies beneath such obsessions. The protagonist is the owner of a failing café, who fetishistically replicates Arab food and styles of dress and covers his walls with pictures of mosques, faux colonnades, and arabesques, but who thinks nothing of treating a Chinese merchant with suspicion and abuse. "[B]elatedly enamored of a style that had gone out of fashion," the owner prepares to close his café with a large party for his customers – a masquerade ball for which they must dress as "Arabs," in aging costumes purchased at the Colonial Exposition decades earlier. Once in costume, the guests begin to regard themselves as exotic objects, taking pleasure in the distance they feel from their identities, at the same time clinging to reminders of their modern Western selves like their watches and eyeglasses. Utterly taken by the masquerade he has orchestrated, the owner cries, "I have always dreamed of being an Arab!" As he indulges in this manufactured distance from his everyday persona, the owner tries to seduce a young woman dressed as an odalisque. But he finds a rival for the woman's attention in a guest described only as the "meticcio" (which David Tabbat translates as "half-breed," preserving the term's harsh, dehumanizing connotations). Alternating between the point of view of the owner and that of the woman, Loria shows how these characters' engagement in racial masquerade does nothing to dispel their misperceptions of the "meticcio," and indeed only deepens their need to reject him. The story ultimately reveals the fragility of the categories of identity and difference to which these characters cling, even in their disguises. In his costume, the owner permits himself to feel the sexuality that he wishes to impute to the "meticcio," while under the gaze of her non-European suitor, the girl ceases "to feel herself the white woman" as she begins to realize a desire she has precluded.

The blurring of masquerade and identity, fantasy and realism accompanies the loss of other defining boundaries in Loria's fiction: between the living and the dead, self and other, desire and repulsion. In "The Rendez-vous" — a fable that emerges from a distant but unspecified past, one that feels as close to Boccaccio as to Poe — a solitary woman cast aside by her family forms a tenuous society with the dead. Dreaming nightly of deceased relatives and old suitors, her brother's amputated leg, and murdered puppies, Teresa abandons her waking life and lives solely for her nightly rendez-vous with "her own thoughts and desires" made visible. In "The Anatomy Lesson," a corpse-bearer in a plague-ridden city eavesdrops on a dissection to "learn how a dead man is made," but he realizes instead that the only difference between himself and the dismembered thing on the anatomist's table is the two *scudi* he holds in his pocket for his own burial.

Cut loose from the categories that might offer easy, if insufficient, definition to their lives, Loria's characters instead become identified with the subtle and complex states of feeling in which they are trapped. The most revealing moments in Loria's fiction are often the briefest and quietest: decisive acts of thought or will which are completed in an instant, but which require complicated prose to unravel. Reviewers of Loria's work have frequently remarked upon the difficulty of his language and syntax, but it is precisely through this densely packed prose that such moments can appear. In "The Wig," two sisters working in their father's shop assist a woman who has come to purchase a wig to cover her balding, disease-ravaged head. She shows them a photograph of herself as a young women. Seeing how beautiful the woman once was, the younger sister begins to feel, incongruously, both pity and envy, and on a sudden impulse, she steals the photograph:

> Having taken it, she felt troubled. The customer's demeanor — at once mincing, imploring, and capable of articulating a carnal horror at her own renunciation of fleshly pleasures — had led the younger sister to such an intimate and sad consideration of her own dilemma, that it inspired rancor towards the other woman, and a desire to find in the image some reason to humiliate her irreparably.

Capturing each woman's view of the other in a single sentence, Loria shows how the younger woman's pity for the older woman produces pity for herself, which in turn forces the younger one to confront her own halfhearted "renunciation of fleshly pleasures," making her rancorous and vindictive. In David Tabbat's sensitive translations, Loria's rich prose offers revelatory glimpses of the need, regret, and indecision in which these characters find themselves buried.

The stories in this collection represent the work for which Loria received the greatest acclaim. During the years of the war, Loria published sporadically and frequently under pseudonyms, while he worked on the manuscript of a novel, *Le memorie inutili*, which was destroyed during the bombings of Florence. The loss of this manuscript was devastating for Loria, "ten years of silent and quite assiduous work,"[6] which he regarded as his "true work as a writer of fiction." But even as his fiction writing tapered off after the loss of his unfinished novel, Loria became a prominent scholar, editor, translator, and lecturer. Throughout the late 1940s and 1950s, Loria translated essays by Bernard Berenson, edited the magazine *Il Mondo*, wrote two plays, and lectured extensively on the European and American authors whose influences are so evident in his early work. Loria's final writings – a book of short, parodic fables, *Sentanta favole*, published after his death in 1957 – exhibit the wry humor of his earlier animal tales like "The Hawk" and "The Goat."

In a memorial piece reflecting on Loria's career, Montale writes: "His material was so rich that we might almost say that he barely touched it. Nonetheless, he did so with a master hand, in an unforgettable fashion." In this first English edition of Loria's fiction, such light and masterful touches form vivid and sharply drawn sketches that are both very much of their time and unleashed from it.

Jennifer Greiman

Notes

1 For accounts of fascist popular culture, see: Barbara Spackman, *Fascist Virility: Rhetoric, Ideology, and Social Fantasy in Italy* (Minneapolis: University of Minnesota Press, 1999); *Fascism, Aesthetics, and Culture*, ed. Richard Golson (Hanover, NH: University Presses of New England, 1992); Jeffrey Schnapp, "Introduction: The Fascist Century," *A Primer of Italian Fascism*, ed. Jeffrey Schnapp; tr. Jeffrey Schnapp, Olivia Sears, and Maria Stampino (Lincoln, NE: Univeristy of Nebraska Press, 2000), vii–xvi; *Qui Parle: Special Issue on Fascism, Gender and Culture* 13.1 (Fall/Winter, 2001).
2 Quoted in Ernestina Pellegrini, *La riserva ebraica: Il mondo fantastico di Arturo Loria* (Reggio Emilia, 1998). All cited quotations translated by David Tabbat.
3 Quoted in: Nicoletta Mainardi, *Il caso Loria: Storia e antologica della critica* (Florence 1998), 130, 196–7.
4 *Ibid.* 130.
5. *Ibid.* 44.
6 Marco Marchi, ed., with S. Loria and L. Meliosi, *Arturo Loria: mostra di documenti* (Carpi, 1992).

From left: Peter Riccio, Arturo Loria, Eugenio Montale, Armenio Jauner, and Alessandro Bousanti, at the Piazza della Republica in Firenze.

Loria (center), with Roberto Longhi (left) and Bernard Berenson (seated).

# Translator's Note

Even the most enthusiastic comments on Arturo Loria's fiction often contain an admixture of frustration with the complexities of his prose style. In a generally favorable review of *La scuola di ballo* in 1932, for example, Eugenio Colorni observed:

> The sentences that emerge from his pen are sometimes needlessly contorted and incomprehensible, or so deliberately dense with recherché ideas as to fall into the grotesque.[1]

It should be said that time has not simplified the complexities of Loria's prose. Writing in 1993, the critic Luigi Baldacci commented – not necessarily in a pejorative sense – on the "inadmissible" elements in the author's syntax and noted "the manneristic bizarreness of his choices":

> We shall limit ourselves to saying that this language of his belongs to his system of defense. Defense against what? Against everything…. It remains to be said that Loria writes this way only exceptionally, but that these exceptions are nonetheless a sign of his discomfort, of his unnaturalness, of his rejection of reality: things which can also take on a positive value in connoting the writer's qualities. Apart from his syntactical puzzles and forced grammar, but in keeping with this aspect, an entire discussion would need to be devoted to his vocabulary which, especially at the beginning, is full of… new coinages [and] obsolete forms.[2]

If, as many important Italian literary figures tell us, Loria's prose style can be difficult and obscure, we may be sure that it is so, and yet, these same writers all insist upon the extremely high quality of his stories. The fact is that, despite Piero Gadda Conti's expressed wish that Loria might write differently, the stories convince and compel in the language in which they are actually written.[3] If this is opacity, it is opacity of a strange kind, for it glows with an intense inner fire, and it creates effects of great vividness.

In these translations, there are passages where readers will have the opportunity to encounter some of the linguistic strangeness and difficulty of Loria's writing: the opening pages of "The Arabian Café" and "The Dance School," for instance, or the description of the sky near the beginning of "The Blind Man and the Beauty." But Italian and English are very different languages as regards their syntactical possibilities. English offers few of those grammatical signposts — agreement of noun and adjective by gender and number, agreement of verb-ending with subject — which just barely enable the perilously perched reader of the original to make his or her way across the dangerous syntactical high-wire of Loria's more complex constructions without falling into the abyss. So, as a matter of practical necessity, in the present translation some of Loria's sentences have been divided in two, and other, analogous choices have also made in the interests of readability.

David Tabbat

Notes

1 Quoted in: Nicoletta Mainardi, *Il caso Loria: Storia e antologica della critica* (Florence 1998), 201.
2 Luigi Baldacci, "I racconti di Loria" in Rita Guerricchio, ed., *Atti Vieusseux 4: L'opera di Arturo Loria*, Florence, 1993, pp. 13-26. (See esp. pp. 22-23.)
3 Quoted in Mainardi, 206.

# The Anatomy Lesson

The new corpse-bearer was waiting, with a curious air, for someone to come along and show him where the devil they kept the bodies hidden in the hospital.

Freshly arrived from the countryside, having let himself out for hire – like his female companion – in the city, he had easily found employment: since people feared the spread of the plague that had broken out in nearby regions, they were constantly hiring men who were willing to undertake any kind of work requested.

He had passed the first day removing beds, mattresses, and blankets from a convent. On the second day, he had turned up at the hospital; and, having received an order without asking for explanations, he stood there on the threshold of the anatomy theater, on the lookout for someone who might be able to put him on the right path.

This work had ceased to be entertaining.

An elderly attendant went by wearing slippers and a skull-cap; he seemed like a walking, constant hawking-up of catarrh. Through the open door, he glanced into the amphitheater.

"Friend, where's the dead body?"

"How should I know? They haven't told me."

"Come along with me, then; it's getting late. If Gregorius shows up in the hall and doesn't find it, we'll be in a pickle!"

They hurriedly descended into a damp, cold basement.

"Here it is," said the old man, opening a door.

Inside, on the marble surfaces of some wash-tubs,

were five cadavers wrapped in shrouds. The air was unbreathable: dry, eaten away by the sharpness of the quick-lime that filled the tubs.

"Gregorius will want the freshest of them. Which one might it be?"

The attendant uncovered the corpses one after another, judging them with an expert eye.

"But whose bodies are these?" asked the corpse-bearer, who had grown very pale.

"Those of the people who can't afford to pay to buy them back. The hospital was out of pocket for these folks, and now they're paying their debt by leaving it their bodies."

"I don't know what the world's coming to," murmured the newcomer.

"Don't worry your head about it! This one seems the best to me. Let's carry him up into the theater. You grab hold of his head. Lift it up.... If it revolts you, keep the whole sheet for yourself."

They left the room with their burden. Where they clasped it, it grew warm, and their own hands felt ice-cold.

In order to close the door, the old man let go of the legs of the corpse, which fell down in parallel, banging the feet on the ground, hard and sonorous like two pieces of metal.

They didn't go back up by the same staircase they had descended, but used another, which was set off in isolation. The newcomer asked why.

"Come on. Do you think we can let those sick people up there see the way that they're going to end up?"

The bearer remained silent; he was convinced.

Having entered the amphitheater through a secret doorway, they placed the cadaver on the large marble table, after having rid it of certain remains that the old man tossed into a basket.

"Remember," he said. "Nothing that's in here must

ever go out, otherwise you'll be in big trouble with the hospital Capuchins. Even if it's in pieces, they want the corpse to be whole."

"I don't know what the world is coming to," repeated the bearer.

"I'm off," said the other. "I've got to be present at an amputation. It's up to you to serve in here."

Once alone, the novice cast his eye on the flat, mean body, not recognizing in it any sign of a man he had already seen: the razor had already done away with its face. Then he had the feeling that the light in the room was too bright for this dead man without a tomb; treading cautiously, he went over to a window, meaning to draw the curtain.

He was brought to a halt by a tramping of feet in the corridor.

The students came in. They were enclosed in black gowns and grave in manner despite their youthful little beards, which were better known in places of amusement than in the Faculty of Medicine.

They arranged themselves along the benches of the amphitheater; and Gregorius, having suddenly emerged from a neighboring room, climbed into his professorial chair.

"Now that the civilization of our times and the wisdom of our rulers allow us to conduct a type of research that was forbidden in other periods, we can follow in the glorious footsteps of Vesalius and study man as...."

The bearer looked at the table, where the light from a window now beat down; he was horrified that the sun played even over cadavers.

"When our science shall have reached its highest point, it will explain to us the true causes of death...."

At this point, he really wanted to listen; but the preview of the anatomical work to be done in the interests of such research struck him as a fantastic catalogue of insults to be inflicted upon the body of a martyr, in revenge for the impossibility of obtaining from him any sooner a truth of which traces remained in the colors of his guts, and in the cuts to be made in his brain and heart: organs that Gregorius talked of opening and studying.

My God! They were starting!

They were all climbing down to gather around the marble slab!

The teacher opened a cloth bag, extracted from it some very sharp iron instruments, and began to flay a forearm, starting from the wrist. He turned the two flaps of skin inside out. Amidst the flesh, there appeared the tendons, taut at the joint.

"As you can see, gentlemen.... As you can see," and he added to this expression a summary of what he had already explained to his listeners, who were now more interested and willingly involved.

Pulling on the tendons, he showed how the fingers moved, while two students repeated, with a slight delay, the rigid movements of the dead hand; they were awkward, inhibited, almost as if unable to command their own movements equally well.

The corpse-bearer shut his eyes, so as not to see the horrible mockery, and thought about informing the priests, the bishop, even the Pope should it prove necessary, of this massacre of the dead.

Gregorius cut into the neck of the cadaver and forcibly detached it from the body, assisted by a smiling youth with a blond beard.

The horrible head, detached and set down upon the marble, looked as though it were made of wax; mauled by hands and warmed by the students' breath, it grinned distortedly.

None present showed any horror: their sensibility was protected by their gowns, but the corpse-bearer, lacking such a defense, was chilled by the disgust and fear that passed over his naked skin like slime.

"The old school, gentlemen, was great; but we have got far beyond it! We study man in his cadaverous state so as to identify the cause of a disease in an anatomical change which finally becomes clear. This is the road to glory!" preached Gregorius with fervor; and the students, seized with anatomical enthusiasm, contended for possession of an organ, red among the yellowish ligaments.

When, as the result of some diabolical trick of Gregorius's, the head sitting on the marble moved its mouth and eyes, the corpse-bearer shrieked in terror.

Everyone turned around, and understood from his shaken aspect.

"You're new here, aren't you?"

"Yes, most illustrious professor, yes."

"Consider yourself fortunate, my good man, that you are permitted to see the way you are made!" Gregorius smiled at the students, who were all initiates by now, and to whom he gave permission to leave, saying affably, "See you tomorrow."

The bearer left the amphitheater filled with a new anguish, feeling painfully offended deep within his poor devil's flesh; and he touched his chest, his flanks, as if to reassure himself that the pulsing of his heart was keeping alive his rights of ownership.

"If we die, our body is no longer ours! It's no longer ours!'" he repeated in desperation. "But why do they have to torture it?"

He didn't believe that the gowned academics were studying in order to learn to heal the living; he had seen them only too happy to apply their surgical instruments to that dead man!

The sick people wandering about in a courtyard struck him as condemned: cadavers in the making, they were awaited for tomorrow's tortures. He felt tempted to tell them so and to lead them – furious rebels – into the amphitheater.

A sick man, who had paused in order to enjoy the sunshine, was chatting of the wine from his farm near the village with another patient who was looking out a window. "They're bringing me a bottle on Sunday! Just wait till you taste it!"

A third patient, dragging along a swollen leg wrapped in bandages (it looked like some beggar's fraudulent appendage), called out to him with a smile, asking him for help in reaching a stool. The bearer satisfied his request; and the man thanked him, promising him a tip on the day when they would let him out of the hospital.

No, you couldn't tell those two how the poor people who died in the hospital wound up; you couldn't tell anyone, since everybody there was living on hope.

He covered his face with his hands.

Wandering aimlessly, he ran into the elderly attendant he had encountered earlier.

"How much do the dead pay so as not to be cut to pieces?"

The man laughed.

"If someone pays two *scudi* for them, they go to the cemetery in the usual way. Why?"

"Ah!"

He swore to himself that for no necessity or temptation of life would he spend the two *scudi* that his female companion kept wrapped up in a handkerchief.

He ran home: the woman was out buying things for dinner.

He began rummaging in drawers; he threw to the ground all the rags that filled a basket and the garments neatly arranged in the closet.

At last he found the handkerchief, neatly knotted and clinking with its coins. He untied it, held the two *scudi* in the palm of his hand, and looked at them, deeply moved; then he kissed them as though they had been the images of saints or the Saviour.

The woman found him stretched out on the bed, sweating and complaining that he felt cold.

"What's wrong with you? What's the matter?"

"Nothing, nothing. It will pass."

He made up his mind to eat, but at the resistance of the spoon, bogged down in the mush of flour and beans, he turned his head away in disgust.

The woman, worried, insisted upon learning why he was so upset. Pretending that he was recounting things far removed from his own torments, he – with the air of a man who leads a full life outside the house – began to tell her what an anatomy lesson was like.

The story filled the poor woman with horror; but the corpse-bearer was enjoying himself, as his own horror gradually left him.

At the end, almost as if to hang onto a bit of horror for himself, he painted matters in dramatic hues.

"The teacher peeled a piece, showed it to those young men, and said...."

Here he wished to demonstrate that he remembered Gregorius's words, since he, too, had understood them; and because he was imitating their tone, he believed himself to be repeating them. Smiling vaguely at his own lost fears, he said: "So you see, gentlemen, this is the way a dead man is made...."

# The Rendez-vous

Struggling along on his crutch, the watchman of the villa crossed the courtyard. It was already dark, and he couldn't make out the visitor's face through the thick bars of the gate. "What do you want?" he asked before opening up.

"Is Teresa here?"

The sound of that voice, already known to him, troubled him so much that he hastily drew back.

"Yes, she's here; but who are you?" His voice trembled a bit as he asked.

"Let me in. I'm Guglielmo. Don't you remember me, Pietro?"

"Certainly. But weren't you dead?"

"Dead?" replied the other, shocked. "I was gone. Gone. Far away to seek my fortune. If I were dead, I wouldn't be here."

"So much the better for you," agreed the watchman; "but that's what they were saying around here. Come in." He opened the gate.

The outsider made as if to shake Pietro's hand, but his gesture remained suspended in the air.

"How about you?"

He observed his old acquaintance, now with one leg the less, sawn off at midpoint.

"I've been through a lot, my friend," the watchman said. He touched his stump; where a round stuffed cushion showed through the worn-out fabric, and added: "My leg has left me a widower, and I'll remain one. I don't want any wooden legs."

Not knowing what to say, Guglielmo kept up a forced

smile; and meanwhile the other studied his well preserved person, with its good clothes, its gold chain, and its showy trinkets.

"And Teresa?" he asked timidly.

"Now I'll call her for you. Teresa! Teresa!" cried the watchman, addressing himself to a window high up on the building.

Hearing no answer, he thought it opportune to warn the visitor: "She's already dreaming at this hour. She won't take it well if we wake her."

But at that very moment, Teresa's head appeared at the window.

"What is it?" she asked in a flat voice.

"There's a gentleman who wishes to speak with you."

"With me?"

Having raised his head, the visitor offered no sign of corroboration: he stared up at the window, trying to see the woman's face.

"And who are you, then?" The voice floated down like a lament.

"I'm Guglielmo. You don't mean to say that not even you recognize me, Teresa?"

The woman repeated "Guglielmo" three times, with a joy that revealed no surprise, and then vanished.

When she reached the courtyard, the two men perceived that she was in her nightshirt; but Pietro made no comment; he hurriedly absented himself, so as not to disturb the meeting of the two former lovers.

All this took place in an atmosphere of muted emotion. Teresa had stopped with her clasped hands pointed in Guglielmo's direction, not daring to come any closer; blocked by a strange emotion, she looked about her in search of Pietro, as though her brother's presence might resolve a doubt she was feeling.

Reassured, she sat down on a bench, and with a gesture invited Guglielmo to join her; embarrassed at seeing her in her nightshirt and in such a dreamy mood, the latter did not sit down and remained silent.

So she too kept silence, as though she might be allowed to speak only after he had done so.

Even though he was uncertain whether she was listening to him, he said, after at last sitting down beside her: "I know that you're miserably poor, Teresa, and that your relatives keep you here as though you were a servant. You know, I'm not rich, but I can help you a little. Will you take them, these two thousand liras?"

She did not reply, but smiled, accepting.

He placed an envelope on the bench – a grayish envelope at which Teresa stared without daring to touch it, almost as if afraid that it might vanish from one moment to the next.

"I haven't much money, you know, and I've done my duty. When you're old, your thoughts turn back to the past, and there are days when you feel like crying." He cast his moist gaze on the envelope, saying: "I've got to go. They're waiting for me at the end of the avenue with a horse." He stood up.

Teresa stood up facing him with ardent, shining eyes. "Will you come back tomorrow night, Guglielmo? Ah yes, tell me you'll be back!" But she didn't succeed in touching him, because he, ever more confused, was drawing back.

"I've done my duty by you," he repeated in order to make himself understood; and, almost running, he slipped through the gate.

The woman remained there in her posture of invocation, having become a stubby courtyard statue; and then she slowly returned to the bench. The envelope was no longer there: in standing up, she had caused it to fall beneath the bench.

She ran her hand over the stone and sighed, as if she had foreseen this disappointment; and then, swaying, she slowly made her way back into the house.

Without his crutch, crawling along the ground, Pietro emerged from the corner where he had remained hidden. He took possession of the envelope, tore up the paper, crumpled it into a ball, and tossed it over the wall; and then he pocketed the money, smiling at the window as he did so.

The next morning, his sister asked him about poor Guglielmo. He sniggered, patting his pocket, and said: "He was a good devil. They say that he died loaded with thousand-lira bills.

"Yes, I think so, too," said Teresa in a sorrowful voice. After her over-free way of life had reduced her to poverty, Teresa had been relegated by her rich relatives to the status of custodian of the country villa, a position which she shared with her brother. She had come to seem a dirty, ill-tempered old maid.

She spent but little time with that scoundrel Pietro, who had been made brutish by wine; she passed entire days on her own, in empty idleness.

After a certain hour, it was pointless to seek her in the house or to call her for any reason whatsoever. She disappeared. She went to bed early, unfailingly, at seven o'clock every evening.

She had a rendez-vous with her dreams, which were her compensation for her sad day, the outlet for the passions of the critical age she had reached. She climbed into bed, shut her eyes, and fell asleep.

Almost immediately, her dreams would seize hold of her. She would see many rooms in a row, with people chattering in each of them. She would go down a corridor onto which the doors opened; but the interiors were too dim to permit her to see who was inside.

They were calling her from the last room. She would enter, and would recognize, in the image she found there, her own thoughts and desires.

Still, this was but the antechamber of the dream itself, which – unpredictable and marvelous – would leave those walls behind.

Very often she would meet up again at night with the dream that had been interrupted the morning before, and she would follow it. Having passed through the usual antechamber, which still seemed warm, she would see herself once again in the same places; and there, once again, she would pick up the conversations, the actions, the loves, as though each day were joined to the next. Her suitor would become less timid from one night to the next, and make a lot of headway, daring to touch her breasts, seize her by the waist, fondle her.

Blushes… protests… there was no way out! Her suit-or would take his place in her room and snivel that it was base to make him suffer so. She would say to him, "Come here," lifting her blankets to let him join her beneath them, feeling herself to be, at that moment, naked and splendid, bathed in light and perfumed air… and then, suddenly, she would awaken panting in the light-filled room, overflowing with desire.

As she got dressed, the intensity of the dream would go off the boil; but during the day she would speak coarsely, pro-claiming to whoever came along the importance of enjoying oneself, praising in no uncertain terms the men of her youth. Strangely enough, however, she would blush in the middle of her speech, falling silent as though on account of some fresh-ly experienced shame.

The shame came upon her from her dreams, from her vain attempts to yield; and so she would promise herself not to act stupid once night had come, but rather to bring matters to a head herself with her new suitor, whose assaults she could already foresee: thus would she overcome the inevitability of the hour when her troubled spider webs should be broken up by daylight.

Over the years, though, her rendez-vous had ceased to be amorous. They had turned serious and seemly, as befitted her age.

Her suitors, having grown old, no longer cherished carnal ambitions; instead, they simply recollected, along with her, the good old days of their amours, reminiscing about their dead loves and their children who had grown up and taken the affairs of the world in hand.

Teresa played lotto with these weary and predictable combinations; but her evil old men were discreet. With their fingers, they signaled numbers to one another in the shadows of the salons. No matter how careful she was, she could never catch them out at it, and always played the wrong numbers.

On account of these disappointments, she kept on promising herself that she would no longer play the fool, but would ask them for the right numbers in the name of their old nocturnal friendships; but once night had come, she no longer remembered this vow of hers, since life can teach nothing to dreams.

Then there came an age at which everything that was dying around her became subject matter and characters for her dreams: relatives, the black cat, the bitch that some wicked person had killed while she was pregnant with puppies, the neighbor ladies – ill-intentioned, second-sighted chatterboxes from beyond the tomb – and even the teeth she was losing, which some friendly hand kept replanting in her mouth....

When her brother's leg became infected and they had to amputate it, it was she who delivered it, heavy and pallid, to the surgeon's male nurses so that they might place it in a certain sack.

At night, the sawn-off leg became a furnishing of her room: a disturbing piece of furniture that hung from the cords of the curtain, delivered kicks, came to stand heavily upon her belly, and grew furious when Pietro was drunk.

The lost leg was kept alive for him, in the first place, through his nervous system, which could not grow used to doing without it and which continued to transmit its orders to non-existent nerves: orders that, having reached the border of the sawn-off knee, delivered such sharp blows as to make him cry out in pain; and, even more, it was kept alive for him by the news of it he was continuously receiving from his sister.

When the leg went beyond permissible limits, Pietro was very pleased and would put on a sly, sneering grin. Then Teresa would yell at him: "You old wizard, if tonight you don't get it away from me, I'll throw it out of the window for you!"

At night, the frightened leg would behave itself, hiding inside a high boot, as if it were a sort of wooden boot-tree.

With two of the ladies who were dead, Teresa had reached a benign reconciliation in her dreams: a reconciliation that allowed her to feel herself deserving of much benevolence on the part of the proud survivors.

Matters had gone as follows.

The two dead ladies had called at the gate.

"Let us come in. Be kind to us, Teresa. Forgive us."

She had opened the gate and led the ladies through the house – which had been considerably altered after their deaths – as far as the rooms where their children were sleeping. Standing on the threshold, the ladies had not dared to come in; but Teresa, with the authority of the living, had awakened the children, who cried out in desperate joy at seeing their mothers once again.

One of the mothers, the haughtier of the two when still alive, had died while giving birth to her fourth child, a daughter.

Once the other woman had left, Teresa said, "Come with me." Holding her by the hand, she led her into a room where there was a cradle.

"Your little girl is here."

"Which little girl?"

"Oh, right! You never saw her. Here she is. Look at her... touch her now."

The dead woman had taken on the hue of life and had been filled with a warm wave of maternal feeling; she stared at Teresa with humid eyes, being unable to speak.

Since that night, the defunct ladies, festively kissing her, showed her their gratitude and revealed such humility towards her that old wrongs were forgotten.


By now, things had reached a point where she no longer exchanged so much as a few words with her brother in the course of the day.

They even took their meals at different times.

She went about her business dully, in a sort of stupor; but in every one of her slow and weary gestures, there was her longing for sleep, so full of life and adventure.

She loved the coming of evening, which set her soul ablaze with hope.

"Tonight I'll know the right numbers.... Tonight I'll have a better understanding of how that business of the inheritance went."

But a terrible thing happened: from one night to the next, she stopped having dreams. Thus it was that she felt herself near death, as do those who believe that their most vital business in life has been suddenly cut off.

Sleep, without its images, became more hateful and upsetting to her than any insomnia brought on by illness.

In her brain certain pairings, certain concomitant thrills, suddenly stopped occurring.

Sleep would come, clad in a white, raw light, a screen with no shadows. It seemed to her that she was sleeping against a wide-open window; and in the uniform white sky there flew not one bird, there floated not so much as a single cloud.

She tried covering her eyes with dark cloth before falling asleep.

She would have, for a moment, the illusion of little circles of fireworks before her eyes; and then the veil of lost color would be ripped open, and sleep would come with its white light.

Perhaps the dead were tired of keeping her company; perhaps she had irritated them with too much chatter and too many questions.

To ingratiate herself with them once again, she visited their tombs in the cemeteries, brought them flowers, offered Masses for their souls.

But they did not return.

A thread had snapped; a transcendental link between her life and their deaths had been broken; and she, an inexpert weaver, could not repair the fabric.

For her, this idea of the broken thread had become so painful, but so clear, that the means, the illusions, the hopes that might tie the thread back together again wearied her brain all day long.

She would have to ask to dead for forgiveness as directly as possible.

And from that day forth, she awaited a new death in the family, so that the dead person might serve as an expiatory messenger or a skilful weaver, one who could tie the thread back together again.

Her brother fell gravely ill.

During the first days of the illness, Teresa watched over him continuously, no longer observing, after so many years, the regular bedtime schedule she had always followed.

At bottom, she was hoping that the hour for dreaming had changed and that her faithless friends would come back to her, attentive and smiling as they filled her room. But nothing happened. She would have settled for seeing the sawn-off leg, swinging from the ceiling like a horrible pendulum; but the dead body part was awaiting the rest, to which it might be conjoined, and no longer displayed its fits of whimsical temper.

Pietro's illness grew worse every day.

Certain by now that he was going to die, his haughty relatives – who were staying in the villa – did not disdain to enter his room; but it was clear that they did so more out of a desire to calculate how many more days must pass before they would be rid of his annoying presence than from any real affection and concern.

She, his sister, desired his death, feeling no doubts or hesitations.

At the moments when the sick man was lucid, she gently caressed him, saying: "You, who are a good person- will you come and visit me, like your leg?" He would grunt and puff.

"And will you tell the others that I've been waiting for them for a long time now?"

Pietro made no promises, but gazed fixedly at her with hatred, pushing her away with his hand; and, if his breath was up to it, he would curse as well.

The doctor declared that the patient's sufferings were about to end: "He won't make it to nightfall." Then he left, without anyone's protesting against the death sentence with a sob or a cry.

And, in fact, at three in the afternoon, Pietro began to breathe so effortfully that it seemed that the house and the entire sky were weighing upon his chest.

The relatives, frightened, stayed away; they wouldn't even venture into the courtyard where, from the barred window, they might have heard his desperate animal efforts.

Teresa never abandoned the dying man. She anxiously awaited a moment when he would be lucid in order to repeat her injunctions to him; and then, seeing that no such moment occurred, she insistently whispered them in his ear.
"He'll remember," she thought.

Outside, evening was coming on apace, and in the room, the light from the candle took on greater intensity. In the adjacent kitchen, a clock chimed out the half-hour.

Unconvinced, she waited for it to finish ringing and then opened the door and went up to the chimney for a look at the clock face.

"Six-thirty!" she exclaimed, as if in fright.

In great haste, she went to call the relatives, who were in the sitting-room.

"He's dying," she said. "I can't bear it. He's my brother, after all. Some of you go in."

She didn't notice that she was issuing a command; and the others didn't notice that they were obeying.

Having gone back with them into Pietro's room, she kissed the dying man's hands and went out silently, without a tear.

"Should we call you?" they asked, when she had already gone out.

"No, no. Leave me alone," she returned to say, desperate at the very idea.

In her own room, she lit no lamp or candle. "Soon it will be seven o'clock."

Slowly she began undressing; then, hearing footsteps, she hastily got under the covers, although she was still wearing her stockings and slip.

Sleep would not come. She drew a black shawl from beneath the mattress and drew it across her eyes.

In her deafened ears, buried in the pillow, there buzzed an indistinct sound, impossible to grasp.

Her chest was swollen with measureless heaves of anguish: the breathing, her brother's terrible breathing, was running along the doors and the walls in a palpitating solitude of escape; it reached into her room. Then, like some wounded animal running away, the effortful breathing calmed down in the distance. In her eyes there spun two black vortices, made iridescent by little gray spots that broke apart as if a rubber band had snapped. The spots threw a blinding white light into her eyes.

The breakage of the spots multiplied.

The hour of the rendez-vous had passed: the screen of her dream was white before her eyes.

But suddenly it was covered with black; it went off into the distance, digging a vortex at the end of which was the antechamber populated by the usual figures, with the addition of her brother, who was adjusting his sawn-off leg at the knee, and smiling at her in friendship.

# The Blind Man and the Beauty

*Here they burned the blind man and the Beauty alive.*
*Having discovered their pure innocence,*
*the peasants put up this cross as a sign of expiation.*

(From an expiatory cross along the road from
Carpi to Mantua)

"Where are we?" asked the blind man.

"Near the climb," replied the Beauty, turning back regretfully to look at the flat, smooth, muddy road they were about to abandon.

"And what time is it?"

At this, the old woman pretended not to have heard.

Peeping forth at this evening hour between the clouds thinned out by the heavy rain, the sun illuminated with false gold the foot of the cloud-towers anchored to the distant peaks and the further, fleecy clouds that had reappeared, dry and white, in another sky, stretching away into the azure beyond the hills.

"It's barely five o'clock," she finally murmured, because the act of saying it to herself would make the hour more believable for her companion, who might grow discouraged at learning that night was drawing near while they were far from shelter.

"Five o'clock? But I've already heard it chime five down in the village!"

The blind man stopped distrustfully at the fork in the road and stood with his hands spread out, letting the air blow through them.

The evening breeze and the chilly calm falling over the countryside, impregnated with humidity, gave him the sense that night was beginning to fall.

"You always want to deceive me," he said querulously. "Do you think I can't feel that it's late?"

Convinced by his words, sick at heart, the old woman offered no self-justifications.

"This way," she said, directing him towards the road that led to the mountains.

The blind man walked along, sometimes touching the ground with his stick, and sometimes the wall along the roadside, while the guitar in its cover rose and fell on his back at every step: a chronic annoyance which he had learned to bear peacefully. Feeling safe under the Beauty's surveillance, he didn't worry about carts or any other obstacles.

The Beauty, a former dancer who had fallen into misfortune – the violent and loudmouthed guest of several shelters from which she had been expelled because of her inability to get along with the nuns – had been the blind man's rival in singing and begging for a living, before becoming his watchful companion. But since the sight of her rags did not move people to pity in the same way as his blank eyes, she had formed an alliance of voices and interests with the blind man, so as to eliminate an excessively harmful competition; she had thereby succeeded, too, in liberating herself from the merciless exploitation of certain shady chaperons.

In the course of their miserable wanderings along roads and through villages and towns – which had left neither her nor her companion with any memory of pitying faces, of the sympathy of other human beings, but only with the recollection of bread, wine, the warmth generated by people reaching into their pockets – the initial motivation of mutual need had matured into a deep, somewhat quarrelsome affection, like that of a long-married couple.

"This year, I didn't feel like making the usual journey," said the blind man, wiping away the first sweat occasioned by the climb.

The Beauty sighed in resignation.

"Neither did I, but where there's famine, there's no bread for us. Keep your courage up! Let's try to remain cheerful. Once we've gotten over the mountains, we'll be in the pink."

As though he were already on the peak, admiring the plains below, the blind man pointed out, in an entirely wrong direction, the road they had to follow.

"If things go badly down there, there's the town with the shelter for unfortunates like us."

"What can you be thinking of? I, return to the shelter?" said the old woman, pushing away his hand, which was stretched out toward a sapling at the roadside. "At the shelter, when they've got too many people, they poison them and then they carry them away at night. I know, because I've seen it. As for you, even if they don't kill you, you'd soon die of hunger in the midst of all those thieves. I won't be there to watch over you. Don't you know the set-up at the shelter? Women on one side, men on the other: the women are pissing all the time, and the men are drunkards. Anyway, who's going to give you wine at the shelter? The nuns? They'll tell you, 'Wine is bad for poor people.' That's how they talk."

The thought of such frightful abstinence must have thoroughly convinced the blind man, because, after a moment's silence, he asked for the wine-flask. Feeling that it was too light, he tried shaking it; but the wine didn't slosh around at the bottom. With a furious gesture, he returned the empty container to the old woman.

"I drank the last drop when we passed in front of that chapel," the Beauty confessed in a penitent tone.

"When we pass a chapel, you've got to tell me right

away, not afterwards," he protested bitterly.

"Would you like some water?"

Indignant at this inopportune offer, the blind man remained mute and hostile; but, stumbling over a stone, he broke his silence, saying: "Look after me, you daughter of a bitch!"

The Beauty, who was not offended, took him by the hand.

Further along, it was almost dark. A white, narrow road intersected at a right angle with the main road. It led to a solitary house in the middle of a field.

At the crossroads, the old woman jokingly let out a piercing cry.

The cry came back broken up into many fragments, as if the echo, in each of its little caves, was holding a child prisoner; it was as though each child, hearing a free voice, consoled itself by imitating the cry, passing it back and forth with a feeble breath.

"Hear that, Tata? They're answering us," said the blind man. Let's go and sing there. They'll give us some wine."

"It'll be a miracle if we find water," said the Beauty with a smile.

"Why? Don't the peasants always give us wine?"

"Try here, and you'll see!"

Having put him on the little road, she let him go on by himself, to play and sing a prelude.

Having taken a few steps, the blind man began his song.

The words covered one another, followed on one another's heels, confused as polyphonic writing divided into too many parts. Astonished, he fell silent. He thought that he had heard, distorted by distance, the Beauty's strophe lost in the countryside.

"Where are you?" he cried.

"Where are you?" The mocking echo interrogated

the entire countryside, deafeningly.

"Tata, I'm here, he yelled, seized with anguish.

The words exploded against the house and rebounded hard and dry like the banging of windows being slammed shut and then falling silent; and then they returned once again, thick and weak, as though the trembling façade were trembling its way into a new equilibrium.

"I'm here," said the Beauty, coming up behind him. He turned around to touch her, but with no anger.

"Ah! Where had you gone?"

"I was right here, you fool."

"And who was singing in front of us?"

"No one: the air."

He understood.

"Let's leave; I don't like it here."

They went back up the road.

A man turned into the narrow way from the main road. He was leading a cow, languid from having been mounted by the bull; she walked slowly, shambling along, already tasting maternity.

"It went very well," said the Beauty happily; she was always interested in that sort of thing.

"Now you're expected," answered the peasant.

And the blind man asked:

"Who's expecting us? Who?"


In their humiliation, the actors had not even tasted the lunch that the innkeeper had prepared for them. Salvante and Olimpia's defection had been a hard blow for them: without those two, the company, already too few in numbers, would be unable to put on a show.

"Betrayal! I say it's a black betrayal," yelled the head of the company, pounding his fist on the table. "They pretended to be sick, those swine, so as to have the time to go meet up with that damned Luigi di Sevo who, taking all the whores he can muster up around with him, makes piles of gold and is ruining us! I won't take them back, not even if they come begging on their knees.... I'll drive them away with kicks, or my name isn't Piero d'Ausiglio."

Just then they heard the door opening at the top of the stairs.

The head of the company leapt to his feet to receive and embrace the two filthy traitors, and the other players, seated at the table, craned their necks, watching anxiously. Up above, uncertain footsteps could be heard. They didn't venture to come down.

A step on the staircase... The feet came together... A pause.

Other, rapid footsteps descended, passing the first ones. There was a moment's halt, and the descent resumed, alternating and rhythmic, as though a cautious person was waiting for his companion to provide him with a description in sound of the staircase before daring to come down.

In the underground room there appeared the blind man and the Beauty.

The actors fell back into their chairs, sighing in disappointment; the innkeeper got up from the bench to drive away the wandering musicians; but the old woman said quickly:

"We have money. We want to eat and drink."

In the darkest, most remote corner of the room, they were served the leftovers from all the tables.

Having barely touched the food, the blind man started drinking. He raised his head while the wine ran down his gullet, and he opened his eyelids, as though his opaque eyes could still express the lascivious lightning-bolt of his pleasure.

The Beauty stuck her long, warty nose into the dishes and, as she chewed, let out raucous grunts of satisfaction. Her teeth covered with bits of food, she smiled at the irritated innkeeper. Meanwhile, at the actors' table, the head of the company was haggling with the impresario, who had come to ask for a large indemnity for the very probable delay in putting on the show.

"If there are just a few of you, jump around in the piazza and don't try to perform in theaters! Just think: counting on you, I turned down the offer of Luigi di Sevo, who has eight women in his company!"

Pale and proud, Pietro d'Ausiglio proclaimed: "Give us time for the others who are still on the road to get here, and we'll do better than he could."

This boast made the impresario very angry. He went out threatening to seize the properties the company had left at the theater unless, within two hours, the show was organized for that very evening.

The actors were weighed down by a sense of discouragement that frightened the innkeeper. In fact, contrary to the usual practice, he presented his bill before the performance. The head of the company rebelled against this infraction of habit as a matter of principle, and defended his point of view with all the resources of voice and posture that his long experience of playing tyrants put at his disposal. But the argument was interrupted by the arrival of the innkeeper's wife followed by a policeman covered with warts and moustaches, who demanded immediate payment, not so much out of a desire to see justice done as from an intention to take his cut of the profits of the firm; and the head player had to hand over the money, despite all his ranting against the inhospitable town and the two traitors.

Having put away their leftovers, the blind man and the Beauty went out into the courtyard in order to enjoy a bit of sunshine, while a knife-grinder entered from the street, pushing his machine along before him. Sitting atop the reservoir of water that surmounted the grindstone was a rooster with dense feathers and an upright crest; a skinny, yellow-furred dog trotted along at the man's heels.

"Ladies, the knife-grinder is here! The knife-grinder.... He's here, he's here, the man who sharpens blades for the executioner of Paris. Out with your knives, your hatchets, and your money!"

His words had the chanting monotony of a street-cry.

Having halted in the middle of the courtyard, the knife-grinder threw the rooster down from his perch on the machine, tied it by a foot to the pedal, and made an agreement with a servant-boy who was not to reveal his presence to the innkeeper.

He had an olive-colored face, long and sharp at the chin, and large, bulging eyes beneath enormous, droopy eyelids threaded with purple veins. Gray-haired, but still quick and agile, he did not look old. He was well-known as a wanderer about the countryside, but he was not as well-liked as certain others – repairers of umbrellas or jars and pitchers – on account of his extravagant, aggressive way of joking. As he sharpened dull blades, he would sing terrifying songs of mutilations; and when he had got them properly sharpened, he would slice the air with them and, bending over, he would stab at it, too, saying, "Whoosh, whoosh, how it cuts!" Although he came from elsewhere, he spoke the dialect of the region, remembered the name of each of his customers, and knew the story of the knives and other tools that they brought to his wheel.

"You say that's rust? Next time, dry off the blood a little better!" he was capable of saying to a hot-headed youth who brought him a knife.

"This used to have a fine handle with your monogram. Why did you change it? Was it dangerous?" he asked another.

He railed against the knife-grinders who had been there before him: they were thieves, eaters of steel, wreckers of utensils.

"Steel calls for a light hand. Look: with your knives, you can even shave." He would provoke a shiver in the onlookers, scraping his hairless cheeks with a butcher's knife and waving it about his face.

He pretended to come from far-off lands and told in detail how the executioner of Paris summoned him to sharpen the cutting-edge of the guillotine. "The year I wasn't there, the prisoners lost their heads after seven strokes instead of one."

He didn't come back to the town on given dates, nor at fixed intervals: whether or not there was work for him, he came back every time the theater was open, whether for comedy or tragedy.

He would station himself at the stage door to spy on the actors, and thought up a thousand excuses to strike up a conversation with them in order to interrogate them about one Gennaro Allori, head of a company of players. Nobody knew of the latter, but from his vague, hearsay descriptions, some of the actors were reminded of another head of a group of actors, whose name was Pietro d'Ausiglio.

"Tell me, is it possible that this Gennaro Allori changed his name?"

"It's very possible indeed; among theater people, it's a common practice."

He had, in fact, just come from the theater, having been informed that Pietro d'Ausiglio was at the inn. He didn't dare go down into the room, on account of an old enmity between himself and the innkeeper. While waiting, he made a blade from a scrap of iron picked up from the ground; the grindstone kept up a constant shrill whine and a spray of sparks. Spotting him from a window, the innkeeper came out to say to him, very brusquely:

"You can go away. I don't have knives for rascally grinders like you."

The knife-grinder stopped pedaling and smiled as if

the insult had amused him. But the other man began to take him to task with harsh words for some obscure business that had taken place years before. The grinder had switched knives on him, and his knife was later found by the police in the heart of a corpse discovered in the mud of the canal. For this reason the innkeeper, believed responsible for the crime, had had endless trouble demonstrating his own innocence.

"In my opinion, you deliberately gave it to a murderer, you filthy executioner!"

"You might let that story drop," replied the knife-grinder who was, by now, very irritated.

He saw that he was having no success at calming the innkeeper down.

"Certainly," he said, addressing himself to some youths who had come, bowling balls in hand, to enjoy the altercation, "while he was going in fear of the gallows, I never came to testify on his behalf. But how could I have, since I was on a journey to Paris and didn't know anything about it? Let's be fair. What rust still clings to me, if it was enough that a girl – there she is, now she's his wife – was not ashamed to go to the judge and say, 'Last night he wasn't at work with his knife, I can guarantee it,' in order to get him off the hook?" How has he been harmed, if everyone has a higher opinion of him than before? Even the police officer has become his friend!"

He accompanied these last words with a gesture, scratching his head with such perfidious gymnastics of the fingers that he formed, as if by accident, horns.

Humiliated, the innkeeper withdrew amidst the laughter of the bowlers, who had scattered in an effort to stop laughing. The knife-grinder sat down beside the blind man and the Beauty and set a table for himself on the low wall, unwrapping his food from a greasy paper wrapper. As he ate, he attentively observed the two wanderers; smiling at the old woman, he showed her that he wished to chat with her.

The actors emerged from the underground room; melancholy and fatuous, they sat down on the shafts of the empty wheelbarrows to swing their legs. Piero d'Ausiglio, who was among them, remained standing and turned his back on the scene, looking out into the road.

And then: "Things are going badly," the knife-grinder said loudly, as if talking to his dog, to which he tossed a scrap of fatty, fetid skin. "Chin up, they'll go better," he went on, untying the feet of the rooster, which began to peck at the ground.

His words didn't please the head of the theatrical company who, turning around slowly to look at him, sat down among his actors while waiting to understand better for whom the allusion was meant.

The knife-grinder smiled.

"Now I hope these good people won't mind too much if I show you my romantic lead who is a dog, and my ingenue who is a rooster."

A rebellious nervousness ran through the group of actors.

"Keep calm," muttered the head of the company. "He's only speaking ill of Salvante and Olimpia."

"Ladies and gentlemen, watch closely," admonished the knife-grinder, who had remained silent in order to enjoy the effect of his own words. "Dog, do your bit."

Something extraordinary occurred.

The dog, hunkering down, stared at the rooster lustfully; then it arose, trembling, and started to circle around it with lascivious intent, approaching the bird repeatedly as though it were a female of the canine species.

The rooster remained indifferent, pecking at bits of food on the ground. But when, with incredible boldness, the dog placed its muzzle among rooster's tail-feathers and began to sniff, the bird, angry and offended, raised a foot to defend itself.

The dog whined and resumed its assault, and the rooster, object of its courtship, drew back, clucking indignantly.

Even the actors were laughing now, as was the Beauty. The blind man, informed by her of what was going on between the two animals, was laughing too, as were all the people in the inn who, their curiosity aroused by the tone of the knife-grinder's comments on the show, had come to look into the courtyard.

Only the strange animal-trainer remained serious. "The damned creature doesn't want anything to do with it!"

He struck the bird with a little whip. Frightened, it flapped about a little on its trimmed wings. At last, the knife-grinder laughed, like a clown who, having finished his turn, is obliged to do so.

Two girls were watching from a window; he tried to shame them by shouting, "This is a show for married women," and then cooled the dog's unnatural ardor by kicking it.

Then he went about with his hat in his hand, but refused with smiles and smirks the coins that those who had been most entertained wished to toss into it, as though his begging were just an agreeable addition to the show.

When he reached the wheelbarrows, he stood before Pietro d'Ausiglio who was awaiting him with a hostile expression.

"I've got something to say to you," the knife-grinder said.

"To me? I don't know you."

"I know, but it's a question of your own interests."

The head of the company stood up and, in order to get away from his curious companions, led the knife-grinder to the end of the courtyard. The latter did not conceal his disappointment at being separated from the group.

"Well?"

"I want to act with you."

"A knife-grinder! What sort of an actor are you? And anyway, why with me?"

"With you or with another, it's all the same; I'm saying it because, knowing that you're short of actors...."

"How do you know that?" Pietro interrupted him, furious that the first outsider to come along should know about his misfortunes.

"My God! Everyone in town knows it, and they're waiting to see how you'll manage this evening. When I'm out in the street and even when I'm grinding blades, I'm always acting. It's a passion that runs in my family. All I dream about is finding myself on a stage and, once there, playing love scenes as a joke, cursing and killing my rival before the public, which holds its breath and applauds when it sees the dead man."

At these last words, Pietro felt faint.

With a look, he assured himself that the knife-grinder had spoken them with no hidden intent, and then he brutally brought the subject to a conclusion.

"Get to the point! I do those things every day, and I don't need you to tell me about them."

"Forgive me, you're right. You're like the man who was irritated by talk about wives: he had three of them." Following these words, the knife-grinder gave a little laugh, that of a solitary man who knows how to appreciate his own wit even amidst others' silence.

"Tell me, friend, did you use to be an actor?"

"No," replied the other with a smile. "You know, I've been asked that by lots of actors who wanted to get rid of me; but they always had a complete company."

Pietro understood from this shot that his man was less unbalanced than he let on. He became instinctively suspicious of the knife-grinder, who added in a humble tone:

"I've read that this evening you're supposed to put on *Mitridane*. It's a tragedy that I know almost by heart. You're missing some actors: I could fill in for one of them. Look for a moment at those two ragged beggars over there. Yes, the old hag and the blind man. Tell me, don't you agree that they seem made to order to play the king and queen who come on dressed as beggars in the first act? They're already in costume! In this way, it seems to me that you'd have three of your actors available for other roles. But this chatter doesn't interest you...."

Pietro looked at the knife-grinder in genuine wonder. The idea seemed so good to him that he was amazed that he himself hadn't thought of using the wandering musicians. Nonetheless, he was repelled at the thought of involving in his affairs this strange volunteer actor who had come to offer him, for no good reason, what seemed like predestined assistance.

"And what part would you yourself like to play in *Mitridane*?"

"The role of Tartaglia," the knife-grinder replied promptly. "I'm ugly and so I'm well suited to play wicked characters." He lifted his face to the sun, so that the actor could see that he was telling the truth. "If you take me," he added, "I can propose certain changes in my part which will please you."

"Are you also, by any chance, a playwright?" asked Pietro, whose unpleasant sense of suspicion had been revived by this strange proposal.

"Certainly not. But as you'll readily understand, a buried passion such as mine makes one capable of anything: even of creating a tragedy."

Pietro, thinking that he could do without this unpleasant person while still striking an agreement with the two beggars, who now struck him as precious, broke off the conversation with a shrug and headed back to join his companions.

But the knife-grinder ran after him and said, loudly so that all the actors might hear: "It'll be the worse for you; it was your only chance of saving yourself."

Extremely annoyed, Pietro was unwilling to offer his troupe any explanation for this phrase – with the result that the actors clustered about the knife-grinder to find out from him.

It was then that Pietro understood the harm that would come of his not having yielded. He was going to have shown himself unwilling to get out of a desperate situation, and the risk was that he would now be abandoned by the few who had remained faithful to him. He had no clear, plausible reasons for turning down the offer; and in the presence of the knife-grinder, he could hardly say that, having excluded him, he was going to steal his idea.

"All right; you'll act, too," he said, with a hostile glance at this skillful intriguer. "Come to the theater in half an hour and bring your friends along for the rehearsal."

Now that the nightmare of the seizure of their properties had vanished, the actors had gotten over their depression as if by a miracle. They wanted to congratulate their new companion; but since he was already busy negotiating with the Beauty, who was seated near the blind man while the latter dozed on a pile of hay, they had to leave the inn, following the impatient Pietro d'Ausiglio. The latter, in order to regain their esteem after having led them into such a bad patch, was now boasting that the use of the two beggars had been his own idea.


Onstage, by the light of two smoky candles, the actors were rehearsing.

Shouting himself hoarse and sweating, Pietro d'Ausiglio scolded his dogs, egged them on, corrected excessively provincial pronunciations, ran after this or that player to get him to move with a tragic bearing.

The Beauty was yelling things that led the blind man to think she had gone mad. After having tried to figure out where the devil she had brought him to, he had fallen asleep atop a chest, with his head hanging down and his white eyes bulging.

Seated at a table, the knife-grinder was marking the script with the changes needed to make the characters' improvisations workable.

Pale, he was unable to control his long shivers, which ended in a rasp on the paper, while the prompter sniggered, irritated that someone else had taken over his job and attributing the other man's trembling to his being unused to the effort of writing.

By bits and pieces, with halts and repetitions, sudden-ly taking wing and then coming a cropper, the tragedy was steadily taking shape amidst the threadbare clothing of the actors.

Prince Mitridane, who had reached the throne by killing his elder brother and exiling his parents, lived in terror, surrounded by armed men and evil advisers, and condemning at least half of his subjects to death or other dreadful punishments. The old king and queen arrived in the palace dressed as beggars in order to approach their youngest son, the good Prince Milo; with his aid, they wanted to organize a plot against the slayer of his eldest brother. Tartaglia, the prime minister, having recognized the former rulers beneath their rags, revealed their pres-ence to Mitridane.

There was a terrible scene of tyrannical fury, with signs of future remorse, and then the decision to put them to death. But Tartaglia recommended a subtler way of getting rid of the three conspirators at a stroke. Mitradane was to hand the wanderers over to Prince Milo as guests deserving of his charity. Then he was to kill them during the night, accuse his brother of parricide the next morning, and deliver him to the executioner.

The tragedy was supposed to end with the killing of the two old people and with Mitridane slitting his own throat, overcome with horror at the crime he had committed.

There was a break in the rehearsal, in order to let Pietro d'Ausiglio catch his breath before this final scene.

The rehearsal had gone on so long that it was almost curtain time; through the heavy curtain could be heard the voices of the first playgoers to arrive and the creaking of the seats.

The head of the troupe was standing in a corner, so as to avoid drafts that might freeze his sweat; the others, having fallen back into their habitual fatuous expressions, were sitting here and there on the tables scattered about the stage.

"Right," said the knife-grinder as he stood up. "I've fixed everything. I really like being here with you; it reminds me of that poor unfortunate, my brother. Do you know who he was? He was Sgandurra, the king of tyrants, a very fine actor. Just imagine! One evening he was supposed to play a man who got killed; he was such a good actor that he let them kill him for real. Yes.... It happened in Madrid eight years ago. He was stabbed, right before the eyes of the public, which didn't realize what was happening, by one Gennaro Allori, who was jealous of him...."

There was a cry, followed by a loud crash.

Suddenly dizzy, Pietro d'Ausiglio, having tried to lean for support against a paper wall, had gone straight through it, falling on the other side.

With the help of his troupe, he got to his feet. Stammering that he felt ill, he said that it was impossible to remain indoors like this.

The blind man, who had been awakened by the racket, complained to some dream figure or other that the Beauty snored at night, and that he himself, even if he couldn't see, felt better than all those people carrying on around him. To shut him up, the knife-grinder spit in his face.

Pietro d'Ausiglio had no intention of finishing the rehearsal; in fact, he was groaning that the performance would have to be cancelled, because he was out of breath; but then the awareness of the disaster that a cancellation would entail for him and his company gave him new strength. The knife-grinder, who was speaking now with an energy that he tried in vain to suppress, made the observation that it would be a good idea to finish the rehearsal. Otherwise, when Tartaglia came onstage to stab Mitridane, as he had decided to do so as to make the finale more exciting and moral (since it would involve the killing of the murderer), Mitridane would not understand the actions that he had to perform in order to let himself be slain.

Having finished saying these things, the knife-grinder seemed momentarily disoriented; but he quickly recovered his self-control, smiling in a manner that signified: Now you know everything, but even so, there is no way you can escape me.

Pietro d'Ausiglio stepped forward, pale and distraught.

"That scene will not be played!" he shouted; but it was evident that the words cost him a great effort.

The knife-grinder held up to the actor's face a candle that he had taken from a table, and mockingly asked: "Do you really mean that?"

With a furious gesture, the other made him lower his arm, and the candle went out.

"And you won't play Tartaglia, because... because... I

don't want any bosses around here."

"Forgive me if I've offended you," said the knife-grinder meekly. "I thought we had an agreement, but it doesn't matter. Everything will remain as you wish. I'm going to put on my ministerial costume: it's time."

And in fact, the impresario came to ask whether he might ring the bell.

Without wasting any more time in conjectures, the actors dispersed to their dressing-rooms. They regrouped in costume in the wings, and the play began.

Here and there, there were some flaws; but suspicions, displays of wickedness, and terrible implications surfaced frequently enough to rivet the public's interest in the obscure movements of the characters' souls, in the reasons behind a word or a gesture demanding subsequent explanation, and the enchantment was not lost. The dark restlessness of the two principals was admirably suited to the tragedy.

Dressed as Mitridane, Pietro d'Ausiglio thundered, the perfect tyrant, but his uneasiness showed that he was expecting treachery. The knife-grinder, magnificently costumed in a collarless tunic that well displayed his yellowish, wrinkled head, stuck atop his neck as upon a handle, made himself hated and cursed by the entire audience. The perfidy of his counsels, the vein of poison in his voice, seemed to torture Mitridane, whose ever-increasing cruelty revealed a crescendo of fear.

Standing near the prompter, the Beauty did not speak her words in each scene, but sang them, which was well suited to a queen disguised as a wandering beggar. The blind man, clinging to her arm, took the constant peregrinations between the stage and the wings for a bad dream and never opened his mouth, since the script only called for his character to speak from offstage.

In the last act, as the tragedy moved towards catastrophe, the public was very tense, in part because Tartaglia's intentions had not yet become clear. The minister seemed to be using the tyrant as a tool for clearing his own way to the throne.

The stage set depicted a prison.

Lying upon their hard bed, the blind man and the Beauty awaited their destiny as deposed rulers and as conspirators.

In the shadows, a man wrapped in a dark cloak appeared through a secret doorway.

He hesitated at the threshold and raised his arms beneath the cloak as though he wished to cast it aside, seeming for a moment as awesome and fabulous as the crime he was about to commit.... He came forward.... Then he abruptly turned back towards the door.

Behind him, another cloaked man had lightly insinuated himself. The first man, who seemed a murderer caught in the act, leapt away, and gestured for the other to leave; but the latter said, "O Prince, I bring you my assistance."

The public recognized Tartaglia's voice and found his line natural and logical. Mitridane, dumbstruck for an instant, hastened to improvise a lame response:

*Stay by the door. Turn your back on me.*
*And drive your dagger into the mother's breast,*
*Since I, her son, would lack the strength to do it.*

The muffled footsteps and the incomprehensible words frightened the blind man who, well aware by now that he was awake, did not understand what world he had fallen into.

*Heavens, what do I hear?*
*Cruel footsteps are descending the staircase.*
*Wife, queen, help me!*

Thus a voice backstage implored on his behalf.
And the Beauty replied:

*Do not be alarmed, my friend.*
*It is but a jailer coming down the stairs*
*With food from our enemy.*

"A jailer? What's gotten into you?" shrieked the blind man, throwing himself off the bed. But he dared ask nothing more, for Mitridane had already drawn near him, breathing hoarsely.

Having fallen silent out of anguish, protecting himself with his hands, he began to move upstage, where Tartaglia was waiting in ambush.

Having turned over on the bed, the Beauty at last saw Mitridane with his raised dagger and cried:

*Help, help! I do not deserve death, O cruel one.*
*He is your father, and I am your mother!*

Stepping back, the blind man had encountered Tartaglia. The blind man howled as he palpated the terrible, immobile presence with his hand.

Seized by the terror of so many unknown things, he leapt forward, accompanied by an outburst of strident laughter that filled with terror not only him, abut also Mitridane, who hurried along behind him like some murderous insect. Then Mitridane was upon him. Having seized upon the blind man – who had by now fainted – as his prey, he covered him with his cloak, dragged him along, and stabbed him, cavorting madly about the stage.

At last Tartaglia came away from the door. Mitridane swiftly held up his dagger to protect himself; but then the other man did his duty as an actor by assaulting the Beauty, justifying his action by crying out:

*"Yes! Kill! Cut their throats!"*

And gripped by a renewed fury, he attacked the king, while the curtain fell on the horrors of bloodshed.


The public's enthusiasm was immense. Through the opening in the curtain, Pietro d'Ausiglio alternated smiles at the applauding audience with anguished glances at the stage, where the knife-grinder, who was being called for loudly, did not reappear.

Then Pietro removed his sinister disguise and, pale and worried, asked one of the company to accompany him to the place outside the town where he lodged. He was the guest of Signora Zelmira, a former actress who was universally beloved for her noisy generosity, even if people mocked her a bit on account of the obvious passions that passing tyrants nostalgically reawakened in her.

Meanwhile, in the wings, the actors were holding aromatic waters beneath the blind man's nose in an attempt to bring him round from his swoon; while in a dressing room the women were dressing the Beauty for the dance. They were costuming her as an inhabitant of Monferrato, as written in the program.

The old woman, excited, was celebrating in a petticoat. She was laughing, clapping her hands, and giggling as she capered about like a mischievous girl of sixteen. "I'll dance until I'm out of breath. I was a famous dancer, I was the Beauty, the Buxom Beauty.... You must have heard the name!"

The women who were dressing her made up for the absence of garters by tying certain red stockings about her thighs with string; then they slipped onto her feet a battered pair of little shoes; after which they all competed to put horribly colored make-up on her lined face and warty nose.

The blind man, who had gotten over his fright and been well informed about everything, was sweating and warming up his voice with resonant, vinous blasts, while three people were fussing over him in order to make him put on a pair of short pants and a green vest with gold buttons. He was to sing and dance together with his companion.

A stagehand came to say that he had reinforced the footlights with five new candles; the violin, cello, and double-bass were already playing the overture, chasing one another at a distance of several measures, as if they were running a race to be the first to reach the recapitulation.

At last they began the monferrina, and the Beauty and the blind man were pushed onstage.

So startled was the public at this apparition that no one in the audience laughed or greeted the dancing couple with applause.

With moves worthy of an old harlot, the Beauty came downstage and, in time to the music, began a weaving of feet, a whirlwind of steps, so perfect that the entire theater, highly amused, cried out: "Brava! Brava, old woman!"

The poor blind man, who had remained near the wings, sang:

> *My beautiful girl of Monferrato,*
> *Show me your legs!*

and strummed at his guitar in the wrong key.

The old woman was now carrying on wildly at the edge of the stage, with a thousand obscene leaps and drolleries, to the resounding, rhythmic applause.

Inebriated, drawn by the public's thousand gazes, the blind man came forward, flapping his arms.

Guided by the music, incited by the calls of his companion, he too began dancing; he would dart first to one side, then to the other, for to him this was dancing. Zigzagging, he advanced, advanced towards the edge of the stage.

No one was laughing any more: the blind man had reached the footlights. The Beauty was backing up amidst a thousand pirouettes. A frightful Bacchante, she disturbed the peace of the Arcadia painted on the backdrop.

As if he had intuited the void from the breathing of the public below him, or been warned by the stench of the candles, the blind man halted for a moment, groping in front of him with his hands, leaning forward with his body; while the violinist, who was afraid that he would land on top of him, swatted with his bow at the blind man's legs, which the latter continued to raise and to drop back rhythmically in the same place.

Still pirouetting, the Beauty came downstage. It seemed that the wide arch described by her steps must lead her to collide with the blind man.

"Watch out! Watch out!" people were yelling at her from all sides. But with incredible precision, she wound up in the minimal space in front of her companion. She pushed him back from the edge, and finished her pirouette on the apron of the stage while spreading her legs in grand style. The curtain fell amidst wild applause, while a certain panic broke out onstage.

Having spread out over the footlights, the Beauty's petticoats had caught fire.

In their desire to come to her aid, the actors hidden in the wings leapt upon her and beat her as though she were made of wood. But the old woman felt nothing: out of her mind at her success, she hadn't even noticed the danger. She wept with joy and hung on the necks of the impresario and of the actors, who were at once amused and a bit moved. When the curtain was raised again on account of the applause in the theater, she noticed the blind man who – in order to have a safe support – had sat down on the floor, with no intention of moving on his own in this cave of dangers. She ran to help him up and dragged him with her to the edge of the stage.

It was raining flowers, hats, silver coins. The old dancer's revenge on age and poverty had triumphed over the public's sense of the ridiculous: the audience was content to be moved and to show itself generous.

It was hard to convince the Beauty that there was no point in bowing to the auditorium even after the last spectators had left. The actors had already hastily left the theater; but the old lady obstinately remained behind to wait for the knife-grinder.

"I have to give him a kiss," she told everybody, and then sang:

*My beautiful girl of Monferrato,*
*Show me your legs!*

and kicked on a bench like an epileptic.

The impresario and the custodians had to lift her up and put her out in the street with her companion.

Out in the open air, the Beauty came to her senses.

"Now let's go and get some sleep," she said, embracing the blind man, who was wobbly with fatigue, with the gesture of a good spouse. "We earned more than five *scudi* with our dancing," she said, putting the money in his pocket. "You didn't believe that I was so good, did you?"

"I heard you, I heard you," replied the blind man. "You even landed on top of me."

The Beauty gave a little laugh.

"If Pietro d'Ausiglio engages us, we'll be rich. I've been thinking for quite a while of returning to the theater to show all those whores who are around today what's what. They don't even know how to pirouette on one foot!"

"Not every day is a feast day," commented the blind

man in conclusion.

Having left the town, they followed a road that could be guessed at in the night like a thread of dawn dividing the plain in two. There was thunder, and the sudden flashes of lightning expanded the boundaries of the countryside for a moment, bathing it in unnatural colors that the subsequent darkness did not erase from the Beauty's dazzled eyes. In its deep silence, the earth awaited the downpour that would cleanse it of the pallor which those arrows of light had left behind them.

At every flash of lightning, the Beauty turned towards the blind man: it seemed incredible to her that his eyes – which turned vivid at every bolt – were not wounded within by any light.

"Where are you taking me?" he asked. "We've been walking for quite a while."

"We're going to Signora Zelimira's house. Today I paid her so many compliments that she promised to give us a bed."

At this moment, the first raindrops fell.

In order to shorten the route beneath the heavy rain, they cut across the ploughed farmland; but they slipped on clods of mire and sank into the soft soil between one furrow and another. Exhausted, the old woman punched her companion and pinched his arms to stop him from throwing himself down in discouragement.

At last they set their muddy feet on the pavement of a small piazza. A lightning bolt showed the Beauty that someone she recognized was coming out of the house.

"Hey! It's the knife-grinder," she exclaimed. "We're here, too."

No answer: only the sound of footsteps mingled with that of the falling rain. A bit concerned, she pushed past the open door and, together with the blind man, entered the house.

"Anybody home?... Signor Pietro... Signora Zelmira..."

Guided by a light, she reached the kitchen. It was illuminated by a candle stuck upon the table, which was covered with open bottles and dirty dishes. She went back to fetch her companion, who had remained in the hallway; she sat him down at the table and poured him a glass of wine.

The sound of hasty footsteps made them turn around. The knife-grinder appeared at the threshold, sopping wet and very agitated.

"What are you doing here?" he asked in a harsh voice.

"Ah! It's you. I saw you clearly," said the Beauty, running over to throw her arms about his neck and give him a grateful kiss.

He pushed her away brutally.

"What's going on here? Won't you tell me why you're here?"

"There's nothing wrong with our being here," said the Beauty, humiliated at this reception. "We're going to sleep here. The lady of the house invited us."

The knife-grinder remained silent and looked at them as though he were meditating.

"Listen," he said, drawing the old woman aside and speaking low into her ear. "Don't you know that Signora Zelmira died this evening of a stroke?"

"What? Oh, the poor thing! In this house?"

"Yes. Don't say anything to the blind man: he might get frightened."

"And where is Pietro d'Ausiglio?"

"He's gone for the doctor, but in this weather he won't be back soon."

"And you? Were you also invited to sleep here?"

"No," answered the knife-grinder, who had given a little start at this question. "Pietro left me here to keep watch over the poor dead woman, but I didn't have the courage, and I was leaving too when you called me."

"Are we still in the theater?" the blind man suddenly asked. The knife-grinder's slightly troubled voice and the mysterious conversation had reawakened his memory of the performance.

Neither of the two answered him; but the knife-grinder poured him out some more wine, and the blind man fell silent at the sound.

"Here you've got shelter. You mustn't leave. I, on the other hand, cannot stay: there's a carter who's going to take me to Mantua. He'll be leaving just as soon as it stops raining."

Thinking that it would be difficult to explain to the blind man why they had to go back out again into the rain, the Beauty agreed to remain behind.

"Wait for me here. I'll be right back," said the knife-grinder, leaving with the candle.

The two beggars heard him going rapidly up a wooden staircase; and then, once he had reached the upper story, they heard him moving effortfully, as though he were dragging a weight behind him. When he came back, he filled a glass for himself and gulped it down in haste, quivering when he felt the whitish, troubled eyes of the blind man upon him.

"If you want to go upstairs, it's the first door on the right," he said, gesturing farewell and disappearing down the corridor.

The Beauty, who had thus remained in charge of the house, lit some brushwood in the fireplace and drank down five glasses of wine, one after another.

"We're alone," she explained to the blind man, giving him another glass. "We can do what we want."

"Then let's go to bed. I'm worn out."

"Bear it just a little longer."

They both kept that voluntary silence that paves the way for sleep; but then the old woman began to speak, more awake than before.

"I've decided that we're not going to wander about any more, singing ourselves hoarse for pathetic sums. You and I are going to be dancers. I saw this evening that you don't know the monferrina, but I'll teach it to you."

The blind man rightly thought that his companion had drunk too much, and made no answer.

"You make good money, and what's more, you also meet up with people who help you to save it. Here everything is ours, and we're not paying a thing. Where else do you think you might be better off? I feel as though I were riding in a carriage." She stretched out upon her chair, which tried to slip out from under her.

In this position, she turned her eyes to the ceiling. Then she remembered that the lady of the house was upstairs, poor thing, dead and abandoned. It seemed to her that, in exchange for the roof, the fire, and the wine, Signora Zelmira had the right to something which no longer struck the Beauty as either frightening or difficult. She took down two candlesticks from the mantelpiece, removed the candle from the table, and wobbled off to go upstairs.

Hearing her footsteps, the blind man thought it was time to go to bed, and trailed along behind her.

On the stairs, she had to protect the candle-flame against a draft with her hand; and she also had to be careful of falling, because the steps, soiled with a thick, sticky, wet substance, were treacherous.

In the upstairs corridor, she opened the first door and lifted the candle to illuminate the room.

On the bed was a human figure, wrapped from the head to the knees in a heavy blanket. Sticking out from under the blanket, the legs, stiff and spread wide, were pointing towards the door; they were clad in black, dusty stockings.

Having lit the candles in the candlesticks and set them by the sides of the bed, the Beauty felt another solemn duty. She knelt on the prie-Dieu and said a prayer for the soul of the departed woman; and, filled with the sincere sorrow imparted by utter drunkenness, she burst out in mindless, desperate snivelling.

The blind man had remained at the threshold. "What are you crying for?" he blind man in amazement. "We've been through worse. After all, it's not raining on our heads." Intending to go over to her and comfort her, he advanced into the room, feeling his way along the furniture.

"There's a bed," he said, touching its edge. "Let's lie down for a bit and sleep; it must be the one made up for us."

"Stop, stop, don't touch it!"

"Why not?" he asked, drawing back from his groping amidst the blankets.

"I'll explain it to you afterwards," his obscure companion replied. Having made him sit down on the couch, which was quite far from the bed, she returned to her task of piteous weeping.

Extremely annoyed, the blind man told her to stop it.

"You stupid woman, why are you crying as though at some misfortune? Haven't we got shelter?"

"Oh, shut up. I'll do as I like."

"Well, I'll show you that I can do as I like, too," replied the blind man angrily. He removed his guitar from its cover and began to sing.

Taken by surprise, the Beauty could not immediately muster up the energy to snatch the instrument away from him. As if struck by some sudden illness, she was seized by a fit of laughter.

"So now you're laughing? See, I've made you stop whining, you stupid thing."

When the blind man struck up the song of the

butcher who kills his lying wife:

> *I'm going to kill you, my beautiful wife,*
> *I've sharpened the knife,*

the Beauty could not help singing the reply at every half-stanza:

> *My husband, do not kill me,*
> *It's not true that I've betrayed you.*

> *There was a hole in the door,*
> *And I saw you through it.*

> *No, my husband, it isn't true.*
> *You've drunk an entire jug.*

Thus it was that, besides this song, others – "The Priest's Daughter," "The Poor Soldier," "The Woman Cut to Pieces," "The Hangman and the Condemned Man," "The Young Man Who Died at the Funeral of his Beloved," "The Girl in the Fig-tree" – also enlivened the wake.

It was still night. The group of policemen stopped on the main road, gathering about the two prisoners.

Someone lit a candle.

"Is this yours?" demanded the brigadier, placing a whetted knife in the blind man's hand. "No. But its handle is like mine."

The Beauty, who had recognized a rusty, chipped knife that she had given to the knife-grinder, prudently chose to remain silent. She kept her eyes fixed on the red, transparent hands of the policeman who was holding the wavering flame.

A gust of wind blew the candle out, and the interrogation was cut off by the darkness.

The town, which was now nearby, was strangely illuminated and humming with voices at this hour of heavy sleep.

"There they are, the murderers!" was the cry from the first window.

"They're the ones who slit the actor's throat and strangled poor Signora Zelmira! Murderers! Cowards!"

"How can they already know about it?" wondered the brigadier. "That knife-grinder must have awakened the whole town to give them the news." He cursed his own stupid error: he had not detained the strange accuser in the barracks.

From the main street there poured forth a yelling crowd carrying funeral-procession torches against the last remains of darkness.

The policemen clustered together to protect the prisoners; but, surrounded as they were, they could not prevent some people from landing treacherous blows with sticks upon the poor beggars.

The Beauty fell down: a well aimed stone skidded along the ground and struck her in the face. She raised her bleeding visage and looked around for the blind man, who was moving his lips and chin as though praying or anxiously asking the reason for this persecution.

Having seen the first blood, the crowd felt such a powerful and noble joy in doing justice that it cried out in enthusiasm. Everyone gathered around to inflict some chosen punishment: blows with a stick, stones thrown, knife-cuts, kicks, spittle.

"Have you got corns?" yelled a massive, ferocious man. Having thrust a pole between the legs of the immobilized policemen, he used it to beat the foot of the Beauty, who, at each blow, let out a prolonged "Oh!" that seemed to express amazement.

Some police reinforcements arrived to reduce the crush of furious citizens, and the rest of the way to the barracks was not so horrendous.

Once the door had been shut and bolted, the blind man and the Beauty, who were near fainting, were made to lie down upon two cots, and their wounds were dressed as well as could be managed.

Outside, the crowd was in tumult, screaming of its thirst for vengeance and its indignation that its prey had escaped it.

Meanwhile the brigadier had had the horses saddled and had sent for the closed and bolted van for the transport of prisoners. "I'm going to take them to the city, because if we keep them here they'll kill them. But there's some mystery in this business," he confided in his corporal. "Did you see how peacefully they were sleeping in that room?"

The van was at the wainwright's for repairs. Two policemen dragged it into the guardhouse without noticing the big bundles of straw that had been tied about the axles while they were passing through the piazza.

When the vehicle with its escort came out of the barracks, the crowd, which up to then had been shouting, opened up in mute complicity.

A wisp of smoke emerged from between the wheels. A lash of the whip for the horses, which took off at a gallop: fresh cries from the crowd, who ran along behind. So as to add an awareness of the tragedy to the tragedy itself, someone yelled, hoping it was already too late: "Fire! Fire!" The policemen did not immediately understand: they stopped after a few steps, made suspicious by a strange odor and by the bolting of their horses, which did not want to stay beside the van. Between the axles of the vehicle, the fire broke out. The policemen leapt to the ground.

One of them threw his cloak among the flames; another used his dagger to cut free a bundle of straw from which, once it was out in the open, there leapt forth higher flames.

"The door! Open the door!" cried the brigadier, who saw the Beauty's hands writhing in the little window.

At that moment, stung by some sparks, the two horses pulling the van whinnied wildly and started to run away.

They crossed the piazza in a flash and headed down the wide paved street that led to the main road. Spurring their horses, the police raced along behind the van, which was by now all ablaze.

The tail of one of the horses had caught fire and was burning rapidly; and the animal, maddened by pain, reared up and then took off at a wild gallop. The movements of the blazing van were so strange and spasmodic as to give some idea of what was going on within. The peasants coming to town on foot threw themselves into the ditches by the roadside and followed the cavalcade with eyes full of astonishment. Mixed up among them was the knife-grinder: he leapt out of the ditch, raised his arms in a great gesture of horror, and began to run as fast as he could behind the van. His dog caught up with him, as rapid as an arrow.

The roof came off, letting out a cloud of black smoke among which there darted bronze-colored flames. The harness, eaten away by the fire, let the horses go free. One of them, exhausted and burnt to the quick, fell down, and atop him landed the incandescent skeleton of the van, cutting through his red flesh.

The other raced off, leaping about in a field, and was observed for a long time as he dashed about insanely, until he disappeared in the depths of the corn.

Like crows, the policemen descended upon the smoking remains.

The knife-grinder soon arrived at the scene of the fire. His dog, having scented the miserable remains, came back to him and stood between his legs, wagging its tail.

"Signor brigadiere, Signor brigadiere...."

The brigadier got off his horse and turned around to see who was calling him.

"Couldn't you kill my dog with a pistol shot? Believe me: I didn't mean for it to turn out this way. I just needed the time to get over the border.... Yes, kill my dog, Signor brigadiere, and eat the rooster to my health."

Having spoken these words, he stood firmly planted, holding his wrists together, and smiled as if to say: "Come on, don't you understand...?"

# The Sirens

She had finished her ablutions. While she was drying herself, it seemed to Edmea, who was completely naked, that she was imprinting her old age afresh upon her flesh; so that, as she pulled the sheet over broad surfaces and intimate recesses, she kept her eyes fixed on the window, where the curtain was swelling a bit in the breeze; and she took only hasty glances at the long mirror on the front of the armoire, where she caught rapid and happy glimpses of pink.

Sure of her own still-intact legs, those of a childless woman, she covered her breasts and belly with the sheet and went over to admire those legs in the mirror. Her red slippers lent grace to her feet by hiding them, overrun as they were with great purple veins, and deformed by stagnant swelling.

Taking her time over this contemplation, she saw herself reflected in a gray, uniform light that showed the objects in the room behind her as instruments of solitude, and which revealed on her dried-up face, amidst the coarse and uncombed curls, a pained expression that had come upon her unbidden, catching her unawares; seeing it, she wondered whether she had not, perhaps, been unconsciously keeping her eyes shut tight for a while.

She sighed in discouragement. No one in that little hotel, selected because she had sensed in it promiscuity and big doings at night, had taken any notice of her, yielding and indulgent as she was. She had not even attracted any attention in those famous haunts of the immense city where she had gone alone late in the evening, hoping to inspire those distracted men – who had only too many offers to choose among – to boldness.

For some time now the night porter, a near-hunch-back with bulging eyes who came, slovenly and still warm from bed, to open the front door, seemed to be mocking her when she returned, a woman alone and upset; and she would hurry up the winding staircase out of fear of him, malicious and filthy as he was. She would lock herself away in her room, almost as if to restore her sense of self-worth after her humiliating wanderings.

Reduced to the vague anticipation of a happy surprise, she engaged in these intimate afternoon washings so as to break up the day and then recommence it with renewed hope that for her – ready as could be, purged of secret flaws – chance might the more easily encourage an amorous encounter, which was to be accepted with no reservations or dangerous delays; and instead, the days went by, useless and uneventful.

A stronger gust filled the curtain, lifting into the air the border that had lain on the floor. Edmea waited motionless for the curtain to fly even higher, thus revealing her to the gray, many-windowed houses opposite, so that she could run to shut her own window and so recover the modesty and self-esteem that were lacking in the vain courage of her erotic imaginings.

Instead, she heard rapid footsteps in the corridor, followed by three knocks at her door.

She felt desperate that she was naked, that she did not know what words to call out to the person who was knocking; then, in a flash, a bold idea came to her. She threw the sheet over her shoulders and said, in a panting voice, "Come in," unable to feel on her face the triumphant smile of a beautiful woman.

"Come in," she repeated in a shrill cry, frightened by her own daring.

The door opened bit by bit, and there gleamed

before her, shining with smiling malice, the eyes of her friend Colomba, set deep in a worn out, painted face.

Edmea let out a yell of anger and ran to throw herself down on the bed, trying to draw the blanket over her nakedness.

"What's the matter? What on earth is the matter?" asked Colomba, pulling the door shut behind her. "I frightened you, eh?"

"Go away, go away. Let me get dressed. Can't you see what a state I'm in?"

"I can see that very well; but excuse me, who was it who said to come in? You thought I was somebody else, eh?" She uttered this last interjection as though speaking to a child, meanwhile shaking her head and, along with it, her large flower basket of a hat. Colomba realized that she was making herself hateful to her friend.

Edmea, with a grim look in her eyes, was now feeling herself strong and capable of revenge.

"Oh, stay here then," she said. "There's time, there's time, I tell you."

Colomba's air of incredulity was not sufficient to hide a certain discomfort: she remained silent and seemed — just as though she hadn't heard the other's words — to be seeking in some void in her memory an important thing that she had to tell her friend.

She approached the bed.

"Listen," she said, "I've come to take you with me on an excursion around the town. I've seen that there's a really fine public garden on the other side of the river. It's always full of people, and somewhere there's a café where two women on their own can get themselves noticed. And I've got another very good idea for after dinner...."

She stopped to look at Edmea, expecting a painful refusal that would provoke an episode of jealousy.

"I was thinking," she resumed enthusiastically, "that

the two of us could go to the famous 'Negro Dance Hall.' How do you like that idea? We'll dance. You know that Negroes invite you from a distance with their looks. They must be really cheery and naughty."

The word "naughty" made Edmea, still hidden under the blanket, give a start. She repeated it, laughing. Then she covered even her face, embarrassed to admit, by accepting this very promising invitation, to the lie implicit in her earlier reticence.

"I like the idea very much," she said with an effort. "It's all fine.... It's just that I'll need to write a few words to leave at the reception when we go down. It's fine, my dear, it's fine. You tell me that the garden is nice?"

Her eyes flashing, Colomba laughed. Then, having recovered from a suspicion, she began looking about the room in order to discover the secret of the other's good luck, a luck which had passed her by.

"Tell me", she said distractedly, "do you spend more or less what I do for your room?"

"Yes, I think so. Why?"

"In my hotel I've got an airier room and a slightly larger bed. I see that it's not in my interest to change." She began wandering about the room, as though carefully comparing other details.

Edmea slowly freed herself from the blanket and got out of bed, trying to make her nakedness seem natural, just a moment of distraction. Embarrassed by her friend's sharp and inquisitive eyes, she laughed with forced gaiety; and having taken her by the hand, she said, "Touch me here: I'm still hard and smooth." She obliged Colomba to feel her, although she made her leave her hand limp, guiding it so as to avoid any more detailed investigation.

Colomba was laughing excessively: she was working up the swing necessary for the blow that she, in turn, intended to deliver. She threw herself backwards onto the bed and lifted up her skirt and slip in order to reveal – she, too – hard, smooth nakedness.

From so much laughing, they both had tears in their eyes.

"We're off to find adventure!" They laughed at absurdity and pain, like incurably ill patients who have decided to make a public show of strength.

The bursts of laughter, the silences charged with hilarity, the renewed outbreaks – all this lasted quite a while. Tired, inwardly fatigued, they looked each other in the face and could find no more strength to laugh: they smiled at each other in unreserved friendship and mutual comprehension, after which, each seemed ashamed of the other.

Edmea began to dress hurriedly, sorry at the same time to be looking so much like Colomba, who was all dolled up in feathers. In just a slip and a brassiere, Edmea felt as free and agile as a young girl.

Having put on her purple velvet dress, she began to deal with her face; and then Colomba, too, wanted to retouch her make-up.

Immersed in the greenish mirror, they competed to see who was the more daring in reddening her lips and in burying the creases and bags under her eyes beneath a layer of blackish grease. Every now and then they stopped to inspect themselves. As they gazed, each envied the other the gleam in her eyes: mirrors reflecting a flame that the senses and the soul doubted could be maintained for long with no backsliding.

Before going downstairs, Edmea seated herself at the table and pretended to be writing a letter. She made a few scratches with her pen; but, fearful lest her friend had drawn near, she stopped to see where she was, covering the page with the blotting paper. Colomba was near the window, ostentatiously looking out. Reassured, Edmea wrote a series of invocations to the ever-awaited unknown one, joined in a design her first tortuous scrawls, and rapidly folded the paper, which was immediately covered with blots from the wet ink.

"Well, that's done," she said, sealing the page in an envelope. "Let's go."

Down in the narrow, somewhat dark hallway, Edmea stopped before a little piece of furniture with numbered slots, inserted the letter into number twelve, and then went her way with the uncertain and pensive air of one who fears that she may have made a mistake. When she got to the door she said, "Wait a moment." She went back, took the letter, and put it in her own box, making sure that Colomba, out in the street, was not spying on her.

Having carried out this empty and pointless deception, she rejoined her companion, filled with the anxiety of one who feels she must explain herself, although she knows quite well that it would be better to remain silent.

"Sometimes men are such bores," she said, hoping that the phrase would somehow justify her maneuvers; and she immediately grew confused at having acted against her own will by adding a comment full of new mysteries.

Colomba turned to look at her in amazement, and then smiled, as if she had taken the comment as an allusion to a husband or lover who was well known to her friend. She said: "Never mind. These are things one has to put up with. They pass."

After having thus spoken to each other in riddles, they were both embarrassed and could no longer find anything real or sincere to say.

As if by tacit agreement, they descended the first stairway into the underground. Aboard the train, during the dark, anxious passage through the sinister tunnels, they were intent upon a complicated exchange of small coins, because Colomba was paying Edmea back an old debt. The white, slightly soiled gloves dealt out the coins with the necessary hesitancy of the elderly; the women insisted upon checking for errors and recounting everything.

When they had reached their destination and climbed back up to street level, the gold of the sky had turned reddish and was already pierced by craters of gray background: the houses and trees had a modesty of outline and color, as though they belonged to a land colder and more severe than the one from which the women had just arrived.

The public garden was just a few steps away, and already dark within the first strip of trees that protected it from the city; it seemed uninviting, on account of the continuous exodus of children, women, and baby carriages through its open gates. As though preparing for the tedium of a train journey, Edmea bought a newspaper and trailed along after her friend.

Having passed through the first zone of trees, they found themselves facing one of the grand marble staircases leading down to the piazza around the basin.

The majesty of the architecture intimidated them a little; they descended slowly and almost with regret as far as the first crunchy gravel.

Stiff in bearing, looking around out of the corner of their eyes, they took a turn about the basin, where some people were intent upon throwing crumbs to the fish in order to get them to rise from the indecipherable depths towards the top of the water, which was still agleam with little bits of grass and dust floating on the surface. When the women realized that they had begun to go around for the second time, they went to sit down on an unoccupied bench near a rectangular stretch of lawn with, here and there, star-shaped arrangements of bushes bearing flowers of a very pure red.

From the upper level, children were throwing bread to the sparrows, while large pigeons waited in stillness, squat upon the grass like animals incapable of flight. The white breadcrumbs fell on the grass and tended to get lost in it. The envious pigeons fell upon them in order to steal them; but they arrived ridiculously late by comparison with the sparrows, whose pecking was infallible. Disappointed or already full from having eaten earlier, the pigeons took off as if for far distant destinations and then perched on the nearest branches or in the treetops, in pompous groups, looking too heavy by comparison with the airy foliage.

The peace of the garden, which made one lose the sense of being in the city, convinced them once again that they had been played false on certain occasions when they had set forth full of fire and hope, only to be led towards a sad and not-fully-confessed torment.

They exchanged a grimace of disdain concerning the basin and made hastily for the tables of a little café beneath the trees. Many of the seats were empty; and those which were occupied were unreachable islands, so much did the couples of lovers sitting there seem to be elsewhere. Off on his own, a solitary young man was reading a book while sipping now and then at his large glass of beer.

As soon as they had sat down, they began to study him as the only object worthy of attention. Each of them had a murmured comment to offer, and yet, they did not speak to each other. The youth, having sensed the annoying weight of their gazes, looked back at them, but stealthily, and almost with alarm.

Convinced that the fact that there were two of them was harmful to the chances of each, they felt a bit like rivals; and they took turns smiling at him encouragingly, like the alternating red and green beams of a lighthouse.

Another young man arrived from the basin to join the first who, in self-defense, had rendered his gaze distracted and dreamy. The two men spoke to each other for a moment, and the newcomer sat down next to the other, who was now all smiles, happy that he was no longer alone; then they looked towards the women with self-assured eyes that were anxious to pass judgment.

Edmea and Colomba, leaning forward stiffly down to their hands, which played with the dangling fingers of their gloves, perhaps provoked the two young men to cruelly obscene imaginings; the youths cast fleeting glances and laughed with the irritation that comes from being uncomfortably seated.

While awaiting events, Edmea perceived Colomba's somewhat heavy breathing, and then her own, which had taken on the same rhythm.

The young men, who had once again turned serious, paid them no more heed; they were conversing, pointing at the glasses of beer in front of them. The first one showed the other some small change, with a nonchalant smile which then turned sad; he blocked with his hand the gesture of his friend, who was reaching for the coins in his own pocket.

That action, observed by Edmea, was a revelation to her.

"Don't you see," she murmured, "that they're settling their accounts? They must have very little money between them.... Perhaps they're thinking that they can't afford to keep us company...." In so speaking, she thought that she had found a consolation for her friend-although not for herself-in the event that the hoped – for encounter should not take place, as she already felt that it wouldn't.

Colomba smiled at their difficulties, drew a wad of banknotes from her purse, and ostentatiously began to count them. Edmea imitated her gesture: she, too, thought that this display of wealth was bound to reassure the young men, convincing them of the cost-free generosity of the women's love.

Once the young men had left and the café tables had been abandoned, Edmea and Colomba remained alone in the shadows of the trees, feeling chilly in the air of the evening which had fallen so suddenly.

The now-deserted garden was once again vast, with its grand marble architecture and its masses of trees. From the interior of the little café there arrived the tinkling of cups and glasses, intimate and calm like the sounds of a country kitchen. To remember the city, they had to listen for distant sounds and noises, or look over the tufted treetops at the great glow of reddish light above the azure.

"Let's go," they said, arising from the cold, damp chairs; then, practically running, they made for the gate, fearful lest they be locked in. Outside they found the city like a third friend who would not leave them alone with their desires, but who promised comfort and easy ways to satisfy those desires. The pleasure of this renewed encounter did not last long.

Without a destination, with the sense of being condemned to renounce everything, they wound up trotting along with their eyes lowered like hunters who, disturbed in the forest by wood-gatherers, have lost all hope that the propitious hour will return.

"Here it's not like home, where everybody goes out for a stroll at this hour," observed Colomba. She didn't want her voice to betray annoyance, since she wanted her friend to accept their fruitless excursion as something inevitable.

"We'll have to stop someplace for dinner," said Edmea. "Let's look for a nice little restaurant." She looked at Colomba, not wishing to be misunderstood: she wanted a cheap, discreet trattoria.

Colomba, weighted down by remorse at having proposed such a miserable outing, straightened up with a decisive air and said, "Come. I know just the place."

The wealthy-looking neighborhood offered only

infrequent luxury trattorias, in front of which they hung around without mustering up the courage to go in, torn as they were between tight-fistedness and timidity.

"Not here. They'll skin us alive, can't you see?" protested Edmea when she saw Colomba drawing too near to the entrances where uniformed doormen bowed and smiled invitingly.

At each refusal, Colomba bit her lips in displeasure and remained silent.

Finally, not caring whether her friend was following her or not, Colomba went up to the threshold of a little restaurant of more modest appearance than the others.

Stiff and stern, she said "Two" to the waiter who had immediately come running; and then she stood there in the street, without finding the courage to point out any one table that particularly struck her fancy.

Edmea, who had now come up to her, remained distant and hostile, quite willing to cut a poor figure just so long as they could get away from the place.

Nonetheless, they let the bowing waiter take their cloaks. They were happily surprised, coming out from under them feeling warm and fragrant, and they let the waiter seat them at a table almost in the middle of the room.

They looked at each other for a moment, smiling in embarrassment, unable to listen to the waiter who was offering advice about the menu with almost ironic benevolence.

"Tomato salad?"

They assented, pleased at the familiarity of the dish, but they felt immediate shame when his pointing finger drew their attention to the fact that they had chosen the cheapest antipasto.

The waiter went off to place the order.

"Don't you agree that this is a good place?" asked Colomba. "They're so nice!"

"We'll see how nice they are when they bring the

bill," said Edmea dryly.

"Ah," exploded Colomba, "how sharp-tempered you are. That means that I'm supposed to pay, since it's all my fault."

"That isn't what I meant; I can even pay for everything myself." She ended her angry speech with a smile, because the waiter was approaching with the dishes.

To distract themselves, they had a look around.

The tables nearest them were unoccupied and white. In the transparent pitchers there shone the magical purity of water; the sparkling knives and forks divided each tablecloth, devoid of plates, into four zones, while the center of each table was marked by a little vase with three drooping flowers. Farther off, all the tables were occupied by people intent on eating. They had a meditative air, almost as though they were intimidated by the waiters standing around, and by the walls painted with dark, vaguely religious figures.

At the only occupied table in the deserted area sat a young couple with a five-year-old child who was sucking on a pear and rebelling against his mother, who wanted to peel it for him.

Having finished their examination of the room, they realized that they had the salad in front of them, cut into red slices. They attacked it hungrily.

The waiter arrived treacherously, asking them what wine they wanted.

As if to astonish him, avenging themselves for any mistaken opinion he might have formed, they both said angrily, one after the other: "Champagne." They were appalled at their own audacity.

"What brand?" asked the waiter, beginning to reel off five or six names.

"It doesn't matter. Give us the one you think is best." They waited for him to leave so that they could breathe freely.

They heard a voice call out a famous brand-name to the man at the counter; and, understanding that it was for them, they had the sense of having made an inappropriate gesture.

After Edmea had been eating for a bit, she stopped, saying: "Tomatoes upset my stomach." Colomba snorted angrily and took some more from the salad bowl.

The waiter came over with the bottle.

Standing before the mute and awestruck women, he went through the ritual gesture of removing the wire from around the cork, at which he then began to tug skillfully, coaxing it out of the bottle.

Edmea and Colomba awaited the pop of the cork in almost physical terror. The man, on the other hand, seemed to be enjoying himself, smacking the bottle on the bottom while the swollen cork emerged little by little from the neck; it was as though he were deliberately keeping them in agony.

The sudden pop gave people at the other tables a start; they turned around to look.

The two women's appearance in conjunction with that delicious wine must have signified something if every-one smiled, including the child, who saw his parents doing so. Unaware and deaf, the women raised their glasses and drank, striving after exquisite poses for their fingers on the stems of the glasses and an elegant manner of drinking from the sparkling rim. But then the red remains of the tomatoes on their plates became, for them, almost shameful: with a gesture, they told the waiter to take them away, ordering sole and refined side-dishes. Their awareness of how much they were spending made them audacious, and they looked about them freely, seeking themselves in the distant mirrors where they appeared as blackish ghosts amidst the vaporous pink of the lampshades. They chewed with gusto, exchanging little bursts of explosive laughter which soon turned raucous.

The child observed them curiously, and they smiled

back and made little gestures of tenderness in the effort to obtain a smile from the mother and father, who seemed irritated and almost apprehensive on their son's account.

After the fruit course they wanted coffee, and after the coffee, liqueurs. They ordered liqueurs of two different brands, so as to reassure themselves as to their reciprocal independence.

Having finished their meals, the customers were leaving; and, given the late hour, no new ones arrived. But the women felt no desire to depart, at anchor as they finally were in a hospitable port. They did not speak: they felt at ease and had no expectations, like people who still have lots of time to decide on their evening's diversions.

Colomba called the waiter, who at first listened to her deferentially as she asked for the strangest information regarding the city and its night-time haunts; then, having assumed an astute and confidential air, he stuck his head between them and, speaking softly and looking over at the counter, he offered them advice.

Distracted, they did not reply: each was following a different itinerary of pleasure. Colomba saw herself at the theater, with the shadow of a man in the discreet, music-filled box; Edmea was in a flower-bedecked barge on the river, leaving the dance-floor and staring at the water as she listened to the preliminary sighs of a man with a black moustache.

Tired of being at the disposition of the two day-dreaming women, the waiter brought them the bill without their having asked for it, saying, "Here you are, my lovely ladies," in a manner that must have amused the last few customers scattered about the room.

Edmea and Colomba paid and tipped him splendidly, out of remorse at having confided in him too much and from their need to appear to him as two grandes dames. While they were wrapping themselves in their cloaks,

Colomba said: "The flowers... the flowers... Can we take them?"

"Who cares? Let's just take them," Edmea encouraged her.

Each woman took a red carnation from the vase in the middle of the table and attached it to her chest. From behind the counter, the owner and two languid waiters looked on smilingly.

"I should say so," murmured Edmea. "When you pay a bill such as ours, you've also got a right to the flowers." She went out without responding to the bow of their waiter.

In order to give themselves an air and, indeed, to maintain in the street the lordliness of the trattoria, they spoke to each other in very brief phrases that meant nothing, but which kept their lips in motion: tiny little movements of an almost intense sensuousness.

From his box, a cab-driver waiting beside the sidewalk gestured at them to offer his services; then he turned upon hearing a far-off whistle, setting off as though he had rejected them in favor of a better customer.

This display of an outright preference once again made them feel alone amidst the enmity of the great city: and then, out of a need to appear sure of themselves and in possession of a goal, they walked towards an intersection brightly illuminated by the cafés at each street corner. They thought of the vaunted ease of city living with a sort of ill-tempered irony directed at themselves. The ministrations of the beauty parlor – the haircuts, the depilations, the roughest manhandling on the part of the masseur – had failed to rejuvenate them or make them more attractive; if anything, these treatments had accentuated, like a poor restoration in a house, the old age which they wished to hide. They admitted it to themselves now: now that the insistently dreamt-of continuous orgy, the new lover every evening, the perpetual display of fireworks were no longer to be hoped for. They thought of a certain big bad youth – a gardener's assistant who had stayed behind in the provinces – as a defenseless creature whom the servant-girls of the neighborhood would forever claim as their own. The homecoming which they had longed for, full of regrets and enchantments to be recounted with meaningful reticence, now looked, instead, like a painful journey, for they would lack the strength to pretend to memories of pleasures they had not enjoyed.

Out of the certainty that their suffering was shared, neither of the two dared to speak or to change course. Having passed through the light-filled intersection, they entered a dark avenue. The pale street-lamps placed here and there beneath the trees, in order to dissipate their nocturnal mystery, cast a silvery light on the lowest branches and leaves, making them appear washed-out and transparent.

There were few people about. They were almost all men who, before meeting the two women, stepped aside, but not out of courtesy; it was almost as though they feared an unpleasant encounter, or as if they did not trust two shadows in such a solitary place.

Further along, quite far from the intersection, encounters grew even rarer. An agitated women flitted along towards them, stopped, and turned back; she displayed the uncertainty of one who is waiting and cannot make up her mind to leave.

They heard footsteps behind them on the sidewalk. Their hearts filled with suspense, like those of two little girls entering a museum of natural history, they kept on walking, because they had understood and they wanted to see. A man passed them: the waiting woman went towards him, murmuring something. They heard an thick and ironic "thank you" from the man who, in order to get away, had to free his arm brutally from a clasp intended to keep him there.

"Did you see that? Did you see that?" whispered Edmea, following intently with her eyes the figure of the woman who, after a weepy chase, had once again stopped in the shadows.

Another man was coming from the opposite direction; the first man stopped near a tree-trunk, out of curiosity to see if the newcomer would yield where he had held firm. The newcomer came forward hesitantly, as if seeking someone. He passed the woman, who began to follow him.

"Let's get out of here!" said Colomba. "He's coming toward us. Just think!"

They fled towards the illuminated city.

Both wanted to escape comparison with the wretched figure they had seen: a comparison which offended and tormented them. To console herself, Edmea thought of the scribbles she had left in the hotel as a gesture of love carried out at the urging of an inner purity.

They were walking in the middle of the road, so as to avoid any new encounters, when a hail from a cab-driver freed them of this fear.

The cab had already halted, but they, startled as if by a fleeting vision, were still yelling for him to stop.

They climbed in and, having closed the door, they were awaiting departure.

The driver knocked on the window and asked them something they couldn't understand.

"To the Negro Dance Hall," Colomba called out angrily, clutching the hand of Edmea, who was trembling. Then Colomba fell back, upset and amazed at having expressed this forgotten desire.

As they looked out of the windows, their shaky knowledge of the city grew ever more confused. Once they had gotten to the end of the very long avenue, the carriage went through crowded, well lit streets of which, after the first change of direction, they remembered nothing but the impossibility of ever recognizing them again; and they looked to see if they could spy, from a distance, less uniform houses or thoroughfares. At an intersection which they thought they knew, they thought about getting out: they knocked on the glass, but the coachman did not hear them. In the trotting of the horse, unfrightened by any shadows, there was the sense of a long and tedious journey.

"But where is he taking us? Did he understand?" asked Edmea.

"Wait. We'll see."

"No, no. I'm going to call him; I want to know." Both of them leaned out of the windows, trying to read the names of the cross-streets, which remained dark and illegible on the white, slightly phosphorescent stone plaques.

Having entered a neighborhood of narrow streets and humble cafés, the carriage frequently changed direction. They thought that the voice of the coachman, who yelled at laggards to get out of the way, would surely draw down upon them the wrathful revenge of the obscure folk, wearing working-class caps on their heads, who had not had time to see what was coming.

When the cab stopped before the door of the Negro Dance Hall, they really thought that the driver had made a mistake; they remained huddled in their seats, waiting. Through the glass they could see a simple café of the working-class neighborhood, the exterior of which was dimly illuminated by some Venetian-style hanging lanterns. On the sidewalk, a group of the curious, glued to the windows – which were defended against their gaze by yellowish curtains pierced here and there by holes – turned to gaze with great interest at the silent carriage.

The somewhat startled driver climbed down from his box, causing the vehicle to dance about a bit on its springs, and opened the door. He said and repeated, as if in ironic reproach: "This is the Negro Dance Hall. This is it."

Edmea and Colomba got out without making any show of resistance and ran to the entrance, so as to pass quickly beyond the gaze of the curious who had huddled round.

Once they had opened the front door, they halted for a moment in puzzlement. They were looking past the first room, with its bar counter, into a large yellowish room where water seemed to be dripping from the dim, painted walls; beyond a wooden gate set up as a divider between the two spaces, they could see the somewhat startling sight of black heads undulating to the rhythm of the dance.

The entrance to the room was made narrower by two tables placed near the gate; at one of these, a black man sat playing with some pink tickets.

They plucked up their courage and went forward; the black man thrust a chestnut-colored hand out from his white cuff and invited them in with a gesture.

Edmea, who was behind Colomba, turned around once they had passed into the second room, and saw the man looking towards the door on the street as though he were expecting someone to come in after them; but she did not immediately understand why. She felt someone touch her shoulder. It was the black man; with a half-sly, half-ferocious smile, he pointed to the tickets. Colomba likewise returned to the two tables. Having opened their purses to take out some money, they looked fixedly at a sign where different prices were indicated for gentlemen and ladies, almost as though they were expecting an injustice or a painful affront from the man.

The black man, imperturbable, tore off two yellow ladies' tickets and took their money. Another black man, immensely tall, dressed in a full-cut light-gray outfit, came towards them, inviting them to a little unoccupied table off to one side; but before they could join him, they had to wait for the dancing crowd to thin out a little when the furious music, full of piercing cries, had died down.

A white waiter, passing by with a full tray, looked at them, smiled at the black man, and entered into the crush, politely asking people to let him through. The black man pushed them along behind the waiter, and they found themselves tossed about and rigid amidst all those bouncing, clinging bodies whose frenzy was regulated by the rhythm. As they tried to break free by pushing their way forward with their elbows, they were startled by the apparition of a pale, white woman's face – it was like a beam of light – close to a dark face with thick lips; it struck them as a strange denunciation of the obscenity of this dancing. They looked where the two bodies were clinging to one another, a bit drunk with the obsessive racket and the animal heat. Once they had finally reached the table, they sat down, the better to observe the crush, and to savor the miracle of having made their way through it.

"Me?" asked Edmea. "Do you really think I could dance like that?"

"One can do anything," Colomba replied in a hard voice. "It's just a question of feeling oneself up to it."

They remained silent for a while, studying the situation in order to understand how introductions and invitations were effected at this exotic ball.

Edmea maintained that they all danced without knowing one another, simply because they were at the ball; Colomba, on the other hand, was certain that they all knew each other ahead of time.

"It's the Negro colony, you see, and they invite one another without making a big fuss about it."

During a break, some people sat down at the table next to theirs. They were a thin black man, on whose smoky, bluish face a little wound near the mouth formed a mark of fire-red flesh, and a young girl with a corrupt air.

The latter looked at them with a satirical frown, and suggested that her companion have a look.

The black man's luminous smile struck the two women as offensive. They responded by putting on wry faces expressive of disdain. At that moment, the dancing resumed; the girl headed for the center of the floor to dance with another man, and the black man, left alone, kept an eye on her. Then he began laughing in childlike fury, choking on his beer and spraying it all over himself.

"Can't you see? Now he's going to come to ask us to dance," murmured Edmea with a kind of horror. "What are we to do? Do we have to say yes?"

Colomba did not reply; it seemed that the expectation of the invitation was a source of anguish to her, for she had grown pale and was staring obstinately into her glass.

"I," she at last said emphatically, "would like to give it a try. It's something I've got to do, or else I'll be left with the desire afterwards, unfortunately for me."

"That's true," said Edmea in approbation. "We've got to try everything in this world. Otherwise we'll always be suffering from remorse at the things we've left undone."

They fell silent, biting their lips, which gave off none of the warmth of a living thing, so encrusted were they with make-up.

The dances went on for quite a while, following one another in intoxicated noisiness, with occasional brief pauses during which the frenzied activity of the dancers came to a halt, as if by surprise; the crowd slowly thinned out at fixed distances during these breaks, as though each person were taking up anew his or her place on the chessboard. Accompanied to their tables, the women sat down, making a gesture around their forehead, as though to drive away something frantic and disturbing. Then there started up afresh the raucous laughter, the confused shouting, a Babel of songs suffocated by the muffled closeness of the room; and then suddenly, like a bunch of scrap-iron, the music would come crashing down into the room; after this initial blow, a flute would break free of the stressful noises, almost as if to mock with its purity the first couple already clinging to each other in the middle of the floor.

Through the little wooden gate, new black people continued to arrive; also whites, who would pause before entering, looking pale with consternation.

Already a bit disoriented, Edmea and Colomba gazed imploringly at the white men as they came in, as if to call for help. They would watch them as they moved forward with laughing faces, fell into the rhythm, and seized black women about the waist; the black women cheerily accepted this brusque invitation.

"We've chosen a dreadful place," said Edmea, who was no longer astonished that no one came over to ask them to dance. She watched her friend stealthily.

Nearby, leaning on an iron column, the black master of ceremonies looked about him, distracted yet always ready to smile into the crowd.

Colomba called to him with a gesture, and he came hurrying over.

In an irritable and sniveling voice, she said, "Oh, but we don't want to dance."

"Dear me! Haven't you got gentlemen?" asked the man, shaking his head in disapproval and gesturing towards the room, to make it very clear that it was difficult at the moment to find men who were not otherwise engaged. Following his finger, they noticed two women in the crush, one black and one mulatto, who were dancing together, draped about each other. A bit taken aback by this advice, they didn't manage to answer him as they would have wished; he had already bustled off.

"Do you see what revolting stuff? He wanted us to dance together like those two madwomen! It's shameful! Ah!"

The black man returned immediately, followed by a little black man dressed in a groom's costume. Having bowed timidly, the little man, uncertain which to chose, asked them both to dance, waving his hand first at one and then at the other.

"You dance, Colomba, since you want to. I'm tired," said Edmea. She turned her back to show her disgust, as if to make her friend feel guilty.

"What's this?" replied Colomba, shaking Edmea furiously. "Do you think I can dance with a servant? Who do you take me for?" She turned to the master of ceremonies and his acolyte and screamed, "Go away! It's disgraceful! Come, Edmea; this is no place for us."

Their neighbors turned around at the shrill sound of her voice, curious and laughing at her last words. The fury of the two women struggling with their cloaks, and the painted wooden dignity of their faces, set off a contagious hilarity, utterly lacking in compassion, that infected the whole room.

For a moment, they thought that the short, abrupt bursts coming from the orchestra were due to the musicians' laughing into their instruments. Pale and trembling, they had to make their way among the dancers; the white, luminous gazes turned towards them rhythmically, looking mercilessly into their faces; they were surrounded by unchecked amusement. An overwhelming hatred drove them to shove and hit the people around them. As they passed violently by, the embracing couples, undulating or standing stock-still on the floor, sniggered and pissed themselves with laughter.

They went through the front room and out into the street, where they found themselves surrounded by the crowd of the curious, who stared at them with the interrogative power of people who are trying to understand an event they have not witnessed. While the women hesitated as to which direction to choose, a general impulse led the people outside the dance-hall to gather around them, eager to know why they were fleeing.

They needed to escape with quick steps, which overwhelming shame soon turned into a run; they chose the dark side of the street, shadowed by buildings in front of which there stood dim street-lights placed at regular intervals, at a considerable distance from one another.

They cried out as they ran, without grasping the substance of their own cries, which sounded in their ears like a high-pitched whistle generated by great speed. Still unaware of her own suffering, Edmea heard Colomba, who was running ahead of her, uttering little shrieks of desperation, while her large black straw hat cast undulating shadows on the shining roadway. She managed to catch up with her; she tried to catch hold of her hand to hold her back, but Colomba fled, breaking free with furious gestures. Edmea stopped to catch her breath, and in a few moments she was alone.

A distant clatter of high heels reminded her of her fleeing friend; alarmed at being unable to catch up with her, she began to cry out desperately: "Colomba, Colomba, wait for me!" Running and calling out, Edmea thought of her friend as the warm and supportive presence she needed if she was not to topple over like a broken thing on the hard pavement which seemed to her, at certain points, too vertiginously steep for her weak legs.

She found her friend standing still at the first intersection, whence immense avenues led toward dark and unknown destinations; but seeing her so shut up in herself, she could not find the strength to embrace her. She took up a position nearby, apprehensive all the while lest she be driven away.

All they could make out of a monument surrounded by sideways-leaning trees was the white base and the dark form of a large bronze lion. They could not remember having seen it before; there was nothing at all that might direct them to a street they already knew. As though they were being chased by an enemy who was undeserving of a change of course, they proceeded straight on their way.

Fearing some outburst of madness from Colomba, Edmea kept her gaze directed downwards, trying not to provoke the first word, convinced that it was her destiny to keep up with her friend. She felt a hand clutching her shoulder in order to hold her back; turning slightly, she saw Colomba's eyes staring into her own.

"Will you come with me to the river?" Colomba cried out, seemingly ready to release her hold, as though disgusted by the contact.

"Yes," replied Edmea hoarsely. She hugged Colomba in desperation.

As if this decision had suggested a clear route, they left the avenue and went down the first side street. It was poorly lit; a white façade at the end, struck by a beam from a lamp, gave the impression of moonlight reflected in a series of mirrors.

"The river. Where's the river? This way, this way." They queried each other, replying according to the dictates of their anguish; they were fiercely determined to find their way without asking directions of anyone.

It was Edmea who, having lost by now all self-control, let herself go in a desperate fit of weeping.

"Oh! oh! oh!" Exasperated by the sobs now coming from her companion, Edmea began to run, pulling Colomba along behind her.

"Let's look calm, Edmea, so that no one will figure out where we're going," begged Colomba.

The self-pity aroused by such words provoked both of them to fresh weeping.

Ever more distressed, they wandered through a hundred alleyways and a hundred streets. At every encounter, they felt humiliated and fell silent, as though they were being strangled. Then the sob that had built up in them would break forth, a strange, isolated cry. They had lost the sense of time, but felt that they had been walking for hours and hours. This feeling suddenly brought on an unbearable weariness, filled with false imaginings. The river became a prize to be won: its waters seemed a mobile yet tenacious support for the journey of two pale Ophelias. They passed beneath all the bridges in the city, finally emerging into the countryside, which was rendered gentle and white by the first traces of dawn.

They had been walking for some time around the fence of a large garden which bordered here and there on dark, tree-lined streets where its contours were lost amidst the leaves high above, and which touched elsewhere on narrow lanes walled in by silent houses; here the garden's borders were so clearly demarcated that the fence itself seemed superfluous. By now they were following the fence, the only route they knew; and the predictably mocking outcome was that they kept on coming back to places where they had already been.

Down below them, the fence curved to take in trees and long, low sheds. A mysterious scent of country air came forth to meet them; a vaster, deeper silence made itself felt in the circular avenue.

Then they noticed that just beyond the fence there were pear trees in flower, forced by an iron trellis to grow with their branches in the form of a candelabrum to the two sides of the straight trunks. The trees were spaced in a row like soldiers, and offered their flowers at the highest point of each of those branches which had grown there from an unnatural effort.

They stopped, with a feminine awareness that here was something worthy of admiration.

"What beauty! What a fragrance!" murmured Edmea; and Colomba, competing with her, said, "How enchanting these pear trees are by night!" She then fell silent, as if aware that her voice had uttered something that was out of tune with the rest.

At that moment, they understood that their fictitious desire to die was no more: the naturalness with which they had paused to admire the pear trees had led them back to life.

On the low wall to which the fence was anchored, a surface, bearing the marks of the stonemason's chisel, remained unencumbered. They sat down upon it, their legs dangling and their backs against the fence, tearful with mysterious gratitude.

They were still thinking about the river, but in hopes of having gotten far away from it in their crazed wanderings; and they were fearful on account of the dampness of the place, where dark waters ran beyond the garden that had saved them.

If they looked inside, past the trellis of the flowering pear trees, they saw an herb garden. In every one of the zones into which it was divided, there stood — where there were, as yet, no stalks or branches — a stick supporting an enameled plate bearing a name. It all appeared very unpromising: the earth looked as sterile as the ashes in an urn. The greenhouses, facing in various directions, looked like shelters for timorous gardeners in love with the night-time sky: through the transparent windows they could see, here and there, the shadows of branches, and confused panoplies of poles and implements.

Feeling cold, they drew closer together and embraced each other, seeking a little warmth.

Observing her friend in the light of a street-lamp, Edmea discovered that she was different now, with her face bare of make-up: an old face, but such an appealing one — almost like that of a crying child — that she herself greatly wished to resemble her. Edmea ran her fingers over the black bags beneath her eyes in order to wipe the blackness away; and she bit her lips until she felt them burning and alive with pain.

When even this struck her as insufficient, she once

again began to moan and sob.

"I wish I could never leave this place," she said; and then she led out a cry as, seeing a cupola, she recognized the afternoon garden.

"How exhausted I am!" said Colomba. "Let's stay here. What could frighten us now? Even thieves or murderers — what could they want from two old ladies like us?"

These words were followed by a silence. They were both seeking reasons for consolation in some vision of the future; but, having seen the garden, they were brought back to the burning pain and stinging shame of their adventures in the city.

"What are we going to do?" Edmea dared to murmur.

"We'll go home. Back there, they still don't think of us as two old women," replied Colomba, with a sudden return of strength in her enfeebled voice.

"Yes, yes," said Edmea approvingly, standing up full of hope. "And we'll start to live the way one ought to. We'll make a better impression by giving up certain things.

"For me, this is a serious matter," she went on, "since there's somebody waiting for me."

"Where?"

"At home. You ought to know."

Since she was thinking of other matters, Colomba did not answer, but she found the silence humiliating: she, too, needed to show off lovers in her turn, so that her intentions to live a pure life should also be based on a sacrifice.

"Gustavo's hairy chest revolts me, if I think about it now," Edmea suddenly proclaimed, convinced that this confession marked the beginning of her new life.

"Me, too! It revolts me, too!" cried Colomba, taking Edmea's hands in her own. "Yes, I want you to know: I've slept with Gustavo too. But you'll forgive me, won't you, Edmea? Anyway, we're both through with all that now, as we've been saying."

She fell silent, frightened by the silence of her friend, who was staring at her, her eyes wide with amazement. Colomba tried to hold on to her hands and said in an anguished tone: "We won't be unkind to him, even if we're turning over a new leaf. Is any of this his fault? If he wants to come and see us, with no evil intentions, we'll keep his things in order for him. He's so disorganized! He always loses all his buttons. We'll be friends to poor Gustavo. Right, Edmea?"

"Oh, do shut up," Edmea begged her. "Why have you told me about this? I'm so afraid that I'll hate you tomorrow. Not now, not now," she reassured her. "I'm afraid about tomorrow," she repeated, almost as though she were talking to herself.

"You're right," Edmea added, accepting her friend's proffered neutrality. "We've got to be kind to Gustavo; he deserves it. We'll invite him for a good lunch on Sundays, and we'll take care of his clothing for him. It's true: it's all dirty and ragged."

"Yes," assented Colomba, her voice betraying the dismay occasioned by the unexpected revelation of a memory.

Edmea squeezed her hands to show that she understood, bowing her head. She was in a great hurry to immerse all that laundry in a washtub: laundry which would be, in a certain sense, her redemption. Cleansed in that tub, it would become white, retaining no memory of the body which had worn it.

Tormented as they were, the two women had no sense of the world around them. They were roused, and embarrassed, by the sound of vast and imperious footsteps. A shadow was coming towards them beneath the trees, hugging the fence.

"My God. Who can this be? A thief? A guard?"

"He'll arrest us. What will we say?"

"Keep quiet."

"I'm afraid."

"Then let's get going."

"I haven't the strength."

"Then work up some courage. Can't you hear that he's whistling?"

A tuneful whistle was performing variations on a popular song; it was carried to them on the breath of the night.

The man himself remained some distance behind this harbinger of his presence, as did the rhythmic sounds of heels and of a walking-stick struck every now and then against the pavement.

"It's someone who's going home happy. I'm so afraid: if he sees us and is frightened, he may attack us with his stick. Let's get out of here!"

But by now it was too late, and they understood that their departure from the fence would alarm the solitary passer-by and make him suspicious.

He drew nearer, showing no concern, in the air pierced by his harmonious whistling.

Appalled at the thought of the encounter, the two women spoke is hushed words, incapable of finding the full, self-assured tone of voice that would have proved that theirs was a peaceful, friendly conversation held in the cool of the night.

The man's footsteps slowed down; he was stomping about, as if before some invisible barrier. Their gazes lowered, Edmea and Colomba felt that they were being peered at and scrutinized.

A few blows, dry and hard, on the sidewalk, almost like a warning; and then the whistling resumed, somewhat hesitantly, on a high note.

The steps came forward with an aggressive rhythm.

The moment of the encounter passed like a sudden

blast of heat. Lifting their eyes, they saw the profile of a young man who went on whistling tunefully as he turned into another street, turning his head to look back.

Mute and fearful, they watched him as he moved into the distance beneath the trees, following the fence.

"He resembled our Gustavo," murmured Edmea.

"It's true," agreed Colomba sadly.

In the darkness they blew him sweet, resonant kisses; then they started on the long journey back, which lasted until daybreak.

The dawn light fell upon two poor, exhausted old women who, lost in the immense city, were looking for their hotel.

# The Hawk

The taxidermist, a specialist in birds, stepped forward to greet the customer who had come in just as it was time to shut up shop. The customer advanced timidly, holding out a little basket with a lid, as though it were a ticket that gave him the right to admittance.

"What do you want? How can I help you?"

The new arrival looked around, pausing to admire the mummified birds on the counter, on the shelves, and in the window, and then said:

"I've got a hawk here, but it's alive."

Seeing the other's surprise, he hastened to add:

"I don't know how to kill it; I'm afraid of ruining it. You, who know about these things  can't you do it for me? Afterwards, of course, the job of stuffing it will be yours, because I want to keep it."

"Well, really," said the taxidermist, making an effort, "I only work on dead birds. A hawk can be dangerous.... What if it escapes?"

"It can't escape," replied the man with the basket, smiling calmly. "Would you like to see it? I've made a hood for it." He began to undo the straps of the lid. "Poor creature!" he murmured, undoing the knots with sudden haste. "It must have suffered a lot during our trip here, but I hope that it's still proud. It was so beautiful. Now look what a state it's in!"

Having raised the lid, he placed a somewhat hesitant hand on the gray, feathered body within the basket.

"It's certainly alive: it's really quite warm," he added, smoothing the ruffled feathers with his hand.

A sort of hiss was heard: a smothered cry, feline and horrible.

"What a state you've put it in!" exclaimed the taxidermist cheerily. "It looks like an old lady!" He leaned over to admire the hawk which, having stood up inside the basket, poked its head out – a head tightly wrapped in frayed and dirty gauze, with an opening just sufficient for the hooked beak, which looked as though it were split in two by a gleaming reflection.

The fierce bird raised one talon to the height of its blindfolded eyes, and then stuck it out to explore the empty darkness; finally, leaning to one side as though lamed, it clutched the edge of the basket with its talons.

"I think that with a big needle...," said the customer, spreading apart the feathers on the chest with a finger: thus did he display his willingness to participate in the operation.

The taxidermist did not reply. Smilingly pointing to his hand, which was protected by a rag, he picked the animal up and placed it on a perch meant for parrots.

"Shut up like that in its hood, it doesn't dare make a move," he said, inviting his visitor to watch the scene; using a brush, he pushed the bird of prey which, flapping its wings, kept its balance on the iron rod.

"Now then," resumed the bird's owner, starting to close the basket. "Are you going to kill it for me, or aren't you?"

"I can kill it, but not now. Can't you see that I'm already dressed to go out? Tomorrow morning, as soon as I open, I'll take care of it. Anyway, it's a good idea to wait: that way he'll clean out his innards."

"But that will make him thinner; he'll become ugly."

The taxidermist laughed. "I'll swell him up with straw and cotton. We can leave him where he is – he's as timid as a newly hatched chick." Having pushed the man with the basket out of the shop, he lowered the shutter, put the padlocks in place, and set off in the company of his customer, who had awaited him on the sidewalk in order to negotiate the price.

The main lamp, which had remained lit because the taxidermist had been distracted at closing time, was blazing blindingly in the shop.

Terrified by the roar of the rolling shutter, the iron-gray hawk remained still upon his perch, hiding his head beneath a wing. He could smell a sharp odor of feathers: an odor similar to that of an abandoned nest, grown cold and incorruptible over time.

His long captivity in the basket had so inhibited his sense of his life as a flying creature that – rediscovering this sense in the odor – he believed himself to have fallen into a stony cave high up on the barren mountain where he habitually dwelt: all that was missing was the long breath of the air that raised his feathers and rearranged them like a caress.

After that first roar of thunder, he heard nothing else that frightened him: he could perceive occasional clanks and rubbing noises in the distance, and every now and then the rumbling of the stormy sky; but it all came from far away, like sounds coming from the plain far below.

Reassured, he tried flapping his wings. He opened them wide and moved them about in the heavy air, arousing a too-immediate resonance, a trembling of mysterious sheets of glass.

The smallness of the space weighed upon his wings, which he timidly closed once again.

With a tremulous and hesitant gesture, he placed his talons upon the gauze hood; having understood that it could be torn, he devoted his energies to ridding himself of it.

With his wild blows, he injured his head and neck several times over. Using his beak, free amidst the loosened bindings, he blindly pursued the ends and unravelings of the gauze, twisting himself into painful positions; while every trolley-car that passed in the street, every cart, was a noisy gust of wind among the rocks, a roar filled with echoes that were new to him since his unremembered fall into this cave.

So as to keep his balance over the unknown abyss that he felt all around him, he waved his wings about frantically, filling the room with rackety whooshing sounds.

Thus disturbed, the air sent back, more strongly than ever, the odor of an abandoned nest. By pulling so much at it, he had wound the blindfold more tightly about his eyes. The hawk stuck his neck out and let out a low-pitched cry, as though challenging an enemy – five, ten times over – and then, exhausted, fell silent and sheltered his head beneath his wing.

When he resumed his struggle, he went about it calmly and slowly: he buried his talons in his feathers and in the gauze, aiming to pick the latter apart from within, with a more insistent grip. He then withdrew his talons, bloodied and trembling from the effort; in them were caught scraps from which he had a hard time freeing himself.

All of a sudden, his loosened blindfold slipped from his head onto his neck. It was as though, along with the blindfold, a great fear had also descended on the bird of prey: he remained immobile.

The blindfold stopped at the first, erect feathers of his neck; and then, by jumping about and making little movements with his wings, the hawk rearranged himself and made the gauze slip further down.

He was free: he opened his black and painful eyelids.

A cry, and he fell like a lightning bolt upon the fat and splendid-looking dove, mounted on a support that imitated a barren branch.

He dug his talons into its back and tried to bury his hungry beak in its throat. From his wing muscles to his neck, waves of effort passed through him in the effort to drive his beak in deeper.

Here was no warm throat full of pulsing blood; no cry, no spasm, but instead a cold and resistant maze.

The hawk withdrew his beak from the wound he had so ferociously inflicted: out came a bunch of straw. Blind, maddened, he resumed his attack on the dove's devastated body, until his fury encountered nothing more than a disorganized heap of straw and feathers.

He lifted his cruel eyes to the lamp, incredulous at seeing the sun after the surprise, and hastened back to his perch.

Ruffled and ill-tempered, he grew agitated at the sight of large birds upright on little pedestals in every corner of the room.

A bright-hued flamingo, a pelican with his large, pendant beak, another horrible bird with a crest: they were all staring at him, immobile and sure of themselves. In the shop window opposite him were other birds with long tails; his hunger was challenged by a nest and a parade of little robin redbreasts.

Silence, such as fell in the woods when he was spotted wheeling high overhead.

He took off like an arrow: his talons collided with glass and, as he fell, he saw a large and frightening shadow.

He had bruised a wing in his fall: it was so painful that now he could hardly move it.

Taking short steps, he took refuge under the shadow of a piece of furniture. From there, crying out and breathing loudly, as if to warn the other birds of his presence, he stuck his head out now and then and had a look around.

All those birds were composed, immobile, and severe like none he had ever seen before. The flamingo stood upright on just one of his brown, minutely scaly feet, with the other foot raised as if seeking fleas amidst the feathers on his breast; the small, brightly colored birds were all frozen in the act of pecking at something in a piece of wood, in a low heap of sand, in a painted piece of cork. Some were grouped – with an air of familiarity unknown in the woods – around a dark-hued weasel; others posed on a branch where a squirrel had stopped, its fluffy tail pointing upwards. A green woodpecker was expecting the weight of his tail to lend him the force he needed in order to drive his beak into a deepcut hole in a piece of wood; an owl, a petrified enchantress, holding her eyes very still within vortical whorls of little gray feathers, was paying no attention to the need to hunt smaller birds or other prey.

In their instinctive poses there was a wonderstruck sense of peace, the certainty that they would not change, as though the atmosphere of the most beautiful morning in the woods or the swamp had accompanied each of them to his pedestal or his compartment in the display window. Even in this limited space, they did not appear to feel any limits: those who were most powerful in flight had their wings open in triumph, with no sense of weight; and if they did not take off, it was from the joy of allowing themselves to be surprised in all their panoply of color, undimmed by air and with their apparent size unreduced by altitude.

Coming out from the shadow of the furniture, the hawk seemed to seek from the flamingo an initiation into this enviable mystery. Finally, having taken two or three little leaps, he flew straight into the latter bird and cautiously rummaged about with his beak among the feathers.

He felt the casing around the false body, empty of blood and flesh.

As though seized by a sudden fit of gaiety after this experiment, he flitted lightly about the room, seeking no landing place. Sometimes the shadow of his wheeling wings hid the incandescent lamp, around which he ended up flying in circles like a moth.

Exhausted, with a green flame in his eyes, he allowed

himself to descend to earth. The odor of the abandoned nest had become more acrid, but no more experiments tempted him. The fixity of his eyes and the deceptive gleam of the glass in the window expanded the borders within which those silent birds remained immobile. Some of them were swollen with the desire for flight, further increasing the anxiety of the hawk, who even heard the rustle of wings. But when he saw once again that everything remained stock-still, he opened his own wings and beat them noisily two or three times.

In the back room of the shop, having found a passageway between the two half-closed parts of a curtain, there entered a flying black shadow. It was a bat, attracted by the bright light. Barely supporting itself on its tremulous membranes, it circled the light a few times and then came to a landing, with a noise of scraping claws, on the lamp's enameled dish.

Alarmed, the hawk watched the swinging lamp while he tried to recall the revelatory memory of that shadow glimpsed on the floor: a fluttering shadow, not firm and strong like his own when, beneath the midday sun, he had enjoyed watching it, large and far off as it ran over the earth. He was just able to guess that the unknown flying creature had gently jumped onto the edge of the lamp.

Frightened, he made a strenuous effort to open his wings and then to close them tightly, like a protective winding, about his thin body. He continually cried out and puffed, low and hoarsely, from the fear that he might be attacked at any moment. The presence of another living being in the room had destroyed his sense that he could lord it over the place like a vandal; now, excluded from that silence and peace, he felt the chill solitude of terror.

The light barely oscillated: the enemy was impressing his movements upon it.

Amidst a clatter of ironwork there passed red and

blue flames on the ceiling, from a glass lunette above the rolling shutter.

It was the call to battle.

The hawk flew high, higher than the light. The black leaf slipped out of the dish and fled in a panic, avoiding the bird of prey and staying close to the walls. After a vain pursuit the hawk, who could not change the movement of his wings so quickly, remained motionless in the shop window, awaiting the enemy. He saw it advancing in the narrow cone of light from the lamp, brusquely change direction, and continue at a lower altitude. He fell upon the bat, hammering away with his beak; but he struck the membrane, which opened up, torn. The bat, having barely escaped from that first assault, changed shape: it now appeared to have three wings and, as it flew, blood spurted from it, red and brilliant in the light.

On the counter, the hawk remained puffed up with tension among the stuffed birds.

The wounded bat tried stubbornly to hang on to the white vaulting overhead; but, its shredded wing not supporting it, it slipped slowly downwards, despite the frenetic flapping of the other, healthy wing. In its fall, it landed on the surface of the counter; and there it exhausted its last desperate efforts in vain thrashings.

The hawk came to finish it off with ferocious pecks. In its trembling death agony, the bat seemed to escape from him, running along the counter in a slippery, blood-drenched space.

Abruptly snubbing his black and bloodied prey, the winner resumed his place on the parrot-perch.

Whether from fatigue or from inability to bear the dazzling light, he shut his eyes; he had a hard time getting a grip on the perch, and had to beat his wings in order to support himself upon it.

Slowly he became short and swollen, with his neck

sunk into his body as though he were cold. He gave a little start every now and then and opened his beak so wide that it strained his membranes, drinking in the abundant air and hoarsely emitting ever-more-effortful cries.

When he reopened his eyes, he stared at the confused image of the birds in the window, and then at the flamingo, with a sort of ecstasy which was followed by an attempt to fly.

The strength of his wings bore him up just enough to make him appear taller and more majestic; but his claws remained tight on the perch as though it were a mounting.

At those moments he was proud and frightening: he looked like one of those emblematic birds of prey, in the pose that taxidermists take so much trouble to get just right.

# The Arabian Café

The owner was alone in the café. Seated on the high-backed chair near the till, he ran his melancholy gaze over the booths and niches of the room, where some vacant tables, lustrous with reflections, attracted his attention, evoking in him the desire to drown in the first evanescent miracles of some unknown image. But at the slightest motion of his head, there lengthened over the lacustrine plane of light a shadow cast by one of the numerous little Arabian columns, dripping like some secretion from the ceiling, or else by a little arch bearing a double row of yellow teeth with poisonous touches of dark azure at their tips – so that all his attempts to vanish into such an unusual mirror were unsuccessful.

The door onto the street yielded to a gentle push and the Chinaman entered, displaying a little green fan that, as his hands played with it, opened into several tremulous corollas.

The owner heard the rustling of the paper but did not turn around. Ever since he had started to feel guilty about a still-secret decision that was going to disperse his surviving customers, he avoided greeting them when they came in; and this lovingly weak tactic had ended up by reducing him to experiments befitting the austere boredom of a sacristan in a church.

The Chinaman, aware that the owner's eyes would have to make a long journey in order to discover his presence, had come to a respectful halt. In his miserably threadbare European overcoat, he had a worn air; but the natural yellow of his skin protected him against sharper suspicions of some slow illness, while the feverish gleam in his little black eyes lent grace to his (perhaps malicious) obstinacy.

The wandering shade of the neighborhood, he dropped in every evening at the café to show off, from table to table, his fans and certain little ivory animals, holding them out in a round box that had once contained lozenges. After persuading himself that there were no buyers for his merchandise, he would leave, calm and resigned, smilingly offering his goods all the way to the door.

Preceded by their voices, a group of four late-afternoon habitués entered; behind them – lively and joyous, as though the new arrivals were his dear friends – came the waiter, who had been out in the street amusing himself. Standing still, the Chinaman waited for the foursome to sit down before approaching them and initiating the rituals of his trade.

It was then that the owner, troubled at the memory of a footfall which he hadn't bothered to follow up, suddenly discovered the Chinaman's presence, along with the image of a very religious mosque that had slowly been taking shape in his own mind. He grew angry at the infidel's sudden appearance in his mosque.

"Get out!" he yelled at him. "What are you doing here? Get it into your head for once and all that you're not to come here any more. Anyway, it's just a matter of days and the café will close." He fell silent and made no threatening gesture, amazed that he had revealed his decision in such an unexpected way.

It seemed to him that his regular customers, gathered around a table in the back, emitted a low murmur of fear upon hearing the brutal announcement. He found himself awaiting the cry, the funereal crash, the catastrophe of cups and glasses that would follow upon his grave words. Instead, the dwindling of voices and whispers into a deep, expectant silence led him back into the painful solitude of a man observed by many gazes.

Nearer than the others, the Chinaman stared at him

in amazed shyness, at the same time desperately holding out the fan to a couple of lovers who, having crossed the threshold, were hesitating over the choice of a table; so many were vacant that no one of them seemed more segregated than the rest.

To avoid troubling these chance customers with his anger, the owner lowered his eyes, grumbling; the couple vanished with the Chinaman into a niche at the side of the room, whence emerged the girl's laughter at her discovery, among the vendor's monkeys and elephants, of a trinket featuring a rooster and a hen, mating. Afterwards, the Chinaman came to the table of the habitués to offer merchandise which must have seemed to him — after the miracle of a sale — rejuvenated and refreshed, just like his obligatory smile, which was wider and more confident than usual.

The owner failed to respond to the Oriental's bow, but not out of any residual anger: he was ashamed of his impulsive outburst, and fearful of the explanations he would have to offer to the four men smoking in secretive silence. Overcome by nervousness, he left the till and began wandering here and there about the room.

The two young people in their corner, trusting the abundant shelter afforded by partitions and little columns, were kissing, and their two joined heads were reflected over and over again in the mirrors on five walls. Here, they seemed nearby and monumental; there, they were reduced to minimal proportions, as though they had been fished up from some dizzying greenish depth.

The owner found himself entering — a third, disturbing shadow — into this combination of reflections. In a little dash, he fled to the table of the four regulars sooner than he would have wished.

They were smoking and staring into their coffee cups, with the mournful yet calm expression of someone who has just heard of the death of a person for whom there was no longer any hope.

"Is it really inevitable?" asked the one who, since he was seated facing the owner, was under the heaviest obligation to say something. Couldn't you redecorate? Find a partner?"

The owner remained silent, hunched over and humiliated. The silence having been broken, the other three joined in, offering condolences and advice – but feebly.

"Thank you, thank you," murmured the owner, lifting his hands from the marble tabletop upon which he was resting them, almost as though he couldn't bear the cold. "I'm well aware that no one could keep this place open. This café is finished. I'm so sure of it that I'm going to close before I go bankrupt." He then returned to the till, in order to show that he had nothing to add.

He felt sad, swollen with repressed rage; so far from upsetting the faithful, his announcement had been greeted as a liberation from a boring commitment. Every new arrival, just as soon as he entered and sat down among the group, was immediately informed of the news. Then and there, the customers began exchanging views in hushed voices, leaning towards one another, warning the others to remain silent – and all this was followed by prudent glances in the direction of the till. By now, the four had become seven: but seven who were alert and taciturn, who asked for their drinks in a crisp voice, without familiarity. In this altered atmosphere, the waiter – who had once been confidential – had turned shy, serving in silence, moving with cautious steps. Every now and then he directed a reproachful glance at the owner, who was self-absorbed and fat as a steer.

The arrival in the café of a personage whom no one knew aroused a hasty curiosity, useful for dissipating the embarrassment that was in the air. His brownish complexion and his garish yet elegant clothing bespoke a person of mixed blood. Gray-haired but still young, the man displayed the chilly and bemused contempt of one who lives at night, going out during the daytime only by accident.

He displayed indifference to the general curiosity: seated at a table near the door, he was undoubtedly waiting for someone. Every now and then, he looked around the room with his too-white, sleepy eyes, as though he were measuring it.

Someone else came in. It was the person he'd been waiting for: the stranger smiled at the new arrival, inviting him with a gesture to join him at his table. The new arrival, an habitué, ceremoniously greeted all those around him, shook the other's hand, and sat down with a smile. He was, so far as anyone knew, a sort of retired sleight-of-hand artist, forced to live on expedients less magical than those of his former profession. He acted as an agent for cabaret singers, put on modest shows in cafés, sold used furniture, made money on others' bankruptcies, provided the addresses of furnished rooms, put together a thin and agitated living. His days were crammed with appointments, trips in and out of town, long waits in the auction rooms where court-ordered sales were taking place.

His huge moustache hid the signs of a hopelessly improvised comedian, given away nonetheless by his emphatic and over-exclamatory voice. One often saw him in the street in the company of beautiful young ladies who needed his help; he seemed to be their down-at-the-heel, exploitative daddy. He had grown fond of those overgrown butterflies, who were always sincere with him. They received him clad in furs or naked in bed in a room not yet paid for; they kept him young, and their slightly intoxicating scent lingered on his faded overcoat. Well informed of all their misfortunes, whether of the flesh or of the heart, he boasted that he was writing a history of modern love as seen without veils: an affair tailor-made for some publisher so daring that it was impossible to find him in the marketplace. Every now and then, he let himself be seen in public with a little gray wife who was always in tears. He would walk alongside her, smiling and happy as any passer-by who didn't know her; when she sobbed, he would turn to speak to her with sonorous gentleness, but one of his hairy hands went to his pocket, where it jingled a large amount of change with an irritated sound that boded no good.

The owner, who had not responded to his greeting, was now doing all he could to avoid meeting his gaze. Since the other had taken on the task of finding a purchaser for the café, the owner nourished towards him the distrust and dislike one naturally feels for the person who has first guessed one's painful need.

On the table-top, the sleight-of-hand artist was making a pencil drawing of a plant; with tired eyes, the half-breed looked on from a distance. All at once the half-breed stood up, measured the room with his steps and, paying no heed to the owner, who stared at him in fury, bent over to inspect the flooring. He removed a couple of chairs from a niche, tapped against the hollow iron of a column, and then returned to his seat, where he murmured something to his companion.

The sleight-of-hand artist came up to the till.

"I'm going to take him into the kitchen," he said, "and also for a look at the covered courtyard. It's necessary. Don't worry, we'll close the deal."

The owner did not reply but – as though authorizing a liberty which it displeased him to concede before witnesses – nodded and pointed to a door, with an air of sovereign indifference. But just as soon as the two had disappeared, he was overcome by the fury of ownership: the need to reconquer, in plain sight of his customers, that which belonged to him. The habitués looked at him, mortified to be present at a negotiation conducted with so little delicacy.

"I'm sick and tired of all these shifty characters who come round for a look at my place," he said. "Some day I'm going to give one of them a good kick."

"No. Business comes first – but watch out when it's time to get paid!" advised, with a wink, a hulking merchant from the neighborhood. "Make them pay cash; don't accept any signed paper. You never know with fellows like that."

"You must think I was born yesterday," answered the owner, and then fell silent. The twosome came back from the kitchen.

When the half-breed suggested that the three of them should withdraw to some quiet corner to discuss terms, the owner refused; instead, he made an appointment with them for the next day at his lawyer's office.

"That'll be fine," approved the half-breed. Having bestowed a farewell nod upon his companion, he went out, staring with a suddenly gleaming eye at the girl, who had emerged from the niche without her boyfriend in order to search the table-tops for an illustrated newspaper.

"Why didn't you want to deal with him right away?" asked the sleight-of-hand artist in a tone of reproof. "You certainly won't get another offer like his. I'm well aware that you're not desperate to sell – but in any case, I want to tell you that, if my acquaintance goes through with the deal, he wants to have the place free by Monday. He's in a hurry to set up his vaudeville theater. The time is ripe. There's money around…"

When his interlocutor made a gesture of boredom, the sleight-of-hand artist left the till and went to sit down at the end of the room among the others, in order to tell them all about the plans for the new theater, where he hoped to be part of the management.

Listening to him, the owner, after his initial rage, fell into a state of miserable apathy, interrupted by intermittent visions of the Arabian Café when it had been jammed with people, back in the days when – in its famous basement room, the Oriental Nights – the dancing, the orgy, and the racket used to go on until daybreak. The downstairs room had been closed four years earlier, killed off by a rapid decline against which four memorable and swarthy rascals had played their Middle Eastern music in vain. When business soured, the owner had found himself liberated from his wife, who – hating him for the city life to which he had brought her and for his lack of success – had gone back to live with her parents in the country, opening the way to freedom and a period of happiness. Too much time having gone by since the Colonial Exposition, the café had been reduced to a respectable meeting-place for bourgeois belatedly enamoured of a style that had gone out of fashion; and the downstairs room had become the exciting alcove where the owner's ancillary loves took on a whiff of exotic atmosphere.

But the city was changing rapidly, along with people's tastes. The neighborhood had gone through some big transformations: banks and art galleries sprang up where a greengrocer had closed his shop; the cafés and dance halls, miracles of lighting and mirrors, were redecorated inside and out every two years. An anachronistic survivor, the Arabian Café remained hidden among so many novelties, its doors opening onto a shabby, empty room, its façade ambiguously encrusted, as far as the second floor, with elements of the bazaar and the mosque. Its clientele had progressively abandoned it. This was why, when he heard the sleight-of-hand artist holding forth about the wonders of the new theater, the owner felt in his throat a lump that every now and then obliged him to cough. Each time he coughed, the nine customers at the back would raise their heads, as though to look at some seriously ill person.

Leaning on the bar, the waiter was lining up some yellow tokens, maneuvering them into piles like chess pieces: there were just a few of them on the marble surface of the till, not even enough to make up the geometric design that the owner was attempting to complete in an effort to keep

himself under control. Here was a clear proof of the meager-
ness of the take, which was insufficient to cover the day's
expenses.

Following this discovery, which he had been making
afresh almost every evening for several months, the owner
felt a sudden need for expansiveness, showy display, and generosity; he wanted to overcome the sadness of his slow march
towards failure. He looked at the shelves, still filled with bottles of fine wines; the placid drinkers of his barley coffee –
which was practically a purgative – never asked him to
uncork one of them. He might as well make a grand gesture:
invite them all to dinner and amaze them with his fine wines
and liqueurs, drowning them in delicious things, so as purchase from them a favorable memory of the Arabian Café.
That way, they would always offer him a friendly greeting
when they ran into him on the street, after he had turned
into an broken-down, nostalgic old gentleman.

He looked around the room and left the till.
Irresolute, he stopped amidst the vacant tables. The presence
of the two lovers – who, seeming to have become curious
about him, were showing their heads above the back of the
divan – made it awkward for him to say what he wanted to
say to those at the table in the back. He started moving once
again and attempted to utter a natural sound, in order to
make certain that his voice was clear and uncolored by emotion. But the distance between himself and the others struck
him as too great to be traversed in silence.

"The Arabian Café will close forever at seven o'clock
on Saturday evening," he said in a loud voice. "At nine
o'clock, there will be a big farewell party for those customers
who wish to accept the invitation. I'm saying this to everyone here."

For a moment, surprise inhibited any reaction; then
the sleight-of-hand artist stood up and came to join him,
crying out: "Bravo! Bravo! That's doing things in style. Let

me give you a hug!"

The others sent up an enthusiastic cheer and promised that they would all meet at the great farewell soirée of the Arabian Café.

"Thank you, thank you," replied the owner. "I count on the friendship of all you gentlemen. I would ask you not to dine at home: you will find a cold meal here." He withdrew, bowing at the applause, while the setting – warm and almost cheerful – seemed to have become his once again.

"Sir, Sir..." The owner turned around, then headed for the niche from which the girl was calling him. "It's true, isn't it, that you've also invited us two? Everyone here, you said."

Surprised, he didn't immediately know how to answer; but her sly smile warmed his heart.

"Of course," he replied. "Everyone means everyone. I would be very sorry not to see you here on Saturday evening, my dear young lady, together with this gentleman who is your friend." He held out his hand to the youth, who sniggered in rather disagreeable embarrassment. "I'm counting on you."

At the table in the back, everyone leaned forward to look at the girl and smile hospitably at her.

The owner went back to the till. Breathing heavily, he wiped away a certain sweat of liberation; he felt that he had found the right way to leave his café with as little bitterness as possible. Looking around the room, he encountered smiles, friendly little nods, winks that signified nothing in particular. Peace and harmony reigned all about his throne: the peace and harmony befitting a king who was generously abdicating.

Little by little, the café emptied out.

The first to leave were the youth and the girl. They bowed to him from the door and left, falling all over themselves in an explosion of laughter that was quickly absorbed by the noises of the street. The next to go was the sleight-of-hand artist, alone, as though in the grip of an unexpected haste urging him towards one of his complicated deals. Then six men came up to shake his hand warmly; and lastly, the hulking merchant, together with two rather elderly high-school teachers, to whom he was explaining the ways in which traders can make money in a hurry. The three barely acknowledged the owner: one because he was busy talking, and the other two, because they were listening to him with that wonder devoid of envy typical of the ingenuous. The fat man, enjoying the effect he was producing, was taking his revenge for many misunderstood intellectual conversations.

They were already out on the sidewalk when they remembered a duty: "See you Saturday," they said, leaning forward to say goodbye to the owner; and the latter felt a sudden chill at the idea that, from then until Saturday, he would no longer see his loyal customers.

"Give me a glass of something," he said to the waiter, who was clearing off the bar, "and turn up the lights."


At about eight o'clock on Saturday evening nervous, and mysterious huddles between the owner and the waiter, the dragging of tables into the middle of the room, the sweeping of the floor right around the last remaining customer's legs, all persuaded that final customer of the afternoon to leave the Arabian Café.

He was a tired old man who had been counting on a long, restful stay in the desolate, silent room. He left his coins on the marble table-top and headed for the door. Without turning around, he felt himself being tailed by four tiptoeing feet. He went out, and was frightened by the racket of the rolling shutters being pulled down behind him, so close that they might have sliced through his shoulders. He didn't look back. He went away, and in his gait, that of a sad old man, there was the hesitation of one who is talking to himself and plaintively wondering about the reasons for an affront, an undeserved persecution.

"At last!" exclaimed the owner. "That old imbecile wasn't going to leave!"

"Well, I did everything possible to make him catch on," said the other. "Who on earth sent him here today, of all days, and at such a late hour?"

But the owner remained silent: the Arabian Café was closed forever, its hospitality dead, its role as a shelter ended with that last mistreated customer. He looked around, gazed at the half-lowered shutter, and could not tell whether he desired or feared the arrival of someone who would provoke the reopening of the café. The waiter, too, stared at the corrugated sheet iron of the shutter with the intensity of a person waiting for someone to arrive; then he went and pulled it all the way down, so as not to have to see the feet of the people passing by.

"That's done," muttered the owner, turning off a row of light bulbs overhead, and then a second series within the niches. He fancied that someone out in the street must be watching that collapse from light into darkness, seeing it as a clear and comprehensible death agony; he thought of the sidewalk, now impoverished for want of the reflected light that the café had offered as a gift to passers-by, to all those who had looked forward to finding themselves in that vivid stretch where they might smile visibly, turn and glance at some woman whose appearance it had been hard to grasp in the shadows; and he felt guilty, as though he had failed in his duty.

Meanwhile, the shutter rang out under a blow struck from outside.

The pair straightened up like thieves caught in the act; waiting, they instinctively exchanged a signal to remain silent. Another blow, but no voice. They were pale, trembling with indecision. The owner exchanged one foot, lifted in anxiety, with the other, and his shoe squeaked; the waiter, still as a lead soldier on his flat feet, wavered for an instant and straightened up again.

Another blow on the resonant sheet metal. Their paralyzed tongues hesitated, for all that they wanted to ask: "Who's there? What's the matter?" With the sound of their voices, a group of passers-by dispersed the imperious silence that accompanies the image of a figure waiting erect before a door. The waiter ran to raise the shutter. No one. The sidewalk was swarming with people running home to dinner. Among the others, one figure was fleeing while emitting atrocious yells, as if from a drunken gullet: a hawker of newspapers. When the pair, having raised the shutter, found themselves once again isolated on the sidewalk, they realized that they had been afraid.

"Let's not lose our heads," said the owner. "It must have been someone. Maybe the newspaper vendor who comes around every evening... As it happens, I had warned him not to come anymore, and he's not the type to knock and keep quiet with that awful voice of his. Now that I think of it," he added, "I think it must have been the Chinaman. He showed up as recently as yesterday evening, and I had promised that today I would give him a bottle of sweet syrup. He's shy: he only knocked."

"He's shy, but he always wins out with those mincing ways of his. I don't trust those yellow people."

"What does he live on?" persisted the owner who, at the thought of the Chinaman, felt profoundly sad, as though he had lost a friend. "I only saw him sell anything once."

"Those are people who can feed themselves on four grains of rice," replied the waiter; and confident in this opinion, he showed that he wished to spare himself any compassionate thoughts.

"What a shame! I didn't think to invite him for this

evening."

"Who? The Chinaman?"

"Certainly! Better him than that damned Mexican! Since he's buying the place, he absolutely intends to come along with that juggler, who apologized to me for not bringing his wife as well, since the lady isn't feeling too well just at present. I'm no longer the boss around here."

He regretted this plaintive outburst: "Go into the kitchen and bring out the dishes," he said, "and also bring me my Arab costume."

The waiter went to put down a big bundle on the marble top of a café table, then helped the owner to set the table festively. When everything was in order, he fled through a door, turning out the lights.

"You idiot, turn them back on!" yelled the owner. But a cool sense of peace had come over him in the darkness, and he didn't persist in calling the other back.

After the sudden plunge into obscurity, the glow that entered the café from the street increased bit by bit, casting its gleam over the mirrors, the shining brass of the bar, and the bottles on the shelves, which emerged one by one from the shadows, showing themselves in unexpected rows as the owner turned his eyes here and there.

As if wishing to taking advantage of the complicity of the things around him, the owner began undressing. He threw off his jacket and vest, slipped out of his trousers and then, after a moment's hesitation, removed his underpants.

Between two slabs of cold marble, he moved about in his shirt; he bent over to untie his shoes, tossing them far from himself. His feet shuffled along at ease in their Oriental slippers. The Oriental trousers came up to the sash, their brown making a crisp contrast with the shirt, tight and white against his belly. After rustling his way into a silken robe, he put on his vest, over which he donned an ample, loose-fitting silk jacket.

In this disguise, the owner stood atop a café table and tried to see himself in one of the big mirrors. He didn't get a good view, because more than half of his figure remained in darkness: he was about to jump down in order to turn on the lights when an unexpected memory gave him a reason for loving that half-darkness, which he unconsciously desired. He held still for a moment, leaned over to get a better look at himself – his eyes having grown used to the bluish glow – and then climbed down to hide his clothes and shoes within a piece of furniture, after doing which he sat down upon a divan.

He was enjoying the soft light that entered, free of cost, through the lower half of the ground glass windows. The side of the room facing the avenue was filled with the shadows of trees: stretching out along the floor, they interrupted themselves in order to fall on the marble table-tops before vanishing into the thick darkness of a corner. Ramifying, they filled a mirror or a niche with fleeting woodland apparitions. The other side of the room, which looked out onto a narrow street, was barren of reflected images. Up above, through the clear glass, he could see the house across the way; on its whitish façade, the warm pink light of an illuminated window seemed to swell in such as way that the whole building responded in sympathy.

With slow gestures, the owner combed his beard, palpated his silk-clad body. Like sudden cries, the intermittent flashes of the neon signs on the avenue broke the stagnation of the indirect light in the empty, resonant room; and each flash was matched by an image buried in his memory, like a white boulder in the blue water of the sea. The owner immersed himself in that wave with the anguish of one who is suffocating, also with trepidation, lest after touching the seabed, he should return to the surface tormented afresh by ancient sorrow and regret. He had already understood the form of the final image, but did not yet wish to see it: fearful that it was too much alive, he kept himself from grasping it by playing little games, pretending to pay attention to the shadows, to the glint of the bottles. He closed his eyes to avoid having to submit to another flash; but by now it was too late to deflect a process out that had unconsciously reached its goal. He saw Susanna; he sensed her insidious approach to those double bottoms of memory which preserve, terribly alive, the gestures, voice, nakedness and odor of a woman once amorously enjoyed.

Susanna was the third-floor tenants' cook. Courted and celebrated by him, by his eye and hand, she had been persuaded to descend at night into his wondrous basement room. The complicitous concierge had opened a door for that love: a door in the courtyard, by way of which Susanna used to arrive, still a servant, still warm from having steamily washed the dishes: a task that left her swollen, reddened hands drained of blood.

He was awaiting her in his Arab costume, donned that first time in order to produce in her the wonder that makes possible – or at least speeds up – the conquest of a woman's devotion. With no kisses or caresses, he pushed her into a sort of dressing room and went down into the basement room to wait for her. It took her just a few minutes to change into a few desert rags which transformed her from a servant into a shapely Arab girl, full of fire and proud voluptuousness. Every time she came to him, he would satisfy her joyous astonishment afresh, wearing his costume and breathing in the scent of dishwater.

While waiting, the owner primped until he was as handsome as a prince from a caravan, carefully arranged the lighting in the alcove, lit sticks of incense that filled the basement with a acrid, whitish cloud which he, in his simple way, felt to be favorable to the feline, silent gestures and guttural cries of passion. When he cried out, he called Susanna "my gazelle," and she answered, "my lion;" and for each of them, there really did come into being, within that stage set, a lyrical freedom of feeling that lent sincerity to their exotic expressions of love. Thus translated into Muslim terms, pleasure made them drunk, carrying them far away, to a place where they could live and enjoy themselves more fully. Such an atmosphere and setting, offered them by chance, acted on them with results not very different from the infallible and exotic bad taste shown by a madam setting up her bordello.

The reawakened jealousy of a former lover of Susanna's had broken the spell in a way that almost ended in a tragic stabbing. The girl had had to go off with the other, enslaved to a bestial overlord whose clouded eyes expressed a dark desire for bloodshed that robbed the owner of all courage and precluded any thought of going to the authorities. The former lover seemed to be just waiting for a legal complaint to be brought against his brutality, so to have an excuse for a vengefully bloody act.

The owner had never really forgotten; instead, he felt a painful sense of inadequacy and humiliation that kept the embers of that old flame warm. Sometimes he thought of the unfortunate girl, respectfully forbidding himself any erotic memories, just in case she was dead. When he put on his Arab costume, he felt capable of avenging her, of inventing atrocious tortures. But these were brief reawakenings, soon followed by the somnolence of a trade that, with the café's decline, had ceased to constitute an activity.

At this moment his senses had rediscovered – in the selfsame light by which he had awaited Susanna on so many happy evenings – her memory and image, but softened by a wise yet painful forgetfulness of the tragedy and its aftermath. He was left with the simple desire for a woman, the wish to say a carnal farewell to his café. In reaction to the difficult step he was taking, his blood desired pleasure: a dangerous compensation for his declining years.

Outside, they were banging on the shutter.

He leapt to his feet, ran to turn on the lights, and disappeared into the kitchen, leaving the task of opening the shutter to the waiter.

The guests, who entered in an initial group of seven, seemed to find themselves in a place that immediately filled them with curiosity and embarrassment. Perhaps they were startled by the elaborately set table in the middle of the room, which gave the place a new shape; perhaps it was the fact of finding themselves guests in a setting where they had always paid.

The waiter alerted them: "The boss is coming right away. He's in there, dressed like a Turk." He laughed, as though such folly brought back welcome memories.

Amazed, the guests wandered around with hat in hand, like visitors to an exhibition. They were seized by the painful sense of having committed an evil action: they had accepted an invitation from a man on the verge of ruin.

"It's too much. Too much!" murmured one of the schoolteachers. "This man wants to ruin himself with our help." The thought of a business going bad, and of other people making a profit off it, choked the breath of the two businessmen in the group, who were busy estimating the prices of the wines while studying the illustrious labels.

The owner emerged from the kitchen: he had added to his costume a brown-and-yellow striped turban. He came over to shake the hands of his guests, who were gazing at him in astonishment.

He said, "I thought that my Arabian Café ought to go out in glory. You gentlemen are kindly asked to go in there and put on your costumes. It matters to me, on account of the overall look."

"Costumes? What costumes?"

"Arabian, like mine. I have a collection I bought at the Colonial Exposition fifteen years ago. I kept them to rent out to my customers when we held Oriental Nights in the basement. Now the time has come to use them for the last time. They're in there." He gestured towards a door that led to a dressing room.

"But why the costumes?" asked the younger of the two teachers. "It's enough that you're wearing one: it looks really good on you." The others smiled awkwardly.

The owner's face darkened. "Do me a favor: get in there. There's a complete costume hanging from every nail. The costumes are fresh and clean: I took them out of mothballs today. Be happy, gentlemen, be happy! Think of the way you used to disguise yourselves when you were young." As he spoke, he pushed them, one after the other, into the narrow space filled with coat hooks.

"What a bother!" he grumbled, slamming the door. Then he turned to greet the half-breed, who was entering the café together with his companion.

The first, sleepy yet malicious, gave the owner in his costume the once-over, smiled, and said:

"Well, it's an idea, you know."

"There are costumes for you two as well," the other answered.

"Listen," said the sleight-of-hand artist. "I've got to apologize for my wife, who hasn't come. It wasn't to offend you, but because she had another commitment. Maybe she'll drop round later to pick me up."

"All right, all right. Go get dressed."

The two opened the dressing-room door. A cry of horror went up.

"What's the problem? We're all men," apologized the sleight-of-hand artist. "But what a wonderful sight! It's like being among the supers in a theater."

"Think what you like, but shut the door," protested a thin little man with eyeglasses who was in his shirtsleeves.

Having spotted a gaudily colored costume, the half-breed took it off its nail.

"Hold it, that one's mine," said his neighbor.

"It'll be too big on you," replied the half-breed, relinquishing his prey. Then he started to undress, after having told the sleight-of-hand artist to find him a suitable costume.

In the narrow space there was a silent crush. Slowly moving men were sighing, bent over to untie their shoes, hunting for fallen cufflinks, undoing their belt buckles.

The door opened: the owner looked in.

"The slippers are all up on that shelf," he said. Those who are wearing long underwear should roll it up above the knee." Closing the door, he vanished.

"Those who are ready should wait for the others," he yelled through the wood. "I want to see the spectacle." The poor devils shut up in that dark hole felt themselves enslaved to a treacherous tyrant who was forcing them into a ridiculous parade.

"He could have told us about these damned costumes," grumbled the hulking merchant. "We wouldn't have come." He hesitated before taking off his shoes and going barefoot in search of a pair of slippers.

By now, most of them were ready, but they hadn't done with fussing. Everyone went back to his own clothes for a handkerchief, a cigar, matches: delicate pretexts for removing wallets and gold watches from pockets. The waiter, who had come in to help, smiled; used to being distrusted, he didn't dare to touch a thing.

"Now let's get going."

As if awaited by a curious public of which they were afraid, the extras lined up in a row. The first opened the door.

"Come on out!" said the owner, standing right there where he could look them over as they went past, like a drill sergeant inspecting soldiers at the barracks door.

"Good! You, you're magnificent! What's that rag hanging down? Pull it up, pull it up! There must be a lace." He went from one to the other, giving advice and retouching the costumes.

"Now sit down. Take your places. There are cards with your names; it's simple."

At that moment, the guests fully grasped that, as customers of the café, they were dead. The owner's awareness that he was, for once, giving something away lent him a slightly imperious tone, making him disagreeably demanding.

The search for the assigned places began. It was dragged out on account of the discontent and reluctance of those forced to sit down to the banquet. Everyone looked around at the mirrors. The three members of the company who wore glasses tried removing them and then put them back on: these instruments had become doubly necessary for rediscovering a lost resemblance to one's usual image of oneself.

When everyone was seated, two places remained free, with no name cards. These were for the anonymous couple, the youth and the girl. It was no longer worth waiting for them: the hour set for the rendez-vous had long since passed.

Everyone gazed at the two empty places in discouragement, as though that absence were a bad sign, or as if it deprived them of the only pleasure for which they might still hope.

"It's already late! They must have forgotten," said the owner in a tone of angry regret.

"They must have had something better to do," commented one of the teachers. Then, fearing that his words had offended his host, he got tangled up in his insistence upon explaining what he had meant by "better," while his face, beneath his turban, lost its habitual seriousness and acquired an air of recovered youth on account of the greedy expression of his mouth, white and barbaric in its sardonic smile.

"They're not coming. You can see that they didn't appreciate my invitation!" yelled the owner. "Start serving, you," he said to the waiter, "but first take away those two place settings: they're getting on my nerves."

Immediately afterwards, they all were faced with the task of eating and drinking without an appetite, since there was no collective warmth to encourage them.

They had not done observing one another. It was as though, unconvinced by the others' faces, every guest were seeking – beneath the others' cloaks and robes – the familiar outlines of normal clothes and the bodies that filled them, while simultaneously feeling himself the only one not in disguise, and therefore authorized to undertake such scrutiny. So it was that, whenever a guest's gaze fell upon his own chest, he started up in wonderment before surrendering sadly to the irreparable common misfortune.

A tall lamp placed upon the table was shining brightly; the smaller ones surrounding it gleamed coldly with reflected light, so that only the middle of the café was well illuminated. The view of the other tables, losing themselves in the shadows of the farthest niches and corners among the little yellow columns, was disturbing, leaving one with the sense that one's back was unprotected; it was like being spied on by invisible witnesses. Here and there blotches on the wall, stains on the floor, electrical wires dangling in lazy abandon betrayed an unsuspected squalor, a ruin that accorded all too well with the café's definitive closing. Behind the bar, barren of bottles, an open door offered a view into a narrow passageway of rough black stonework, like the entrance to a grotto. This was the route along which the waiter ran into the kitchen, returning laden with dishes; every now and then a sudden call from the owner made him reappear with a half-curious, half-frightened face, while the napkin that was the insignia of his calling waved in his agitated hands.

Once, upon returning to the room, he wore his rolled-up napkin as a turban. Thus disguised, he hesitated to approach the owner; then he worked up his courage and smiled at himself, pleased at having gotten away with it.

None of the guests dared to speak. Only the half-breed exchanged a few words with the sleight-of-hand artist seated next to him; and in their complicity, they looked like a dissolute prince and his crafty confidant, who had entered incognito into the house of an upright merchant. The others ate, discreetly watching the brooding, surly owner; then they looked away, afraid that he might suddenly leap to his feet, brandishing a bottle like a bludgeon, overturning the table and massacring them in a fit of insanity brought on by remorse at having thrown his money away.

Suffering because his dinner was going so badly, the owner tried to react to the disaster: he began to chew and grunt with an exaggerated pleasure, so as to celebrate the food and create the cordial, unbuttoned atmosphere appropriate to an all-male gathering of connoisseurs of good cooking.

"My dear gentlemen," he said, seeing that he wasn't getting anywhere, "we must drink. Why all this abstemiousness? It's true we're Arabs, but we still don't give a hoot about Mohammed!"

At last, the group laughed in relief. The idea of pretending to be Arabs drinking wine despite the Koran had, for all of them, an odd, childish, geographical fascination.

Padding around the table, the waiter filled the glasses with fine red wine. Each time he stopped behind one of the guests, he stamped his foot, smiling at his own spontaneous contribution to the gaiety. But a glare from his employer made him as rapid and silent as a reptile. Discouraged, he planted the bottles in the middle of the table and took off to do something else in the kitchen.

Then came a moment of dangerous silence.

That was when everybody's eyes followed the intense stare of the owner.

Beyond one of the large windows looking onto the

street, one could make out the shadow of a head, stock still and spying on them. It left the window and returned; now and then the shape of a hat emerged in the clear pane above the arabesques in the ground glass, and it looked like the cap of a policeman who had been made suspicious by finding a café closed at such an unusual hour, with a good number of people inside.

The guests immediately felt that they must be breaking some police regulation, and they feared a half-ironic, half-brutal investigation of their banquet and their disguises – which, in their troubled imaginations, suddenly lost their innocent aspect. A mystery sprang up at the table: each one felt that he was participating in a rite, a strange secret initiation ceremony from which women were excluded. In the complete silence – as they all watched the owner so as to make the matter his responsibility – a multiple ticking became audible, like the voice of a termite colony within the table.

It came from the watches they were wearing on their bellies, tied to various laces within the Arabian costumes.

It was a reassuring surprise, like falling back into the bourgeois Occident. Their hands sought the places where these instruments of civilization were palpitating, almost as if they wanted to be ready to display them as a proof of identity, a document testifying to rectitude and good behavior.

"I'm going to go tell that curious fellow a thing or two," said the owner as he arose from the table. He ran to the window where, standing on tiptoe, he tried to look out.

The others saw him jump with sudden joy, while the black shadow fled in fear. At the owner's brusque command, the waiter hastily pulled up the shutter and the owner hurried into the street with a rough cry. One could hear his slippered footsteps running along the avenue amidst the hilarious exclamations of a few cabbies seated on their coach-boxes, and then silence returned.

"Here she is, our guest!" the owner cried out in triumph. He went to give a twist to two or three knobs, turning up the lights, the better to show off to the rest of his admiring and curious guests the girl they had seen in the café a few days earlier.

The lamps illuminated her embarrassment; she covered her eyes with her hands. Standing thin and afflicted, she gave the lie to their happily luxurious memory of her: now the low-cut dress that appeared through her open coat revealed a false wealth of glass beads, poorly sewn to a fragile fabric. Her misery was physical, as though she were recovering from an illness.

"Come here, come here," the owner encouraged her, pushing her towards her assigned seat. "Open your eyes, look at us. We Arabs are real gentlemen with women. We're looking good, aren't we?"

Her sly curiosity about what she had already glimpsed led her to uncover her eyes and look about her with a smile. The Arabs sitting around the table made gravely respectful bows to her.

"You are the gentleman who was sitting over there the other evening."

Her voice, fresh and close to laughter, made a pleasant impression on all of them. In order to show his satisfaction at having been recognized, the guest thus addressed arose halfway from the table and opened his cloak to reveal the European clothes he had on underneath: he uncovered only a great tangle of strings and his trousers, which were slightly open over his belly.

Everyone laughed and settled down more comfortably upon their chairs: the half-breed and his sidekick looked like two refined spectators, shedding the boredom induced in them by the rest of the show in order to watch the only act that interested them.

When the girl's gaze chanced to meet that of the

half-breed, he undressed her with his eyes in such a way that she gave a start and lowered her head.

"And how is it," asked the owner, who had remained standing near her chair, "that your friend isn't here? I invited him, too."

She lowered her eyes and didn't immediately answer.

"I haven't seen him since Tuesday: I don't know where he is."

A silence followed this confession, as though the assembly of tribal chieftains were listening to the survivor of a shipwreck telling of brutal treatment at the hands of a neighboring people; then the owner could no longer contain himself.

"Don't take this amiss," he burst out, "but he's a real bastard... That's no way to ditch a girl like you."

All the others expressed their agreement without speaking. It was as though the silence had been created so that she might cry freely, comforted by them in her shame. Unable to resist such an invitation, the girl broke out into sobs.

"He hasn't been round: I haven't seen him since then. I hoped to find him here, because I remembered that he wanted to come."

"Maybe he'll come," said the thin one with glasses, looking at her from beneath his lenses with enormous, too-white eyes. "But meanwhile, eat something. You look famished."

The owner spoke up. "Let's tell the truth, my girl. How long has it been since you ate?"

"Me? Why? I've eaten... I've eaten."

"Maybe, but I don't believe you. The young gentleman has gone off without even leaving you enough to eat. That's what they all do, these young people!"

She raised no objection: she relaxed the hand that was grasping a piece of bread, and dropped her fork onto the tablecloth as though disgusted by some over-costly food.

"No, no. There's nothing to be ashamed of. What's true is true. We're glad for ourselves that you've come, aren't we? So eat, and think happy thoughts. You, pour her some wine and set a place for me over here, next to her."

The waiter hastily obeyed and suggested: "Wouldn't it be a good idea to warm up some broth first for the young lady?"

"Absolutely. Run to the kitchen and bring on the broth."

While waiting, she began to eat a sandwich. She took small bites and chewed slowly, as through already full. The men watched her as though they had discovered a woman who was eating for the first time; they exchanged glances of satisfaction at every bite she swallowed, like children feeding a sparrow found half-dead in the snow.

Untouched by all this emotion, the half-breed was studying, with the sharp eye of a connoisseur, the girl's naked arms and her torso. Having spotted a danger, a self-assured will, she avoided turned her smiling, still-tearful eyes in his direction.

Observing this interest on the part of the half-breed, the sleight-of-hand artist finally understood his desire to take part in the dinner and the disappointed apathy he had hitherto displayed. Moved by his courtier's instinct, winking and whispering, be began to formulate opinions and speak flattering words about the girl.

"She's a real type, don't you think? We should train her and then launch her along with the new theater. Spend a little money on her, sharpen her up a bit, and we'd have one hell of an attraction. Take a good look at her: she's thin in the way that's popular right now. Try to talk to her later on. Girls like that don't dream of anything else but getting on stage."

Still silent, the half-breed smiled, and the owner, having noticed what was going on, kept a jealous eye on all three of them. He, too, was starting to make plans of his own for the girl.

He stood up to get something from behind the bar, and came back displaying an Arabian costume for a woman. It was white, with silver embroidery.

"It's for an odalisque," he said, and began to display it in detail to the girl, who cried out: "It's beautiful! Just beautiful!" lovingly running her hand over the silk.

"Put it on, then," he said. "It'll look great on you."

Curiosity to see this new apparition led everyone to demand that she disguise herself.

Even the half-breed emerged from his silence to say: "Oh, yes, dress yourself up as an Arab, Signorina. You'll look prettier than most of the ones at the Casino."

"I don't think so, but where do I go to change?"

"Over there, Signorina," said the owner. "I'll come with you to turn on the light."

The pair's departure from the table left an impressive gap. Everyone looked towards the dressing room, where the owner, throwing suits and shirts to the floor, uncovered a mirror.

"I'll leave you to it; I'll close the door." Without delay, he returned to the room, wearing the expression of a virtuous cavalier.

By now, everyone was watching the yellowish door, in which the keyhole opened its jagged black jaws. The awareness that a woman was undressing just a few meters away acted as an intoxicant. Conversation was interrupted by little bursts of laughter, winks, nervous smiles. Only the owner remained impassive, determined to seem the most discreet of all; but he sought to overhear the words exchanged between the half-breed and his companion who were, as he had already understood, powerfully hostile to his intentions.

"I'm almost ready," announced the girl from beyond the door, arousing visions of a sparkling disorder, in the midst of which her beauty would flower in its ill-disguised nudity.

"She's almost ready," repeated a voice, and everyone laughed, discreet fauns, sure of their self-control.

At last she opened the door and appeared, dancing and waving a green veil. Happy to wear the costume and, at the same time, a little confused by her own courage, she was very beautiful.

The owner, pale and with his mouth agape, stared at her without a smile, enchanted by this overwhelming vision, which overwhelmed all his memories.

"It's too much!" he cried out, to general amazement; and then, repentant, he lowered his gaze. A perfection long dreamed of, an odalisque worthy of a great prince, was before his eyes. He felt himself blinded, dazzled. He took a drink, stood up, drew near to her – his cry had frightened her – and murmured: "Brava! Brava!" in a hoarse voice that made the other men feel disgust and jealousy.

"Brava!" he repeated. "Let us have a look at you, odalisque. This is my poor Arabian Café's greatest night. I've always dreamed of being an Arab!" he confessed, overflowing with mixed feelings. "Love must be more beautiful for them."

This comment provoked a dry, ironic hilarity among the guests and an irritated protest from the thin man with glasses, who started explaining that every people has its own mistaken notions about other races. In his vindictive outburst, he dared to say that many men understand love only when it wears a mask, thus revealing themselves as worthy members of one category or another of perverts.

The girl, who had gone back to her seat to eat her dessert and fruit, seemed to have been made thoughtful by this outburst against the fascination of the Orient. Towards her second self, her joyous companion in this adventure, she felt both slightly angry and somewhat amused.

The half-breed was sniggering with the teachers and

the businessmen, claiming that the cities of Europe had much to teach all peoples when it came to love – they  even had lessons for him, a mixture of lascivious and highly refined races. The owner remained silent, uncertain as to whether or not he should take offense at the thin man's speech. However, since he was sitting next to the odalisque, he exploited his position as head of the assembly, keeping his hand on her shoulder; she paid no attention. Every now and then he stood up and offered wine to the others, so as to remind them that they were his guests.

There was a knock on the shutters.

"It must be my wife," said the sleight-of-hand artist in order to sooth the fresh anxiety that everyone felt upon hearing the sound. "She's come to pick me up; that was our arrangement."

In the meantime, the waiter had opened the shutter.

The gray, shabby little woman hesitated at the threshold, stunned not to recognize any of the men in their disguises.

"Come in, come in quickly," roared the owner. "Are you afraid, or do you want everyone to stick their nose into our business?"

Fearfully, she advanced; she scrutinized everyone with the red eyes of one given to weeping. At last she discovered her husband: she ran up to him as though to a safe haven.

"Well! Sit down, eat, drink, so long as you're here," said the owner, irritated by her miserable presence, which seemed a bad omen. "And you, introduce your wife to these gentlemen. I'm truly sorry, but I haven't another odalisque costume for her."

Everyone burst out laughing: even the sleight-of-hand artist, who had sat his wife down at the table and was offering her dishes of dessert, as if to say, "Here, enjoy yourself, and then go tell people how bad I am!"

Her gray head trembled with anger. "I don't want any," she said humbly and, tilting her head back, began to cry.

"You're mean," said the girl to the owner, and then started to move towards the old woman in order to console her.

He held her back, apologizing for having wanted to make an innocent joke, with no offense meant to anybody. He poured out some wine for his victim and tried to stuff her with biscuits from a large black bag of waxed cloth, showing his friendship with words and little caresses.

Once the old woman had calmed down and all the polite phrases had been spoken, he announced that coffee would be served in the basement room.

"Many of you don't know that room, because you've never dared go down there when there were happy doings. Shall we?"

At the back of the room, a railing offered protection against the risk of falling down a staircase that descended from floor level.

The host led the way. At the bottom step, a doorway cut into a niche bore the words: "Oriental Nights."

"You see?" he asked, turning around to look at the guests who were coming downstairs behind him. He pushed the door open and turned on the electric lights.

Along with the slightly disagreeable cellar odor and the smell of stored fabrics, there emerged from the cave a dim light – green, red, and blue – that divided itself up into oily patches on the stones of the stairway.

"First of all, the odalisque," said the owner. He heard the girl laugh, pressed by the men, who were full of flattery as they brushed up against her.

She broke free and was the first to enter the basement. It was a square little room with a vaulted ceiling painted with gold stars and arabesques against a dark background: in the wall facing the entrance, a large niche contained a sort of throne or alcove, surmounted by a baldaquin bearing silver-colored crescent moons.

Around the dried-up bowl of a little fountain in the center were divans and small tables. Upon the tables rested enormous, dust-covered brass trays that sent back veiled reflections of the composite light coming from the colored glass lamps hung all around the room. The carpets and cushions of the various areas where one might sit or lie down gave off a dry dustiness that invaded the nostrils, provoking a faint itch in those parts of the body that would have to take their places upon those surfaces.

The owner turned a knob hidden by a trap door: a gurgling and effortful stream shot high up above the fountain, stopped for a moment, and then returned to a height where it took on candied hues of green and red.

"Great. It's beautiful!" approved the guests; but they remained standing, wandering among the divans and tables as if seeking an excuse to leave.

"Be seated, gentlemen. We're going to have coffee and liqueurs down here."

Having overcome their hesitation, some of them started to sit down on the creaking divans, provoking a shower of minute fragments of stuffing which fell to the floor in a fine drizzle of dust.

The alcove was still free. The owner led the girl to it, desiring that she should sit there. His eyes were gleaming a little, and he kept a caressing hand on her back.

The coffee and liqueurs duly arrived.

The sleight-of-hand artist's wife, a suffering being who could find neither peace nor a place, sought only to stay close to her husband, while he tried his hardest to avoid her, unhappy at seeing his half-breed so grumpy. Every time he changed his place, she followed him tenaciously. Looking at her threateningly, he kept offering her little cordial glasses filled with liqueurs – a sign of exquisite attentiveness – and then trying to abandon her next to the tray with the bottles. When he saw that his maneuvers were useless, he threw himself down furiously on a sofa and pulled her down after him, faking one of those sudden accesses of tenderness that come over old married couples when they are in company.

The sound and the sight of the water generated a feeling of freshness that filled everyone's nostrils, joining the odor of dusty, moth-eaten fabrics. At this moment of stillness, everyone took on an indolent, middle-eastern aspect. Those already leaning back on a divan now stretched out comfortably, head down and legs raised on some support or other, letting their gazes lose themselves in the clouds of fragrant smoke arising from the incense that the owner had lit next to the alcove, or contemplating their own feet encased in embroidered slippers. The voices had become discreet, veiled. There fell a silence that was an invitation to dream and sleep – brusquely interrupted by the footsteps of the waiter coming downstairs.

Everyone resumed a more dignified posture and looked toward the alcove. The owner and the odalisque were sitting at a decent distance from each other, meditating with a very serious air. There nonetheless hung over them a sense of tension kept under control, such as follows, perhaps, upon a woman's rejection of an overly bold overture. Her dreamy immobility might have hidden indignation. His almost painful fixity revealed the attitude peculiar to a person enduring punishment while asking forgiveness, in hopes of renewing his attack with the advantage of a tacit understanding that matters have gone beyond the first modest preliminaries.

At any rate, they were all aware that a task of small-time seduction had been undertaken while they were resting; and envy created a sense of anger that snaked from one to another – all the more so because the girl had turned to the owner, who was still wrapped up in his own affliction, and smiled as though to grant him his forgiveness.

The male guests were filled with a subtle desire to

undo the tacit understanding and take their revenge. Made shamelessly happy by that atmosphere, the old woman laughed and threw her gray head upon her man's chest; but after a few words from him, whispered in her ear with a tigerish smile, she wound up weeping in a way that was even more annoying than her earlier sobs.

The owner had taken the girl's hand and was caressing it with a smile. The couple seated in the alcove isolated themselves, with no thought for the others, who felt themselves treated like dear old eunuchs, forced witnesses to the preliminaries of love.

No one protested against the horror of the image with a cry or a gesture; but each man nonetheless got his vengeance by staring at the girl, shamelessly expressing his own need for physical consolation, piteously asking – begging – for a sign, a nod, that would designate him as the favorite.

Troubled by his memories and the wealth of new impressions and hopes, the owner had grown distracted, but he kept his hand on her shoulder.

This collective display of desire and passion was a sudden revelation for the girl, who gave a frightened start. Her companion, thus alerted, laughed imprudently, with the quickness of one who has just scalded himself; and the others grew even angrier at having been discovered in their crafty scheming.

Everyone laughed, but silently, as though they had understood their misfortune and, disenchanted, were resigned to it. But they had achieved a result: they had made the girl conscious of her position. Now she was smiling, not knowing what else to do; and everywhere she looked, her smile was lovingly answered with a commitment to feed her, clothe her, keep her, love her like a wife. All this selfishness gave off a goodness that was new to her, accustomed as she was to young men. Refusing to torment her with jealousy regarding her past, they were generously understanding, promising more attention than passion, and she understood her own value to the men around her. They no longer looked old, nor did their offers seem repugnant, partly because their Oriental costumes saved them from a precise revelation of their desires, allowing them to behave with the fantastic freedom of actors in a pantomime.

But there was one among them who troubled her: it was the half-breed. In his case, the disguise had no influence: he was clearly promising ample rewards. And yet, with his dark skin and harmonious movements, he struck her as handsome. She sensed that his success with the envied women of the stage would constitute a future danger; she felt his fascination as a man of the night, a man whose dancing and drinking were vices. She was tempted and provoked by the way he was calmly waiting, and would have liked to see him as jealous and ridiculous as the others, so as to find herself faced no longer with the risk he represented: the risk of a way of life full of the horrors she had learned about as a child, listening to her family talk of them with insults and curses.

She had to turn her gaze to the others, in order to feel herself the white woman who has chanced into an oasis of cuddly, paternal predators.

"It's true," she freely confessed, "I was hungry this evening. I hadn't eaten since yesterday morning." It seemed to her that, by speaking these words, she had renounced all her attraction to the lustful half-breed and returned to a world capable of feeling compassion for a good girl's miseries. An unhappy sigh reminded her that the owner was sitting next to her. She turned to look at him and smiled with gratitude when he murmured, "Poor thing, poor thing!"

Leaning her head back, she saw the fine Arabian woman's costume she was wearing, and felt ashamed; she wanted to deflect from herself all those gazes that, after her confession, had turned hopeful and vivacious, as though from the effects of a heady liquor. A bit worried, she sat back, pulling herself together with a gesture of modesty. Then she saw the other, gray-haired woman as a protector, an anchor in a storm; with a gentle gesture, she called her to her side.

The woman came running: her husband looked at the half-breed in triumph.

From that moment, the owner feared the old woman's evil arts, and could think of nothing but the quickest way to get rid of her and of all his guests. He arose and went upstairs into the café.

Everyone waited in silence.

The old woman embraced the girl affectionately. "My child," she whispered, "you must seize good luck by the hair! There's a man here who can give you a future. Just think, in a few days he'll be the owner of a vaudeville theater. Do you understand?"

Meanwhile the half-breed had drawn near, pretending to study the arabesques painted in the alcove; but none of this escaped the others, who smiled and winked, although the sleight-of-hand artist claimed through his gestures that he couldn't see what they were going on about.

Silent and monumental, the owner reappeared at the basement door. He grasped the plot that had been going forward during his absence: the hag was tempting the beautiful girl in the interests of his rival, but he kept calm, so as not to compromise, through an error, the victory he felt he deserved.

"I'm very sorry," he announced, "but it's past closing time for a business like mine. I don't want to get in trouble."

Everyone stood up.

"No, no: there's still time for a little glass. I just wanted to prepare you."

The thin man with glasses advanced resolutely towards the alcove.

"Signorina," he said, "I am most grateful to you. You've put a bit of a smile on our faces: the faces of men who are not usually very cheerful." He respectfully kissed her hand. "I hope to meet you again." He bowed to the owner.

"We will cherish the memory of this lovely evening. I hope you will soon begin some fortunate enterprise."

The two schoolteachers were brisker in their farewells. They followed the thin man upstairs.

"Learning has departed," cried the owner; and his voice betrayed the calculating hope that industry and trade would soon depart as well.

The remaining guests understood and came over to say their goodbyes to the girl.

"It's late," she said, climbing down from the alcove. "I should be going, too."

"Well, then, young lady, my wife and I will accompany you."

The owner glared furiously at the sleight-of-hand artist, but found him armored and imperturbable. It was then that he made a last-ditch attempt to save his treasure.

"I'm telling you that I'll be the one to show the young lady home. She lives far away, and I mean to take her back in a carriage."

"If that's how things are, I give up," said the other, seeing that the half-breed was signaling him to let it go. He and his wife headed for the stairs, followed by the half-breed, the owner, and the girl.

When they were upstairs in the café, the voices of the men crowded into the dressing room reminded them that they had to change their clothes.

"The young lady will wait until the gentlemen have finished," said the owner. His words had the tone of an order. He pushed them all, including the old woman, into little passageway. "Go help your husband," he commanded.

No one had closed the dressing room door. The

guests crammed inside threw off their mantles and vests, remaining in their shirtsleeves and showing an acrimonious, deliberate lack of respect towards the woman who was meant for another. Some of them came into the café with their flies still open and buttoned them up out there, coughed, and returned to the passageway – from which another man emerged already dressed, returning to the bleak limitations of everyday life.

The farewells were courteous but devoid of gratitude. The half-breed came to shake the owner's hand, smiled at him as at a fair winner, and then turned to the girl. She felt him to be so sure of his future victory that, with a vague gesture, she promised it to him then and there.

"When they're done, I'll go get dressed as well," she said.

"What? You, too?" murmured the owner, softly but desperately, looking about him to make certain that no one could hear. "Stay on for a bit, I beg you. I've got something to tell you." He hurried off to help a guest who was having trouble getting into his jacket.

While everyone was saying their last farewells, passing under the half-open shutter, he stayed close to her, watchful and suspicious as a prison guard who fears that he has given the visitors too much leeway. The last black-clad back passed beneath the sheet metal: he grabbed the handle, pulled it down forcefully, and pushed it right down to the bottom, helping himself out with his foot.

It was then that he noticed the waiter. "How did you make out with the tips?" he asked.

"Badly, to tell the truth."

"Take whatever's in the till and go get some sleep. We'll settle our accounts tomorrow morning at my house."

Touched, the waiter hugged his boss, then bowed to the girl in order to express his devotion to her as well. He took his time leaving, standing still in the middle of the room, as though he wanted to say a melancholy farewell to the café. At last, feeling himself superfluous, he disappeared silently along the kitchen corridor.

"And now, let's go back downstairs," gently proposed the owner. "We can talk better. You're my gazelle, aren't you?" His voice shook with anxiety.

Without waiting for an answer, he turned the knob that extinguished the three rows of lights in the room. Outside, the others saw the café vanish into darkness, and the house recompose its architecture all the way down to the sidewalk: beyond the windows, there remained only a glow that came from the deep mystery of the Arabian night.

# The Dance School

The quartet room was nearly empty: a piano, some chairs of delicate cane, the four music stands. The voices of the instruments could better pursue one another along the pallid walls, dense with the forms of small paintings and miniatures. The music stands were in the center, all contained within a rose of dizzying little red and white squares painted on the floor; the stands were made of a sonorous-looking old material, a light-hued wood cut with precision and astuteness. Empty in the morning, the room remained closed until it was time for the evening rehearsal, when just a little light was poured out onto the players' pages, while in its dark corner the piano made it clear, by the vibration of its strings, that its musical belly suffered from remaining silent.

In the daytime, during those hours of respect and waiting, the mistress of the house withdrew into another room near the entrance door in order to give her singing lessons, helping herself out with another piano, an upright – a muffled finger-breaker that she alone was capable of taming. Those were the days when the other tenants, generally undisturbed by the lessons, were astonished as they trudged up the stairs by certain high notes which, breaking through the skylight and escaping into heaven, made the wearisome aspect of all those steps look at least three flights higher.

By the accent, the nuances, the different type of resonance, some of the tenants distinguished native throats from foreign ones, perplexed that a woman's voice should thus be able to perforate the whole house, like a pipe full of moaning water.

The singing teacher had four daughters, but only the

three eldest studied at the conservatory. They returned home with their scores rolled up under their arms, and often with their instruments shut up in dark cases, having enjoyed hearing people murmur in the street: "The violinists, the violinists," like a public recognition of the virtues that a hoped-for diploma would confirm. They were a bit graceless and wan; and only experience with a full-blooded man, and the fertility that would follow from it, would be able to make them desirable, healing their monotonous and repulsive way of skipping. Perhaps, had you thrown one or another of the three skinny, freckled daughters down onto a bed, you would have discovered that she had a dry and resounding belly like that of a cello. They were creatures born to unhappiness, brought up by a mother who was all rhythm, desiccated music reduced to the bone.

Their mother exercised over their studies a nagging vigilance which it was their duty to appreciate as a gift. When her daughters played at home, she was incapable of holding still, running to their doors to beat the rhythm more strictly, intoning the melody with the incredibly out-of-tune voice of one who teaches singing, until, no longer able to restrain herself, she arrived behind the performer and repeated a phrase that had been treated too freely.

Her authority and dominion over her daughters derived in part from the solid piano studies she had carried out under the guidance of a fabulous old provincial teacher who had remained in obscurity despite a talent adored by his female pupils, and in part from her manner as a teacher of an art which they, too, cultivated.

The only one who escaped was Amina, the youngest. In a family nourished on music, Amina had grown up indifferent to the tidal wave of sound that filled the rooms of the house with insistent, ecstatic fiddling and singing. Having refused obeisance to solfeggio since early childhood, with a stubbornness that had discouraged her mother and horrified her diligent sisters, Amina had afterwards liberated herself from every form of domestic obedience. She lived with the four women as her own mistress, subject to no surveillance. Following her very happy schooldays, she had learned how to decorate luxury garments with embroidery, a task she found odious, at which she worked with commitment only when her sisters played: the commitment of one who felt that she was working seriously in the midst of genteelly absurd idlers.

She went to the concerts so as not to remain alone in an empty house filled with disturbing noises. She was always the last to enter, hoping, in such a crowd of people, to be forced to remain at the threshold. She was ashamed at the self-confident manner her mother and sisters had of making a place for themselves, of taking the best seats: priestesses, waited for and indispensable to the rite. Standing near her door, she held herself aloof from the game of greetings, from the signs of complicity and pleasure her sisters exchanged with their female classmates from the conservatory, who formed, along with their fathers and mothers, a group of ravenous connoisseurs, disdainful of novelties.

Every now and then some virtuoso had the power to enchant them; and then, at the end of the program, everybody crowded around the podium to request encores, excited by a fever hateful to Amina, who envied those who had already made their escape.

She didn't like the girls from the conservatory, who talked too much of music and of lessons to be mastered. If anything, she listened to them when, having reached the point where they talked about their teachers, old or young, she discovered something loving and devoted in their harsh voices; then she smiled with satisfied malice. The conservatory, of which she knew only the atrium and the first corridor, she saw as some extraordinary monastery under the spiritual guidance of sentimental singing monks, abbots, and novices.

Once she had overheard, there in the atrium where she was awaiting her sisters, the chanting of the solfeggio class: the exercises of a nasal church choir, stupendously well suited to give her an everlasting impression of something that had hitherto remained vague. She had developed a taste for concerts only at sixteen years of age. Those halls had revealed themselves to her as the places where, week after week, it was easy to foresee that the most graceful and best-dressed people of the city would meet. She quickly came to believe, as a reaction to the setting, that beneath a love of art the majority hid a calculation that led them to take advantage of the special atmosphere created by the music. Amused by the idea of having discovered a truth which she was inclined to exaggerate, she had become, on account of her desire to unmask the most varied types by means of flirtatiously ingenuous glances, a seductive will-o'-the-wisp who troubled the fattest bellies and the boniest, most hollowed-out adorers of the minor mode.

Some of these people, encountering her alone in the street, had followed her and tempted her with apparently obscure speeches. Amina laughed at them, considering herself well protected by her own precocious artfulness, and returned home full of an amused compassion for her sisters who were ruining their necks by rubbing them against the ribs of their violins. But she kept silent, certain that she would be unable to convince them to make themselves beautiful instead of scratching away all day at their instruments. When you came right down to it, she didn't count in the real life of the family. Her mother and sisters — on the recurring days of high ill-temper and harsh words — did not hide the fact that they were expecting from her some bad news, some huge mistake; but expecting it with resignation, as though anything were possible for one who did not belong to their noble world of artists. Perhaps this was their way of punishing her for being the only one who gave a sense of having a carnal life, of seeming a ripe and juicy fruit among dried nuts and almonds.

The few visitors to the house were old friends of her father, an unfortunate composer who had died young with many sketches and a completed opera in his desk drawer. They were musicians and private teachers shut into their touching, petty world of memories and missed opportunities to achieve the fame they envied in others: a fame which they pretended to believe was the result of cheekiness rather than real talent.

As for the voice students, the mother kept them far from the rest of the family, with the exception of Carmen, her favorite, who happened to be the only one Amina liked. The girl had a stupendous voice, one of those voices that enchant teachers and make them as humble and relentless as lovers. Carmen was beautiful, rather plump, and striking. Mature men liked her on account of a certain way she had of invading them, of taking their hand while talking, of interrupting the most serious and threatening speeches with resounding, stagy laughter which deflected anger into sensuous surprise. One could not help but laugh, forgive her, love her even more. She came into town for her lessons from a suburb; but she had beautiful clothes and jewelry, the suspect gifts of a relative who was helping her while awaiting the triumphal career that connoisseurs predicted for her.

In order to prepare for her debut, the singer attended a dance school where an old teacher of hers, once a celebrated ballerina, was teaching her how to move gracefully and perform dance steps.

Amina came upon her one day while, waiting for her voice lesson, she was dancing in the sitting room to the tune that she herself was singing with such freshness. With head abandoned backwards and eyes half-closed, she seemed to be enjoying the joy of her own rich body and, thanks to the song, an escape from the gray room; Amina stood and watched her, suffering from a sense of envy.

"Brava! What are you doing?"

The other turned around, a bit disoriented; but recognizing Amina, whom she trusted as a friend, she smiled.

"So you dance?"

"I'm not dancing: I'm practicing for my debut. A singer has to be able to occupy the stage without looking like a statue."

"You're really good. Where did you learn?"

Carmen told her about her dance teacher, who was very old but still full of energy – the last custodian of a now-dead tradition.

Amina remained silent and sighed. "Will you take me there?" she finally asked. "I would like to talk a bit with that lady. Don't you think I could be a dancer? Or maybe I'm too old?"

The other looked her over from head to foot with an inquisitive eye.

"It depends...You've got very good legs..."

"Do you know much about dance?" asked Amina, to put an end to the scrutiny, which was embarrassing her.

"No, but I can see very well that you've got the physique for success. You're bound to please. You, too, will find a rich relative who will help you," she laughed, glad to confess to her younger friend the truth that the latter must have frequently suspected.

"Thanks," Amina joked, since it seemed to her naive to take offense.

"Enough said! Pay no attention. But men of a certain age are so sweet! Tomorrow you'll come with me to my teacher. All right?"

The next day Amina made the acquaintance of the dance school and of the old woman who ran it.

The school, on the second floor of a run-down old palace, was a big room where the teacher gave lessons to mixed classes of youths and girls. Amina and Carmen arrived as one of these group lessons was about to finish.

The singer, leaving her companion to torture herself with anxiety while waiting at the door, entered the room and approached a white-haired old lady, very thin and dressed in black, who was standing still in a corner and watching the dancers.

The woman turned, smiled at Carmen and invited her to sit down next to her on a long and narrow cushioned bench. In amazement, Amina saw the old woman cross her legs and start tapping out, with the foot that touched the ground, the awkward and stilted rhythm, a slow, languid ballabile, that a middle-aged woman was intent upon squeezing from a suffering piano. She understood that, in the meantime, they were talking about her: she saw her friend make a sign to the teacher, who turned to study her with hard black eyes set in a nearly waxen face, and the gaze confused her so that she would happily have run away.

The two woman called to her. She approached, crossing the room in the spaces between the couples who, enchanted by their own undulation, dragged their feet along the platform with an insistent, mysterious murmur.

"Come here, Signorina. Sit down with us," was the teacher's greeting. The voice was hoarse, but the tone was benevolent. "So you want to become a great ballerina? Do you know that it's no profession for modern times? At any rate, let's see. Do you know music, do you understand tempo?"

Intimidated, Amina replied with an evasive gesture.

"Guglielmo," the teacher called out, "come here."

A youth dancing with a girl whose red hair gave the sensation of fire separated himself from his companion and approached with a smile.

"Do me a favor, Guglielmo: try to dance for a bit with this young lady. Don't do complicated steps. Here, let me introduce you: my pupil Guglielmo Tassi, Signorina...?"

Red with confusion, Amina stated her surname.

"Come on, kids, get going, I want to see."

Some of the dancers, curious, turned around to enjoy the experiment; Guglielmo's companion had remained in the middle of the room as if still awaiting him, and looked at herself, proudly, in a mirror.

Dominated by the tone and gaze of the old woman, Amina yielded to the embrace of the thin, loose-limbed young man, who was wearing slightly droopy clothes that smelled of tobacco; clinging to him, she took her first steps. Not knowing where to put her head, she held it tilted back with an effort that caused a bit of pain in her neck, but she was surprised by a sense of happy lightness. The floor was always free; her feet never encountered those of her very agile companion, who embraced her with a languid gesture, indicating with a barely perceptible pressure the movement in which she was to accompany him. Obliged by her position to look him in the face, Amina never saw his expression change, nor did she see the heavy lids move over his black, sleepy-looking eyes.

The music ended; the couples separated.

"Brava, Signorina!" said the young man, leading her back to the teacher. "Who taught you?"

Amina, afraid that he was making fun of her, did not answer.

"The predisposition is there," said the teacher. "Naturally you've got to improve your ear. Come to my school whenever you want. You'll dance with these young people; then I myself will teach you something suitable to you."

"Thank you, Signora," Amina murmured.

The old woman was no longer listening to her: she was advancing threateningly towards a group of students who were demanding another round of dancing. "Have you or haven't you understood that the class is over? I've got other things to do now. Get going, free up the room. Quickly!"

The voice was rough and irritated. It frightened Amina, and made a chill come over her. She left the room with her friend feeling as though she had suffered a brutality: dancing with a man, carrying out an act regarding which she had received no intimate advice and made no free choice.

From that day onwards, she attended the school assiduously. At home she said that she was going to the house of a friend, a good girl who lived on embroidery; in reality, Amina hadn't seen this friend for some time, because the distrust of the other's fiancé towards her had come between the two girls.

Amina soon became so skilful that she helped the teacher to break in the new pupils. She took them by the arm and, following the rhythms of the out-of-tune piano, dragged them here and there on the worn-out platform, with the vacant expression of someone carrying out a boring task. This accustomed her to dominion over the awkwardness of males, to a deliberate fashion of treating them and rejecting them that persisted even away from the school.

The promised classical-dance lessons never materialized: the teacher had so much to do, and Amina lacked the courage to remind her of her promise. She had entered an environment that suited her tastes, and didn't want to risk an imprudence that might ruin her relationship with the irascible old woman. The latter was still so full of life that a trifle was enough to set her to yelling and cursing, and then she reverted to her Milanese accent, a sign of her membership in the noble race of old-fashioned ballerinas. The person who suffered the most from this harshness of manner was a sister of the teacher's, a bit less old, but filthy and servile, who opened the door, performed other services, and did the cooking at the far end of the apartment, which consisted of a few dark little rooms.

The dance studio, which had formerly been a billiards-room, still had on its walls, between the mirrors added afterwards, racks for the cues and, higher up, two-light fan windows designed to limit the light that fell on the rectangles of green baize. Along the sides of the room ran two very long cushioned benches. At the end, opposite the window looking out on the street, was a white door with a glass pane at the height of a man, rendered impenetrable to the gaze by a yellowish curtain. This door opened onto the teacher's bedroom. Entering the latter, one's nostrils were assailed by a rancid odor, a suspicion of old urine forgotten in a night-table. This was the girls' dressing room: a dressing room that put one on terms of intimacy with the teacher, but without repugnance, on account of women's natural tendency to put up more easily than men with both the elderly and children.

Men were forbidden entry; but some came in by way of the kitchen, under the protection of the servile sister, and were thus able to embrace their complicitous girlfriends under cover of a favorable semi-darkness. When the old lady discovered such misdeeds, there were frightful but brief flashes of anger: her black eyes flamed, her voice suddenly took on a harshness that recalled life backstage, with its requirement that rage be given full expression during the few minutes of the intermission. The next day, she already appeared to have forgotten the guilty parties, treating them as well or as badly as she did all the others.

At the school there gathered young men with some money in their pockets; sons of good families, ashamed of not yet having a lover and capable of the most treacherous calculations in order to obtain one; a few fat innocents who needed to dance for physical exercise; and many girls who were poor, or orphans, or on bad terms with their families. These girls avenged their unhappiness at home by dancing and carrying on in a dangerous fashion. Most of the girls did not pay, having become the teacher's assistants both in attracting people and in instructing them.

Amina enjoyed this environment, full of surprises and a bit mysterious; the only thing that startled her was the ease with which certain of her companions got involved in messes and tragedies. The fact of finding themselves frequently in the arms of men led them into rapid love affairs. Having two lovers turned them into women who lived a life of anguish, always in a hurry, awaited in the farthest and most inconvenient parts of the city, which was not, in any case, very large. They turned up pale, exhausted, suffering from pains and unusual malaises, in need of long confidential talks with the ballerina's sister and the pianist, a creature – even more servile than the other – who always smiled at others' misfortunes, as though these might compensate her for the obstinate accumulation of her own, which were very bitter indeed.

The dance school brought misfortune. It was no longer possible to count the rash actions, the futile moments of abandon shared with certain insinuating and sneaky young men who were older than the majority of the pupils. These men came in groups, as if they had received word, like bandits holding up a bank. They would attend assiduously for a week, rendering the teacher powerless against their numbers and authority, and then disappear; and a long while would go by before they put in another appearance. During their dominion, and afterwards as well, there was a corrupting poison in the air: a desire for something new in life, for excitement aboard automobiles driven at full speed along the hillsides at night – a desire that led the girls into dangerous missteps.

Amina always remained unscathed. Her singer friend had taught her a series of sung distractions that alarmed the young men who – incapable of enjoying them – acted harshly and made themselves ridiculous in order to wound her in turn, with the result that Amina lost all respect for them and had no inkling that they might have their charms.

Every now and then, a nephew of the teacher's joined the teaching staff. He had a white-collar job and was around forty; he wore a pair of pince-nez glasses behind which his eyes bulged and always seemed to be looking in the wrong direction. His smooth head showed dandruff where he parted his greasy hair; and his short moustache, clipped to form a hard line, made his red lips, criss-crossed by little wrinkles, look all the fleshier by contrast.

He danced too: he moved with a dry but precise rhythm, like an automaton, maintaining the sense of a geometrical, rectangular surface as he went dancing about the room. The girls thought of him as little more than a piece of furniture, but Amina didn't trust him. He turned up too frequently in his aunt's room, as if to search for something he had forgotten, carrying out troubling, hasty and intimate investigations around garters or other undone items of lingerie. In the mirror placed over a big chest, he looked like some awkward black bird: he excused himself with an incomprehensible mumble, and took off as if horrified by his own inopportune entry.

With hostility and contempt, Amina had noticed that he started up only with girls who were saddened or disillusioned on account of their having given themselves to loveless egotists. He got round them by speaking the words of a dictionary not his own, trying to put into his voice the soft sweetness of a man in love and inclined to forgive the error committed with another man more handsome and charming than himself. He contented himself with making advances, since this was the easiest course and, perhaps, because he was aware that he deserved no more.

A few girls had fallen, conquered by his nearly disgusting displays of compassion; but afterwards, they no longer showed up at the school. On the basis of hints, of tales or fought-back tears, Amina had formed an idea of his cruelty, of morbid explosions of passion that must have terrified her schoolmates.

Where Amina was concerned, he appeared to be waiting for someone else to drop in before starting up with his tactics of a pitying second lover: one who did not demand those first fruits already given away, and in such an unfortunate manner. Now and then he looked at her; and he blushed when she cast upon him her inquiring gaze, as though she had surprised him in the midst of his calculations.

In order to give the pianist a break, he would sit down at the piano as soon as he arrived from the office and, playing a *ballabili* of his own invention that seemed to come from his knuckles, repeat them every time with such stereotyped exactness as to make one miss the lady's mawkish diminuendos and wobbly rhythm. The old ballerina showed no signs of pleasure at seeing him; sometimes she didn't even respond to his ceremonious and humble greeting.

Nonetheless, the memory of the dance school was enough to console Amina for the reception that awaited her upon returning home. She sat silently at table and, as if to mock her mother's and sisters' suspicious gazes, listened in her head to the echo of those two or three endlessly repeated rhythms, smelling the odor of tobacco and hearing the rustling of feet on the platform when, once the lights had been turned on in the evening, the veteran students of the school took a languid turn about the floor, holding each other close. The room filled up with undulating couples, doing their best to surpass themselves under the eye of the teacher who, planted to one side, observed and marked the right tempo by beating her black hoof on the floor. With the partner she had chosen after turning down those with little experience, Amina – once again a woman who wanted to enjoy the dance, no longer a schoolmistress – almost always won the improvised contest. Applause broke out, and she was happy, still held in the arms of the young man who, once the music had stopped, pretended to be distracted.

At that time of day, you paid a small amount for dancing. Some of the men, more as a joke than from stinginess or lack of funds, tried to elude this obligation, protesting that they had only come along to watch; but if a youth took even one turn about the floor – which was sufficient to annul his legal status as an onlooker – the teacher's sister would put in an unctuous appearance, reminding him of the fee, almost as though she was hastening to acknowledge the other's haste to pay it. If, in the confusion, she failed to obtain payment, she took up a position on the landing near the exit, and the young man either had to cough up, or else his trickery would be repaid with a stinging and sibylline phrase that would follow the escapee all the way to the bottom of the stairs.

These and similar memories brought Amina sudden moments of gaiety, which came close to giving her away when she was faced with the hard gaze of her family.

It was at this time that preparations were being made at home for a long-awaited event: the formation of a string quartet. The sisters had had a fortunate encounter with the missing fourth instrumentalist; the mother, filled with joy at the thought of completing the two violins and viola that her family was already able to offer, was dreaming of a grand musical evening, for which she would invite friends and acquaintances to a house ennobled by such a fiery passion for art.

The cellist was a chemistry student, with a very ugly but genial face. He was a bit of a musical jack-of-all-trades: he could play the piano, read scores, play various string instruments, transpose an accompaniment – and personally, he seemed to dream of nothing but full symphony orchestras and balconies full of symphonic enthusiasm.

To Amina, the first time she saw him, he seemed horrible: the sisters, on the other hand, recognized him for what he was, a companion and colleague so cultivated and skilled as to inspire respect. He loved the classics, but had two or three favorites among the moderns, which scandalized them a bit but also gave them the sense of a free, self-assured personality.

He arrived, late one afternoon, for the first rehearsal of the quartet. He seemed awkward, but once the parts had been opened on the stands, he found the words of a captain. The character of the first movement was gay, scintillating; that of the second movement elegiac, with echoes of triumphal nostalgia; the third was lively and fluent, as befits a Classical rondo. He was sure of himself when he spoke, supplying examples by singing a little in support of his interpretation, just like a teacher. The sisters and the mother, who sat at the closed piano, remained silent, admiring and a little offended. Perhaps he noticed this, because, in order to banish any sense on their part of having to put up with bossiness, he said gently: "I may be wrong, but this is a quartet I know well, one I have heard performed several times by great artists." After the first phrases, he brought the music to a halt: the rhythm was not as secure as the score specified it should be, an accent didn't fall in the right place, the legato failed to do justice to the sweetness of harmony desired by the composer.

Standing in the doorway, Amina enjoyed the schoolgirl blushes of her sisters, thus overwhelmed by a greater talent. She began to admire the young man, who every now and then looked at her with a curiosity that too soon had to yield to the unceasing need to look at the pages and the strings of his instrument, which vibrated and resounded under his resolute bow.

Amina, a little intrigued, thought that a man so

caught up in his musical interests, so intensely committed to finding the way to make all the parts of such complex compositions clear and to express what they contained, must be invincible.

The rehearsal lasted a long time, and offered many incidents that cast light upon his manly strength. He clearly showed the mother that he found certain rests too long, inasmuch as it was no accident if the composer had not put holds over them; he changed the bowings of the eldest sister, who played the violin, suggesting to her a gentle way of coming in that seemed a happy and unexpected novelty on the part of the bony girl. Amina opened her eyes wide in wonder. The man who could dominate those proud, haughty women had finally been discovered and had come into the house. She had the sense that the light was being turned down when she saw him put his deep-voiced instrument back in its case and prepare to leave.

At last, after a consultation conducted through the eyes, he was invited to stay to dinner. He accepted as though it had been owed him. Two sisters flew to the kitchen in order to dress up the evening eggs with spicy sauces; the third went out into the street to buy cheese, a necessary addition to the table for the guest's sake.

It was a merry dinner, one which left in the whole family, Amina included, the troubling sensation of having passed a few hours in the presence of a delightful danger. The sisters all laughed without knowing why; the mother, having shed her habitual solemnity, interrogated him, humbly questioned him, and took such a satisfied pleasure in the self-assurance apparent in his answers that, at long last, the woman even in her was revealed. So as not to turn the conversation away from music, the young man told stories of famous composers, their loves, their professional jealousies, and he told it all with perfidious wit. It was another world: an opening of vital perspectives made up of flesh and blood, whose existence they had never before suspected in the scores with their icy precision of bar lines, rests, marks indicating dynamics and articulation. He threw out daring phrases, and the women split their sides with laughter, wriggling as though at a caress; they were caught up in a collective madness by which Amina, too, let herself be pulled along, perhaps, in part, out of a sense that she understood, like him, more than the words were saying. The young man confessed that music had made him fall in love first with a singer whom he had vainly adored from the balcony, then with a violinist to whom he had offered flowers after a concert. He seemed to feel sorry for himself on account of such episodes, but spoke in the tone of someone who was ready to go through it all again, giving each of the sisters a shiver of vague hopes, of sudden ardor for a man so warm and generous.

When he finally left, the astonished family realized that it was past eleven o'clock, but the new understanding among the women persisted. One of the sisters spoke of a painful episode which had befallen her, without making the usual mystery of such matters, and met with ready compassion, as among animals conscious of and resigned to the same misfortunes.

Such an orgy had no sequel, but the young man became the pillar that sustained the quartet. Rehearsals took place three times a week. When expecting him, the sisters were nervous, awaiting his arrival with obvious anxiety. They received him as a liberator to whom they might recount the thousand banalities of the conservatory. Amina was tormented by the presence of the student, who barely greeted her, as though he had well understood her situation in the family; and she made an effort to find him ridiculous, in the midst of all that reckless admiration on her sisters' part. But in reality, it was only the sisters who seemed ridiculous.

His fine teeth gleamed when, bending forward, he

smiled as he listened to the low notes of his instrument, so masculine amidst the virtuosic slenderness of the two violins and the nasal, still feminine voice of the viola. Those teeth led Amina to suspect that ugliness was merely a preliminary deceit on the part of those who are truly beautiful; and, from the threshold – tacitly forbidden her – of the musical sanctuary, she spied on the young man, studying him to the point where she had impressed upon her mind and flesh a tormenting image that frequently appeared to her in the uncertain state between sleeping and waking.

The student had begun to default on the quartet rehearsals, which took place in view of the mistress of the house's ambitious plan. He was never happy with the program that had been chosen; he recommended that they put together a small repertory among which they might choose; he frequently failed to show up, adducing the heavy commitments entailed by his scientific work.

Amina had realized, meeting him alone on the stairs, that he behaved differently when they were alone than when he reigned over the quartet room. He had said to her: "Oh yes, you're going out for a walk," in an envious tone that disagreed with his musical ardor, but which was sincere. When she came back early that day and appeared at the threshold of the room, he had smiled at her in gratitude. Amina had convinced herself that there was some mystery which, shortly afterwards, he revealed to her. She had gone to the dance school, guessing from her sisters' harsh nervousness that he would skip the rehearsal. While teaching a difficult step to a rich but rustic youth, who was intimidated by her only when he viewed her as a teacher, she saw the student appear in the room.

He looked at her, after a circular gaze that was undoubtedly seeking someone, and smiled.

Amina let the clumsy dancer go on by himself, clownishly turning to the rhythm as it was beaten out; she ran up to the student, aggressively.

"What are you doing here. What about the rehearsal?"

"I'm here for various reasons which I'll explain to you later," he said, smiling almost threateningly. "We can both say we've seen each other in this room, but I don't know for which of us it will be worse at your house."

She perceived an unpleasant element of blackmail in this announcement. She looked into the eyes of the student, who was now laughing, so as to dispel any doubts she might have.

"To me it seems better," he added, "that neither of us should say where we met. Do you agree?"

Amina, still perplexed, remained silent.

"Don't misunderstand," said the young man, varying his approach in a fashion that showed his experience as a musician who is used to changing the tone. "It was you I was looking for. I wanted to see you at last outside those sad walls."

Amina felt in these words a compassion that pleased her: she didn't know how to answer. The old teacher intervened.

"Bravi! You already know each other? This gentleman came this morning to ask me for dancing lessons. You start off with him. Get him to move a bit. We'll see!"

The two embraced for the dance. He smiled, as though to excuse himself for receiving over-competent that help that he hadn't requested.

"One, two, three, four."

The student was stiff in his movements, but was sure of himself, unlike the others who were always victims of their inexperience. By the end of the dance, he was no longer bumping against Amina's feet, although he held her ever more tightly.

They laughed, looking into each other's eyes: they understood each other. They both had the sense of gaily betraying a boring and hostile world.

"The quartet..." he murmured, ironically, but the allusion was too direct. Amina became serious once again and, to regain a bit of control over him, she began leading him here and there, as if she had realized that he was there for a dancing lesson.

After a second dance, he asked the teacher to introduce him to the other girls in the room. This displeased Amina, who saw that they were curious and interested in a young man who was also an acquaintance of hers; but, pretending to be cheerful, she helped out through playful expressions, with the reciprocal handshakes and the repetition of names. When the lady pianist took a break, the young man sat down at the instrument and played, with perfect expression, a dance he had learned by listening to a foreign recording. No one danced: they all stood there immobile, listening.

When he left the instrument and returned to Amina, she admitted to herself that she was proud of the student and desired his company. The other, aware of his success with her, decided to turn nasty in order to attain an even greater one. He didn't ask to accompany her home; he said a respectful good-bye and left, calm and self-assured, like a man who has limited time for frivolous entertainments.

To Amina, the room seemed empty and sad, and dancing an activity inferior even to schoolteaching. A little later she left too; and on the way home through crowded streets, full of shops selling fragrant, already-cooked dishes, she felt a strong desire to live in a tall, narrow room and to go out at this hour to buy the dinner that a young man, bent over his books, was awaiting amidst a cloud of tobacco smoke.

From that day forth they met frequently both at the dance school – of which he really did intend to take advantage – and outside, for long walks. Meanwhile, the quartet and the sisters languished.

The young man had a strange way of behaving with Amina: he wanted her kisses, condemning her reluctance with a stream of sarcastic words; but he never spoke to her of love, almost as though fear or calculation kept him far from such a confession.

Bit by imperceptible bit, Amina came to grant him a familiarity with her own flesh, so she was not frightened when one day he asked her to come to his room. She went, thinking that once the two of them were alone within four walls, the words as yet unspoken would find their way out. Later, on the way home, she meditated on what an error it had been to give herself to him, who had never spoken of love; she felt herself similar to many other women who are nothing but men's accomplices in pleasure, but this was not a reason for which she wished to cry or deprive herself of an enjoyment of which she had only her first troubling experience. Bitterly offended and full of self-contempt, she had maintained, while yielding, an air of conviction that astonished her lover. She had returned caress for caress, kiss for kiss as though observing the terms of a contract. She had pushed her boldness just so far as he had pushed his own, never taking the initiative or showing passionate vacillations. It was her wish to follow him along the road of selfishness, convincing herself that she felt no love for him.

Afterwards, she felt self-pity, as for a girl destined to be unhappy because she had made a mistake in choosing the man to whom she had given herself. Perhaps, that day, she had forgotten the value of an act that could no longer be repeated, not even once true, cherished love should have come into her life – for the past has, for a woman, a weight like that of some horrible remorse. On account of his insufficient reaction, her hidden life with the chemistry student thus became, from the first day onwards, a chain she must drag along. The absence of a shared way of living, self-sacrificing but secure, made her envy her sisters.

Most of what she had formerly admired in the student had turned to ashes, but there remained his musical gift, compared to which she could only find laughable the manufactured, dry talents of her family. This was her last resource, her refuge against showing her mother and sisters the spectacle of her abasement.

She had understood him well: he was selfish and rigidly intent upon arming himself in order to escape, as soon as possible, from a difficult situation of near-poverty. Amina felt that even the greater attention which he had, some time since, begun to devote to the care of his own person was not meant for her, but was rather the fruit of purchases and calculations made as the result of keeping company with persons richer and better dressed than himself. Through a research project commissioned by a pharmacist, he had earned the money to buy himself a showy dressing-gown. He kept it hanging from a nail, in plain sight; but for Amina he dressed in his usual frugal clothes, displaying a miserly jealousy of the dressing-gown, for which he had paid a high price – while he was eager to dress well for other men, so as to show himself their equal. And the young man would not even permit her to distract him, on an amorous whim, from his intense studies: studies carried out with no passion for science, but solely in order to obtain the position he desired in an industrial firm headed by the father of one of his classmates.

After the first flame of passion, the young man had been, for some time, doubtful and circumspect; he was troubled by the contrast between Amina's ready availability and the hostility of her mouth, which always remained shut, as though she were holding herself back from saying harsh and bitter things to him. Afterwards, having recognized that she belonged to the stupendous race of women who never complain, who never make a tragedy of an abandonment, convinced that the fault is mostly their own, and who go through life hating themselves for their mysterious inability to choose that which would best suit them, he had once again become sure of himself, and accepted Amina's devotion as something never to be doubted, something that was his by right. In the end, he viewed his part in their love affair as a concession of himself, granted only because his talons were not yet fully developed: a decision made in the interests of economy and safety, as against those other outlets that he despised his peers – always wasting their time in bordellos-for choosing.

During this time, Amina had not interrupted her attendance at the dance school, where the teacher looked at her inquisitively and sometimes treated her brusquely, as though she had disappointed certain expectations. Perhaps the old woman had guessed everything and, in her wisdom, felt sorry for her; perhaps she also felt a bit guilty towards the girl, whom she had come to love.

But the one who really knew and understood was the teacher's nephew who, as if liberated from some more burdensome task, threw himself into his efforts to possess her with maneuvers that the distracted Amina did not even notice. But one evening, the dance school revealed itself to her as a terrible place: in her room, the old lady was inveighing in broken words against her nephew and the latter, pleading with her to keep quiet, was weeping. Amina heard her own name mentioned.


Amina was anxious to observe what would happen at home when the student came back for quartet rehearsals. Enthusiasm for the great evening had been born afresh. The growing ill-feeling between Amina and her lover had led him back to her house, as before.

During rehearsals, when he sang with his instrument,

Amina felt that her sisters were being pulled into a vaster and warmer musical world. It was as though the warm breath of a man blew on the nape of their necks, sending them into ecstasies and melting their usual frigidity; and Amina envied them their ability to yield to the illusion. After a while, unable to bear the torment of feeling his presence in the house, she took refuge in the farthest room; but even there the voice of the cello pursued her so as to wound her. Among her sisters, the man was so moody and incomprehensible that she felt the need to meet him in the hallway as he was leaving, in order to take a good look at his face. Afraid that her looks might betray him, he fled in a hurry, slamming the door.

Amina saw him again in his room when she complied with the agreement – never explicitly stated – that they should meet on the same day every week.

He, who had been awaiting her, embraced her, assaulted her, leaving her no time to ask him anything or to talk. Amina left feeling that she needed a doctor who would put all her limbs back in order, that she required a much longer truce: the next morning she was healed, but she felt base for going on this way.

In order to make absolutely certain that she would, for the first time, miss a rendez-vous, she had promised the dance teacher to help her with a group lesson for some schoolchildren who were preparing for their annual party. It was during those lessons that the teacher revealed herself to the girls as a magical, supernatural being. The most devoted among them never missed these lessons; they agreed to meet at the school as though for some stupendous show, turning up on the flimsiest pretext.

The old woman appeared before the little children in a black skirt, shorter than usual, which left her legs – still rounded, clad in black stockings – uncovered from the knees down. She danced the first steps of a gavotte, swayed gracefully, shifted her weight from foot to foot with admirable sureness. She was like an old marquise with her grandchildren: she knew it, playing her role with all the experience garnered in the theater. Moving slowly, the children obeyed the rhythm and its patterns, bending over in bows that had a tradition behind them.

"Farther apart, children. Leave room for the pirouette."

Already freer and more sure of themselves, the children executed the difficult step to the four endlessly repeated beats.

The girls acclaimed her: still, in old age, a hard-working teacher of grace, as straight and upright as a sword, she seemed to them marvelously enchanting.

"But Signora, when do you practice?"

"At night, my dears. I come here into this room and dance with my memories," she laughed, protecting herself against so much admiration; but she was happy and, at the same time, veiled in sadness before the girls, who felt moved.

Something in her was provoked to action. Forgetting for the moment the children, who crowded together restlessly during the break, she resumed dancing. She moved her skirt here and there, gathering it up with a gentle gesture that seemed strange coming from her, who was so rigid; it was as though sweet, pure music were to emanate from an old, broken-down carillon. Her arms were raised and arched, almost as if to resuscitate the pride of her breasts, while her face took on a childish naiveté, perfect and horrible. Looking at her legs, still full and skilful, one was reminded of a picture of herself as a ballerina that she kept in her room: the wrinkled face and white hair finally broke, for the girls, a spell that had lasted too long.

That day, the teacher's performance had been even more significant than usual: she had finished with a whirlwind of pirouettes, amidst the applause of the girls and the cheerful yelling of the children. Exhausted and moved, she had then retired to her room to lie down on her bed. Looking at the time, Amina realized that she had missed her rendez-vous and was happy to have taken a first step towards freedom. She helped the children get dressed and watched them leave, counted one by one by the two elderly, worried women who had accompanied them there. She returned to the students' little dressing room, not knowing whether to leave or stay; uncertainty about her own courage began to torture her. She felt like going to the young man's room and offering an excuse for her lateness. He certainly would have no more time to concede to her; on the other hand, she was tempted to see what he would be willing to give up in order to find the time.

She heard footsteps coming up the stairs: the foot-steps, well-known to her, of the teacher's nephew. This was not an hour when the office worker usually appeared, and she wondered why he was turning up this way at the school.

In the classroom, it was a moment when everyone was taking a break after the departure of the children. Against the gray light that entered through the window, the dust slowly migrated, swirling more quickly whenever a breath of fresh air entered the room. At the piano, the lady pianist was banging out a romantic piece, full of octaves and arpeggios, as if letting out her frustration at her boring job, or showing off an unrecognized talent.

Amina, guessing that the nephew had stopped in the classroom, went to the door of the dressing room and lifted the curtain a little. She saw him sitting on one of the long benches and almost cried out in surprise. A black bandage, covering even part of his nose, concealed an injured eye: the brother of the other bad one that rotated in a socket with reddened lids. The obscene quality of the disease or wound that had made such a wreck of his face was plain to see, as though the bandage didn't exist.

He hadn't realized that he was being spied on. He seemed to be waiting for someone. His eye turned downwards to look at the watch which, having been extracted from his pocket, rested pendulously on his belly; the eye looked nervously upwards, towards the door of the teacher's room, while his hands opened and smoothed a newspaper.

Then the man bent over to read. Every now and then he raised an arm to touch the black bandage. The other arm dangled, its fist clenched and threatening.

The eye looked cruel and staring above the page folded in two; and the yellow teeth, clenched and crooked, barely opened in a faked yawn.

"Is Signorina Amina not here today?" he suddenly asked, turning to the lady pianist who, having finished her piece, was putting her sheet music in order.

"She must be in there, in the Signora's room."

The unexpected question and the interested tone of the reply gave Amina the shivers.

The man was pleased: his eye gleamed and disappeared alarmingly into the extreme limit of its socket, almost as if he wanted to enjoy a dark exultation beneath his black bandage.

"She doesn't come very often, the Signorina, does she?"

"On the contrary," replied the woman, "now she comes as frequently as she used to. You can see that the great business she was involved in has come to an end."

Hating this conversation, Amina opened the curtain and advanced into the room, heading towards the man.

"What have you done, Signor Muzio?"

He stood up to greet her, couteous and formal, and then said: "It's a summer allergic reaction that I've got here in my eye. The doctor told me to keep it covered." He attempted a kindly, resigned smile.

When she sat down, he seated himself next to her.

From the piano the woman watched them, puffed up like a frog with astonished curiosity. His eye had become benevolent and devout, but it seemed to Amina that the other one, safe under its shelter, was fierce and bloodshot. She understood that he suffered from not being able to hide his lone eye, which looked frightfully naked alongside the black bandage.

He looked for something, rummaging around in a pocket: at last he seized a little round object, glanced at it, keeping it hidden in his hand, and then put it back in his pocket.

"What is it?" she laughed. "Do you want to give me a present?"

"If you like," smiled the nephew. "It's a little mirror."

"Thank you. What do you expect me to do with it? Here in this room, there's no lack of mirrors." She gestured towards their image, reflected in a large, gilt-framed mirror.

He looked and became worried: he tried to change his place without appearing to, so as to get out of range of the mirror in which she was watching him.

"I don't feel too well today," he said as a justification for his movements. "I can't get comfortable. I left the office earlier than usual: they gave me permission."

"Why don't you ask for some time off?"

"It's not easy to get it: there's a lot of work, and there aren't many of us to do it."

He was finally out of the mirror: only an elbow came and went as he gesticulated while talking.

"I wanted to go to bed, but I came here," he added. "I like company," he said effortfully, and it seemed that his tongue had become thicker on account of something obscene that had occurred to his imagination. "I like it, here at my aunt's place, because people dance. It's true that I'm not a good dancer, but you, I must say, are kind enough to put up with me."

She shook her head to prevent his going on in this piteous tone, which he had adopted only as a blandishment.

"You dance better than many others who come to the school," she told him. "You can be sure of that."

"Perhaps, Signorina, but it's all your doing. One has only to look at you to feel inspired and…"

Amina stared at him, trying to understand what he was driving at with these words.

"You're looking at me, Signorina, as if you were seeing me for the first time," he said bitterly. "Don't you think that, even ugly as I am, a woman might like me?" He had put on a nasty and aggressive expression, and reacted to his own desire to look at himself once again in the little mirror he held in his hand.

"I haven't said anything that might offend you, Signor Muzio. I'm convinced that it's the same for you as for everyone else."

He remained silent: he feared that he had committed an imprudence which might make her angry.

"We don't know each other well," he finally said. "I know that you are kind and generous: perhaps too generous. But, you see, this isn't enough to win me your esteem. I don't have the talent of certain young men!"

Amina leapt to her feet and stared at him harshly. She had detected an allusion to the student in his speech, and wanted to make sure of it.

Before she had spoken a word, she turned around, because someone was touching her shoulder. It was the dance teacher, insisting through the pressure of her hand that she should leave this spot. The nephew, standing up respectfully, kept his head down. The old lady began speaking to him in an excited tone, as if reproaching him: the other was humble and pleading in his replies.

Amina, displeased by this help given her against a man before whom her solid sense of security was enhanced by the repulsion she felt for him, left the room and went into the kitchen to drink a glass of water. There she encountered the teacher's sister, who greeted her in so exaggeratedly festive a manner that it put her on the defensive.

"Dear, dear Amina, the world belongs to those who know how to seize it. Enjoy yourself now, while you're young. Enjoy yourself; anyway, the first man who comes along is no worse than one chosen with every precaution. There's a remedy for everything: you've just got to be a bit adaptable."

Amina left the dark and smelly kitchen, disgusted by this speech made in order to console her for an unhappiness that she had been unable to keep hidden, and perhaps even more to remind her of Signor Muzio's solicitousness: he was always deep in confabulations with his second aunt.

In the classroom, other people had arrived. More of them turned up every minute. Then the piano began rumbling: the lights, which had been turned on, created intimate greenish reflections in the mirrors, and the first couples started dancing.

Even though his aunt was keeping an eye on him, Signor Muzio dared approach Amina and ask her to dance. She could find no way of refusing that would not be too discourteous. The man must have had hopes because, holding her tight in his arms, he smiled, and Amina guessed at his satisfaction. She realized immediately that he was trying to keep her away from the teacher; for this reason, with monotonous insistence, he kept coming and going, coming and going, repeating the same series of steps.

"Women feel comfortable with me," he suddenly said. "I know how to understand and forgive. Besides, I don't ask for much: it is they who grow to like me."

"Perhaps," Amina replied, trying to smile sarcastically but failing, because she was afraid of him as he bent over her, staring at her with that single heat-emanating eye.

"A month ago, a married woman wanted to run away from home in order to come to me. I was the one who was against it. Don't you believe me, Signorina?"

"I don't care whether I believe it or not! Why are you telling me these stories, Signor Muzio?" As she spoke, she twisted so as to escape his embrace, which had become too tight and hot, and she didn't hide her revulsion at the contact.

He loosened the knot of his arms.

"You're right," he said. "I sometimes say stupid things. Forgive me." He waited to see whether this tone would give him an advantage over her, moving her to pity.

"All right, Signor Muzio: let's talk about something else."

They danced in silence, caught up in the motion of the other couples. The mirrors showed Amina her own pale image alongside that of the man with the bandage, who was smiling and dry in his movements, as if obeying the rhythm of some silent counting.

"I'm very sorry to have spoken in such a way as to give you a wrong idea of myself, dear Signorina. You can't imagine how much I regret it." He had lowered his voice, speaking in a veiled tone – as though, speaking to a woman under a spell, he wished neither to opportune her nor to allow her to forget him.

She didn't bother to answer: she could tell that liberation would come soon, to judge by the special inflections that the lady pianist used when nearing the end of a piece.

They separated. Summoned by the teacher, Amina flew to join her at the other end of the room.

"What was my nephew saying to you?"

"That he doesn't feel well and that... many women are madly in love with him."

"Ah!" The old woman stared at Amina as though the latter had spoken to her of a well-deserved punishment. "If he keeps up these stupid speeches, let me know. He needs me to put some seriousness back into him. Now, go and dance a bit with those new boys."

Perplexed and annoyed, Amina obeyed. If she perceived a danger in all these maneuvers centered on herself, it was that, at a certain point, the teacher might stop protecting her, considering her one of the girls who threw themselves into Muzio's arms. But this was an imaginary peril: the teacher clearly demonstrated her dislike of her nephew.

The latter, sitting on one of the benches, was watching the couples with indifference as they went by. When Amina passed before him, he glared at her with a sort of emnity that was ready to turn into a smile. Then, lowering his eye, he looked at it in the little round mirror, where it appeared all by itself, magically isolated from the face; it was as though he were expecting it to be harmed at any moment by the same injury that had already damaged its companion.

The old teacher was ill. It was several days since she had taken to her bed, wan and hovering near death. But this was not enough to shut down the school. The continued presence of a certain number of pupils was guaranteed by the efforts of several girls such as Amina, who were devoted to the sick old lady. Classes began only in the afternoon; and the piano, rumbling away for hours, accompanied the nightmares of the patient, who was so used to the sound that it didn't disturb her. Every now and then the young teaching assistants disappeared from the classroom to keep her company, help her change a position which had become uncomfortable, make her drink something.

Thus was their attachment to her revealed: the sort of attachment that girls occasionally feel for a teacher who has, in some way, helped to free them from a home atmosphere that has grown oppressive. At her bedside one might have observed a solicitude, a care, a patience that some of the girls would have been incapable of showing for their own mothers.

Since learning that the old lady was doomed to fade slowly away, her young friends realized, almost with wonder, that she was not a creature who had lived only on dance and lessons. Intimacy with the patient gradually modified the image that Amina and her classmates had of her. The teacher frequently cried, as though, during her lifetime, she had been ready to yield to such a lovely weakness; she welcomed flowers, wishing to have them in a vase on her night-table; she spoke of the girls' self-sacrifice in staying with her when the springtime weather outside was so fine. She overflowed with a poetry that had hitherto remained hidden; they were convinced that her past had been very difficult and painful. These moving discoveries, discussed in  murmurs in the classroom, provoked weeping and further impulses toward devotion. The girls felt that they were consoling, in her final days, a being who deserved much better than what life had given her; and they imagined her glorious and bitter youth, the disasters of her maturity, her resignation at having to give lessons for so many years.

In her bed, exhausted and drawn, the old lady re-acquired a resemblance to her early portraits, taking on – in the girls' future memories – a gentle aspect.

Every now and then, this atmosphere of beautiful death was brusquely disturbed: in a moment of strength, the old woman would burst forth into abuse and curses against her sister or her nephew on account of some irritating circumstance or some slowness in carrying out one of her orders – which she always gave to those two in a harsh voice. It was as though she were taking advantage of her brief moments of rebirth in order to express her resentment at their oblique and tormenting requests, which had always been made with the awareness that, sooner or later, she would give in.

The girls were dismayed at these displays; and the servile and awkward sister, driven from the room with a fury that was frightful coming from a body which grew feebler every day, had a hostile and ironic way of looking at them, as if she considered them the victims of some deceit.

These were the gaps, the appalling interruptions in a process of dying that ought to have remained gentle and calm. In the evening, after classes were over, the sister came to count out the proceeds on the patient's bed, and Amina and her companions observed the old lady's perfidious, deeply distrustful manner of checking up on her sister. They were forced to defend the latter, backing up her protests. Once the sister had left, the teacher had one of the girls bring her a little chest; she put the money in it and wrote down the amount with a pencil in an account book that she kept, along with the key to the chest, under her pillow.

One evening when she was feeling better, she wanted to make Amina a present of an ostrich feather. From the bed, she directed the lengthy search in a big chest full of bric-a-brac mingled with fragrant sachets of camphor and naphthalene. At long last, Amina found the feather, wrapped in several layers of light paper. The gaudy, bright-red feather trembled in the old lady's hand.

"I'm giving it to you because you're the kindest. It may come in handy – who knows, one of these days it may come back into fashion. Make sure you stay virtuous: you have everything to gain by it. Do you understand?" Amina started crying, feeling all the weight of her shame under the gaze of the woman, who was gazing at her steadily. So the teacher knew; she had caught on. However, the dreaded, hoped-for moment of confession did not arrive; the patient looked tired and, while Amina sobbed, closed her eyes. After a while she asked in a harsh voice for something to drink; and when she spoke, she spoke of other matters.

The nephew, coming back in the evening for his

daily visit, approached the bedside hesitantly, asking for something with his gaze; then, intimidated, he lowered his face. The old woman barely replied to his greeting. He sat down in a dark corner, destroying with his breathing the atmosphere of intimacy between the two women. Sometimes, if Amina leaned towards the bed together with the nephew, the old woman hesitated, uncertain whether to include the two of them in a benevolent smile; but then she turned hard once again, after struggling against another type of gaze. With a skilful eye, she made sure that no understanding had yet come into being between her two attendants. Signor Muzio looked distractedly at the ceiling; but his hand clutched at the folds in the blanket, which he had touched, at first, as delicately as possible.

Sometimes, if he had to stay the night to watch over his aunt, he ate something from a little bedside table upon which were a plate, some bread, and a greenish bottle within which the red wine took on a rotten, false hue. Signor Muzio drooled a bit as he ate, worrying about being overheard; and the old woman grew exasperated but said nothing. When he finally went into the kitchen to chat with the other aunt, the old woman sighed in relief.

One evening, when Amina went into the kitchen to fetch some hot water for the old woman, she found him and the teacher's sister seated at the marble-topped table; they stared at her, interrupted in their whispered conversation.

"Would you like something to eat, Signorina? Would you like to stay here until it's late? My nephew can go to your house and tell them so that they won't be worried."

"No, thanks; I'm leaving in a few minutes. I wanted some hot water for the Signora."

"All right."

In the dark, narrow kitchen, a pharmacy odor won out over that of the foods and the sink. On the stove meat and vegetables were cooking, while herbal teas and linseed paste were boiling away. A pot blew its lid, which fell on its rim with a metallic clang, while a little trail of steam escaped, immediately turning into drops of water against the black metal of the stove.

The nephew stood up almost immediately to return to the patient, and the sister, now alone with Amina, resumed a discussion regarding him that had remained interrupted for several evenings on account of the girl's cleverness in finding pretexts to escape.

"It's easy to see how kind that boy is. And just think, my sister can't stand him, because he's so ugly. And now that he's got a sick eye, she's treating him worse than ever. There's no justice!"

Speaking of his goodness, she clenched her teeth, as though keeping an agreement and making an effort not to remember the tensions that might induce her to change the direction of her speech.

"If I say this, it's because I can't forget that Muzio is the son of my other sister – poor dear, she was good as an angel."

She drew near to Amina. She was thrusting her face forward, as though offering up a secret. "The Signora had a son, too, but he died. That's why she doesn't like her nephew."

The revelation didn't upset Amina, who remained silent.

"She had him when she danced half-naked in the theater, but she really took it out of us if anyone looked at us in the street. That's the way it always was: she was allowed to do everything, and weren't allowed anything. We were servants, we were, servants of her fame. She must have had the son in a moment of carelessness, because she was always stingy with men, too, except for the last one, who ran through all her money. I grant you that she was no longer so young, then – the great ballerina!"

She noticed Amina's harsh, hostile stare and interrupted her outburst.

"Now, don't get angry with me for telling you this. I wanted to tell you because it seems to me that there are too many illusions around here. Want to know what I think? You oughtn't trust those two: yes, my sister and my nephew. They've always got what they wanted by adopting the policy of waiting for the right moment. Don't you see how they've crushed me? What right has my nephew, whom I dangled on my knee, to treat me like a servant? Is he a great dancer too? Oh, but as for you, Signorina, you're too proud and lofty to understand these matters."

"That's not it: I only ask that you don't treat me as an outlet for these things. Understood?"

The other suddenly became humble.

"Don't say anything, for heaven's sake."

"Rest assured, I won't say anything," Amina promised. "But why do you always try to put the Signora in a bad light?"

The woman whirled around ferociously.

"The 'Signora'? She's the Signora for you idiots who come here to adore her because she's got old dresses with sequins, beautiful white hair, and shows you how to dance the minuet! To me, she's a witch who has ruined my life. I knew how to dance better than my sister, I did — and the other sister was better than either one of us. But there was no way we could break in. It was she who barred our way. I had a temperament that was — shall we say — fiery. But she kept me a prisoner if I wanted to eat, and so I always had to settle for the first man who came along, whether it was the milkman or some servant delivering flowers for her. I thought I was the clever one. But it was she who wanted things to be that way in order to abase me, so as to be able to scream 'Servant! Servant!' at me and keep me in her house to serve her the way I do now. That's enough. Don't say anything. I'm going through some difficult days."

These rays of light cast on the teacher's distant past did not destroy Amina's devotion to her; nor did the allusions to the nephew's calculations increase the suspicions that she already nourished regarding Signor Muzio, who – no longer trusting his aunt in the kitchen – no longer assigned her the task of painting him in glowing colors.

When Amina left the sick woman's bedside in the evening, the nephew accompanied her through the streets and, finally, all the way to the staircase of her home; holding her hand in his own sweaty one, he would express the greatest gratitude for her attention to a person so dear to him. He seemed sincere. He added that his aunt's death would leave him alone in the world, since, on account of a very pure love, he had rid himself, a while back, of all those women who were mad about him.

It was just a moment; but in that moment, he once again became repellent to Amina, who fled quickly up the stairs, feeling herself lusted after by the flaming eye of the Cyclops down below.

With her family, she was barely able to find excuses for the days she spent almost entirely away from home. Besides, she had no great need of them: by now the quartet was rehearsing every day and making rapid progress. Fearing some unwelcome surprise if things were to go on as before between himself and Amina, the student tacitly accepted the separation and no longer asked her to his room. Conversing with Amina's mother and sisters, he let slip that he had accidentally made a discovery. Amina, out of devotion to Carmen's dance teacher, was lovingly tending the latter during her painful final illness. It was a beautiful gesture: they ought to understand this, without asking the girl too many questions or otherwise tormenting her.

Thus protected by him, Amina found herself received at home with incomprehensible, almost sweet smiles.

A bit awkward in rustling new dresses, Amina's sisters were greeting the guests at the concert, guiding them to the bedroom where they could leave their coats; accepting, with timid blushes, the anticipatory compliments of their public of classmates and their parents.

That first shyness disappeared when, once the black-clad student had arrived, they sat down with their instruments before the four stands. They seemed ready for battle, and took their time in tuning their instruments, with a sense of mastery that increased the expectations of the small audience crowded into the room.

With a little cough, the mistress of the house finally appeared, with the sickly air of a woman who has borne heavy burdens, wearing a gown that left certain parts of her body uncovered. The doors were closed: silence reigned in the room, where the light was gathered only above the four players.

Amina, likewise dressed for a festive occasion, remained standing near the door, worried and unhappy at having yielded to her mother by returning home rather than remaining at the bedside of the old woman, whose condition had worsened during the day. The instruments, now tuned, tried their voices in little individual attacks, while the student, seeking Amina with his eyes, desired a confirmation that she would return to his room within the week, as he had fleetingly asked her to on the landing; but he obtained not so much as a glance.

At the end of a hallway, a far-off doorbell rang. Amina made a sign to her mother, who jumped up furiously and followed her out of the room. The musicians remained with their bows poised in the air, ready to begin; then they desisted, waiting, already far away from the little audience that, no longer able to keep perfectly silent, murmured and shifted on the creaking chairs.

Amina had opened the front door. Someone was running up the stairs. It was the teacher's nephew.

"Signorina," he begged, when he was near her, who had gone down to meet him, "come, for heaven's sake. My aunt is very ill: I fear that... She doesn't do anything but ask after you."

"I'll come right away. Wait for me."

Back upstairs, she defied the cold and hostile gaze of her mother.

"I've got to go," she said. "My teacher is dying and wants to see me."

"And the quartet?"

"What do I care about that? You know perfectly well that it isn't stuff for me."

"Do as you wish. Anyway, you're not a daughter like the others."

"This isn't the moment," pleaded Amina. "Go back in there, where they're all waiting for you."

The other headed back towards the music room with hard steps that rang out on the tiles of the hallway. Rummaging in an armoire for a coat, Amina heard the door close gently. Then the quartet began. Gentle and sure of itself, the cello set forth a phrase; with their thin voices, the first violin and the viola – a bit effortful in their rhythm – took it over. In her mind's eye, Amina saw her sisters handling their bows with the graceless movements of their bony shoulders, and felt a stranger among them and their mother, whom she imagined smugly happy among the smiling faces of the professors seated in the front row.

"This can't be my house," she thought.

The nephew was awaiting her at the door; he was still breathing heavily from climbing the stairs in a hurry.

"Thank you. You are very kind."

"Let's get going, Signor Muzio. Tell me: is she in a very serious way?"

"I fear she is: she's had two attacks in the last few hours."

"Will we find her alive?" asked Amina, climbing into the taxi waiting in the street.

"Let's hope so. She was calm when I decided to come to you. Forgive me: I didn't know that there was a party at your house. I'm truly sorry."

"No, it wasn't a party. You were quite right to come." After these words, she felt the other gently lifting her hand to his lips. She withdrew it, but without violence, troubled by a gesture of which she would not have believed him capable. In the darkness within the cab, broken only by infrequent encounters with the stark streetlights, she felt herself too close to Signor Muzio, whose face she could not see, and moved away. He emitted a sigh of humiliation.

The roads, made slippery by a fine, insistent rain, forced the driver to go slowly and to brake repeatedly.

They finally arrived.

Signor Muzio remained on the sidewalk to pay the driver; Amina ran up the half-dark stairs. On the landing she was met by the teacher's sister, uncombed and a bit distraught.

"How is the Signora? Tell me, tell me."

"Don't worry, she's not dying. That one's not going to die." She laughted sardonically at Amina's concern and at her own disappointed hopes of liberation – which nonetheless filled her with apprehension.

"You're mad," Amina screamed at her. "Mad and ungrateful."

"Child...," the other threatened her; but then, hearing the nephew coming up the stairs, she fell silent, continuing her threat with gestures.

Amina entered the classroom: a feeble light filtered through the square glass window in the door of the sick woman's room and fell upon a little table covered with medicines. She took off her coat, opened the door noiselessly, and advanced towards the bed with cautious steps, followed by the nephew as by a shadow.

The old woman raised her cloudy eyes without recognizing her; then, bothered by the veiled light falling upon her, she turned her face away on the pillow, falling asleep. You could count the hairs on her skull, which was red and corroded with spots. At the foot of the bed the sister, who had come in through the other door, stood staring at her, afraid that the old woman might see her and recognize her: it seemed that seeing the old woman in that condition made her curious, and every now and then she smiled at Amina in embarrassment.

"She's really in a bad way," she murmured, but an angry gesture of the nephew's made her regret having said it. She no longer spoke a word, but persisted in her investigation with ever-increasing agitation: she seemed to be convincing herself that death was near, and felt, at its approach, a superstitious horror, a revulsion that filled her eyes with tears.

Signor Muzio, who had sat down on a divan not far from the bed, was waiting with anxiety and clenched teeth for the sick woman to regain consciousness, as though he were struggling to fend off the end.

The first sign was a moan that made the three bend over the bed; then, unsure of herself, the sister tiptoed out, closing behind her the door that led into the kitchen.

"She's suffering, she's suffering a lot," murmured the nephew. "I hope she doesn't die without regaining consciousness. The doctor said that she may make it through the night and, perhaps, part of tomorrow... Who knows? But her condition looks very serious to me. And to you?"

Amina sorrowfully assented. She took a chair, brought it soundlessly to the bedside, and sat down to wait. "You can go and get some sleep, Signor Muzio: I'll watch over her tonight."

"Never! I'll stay here in my clothes. That way I can go for the doctor or the priest. Don't you agree?"

"Just as you wish," she answered; but in reality, she was glad that his presence would comfort her in case of need or during the catastrophe, should it come. He lay down on the divan, which creaked beneath his restless weight, and covered his face with his hands. He seemed to be meditating; but he was really watching her through his open fingers and rubbing, beneath the black bandage, the burning rim of his torment.

Believing herself free of his gaze, Amina made an effort to look at him with pity; then she began to scrutinize the emaciated face of the teacher, alternately hard as stone and deranged by sudden shocks and grimaces of atrocious physical anguish. Almost an hour had passed since she and Signor Muzio had last exchanged words. Her examination of the teacher's face lasted so long that, when she came back to herself, she realized that she was cold. As cautiously as possible, she went into the classroom to seek her coat. A dark shape lay on one of the cushioned benches. It was the sister who, having heard her footsteps, raised her head.

"How's it going?" she asked. "Has she spoken?"

"No, she isn't moving. She's barely breathing. But why don't you go to bed, instead of staying here in such discomfort?"

"I can't. I'm staying here because she is my sister, after all, and I don't want her to die without saying something to me. Today, during her attack, my sister kept talking about you and my nephew. After all, you two are the ones who look after her."

She saw Amina make a gesture and added: "I'm well aware that I'm not suited to it: I've no patience. And what's my nephew doing now?"

"He's in there. I think he's sleeping. There's no point

in awakening him."

"He's like a cat, that one: you can never tell if he's asleep or awake," the other murmured mysteriously, waiting to see the effect of her words. But Amina, breaking off the conversation, went back into the bedroom.

She sat back down next to the sick woman. Hearing the creaking of the chair, the nephew freed himself from the bonds of an uncomfortable position, and showed an eye full of interrogation.

She gestured to him that everything was as before: the man lay back down and let out a sigh, as if he were really sinking into sleep.

A little while later, Amina was convinced that he really was sleeping, because he had turned his open mouth to her in such a repulsive fashion that, had he been awake, he would have avoided doing so.

From that moment onwards, the night began slowly to drip away. She did not dare look at the old lady, but followed the complicated pattern of the blanket here and there, where the light revealed it. She was afraid. She felt alone, caught between two wills, each of which was, in its own way, her enemy; she was without the comfort of the only one who could defend her. The nephew's breathing and certain tiny sounds from the classroom gave her the sense that she was no longer the teacher's guest, but only a guest in the teacher's house, already occupied by hostile forces. She hoped that the sick women would, upon awakening, beg her to go away, to leave her alone to do battle with those two who – right down to the last breath – could do nothing to harm her; but the sick woman did not move, rigid in a spasm that left her eyes frenzied and her hands contracted on the border of the blanket.

Through the little window that looked out over the courtyard, narrow and deep as a well, water dripping from a roof onto a piece of sheet metal struck the ear with a dull sound that sometimes seemed tremendously close. At other moments she noticed a tick-tock: there was, in the room, only a pendulum-clock that had stopped two days before: the sound must be coming from the vest of the sleeping man. Amina was tempted to approach him furtively and extract the watch from his pocket to find out what time it was, but she resisted out of fear of finding herself under the gaze of the nephew's eye, surprised and, perhaps, filled with joy at the confidential gesture.

Yielding to fatigue, she leaned her arms and head on the bed and slept.

When she shook herself and reopened her eyes, she realized that a long time had gone by: the others' sleep seemed to have emptied the house. She was on the point of standing up; but she saw her own hands near those of the sick woman, which were white with a dark shadow around the wrists, and felt chained to that death-agony. She remained.

Like a sky heavy with clouds, the opaque curtain cast a pall over the wan light that came from the classroom and filtered across the threshold beneath the wooden door. It was the hour when the sleepless feel most exhausted – the hour of uncontrollable laughter, of that pointless weeping that makes men feel once again like children frightened by the silence and the surrounding emptiness, with no awareness of their own strength.

All at once Amina shivered, holding back the scream that arose in her throat. The old woman had taken her left hand and was holding it tight. Every now and then the grip relaxed, remaining around her soft, plump hand like a tepid strip of cloth; and then, all at once, it would tighten once again, and Amina felt the power of the sinews and veins by way of which the grasp reached her from the teacher's heart. The old lady had her eyes open now; in them, the fog was lifting. Her breathing was more regular. At last she started up in the bed, as though she had fallen into it from a dizzying height; she twisted and turned, as if seeking a painless position; and she drew Amina's hand near to her face. Amina had to bend over yet nearer the bedside. The old woman let out a hoarse sigh and, having straightened her head with no apparent effort, looked Amina in the eyes.

Slowly, as if the heart's commands took a long time finding their way to her lips, she smiled, and her mouth looked as though she were going to weep with gratitude. It was just an instant, because the old woman regained control of herself and looked about for her nephew. Seeing him, her eyes filled with an indefinable expression of pain; then she appeared to sink back into nightmares and spasms. But she went on caressing Amina's hand; and Amina, empty of thoughts and desires, believing that she was being invited to rest, lay forward with her torso on the bed in abandon and shut her eyes, despite the uncomfortable position.

But then she felt her hair being caressed: caresses and rootings about that were like a martyrdom. The old woman wanted her awake. Painfully, Amina straightened herself. With a gesture, the woman told her bring her ear closer. At that moment, Amina thought she heard the divan creak; like her, the teacher turned around with a worried expression. In his sleep, the nephew had thrown his head back, so that it was now hidden in the shadow cast by the backrest.

For a bit longer, the old woman remained silent: she was gathering her strength and her ideas before saying what she wanted to say.

"Listen," she began, "I must ask you to do something." Her voice was new, raucous but resonant, as though she were no longer capable of calculating a low, discrete tone. "You see my nephew over there?"

"Yes, Signora."

"He's a poor, unhappy man." She halted for a moment. "You are so good," she resumed, "and you've already given yourself to the wrong person. Don't cry: it's the truth. I know everything and understand everything. You're on the road to becoming a hard-luck case like so many others. Do what I ask of you. It will be an act of kindness: I repeat, he's very unhappy. When you get to know him, he's kind. And yet, he never finds a woman who isn't repelled by him. You must pay no attention if he carries on, if he tells you about this one or that one: none of it is true. He wants to make people believe in what he's never had. Do you understand?"

"Yes." The word fell heavily, like an entreaty not to go on, but the old woman did not relent.

"Now you know everything. I leave it up to you to decide whether to make him happy or not. Who knows? Afterwards, he will become even kinder. As matters stand, he has to do without everything he would need in order to live well. Do you understand?"

A silence followed. As if fearful of forcing Amina to decide, the old woman was no longer looking into the latter's eyes. Her breathing was effortful.

A helpless sob suddenly emerged from the shadow on the divan; it was followed by moans and groans.

Aghast, the two women trembled.

It was the nephew. His form shook convulsively with the effort to find speech: if all this was sincere, he must have suffered from a desperate self-loathing from which he was seeking redemption. "Why have you told the Signorina these things?" he finally yelled. "Now she will feel even more contempt for me. And you, Signorina, forgive me: I really am unhappy. I would sooner die than feel this way, like a worm, before your eyes."

The old lady's raised hand imposed silence on him.

"You were the one who asked me to speak. You've been tormenting me about it for a month.

"No," he gasped out in rage. "Keep quiet, keep quiet, Auntie, if you don't want me to go mad."

In the classroom something – moved by a foot or a hand – made a sound. A chill came over Amina at the thought that the outsider was spying on them.

"That's enough," murmured the old lady. "I've done my bit. It's up to you two to decide how you feel. I can't go on much longer..." She fell back on the pillows, panting.

"Yes, Signora," Amina wept, speaking into her ear. "Yes, I'll do everything – but look at me, tell me you're pleased." She made this promise solely in order to bring the torture to an end, but the dying woman seemed not to hear her.

Once Amina had spoken, the man's sobs soon came to an end. Then, like a child who has gotten over a momentary embarrassment, he approached the bed, took Amina's hand, and kissed it as if taking possession of her whole flesh. She felt herself falling into an abyss, but could not find the strength to withdraw her hand, to break open that dandruff-covered head with the first object that came her way. The man suddenly stepped aside: the old woman's intense gaze was fixed upon him, holding him prisoner, forcing him back into the shadows.

Amina, stunned, was watching the daylight – enemy of her intense desire to rest – as it broke through the curtain. One could already detect the curtain's yellowish hue, with zones of shadow within the folds, still swollen with dark gray.

By now too exhausted to be able to speak, the old woman gestured for Amina to throw herself down on the bed, to let sleep overcome her. When she saw the girl rest her head upon a pillow at the foot of the bed, the old woman lost the stiffness of her last effort to keep Amina away from herself. "Are you comfortable there?" she managed to say. "Sleep."

Having lain back down, the man was sleeping, or pretending to sleep, black and stocky on the divan. Beyond the curtain, the ever-intensifying light was glitteringly alive:

points of whitish brilliance were dancing everywhere. In the silence, the man's breathing grew lighter, happier. Amina sank into a sleep that liberated her from a nightmare; while the old ballerina, her head erect on the pillow, looked at her dozing nephew and the girl with the hard expression of one who, no longer recognizing those around her, is all alone with the enormous fears that come over one while waiting.

# The Repainted House

The housepainters' arrival caught Anna by surprise: she hadn't been expecting them so early. It seemed to her that repainting the gray, time-soiled façade pink was a form of celebration, rather than of mourning, so few days after the old man's death. And yet, she didn't say anything to Lucrezio. She sensed that, having become master of his father's house, he was anxious to turn it into something else, to cover it with a hue of pink as cheerful as the one used for wishing joy to a bridal couple – almost as though this were his way of giving vent to his anger, of taking a prompt revenge for his sad youth, passed under the old man's domination.

For two days the painters were lords of every room and window; then, having made holes for their scaffolding and set up their swaying suspended platforms, they went outdoors, hovering about the façade like a populace of hardworking parasites.

The rooms – with their shutters closed and sealed with paper against the dust raised by the scraping-off of the dirty old painted plaster – were dark and resonant with hammering, thuds, and rasping: sounds upon which, every now and then, a tranquil male voice or a burst of song conferred the reassuring significance of a work of peace rather than destruction.

Anna and Lucrezio were awakened early each morning by the painters as they started work, maliciously pleased to pound hard upon the walls that protected lazy sleep. Lucrezio would become restless in the dark room and shift about in bed, intending not to listen and to go back to sleep; she imitated a sleeper's breathing and enjoyed with a shiver the scratching of the dry plaster against the shutters and the rustling paper. She listened to the workmen's voices, waiting, curious to catch a joke or a coarse word that would cheer her up as she lay in warm contact with the flesh of her man. A hammer pounding on the wall grew deafening: as though aimed straight at them, it seemed meant to open up a gap and reveal them in their intimacy.

She smiled, a bit perturbed; Lucrezio, his eyes fixed on the wall, watched as a crack took shape. When silence returned, they furtively exchanged a caress.

To put the shutters back in order, it was necessary to dismantle them and take them away. The façade was left bare and ignoble: the windows looked like eyes without eyelashes.

Lucrezio was tormented by the idea that the men might look down into the rooms from their scaffolding. In the bedroom, a white curtain covered the windowpanes; but because it let so much light through, the curtain could not banish the suspicion of prying eyes. As soon as daylight came, he arose and, through his reserved demeanor, obliged Anna to get out of bed and dress. She obeyed lazily but afterwards remained – wrapped in shawls, awaiting the less chilly hours – sitting in an armchair, motionless and fixed as though suffering some great sorrow. Lucrezio would go out into the street and head for town, then turn back and reappear at the bend in the road, anxious to see the men who had climbed onto the scaffolding resume their task and make progress at it: he expected its completion to mark the beginning of a new and happier life.

It was still too early. There was no one on the scaffolding. From a distance, the house looked as though it were being taken to pieces: amidst the poles, in the shadow of the platforms, the little windows seemed to carry an internal current of darkness to the transparent surface of the windows. Beneath the roof's protective eaves, the house was already painted pink – a pink that, revealing itself to the morning sun, disappeared at its lower edge into random brushstrokes applied to the old gray and to brand new stains and patches. Out of obedience to some strange method of their own, the painters were now working at applying the new color much further down, without thinking, for the moment, about joining the two zones. Lucrezio suffered as he awaited that union, but feared to make himself ridiculous by demanding it immediately.

Afterwards, returning home beneath the astonished gaze of the men arriving for work, he would find Anna asleep in her armchair. Then he would be seized by an intense remorse at his abuse of her docility: he would awaken her and beg her to go back to bed.

"No, no, I know very well that you don't want me to. Anyway, it's late and there's a lot to be done around the house, to keep it clean with all this dust."

Following this or some other, similar reply, he lacked the courage to insist, as though she were forgiving him for the symptoms of some disease of which she knew he could never be cured.

At mealtimes Lucrezio feared that indiscreet gazes might fall upon the foods, which he felt were likely to be envied by the workers, who had just climbed back up after eating a piece of bread with little else to accompany it; he gobbled his meal hurriedly and badly, stopping whenever a shadow passed by the window or a brush began slapping against the nearby wall, indicating the presence of the hard-working man who was handling it.

After lunch, Lucrezio would leave, heading for the Home for the Elderly Poor, where he had taken on the role of director, succeeding his father. Once out in the street, he would turn around for a look at the house. The hidden labor of a workman who had spent the entire morning on a single point on the façade revealed itself at last: it was a chipped window-frame, now becoming whole once again; the place where a pipe embedded in the wall had caused a swelling, now evened out beneath the fresh plaster – a dark scar amidst the dry marks left by the rub of the rasp. At the bottom, the plaster and paint ran down, halting on the house and the poles like big raindrops when it first starts raining: soon dry, they formed a crust of color.

Once Lucrezio had gone, Anna took refuge in the rooms whose windows faced away from the street. They looked out on square little gardens where the poorish vegetation was oppressed by the shadow of the buildings. The fruit trees were practically barren, and if an apple or pear chanced to hang from the bough like some miraculous excrescence, all about there was lacking that sense of expectancy that reigns where ripe fruit may detach itself and fall to the ground.

Farther off, above the numerous low dividing walls, one could see the garden of the Home for the Elderly Poor. It was the large garden of an old villa that had been donated to the institution. In its solemn avenues, covered with abundant gravel, there wandered the elderly poor, dressed in gray like beggars who had all been made equal, with no hope of receiving a valuable coin handed out by mistake. On sunny days they sat on little iron chairs around the basin of the fountain until, warmed at last, they merrily began to play like children. A paper boat would leave the shore, and the sticks that made waves would push it towards the radiant spray in which it would be shipwrecked.

In these games and maneuvers there was an order, an awkward common enjoyment of the same distraction on the part of the old people, who were dominated by poverty and fear, and made equal by the strict rules of the Pia Casa. They put their sticks in the water with a dreamy air, almost as though ashamed in front of one another – and then they moved their sticks all together with brusque gestures, shaking their heads as if making a great effort, driven by paralytic anger. A bell would ring and they would all rise and head for the refectory.

Awaiting Lucrezio's return, Anna would watch them from the window, but without that proprietary sense towards them created in the house by Lucrezio's father, the institution's director for over twenty years. Quite the contrary: at the thought that her husband spent his days there, she felt that the old people were themselves like proprietors who made one sad, and the director's role – which she could never separate from the image of a red-faced, ferocious senility – struck her as the enemy of love, of having children, of the youthful enjoyment of a few hours of life. She had bad memories of the old man. As soon as she had entered the house, she had been seized with a terror of him who, through his dominion over those weak and miserable old people, had lost the sense of both youthful life and his own destiny, ending up with an angry contempt for old age which he did not feel applied to himself. As his daughters had done until they married and left home, Anna, upon hearing his footsteps, would flee to the bedroom to await an explosion of rage and sarcasm that Lucrezio, while quivering, would take in silence.

At bottom, although she dared not admit it to herself, she was glad that the old man had died – only, she couldn't see that it had had any beneficial effect on Lucrezio. It seemed that, for him, the death had put an end to a situation which he had hoped to break out of on the strength of his own abilities and energy. Perhaps he had been left with a sense of bewilderment at the steps he had not taken while his father was alive, or remorse over the mute resentment nourished over long years: a resentment born of his own weakness when faced with his father. When he spoke about him, it was as a man from whom no one had been able to lift a bit of the weight of crushing family responsibilities – an isolated man, whose isolation had made him arrogant even towards his fearful, evasive sons. This beneficent investigation of the dead man now struck Anna as full of contradictions dangerous to Lucrezio who, out of hatred for his own mass of unpleasant memories, had decided to repaint the house, in the same way that one erased old marks on a blackboard.

His days were taken up with the affairs of the Home. If he came home in the afternoon, it was not to see her, but rather to look at the work on the façade which, bringing him close to the realization of a deep-rooted, long-cherished desire, made him as anxious as the preparations for a departure on some important journey.

A need for harmony, for things well finished and properly done, drove him to the work site, where he evaluated the day's labor done by a man on the scaffolding, the area that might be colored by a can of paint, the patches that could be made using a pile of lime dried out on a wooden plank. He carried out these studies almost secretly, from behind the windows, making up for their miserliness by dreaming of the whole thing finished, disencumbered, bearing no marks, like an artisan who, during the unpleasant task of heaping up pieces of material, frees himself by thinking of their final cut and the fixed place they will have in his finished work, forming its smooth, unified surface.

When he returned for supper, he told Anna about the miseries of the Home. Solicitous charity made the old age home a prison; the staff was brutal with the old people, who were full of whims and manias. A bundle hidden under a bed, chestnut skins tossed into a corridor, were matters calling for his personal intervention, lectures and threats of punishment. Discipline having been relaxed by his willingness to listen to everybody, the old people grew lawless. They would await him in the atrium or in the garden to make their urgent requests or complain about an attendant. They gave him no peace, following him in a row all the way to his office beneath the scornful gaze of the bursar and the attendants.

Listening, Anna understood that he was remaining silent about his most secret humiliation: the perception that his own generous plans were a failure, and that it had to be admitted that his father's methods had been right. Perhaps some people at the Home, comparing him unfavorably with the old man, viewed him as a degenerate son.

After supper, Lucrezio would work on a speech for the anniversary of the charitable institution.

Saddened and embittered, he would sit down at the desk in his father's study, where he passed lugubrious hours distilling his sentences one by one; and while he sensed that they were a compilation of rhetoric, he discovered – as he struggled to link each phrase to the next, the words coming only with an effort – a series of images in which the Home passed before him, corridor after corridor, room after room, giving the lie to the rosy picture painted in his speech, bringing him back to the cold tedium of the walls, the misery of the dirty little beds, the rancid smell of the refectory. He heard once again, as a reproach, the dragging footsteps of the old man who came into the office to receive a reply in which the generosity of the rich benefactors was praised to the skies.

Lucrezio felt as though he had become that bent, tired old man's inquisitor. It seemed to the new director that when – having got tangled up in re-iterations of his little lecture – he was forced into long and boring repetitions, the old man submitted with a gaze expressive of a rancor, born not of strength, but all the more fearsome because it aroused pity.

The presence of Anna – who would come into the study and sit down beside him, giving him her hands to caress – distracted him from such melancholy visions But why are you suffering this way, my love?"

"Poor Papa," he would murmur, so as not to reveal that he was the victim of such sordid necessities and, at the same time, to put an end to her investigation by requesting respect for a sacred sorrow. Then he would shut his eyes and reopen them with a confident air. "We'll have the pink house. Things are moving ahead."

And he would smile at this confirmation of a promise made to her and to himself; but Anna suffered at hearing that he was so intent upon a change that concerned only the façade of the house.

The tallest scaffolding had already been taken down; the shutters, painted a light green, were ready, piled up in a hallway. The brushes were at work beneath the level of the windows; indiscreet gazes were no longer to be feared; the hammers fell silent; every now and then the rasp screeched over old wounds in the architecture that needed to be healed before the paint was applied.

The rainy season hindered the work. The men, having arrived early in the morning, remained out in front of the house with their jackets over their shoulders, sheltering under the scaffolding. They would gaze at the sky with an incredulous air, chatting as they waited, until a man on a bicycle came along to summon them to other tasks in a covered workplace.

During those days, Lucrezio suffered from a sense of unfillable emptiness. He tried to stay close to Anna, realizing that he had made her unhappy, that she was living with no energy, despondent because she had no children, intent on transforming her love for him into an almost maternal love: one that was too demanding if, thus purified, it could admit of no intermittences.

Then, in order to re-establish the equilibrium lost through his failings, he thought of taking her away on a long journey, in the course of which he might once again discover in her a lover among strangers, thus beginning a new and happier cycle. That pink that was blossoming on the façade would come into the house, shimmering in the cold interior.

The weather having changed from rainy to dry in the

late afternoon, the forgotten moon, full and shining, reappeared in the evening sky.

Entering the bedroom to lie down, Lucrezio and Anna saw that it was illuminating the middle of the room and half of the bed.

He didn't want to draw the curtain over the windowpanes, nor to turn out the light. Undressing on the other side of the bed, Anna looked like Diana to him, giving him a freedom of imagination that prepared him for a nudity not domestic, but miraculous in his woman.

Embarrassed to see him spying in the shadows, she plunged under the bedclothes. Without a word, Lucrezio lay down as well. He wanted to speak with her, to plan the journey with her – but he remained silent, enchanted by the moonlight that augmented like a great breath, polishing and silvering the things in the room. Raising his head, he saw the white plain of the bed reflected in the mirror, his own dark shape emerge, the stain of Anna's hair reposing further down. He enjoyed the way the folds and cut of the shadows created an unknown landscape, enveloping it in a liquid, penetrating blue.

It seemed to him that he had surprised in the mirror the image of two beings who entirely resembled himself and Anna, but who were immersed in an unaccustomed light that he nonetheless knew and could find in the gelid memory of certain moments of anguish.

The light's fixity made the spectacle appear even more immense to him. Little by little he realized that he found it frightening: it was the same fright that he felt when, hearing others speak of terrible vices or of madness, he had been struck by the thought that the seeds of these things were in him. He wanted to destroy the immobility of the image through gestures. His futile gestures passed in the mirror like a battle among shadows; but when he pulled himself together once again, the gelid quiet of the shapes reappeared unchanged. He sighed and was on the point of weeping, overwhelmed by a presentiment.

Anna raised a silver arm above the covers: he was amazed, feeling it about his neck, that it was soft and warm. Then, as if to return to land, to reaffirm an imperiled right to life, Lucrezio drew the woman towards him and made her his own.


Lucrezio passed the morning of the Home's anniversary at the institution, overseeing the preparations for the celebration.

Coming out of the house, he halted to look at the façade in order to judge its effect, now that the pink had been brought down almost to the point where it joined the brown strip on the ground floor. The house was rejuvenated, but had become vulgar: a ballerina on stage when compared to the others nearby, jealous custodians of a dusty gray that turned silvery in the morning air. In certain places between one window and another, perhaps on account of the color that was not yet dry, one could see brushstrokes, points where work had been resumed, and spongy-looking places where holes had been filled with non-quite-smooth lime. Lucrezio had felt an irritated disappointment, followed by the sense of emptiness that comes to one who cannot manage to imagine the hopeful commitment to a new, long task, or the company such a task provides.

At that moment, he had forced himself not to pay too much attention to his disappointment; but as he went on working to embellish the room for the ceremony, he felt betrayed by something that was gradually identifying itself. Changing its color bit by bit, day after day, the house had not allowed him to make the clean break he had hoped for; it had used up his expectation of a great moment, of a great decision leading to a new life. The house was almost finished and he found himself unprepared to live in it: an old man from a dark house that was gray and dirty, the way his father had kept it. Observing the way the elderly poor enjoyed the air of novelty created in the Home by festoons and flags, which were unable to change anything for him, he realized that nothing would change. He thought that perhaps the entire house should be restructured, including the interior walls, the furniture and decor; and then he smiled, feeling sorry for himself because he needed, by now, so much in order to go on living.

At lunchtime he returned home. He did not feel like eating, and snubbed the various dishes. Anna spoke to him of a partial payment requested by the housepainters. He began to inveigh against their money-hunger and their bestial way of doing their job; then, having mastered his sudden burst of anger, he gave her enough money to pay not just a part, but the entire price agreed upon.

"I don't want to think any more about this business. Is that understood?"

Anna, concerned at his worried air, did not dare point out to him the lack of consistency he was showing. She let him leave for the Home without saying a word to him, offended and humiliated that she had no beneficial power over him. Later on she dressed to go out and join him before it was time for his speech. At the door of the house the head painter came up to her to ask about the outcome of his request for partial payment. Like an automaton, she gave him all the money. Astonished, he signed a receipt, then shouted an order to his men. As she left, Anna heard them taking down another part of the scaffolding: people who had already been paid, in a hurry to finish a job from which they had nothing more to expect.

She was surprised to find herself understanding them and almost envying them. In just a short time the house would be entrusted to her alone – pink, but more unlivable than before.

When she reached the Home, everyone was already in the large room used for parties: an old armory where, the weapons having been removed from the shelves, the walls remained, decorated with reddish coats-of-arms and warlike trophies painted on the doors.

Facing a rostrum were several rows of armchairs for guests and various benefactors; further back there began the bare white chairs for the old people. In a little room off to the side one could see the refreshment table, heavy-laden with desserts and fruit.

When Anna reached the room Lucrezio, dressed in black and grave with a gravity recalling his father's, was bowing as a group of elderly gentlemen entered. She did not dare to cross the rows of armchairs that were already occupied: she took up a position in a doorway, leaning against the jamb.

The seated old people stared at her, astonished to see so beautiful a lady remain standing: first one, then another, arose to offer her his place. Upon her gracious refusal, the nearest devoted a curious attention to her, as though she reminded them of something, but then they were distracted by the arrival of two attendants carrying trays heaped with biscuits.

Lucrezio climbed onto the rostrum. Anna suffered at the immediate silence, almost as though he were exposing himself to a grave danger. She suffered while he was speaking: she felt the effort he had made to put together that tear-jerker of a speech, to which the old people listened as attentively as children pleased with fluent words.

After Lucrezio, spoke the elderly poor man whom he had instructed. His babbling soon came to an end: the old man stepped down from the rostrum, made tender-hearted by the applause and the handshakes that seemed to assure him of a future as an orator. Having returned to his companions at the back of the room, he talked so loudly that it was irritating, while one of the benefactors began to speak.

Once the speeches were over, all the people in the armchairs went into the refreshment room while the old people remained where they were, exchanging the smiles of poor people who believe they are being hoaxed.

Lucrezio joined Anna.

"What are you doing here?" he asked nervously. "Come with me: I've got to introduce you to a lot of people."

"It's the director's wife," murmured a nearby voice. She heard, and it struck her as something sad.

While Lucrezio and his staff were accompanying the benefactors and authorities to the exit, the elderly poor entered the little side room and made themselves masters of the crumb-covered, soiled tables, the wines, the desserts, the fruit.

Their yelling and the clinking of glasses could be heard as far as the atrium; then they began shushing one another and laughing like escaped prisoners who are not quite sure of their freedom.

Lucrezio realized with horror what an error it had been to leave them unsupervised. Having bowed deeply to the last departing guests, he ran to the little room in order to try to calm the inmates down through his presence. Anna stayed right behind him: she feared an outburst of anger, some unfortunate and saddening excess.

The press of old people around the devastated tables grew wilder. Some, equipped with bottles of wine, were serving as bartenders in the crush, pouring drinks for those who pleadingly held out their glasses; then, with a wink of affectionate complicity, they themselves drank straight from the bottle.

In their furious desire to grab something, most of the old people engaged in bestial struggles over the wine and the desserts; others, having drawn off to one side, spit out hard bits and orange seeds or awkwardly made off with their booty while, beneath the frocks they all had in common, appeared a disturbing reflection – whether sweet or coarse – of the men they once had been.

Lucrezio's voice and gestures were powerless. Coming up to him, the bursar said:

"You wanted to do things in style. Now look: who can restrain them?" He pursed his little mouth in suffering, following with a policeman's eyes the hands that he had seen fall rapaciously on the biscuits and a fruit dish.

"I don't give a damn!" Lucrezio shouted in his face, dragging Anna out of that unbearable environment.

When they were in the garden an attendant, red with fury, ran up to them with a busy air.

"Signor Direttore," he said, "down there at the bottom of the garden, five or six of these rascals are drinking wine they've carried off from the room. Three bottles, they've got. I tried to get them back and, right away, I got hit over the head with one. What am I supposed to do?" His angry question clearly expressed his desire for revenge.

"I'll go calm them down," replied Lucrezio, who was very pale. "Anna, you stay here: I'll be right back."

Anna remained alone at the meeting-point of two avenues: Lucrezio and the attendant disappeared around the first turn.

She felt painfully worried. It seemed to her that Lucrezio had, by now, accepted even the poison in his situation at the Home as an evil he had foreseen – a petty evil as compared with another, greater one, he awaited with fear.

Three old men, coming out of the villa, made their way towards her. Two stumbled as they walked, sniggering; the third hurried after them with precipitous little steps, in constant danger of falling on his face, unable to stand up any longer. They must have drunk a lot and played a trick on someone, because they were so exhilarated that they could not contain themselves.

The first threw himself down on a bench to catch his breath. He was coughing and laughing: the other two suffered through their long, singing fit of laughter while remaining standing, wobbling nearby.

Two more old men emerged from the villa. They were laughing and shoving each other, putting their hands on their swollen pockets, over the tops of which peeped the yellow heads of oranges stolen from the tables.

The new arrivals noticed Anna standing still against a hedge.

"The director's wife is here," they warned, frightening the first group, which abruptly stopped laughing.

She tried to reassure them with a smile. A bit hesitantly, the old men gathered around her. She attracted them: they stared at her with wan eyes beneath reddened lids, trying to let her know that they were amazed and happy.

Anna went on smiling, but she was afraid: she wanted to leave, caught as she was within a circle of lined faces that opened up in pink smiles, wet with gums.

"Let's offer the oranges to the lady," proposed one.

Their trembling hands offered the fruit.

"Signora, signora, take one from me, too," implored the generous and somewhat drunken beggars.

She accepted the oranges.

"Thank you, thank you, not so many. Keep them for yourselves; you can eat them while you stroll about." She hated herself for these words, worthy of a true lady director.

She made them a friendly sign. The old men opened a passage for her and then, as if some new liquor were running in their veins, burst out laughing.

Anna turned around when she was already far away. The old men were throwing the oranges back and forth among themselves. The golden balls flew through the air, as in a game played by happy children.

Lucrezio, who had emerged from a path along with the attendant, was watching too. He joined the woman and, touching her, said: "Look, I've turned the Home into a kindergarten, and my father will never forgive me for it, through all eternity."

She laughed, but was afraid.

Once they had gone out through a gate, Lucrezio headed for home. They had to walk along short stretches of road and make three turnings along the walls before reaching an open space from which they could see the house. At the last turning, the building's free-standing side appeared: a lugubrious slice, covered with tar to protect it from the weather.

There was something new in the air: on the last bits of scaffolding, seen obliquely, played the red reflections of a large sun about to set.

"Given my poor showing," he said smilingly, "they'll accept my resignation as director. I don't have the strength to go on this way," he added to explain his last words. "I feel that, to do this job, you'd have to become like my father: a hard old man, deaf to everything."

To show her approval, Anna squeezed his hand.

All at once he left her and ran on ahead: he stopped after a few steps, there on the sidewalk. He was looking at his house.

The pink façade was drinking in the setting sun that enriched and expanded it, turning it reddish and setting it apart from the other houses, all bleak and neatly lined up. The sun, a solidified ball of fire, was shining directly upon the panes of a window rendered impenetrable, but so incandescent that the eyes could not bear the dazzle. In comparison, the other little windows were holes in the wall, poorly aligned by the wooden crosses dividing their panes. Passersby raised their heads towards that golden light, amazed to find it in the city, in a sad, remote street; and then, noticing the couple standing stock-still and seeing her beauty, they went their ironic way, thinking of the risks entailed in having an overly poetic husband. He, his face pale, fixed his enchanted gaze on the stones, the corners, the window-sills, rich with an intimate, sweet fire, like red-hot steel that is cooling down.

"Look," said Lucrezio, touching Anna. "Think how beautiful our room must be with that sun inside it; but perhaps the window only reflects it. Let's go see." He paused for another moment to gaze on the source of light, which was shining less vividly and securely: here and there the glass had recovered – amidst its cold, vertical, mirror-like hues – its dark transparency against the interior.

They ran into the house. He opened the bedroom door. There was no sun, just a gray light barely touched by pink reflections. Lucrezio held Anna tight, clasping her to himself with the strength of anguish.

"What are we doing here, in this house where I feel myself dying? Let's go away! Let's go away!"

She made a gesture of desperate grief and followed him as he fled towards the stairs. She took his arm and led him out of the house, toward the sounds of the city, as though he were already an old man whose uncertain steps were numbered – a man who, this day, is allowed to gaze upon the spectacle of other men's novelty, so as to afford him a memorable view of the world he is preparing to leave.

# The Tired Bricklayer

The father and his son climbed out of the dormer window onto a level catwalk running along the base of the pyramidal roof: like a coldly mineral hat atop the building's architectural humanity, the roof aroused a sense of alarm, like some inaccessible mountain peak.

Looking about him, the bricklayer located the chimney damaged by the storm. It emerged, solitary, from an area of the steeply pitched roof where little squares of new slate sent back icy reflections of the sky, amidst the opaqueness of the older slate – new and old were distributed in a disorderly checkerboard, whose pattern the eye sought vainly to complete.

"It's almost at the corner," he said. When he fixed his gaze on the chimney, the heavily clouded sky seemed brighter over the villa than elsewhere, and this increased his sense of the void at his side. He nonetheless proceeded with calm self-confidence, turning around to watch over the boy, who was challenging a barking black dog that had remained down there on the gravel-covered ground.

"Let it alone."

"It's got it in for us," replied his son, who bent over to pick up a fragment of slate that he tossed down near the animal. The dog soon stopped barking and started hunting about for the slate.

The father smiled and then said in a severe tone, "Keep moving."

When they reached the chimney, which emerged directly from the pitch of the roof, they put down their materials and tools. The bricklayer realized that the job was a simple one.

"Go bring me the water, and be quick about it," he ordered. "I'm afraid it's going to rain."

The boy set off towards the dormer window, while his father kept his eyes on the sky. Rain looked imminent: the clouds were shifting, and their white gleam was giving way to great, still, heavy waves of gray. As the darkness gradually increased, the forest that spread all about lost its airy hue, turning dense and uniform as grass in a field. Close to the villa, the tops of the park's first trees were reflected in the little lake, and the water containing these images seemed to climb heavenwards and draw nearer.

In order to overcome this disturbing illusion, the bricklayer calculated the real distance with an expert eye; then he began to remove the tottering bricks from the collapsing pile, keeping at it until he had reached intact, healthy masonry.

The boy arrived with a container full of water, and prepared the mortar on the board.

His father turned to him with a smile.

"I don't need you now. Why don't you go down and have a look at the garden? There are swans in the lake. Go on, you're not going to get another chance. Watch out for the dog and don't touch anything."

The boy was a bit hesitant to set off on the adventure he had been ordered to undertake, as though fearful that he would encounter opposition along the way.

"If you meet anyone, just say you're my son," the bricklayer shouted after him; then, finding himself alone, he realized that he was in a hurry to finish the job and get down off the roof.

The sky threatened rain; the wind fell silent now and then, as if to encourage the downpour; but on the nearby trees, some of the leaves – driven by mysterious, invisible air currents – continued to blow about with a rustle, while others remained still.

There were moments of absolute silence, when the bricklayer heard his own breathing; within the hollow shaft that he was rebuilding, it sounded like snoring. He felt like whistling down that thick black throat, as into a flute. The sound would emerge through the open fireplaces of the superimposed rooms below, replying to the vague noises that reached him: noises that seemed at times to come from a festive dinner, and at others to suggest flights and chases enacted by barefoot people along endless corridors.

He refrained. But he did beat mischievously and loudly with his resounding trowel against the bricks as he laid them into the mortar he had spread to receive them. Then he stopped to listen; he was disappointed that neither an orgy nor a bacchanal was really taking place within the villa, as he would have wished. As the pile grew taller, he could work in a less cramped position and look about him without straining. Someone was running down below in the park down, followed by the joyously barking dog. He recognized his son; he had a glimpse of the boy at the lakeside, admiring something that remained hidden from his father; then he lost sight of him behind some tall stacks of fresh-cut wood. The pile of bricks continued to grow, and the sounds from the house seemed ever more muffled, strangled by the moist new building material. The masonry was contracting and solidifying: scratching with his finger along the interstices of mortar, the bricklayer assured himself that his work had already taken hold.

"Now let it rain," thought the bricklayer, as he adapted the new black tin hood to the chimney. As he stood up from the uncomfortable crouch he had adopted in order to gather up his tools, he felt an unsteadiness, a slight dizziness. His gaze had run over too much sky and forest in those brief instants, and the images collided with one another; he was unable to sort them out. He smiled and fixed his eyes on the horizon, in search of a strong, straight line. Rain had already begun falling upon the blurred and distant reaches of the forest. He discovered that his perfect solitude was a danger. The new bricks of the chimney, bright red upon the grayish old pile, gave him the sense that he had added something garish and hostile to that steep, skywards-sloping roof; and he felt a sort of angry bitterness.

He set off towards the dormer window leading to the attic. After two steps he stopped, trembling. An inner coldness, a sudden lack of strength, forced him to lean against the sloping roof, while his tools fell from his hands. The weight of a hammer upon his foot reassured him that, dizzy as he was, he was not moving, and that he was supported by a solid surface.

"I'm tired," he thought. "I'll get over this." He fixed his gaze on the distance, at a level above the trees, in order to avoid the attraction of empty space and the repulsion aroused by the smooth roof.

He overcame his dizziness, but self-confidence did not return: with his hands glued to the slippery slate, the bricklayer explored what was below him, in search of his former security. He saw the little lake off to the left, silvery in the middle and dark with black water near its shady banks. The swans were emerging from a hidden inlet. Three, white, all in a row. They moved smoothly through the dark water, breaking through barriers of floating leaves with their breasts, and seemingly headed for distant destinations. He measured the boundaries of the lake ironically. Every now and then the birds opened their wings, like boats raising their sails, and maneuvered with their long necks so as change direction.

They reached the middle of the lake, where they turned gray and practically invisible in a silvery reflection.

His attention captured by another attraction, he forgot about them.

An unharnessed colt was galloping nervously in a fenced–off area of the park. In the silence, one could hear his hooves striking the ground; the sound drew closer when the animal was hidden by the trees; he would reappear as he ran, brown and fast against the green grass.

It suddenly started raining.

Keeping his eyes on the horse, the bricklayer managed to return to the chimney without suffering from a sense of the void, but he was panting as though he had escaped a danger.

He remembered that not far off, around the corner, the noble building was joined to a lateral wing with a flat roof, from which it should be easy to reach a dormer window or a skylight.

Blinded by the downpour, he went down on all fours upon the catwalk, so as to proceed along a safe path. He heard the gutters gurgling; from the pitched wall of slate, the water ran down in sheets that were alternately opaque and luminous.

In this way he reached the flat roof, which was a little lower than the catwalk, and he climbed down onto it; having finally reached safety, he sheltered beneath the protruding eaves of the pyramidal roof.

The swans were no longer swimming in the lake. They were huddled along the shore, opening and shutting their wings, never content with the way they had reorganized their feathers, which were being drenched from on high.

The colt, no longer visible, had ceased galloping. Standing still, he pawed the earth and neighed stridently at his own suffering: he was a prisoner in a shut–in, rain–soaked space.

Amidst grumbles of thunder, the rain stopped.

The bricklayer came out from under the protection of the eaves, anxious to verify whether what he had glimpsed was true. The flat roof was completely lacking in dormer windows and skylights. There were large, equidistant panes of transparent glass, sustained by a skeleton of crossed pieces of iron. Against the inner surface of the glass, there arose from within the house a light that was gray and dense as a gas; and the whole weight of the roof seemed barely adequate to contain its exhalation.

The only solution was to go back, but the bricklayer felt as tired and as uncertain of his own strength as if he had just gotten over an illness. He remained on the wing of the building, from which he had an oblique view of the rear façade; and he sat down to wait. He imagined that if he could speak with someone, or see his son once again, his malaise would vanish. For this reason, he fixed his gaze now upon the places where the park opened onto the graveled open space surrounding the house, and now upon the façade with its many windows, in the hope that a servant might open one of them.

Where the curtains were drawn aside, he could catch a glimpse of the interior of the rooms, the furniture, the gilded picture-frames; and each of these objects brought him repose, a defense against emptiness and altitude, those enemies of the heart. They put to sleep his awareness of the mortal risk entailed in trying to reach them though a premature attempt.

Through the deflated clouds, there appeared a bit of false sunlight that made the forest, the glades, and the park seem unnatural. Everything looked detached from the ground and suspended in the midst of movement; the air, quiet upon the treetops, brushed his face with an undulating motion. Everything was near, and would be easy to touch. A step, a leap should be sufficient to send a man flying onto the peak of the roof or the tops of the welcoming trees, into the glades, next to the resting colt.

The illusion that he had merely to hurl himself into

the void became so insidious that the bricklayer had to make an effort to overcome it. Once he had regained an awareness of the weight and height of things, there remained in him a feeling of bitterness, like a regret at having been incapable of seizing a proffered fortune.

He thought of calling out, but the silence, the tranquil air, and the majesty of the building held him back. Resigned, he hunched down with his hands on his knees, his eyes glued to the horizon.

The golden air turned him into a drawing of solitude, even for himself. His hands had a halo of gold; the soaked, hard fabric enclosed him within a luminous line that made movement alarming to him, as though he were clad in a rich new garment not his own. Within that luminous outline, he felt alone and condemned to immobility. He imagined that, from afar, he must look like a mass of old stones, a collapsed chimney; and he despaired of this, as though he were a wretch betrayed by an evil magician.

The sound of a window being opened caught him by surprise and made him turn his gaze to the façade.

In the opening there appeared a completely nude woman. She seemed to have come to the windowsill to breathe the new air left by the rain. Around her, warm steam emerged from the window. Her face was serene, and she was drying her breasts with distracted, delicate gestures, lost as she was in contemplation of the countryside. She vanished for a moment, and then returned with a white comb in her black hair; the gesture of combing her hair back swelled out her splendid nakedness.

The bricklayer held his breath and lowered his eyelids, out of a fear that his thirsty, heavy gaze might make itself felt; the woman was looking at herself in a little mirror, which she then set down on the window-ledge in order to tie up her hair. A cloud changed its position, causing the explosion of a fiery lake of sunlight in the sky. It seemed to the bricklayer that the woman could no longer move from her place; she was the reward for his suffering and patience. He laughed happily, and the sun entered his mouth, bringing more joy even than oxygen itself; then, feeling his cheek illuminated like a mirror that might give him away, he lowered his head and hid it between his arms. He let his gaze wander over the scene below, beyond the graveled area and the green planters for the lemon trees. On the grass of the lawn, stock-still like a sapling covered with gray rags, his son stood looking at the naked woman. In the boy's face, hypocritically turned downwards, one could see his upturned white eyes.

Then the bricklayer felt irritation and anger. With his hand he gestured to the boy, who did not see him: "Go away, go away!" And then his own gaze returned nervously to the woman. She was looking upwards, and so hadn't noticed the new shadow on the lawn; but the bricklayer could no longer enjoy her as he had previously, because of his inward shame at sharing the spectacle with his son. He envied him that voluptuous vision granted to the dreams of adolescence; while for him, the woman's nakedness had already been robbed by the boy of all its miraculousness. With confused sadness, he felt that his son was guilty of something for which he, as the father, could not punish him; at the same time, he could foresee the brutality with which he would push him into the arms of the boy's shabbily dressed mother, and the reproof in her question: "What has he done?" He preferred to tear his gaze away and direct it to some randomly chosen part of the park. In the lake, he saw the swans advancing, dawdling like choristers preparing to sing; in the enclosure, the colt was lying, tired and heavy, on the grass. But these images gave him no relief from the desire to spy once again on his son.

The latter was still standing, small and shapeless, on the dark grass; here and there he was white with plaster, like some piece of fruit within a multicolored peel. Turning her happy gaze here and there, the woman might encounter him. But she — although she was now looking down — seemed to be searching for something among the trees that sheltered the pawing colt. Stunned, trembling, the boy was no longer showing his eyes.

The bricklayer felt a sort of satisfaction at seeing the boy already somewhat punished; but the paternal instinct to protect him brought back the tenderness that had been driven out by rancor at having been distracted from his own felicitous discovery. He measured the woman's gaze, spying on her to see where it was turned, forgetting that she was beautiful and naked.

Ending her long pause, the woman withdrew and shut the window. A rosy shadow remained at play behind the muslin curtains.

The boy was still standing there, as though expecting the vision to return. Then the bricklayer gave forth an unconscious shout of anger: it provoked such terror in the boy that he fled towards the trees, weeping noisily.

Liberated, the bricklayer followed the nakedness behind the curtains with the desire of a man who completes and magnifies the image. The shadows in the room were his accomplices; but the white lingerie that the woman turned about as she prepared to put it on created intensely luminous zones that fell on her body, grew dimmer, hid her. At last she vanished into the room's dark interior; he remained staring at the window until a flash of light at the back of the room told him that a door had been opened and closed.

He looked about himself joylessly, and thought once more about his son, with a strange kind of anguish. Rapidly and securely he leapt onto the high roof, reached the chimney, ran to the open dormer window. Having dashed down the stairs and thrown open the glass-paned doors in the atrium, he found himself on the graveled open space before the house. There he began calling out to his son as he ran towards the trees. He now felt remorse over his cry from the roof, and he imagined some disaster, thinking that the boy, in his flight, might have believed himself discovered by someone from the household.

He reached the lakeside without having heard any response. The swans were gliding smoothly through the black water, which turned limpid and yellow wherever there was a patch of sunlight. Hearing his renewed calls, the swans split up and then gathered anew in a tranquil inlet beneath the bank, where there grew a tangle of briars. He went on, his anguish increased by the sight of the round, evil eyes of the white birds. Among the trees, he lost his sense of direction: he wandered, deluded by voices and sounds created solely by his desire to hear them in reality. He found himself at the fence of the enclosure where the colt stood up nervously, fearing the trainer's whip.

Persisting in his desperate calls, the bricklayer went down a path that lead into a thicket. He was stopped by a shape: something gray at the foot of a tree.

The boy's frightened eyes no longer seemed those that had admired the beautiful woman; not even when, standing up before his father, he said: "The swans, Dad, the swans! I think I've killed one of them with a stone." His father discovered that he was resigned, ready to listen to the modest lie of another man like himself.

# The Wig

Having gathered up, amidst the water that had collected on the floor, the buckets and sponges he had used for his ablutions, the coachman was dressing in a corner of the coachhouse; a protruding section of the wall hid him from those who might see him through the wide-open door. So as to offer the spectacle of something naked to the theatrical wigmaker's daughter, whom he guessed to be spying on him from the shop-door, he stuck out a thick and hairy leg from his hiding-place, kicking the air and wiggling his toes so that they seemed a row of bowing monks. Alone as he was, he sniggered at the sensual anxiety of the joke.

A glance outside was enough to disappoint him and take away his desire to laugh. He immediately withdrew his leg into the shadows; it had turned pale and puffy in the cold, vacuous light entering from the street. He clothed it hurriedly: it was the one that hurt on rainy days.

With no more delays, he finished putting on his black outfit, and then went to look at himself in the mirror. As he adjusted his three-cornered hat on his head, his beard — not freshly shaved — struck him as a sort of mourning-band, lending his face the black gravity his position called for. Satisfied with the results of this examination, he locked the door and went out to the carriage that was waiting a bit further along, where the street grew wider.

Before climbing up onto the box, he turned his gaze towards an odd little shop: a girl with a faded, suffering face had appeared on the threshold. The coachman smiled at her, but she did not respond. She was staring at the black horses, adorned with plumes, who were keeping their heads down and breathing heavily down near the pavement, revealing, out of their distaste for the bit, ferocious red mouths which looked as though they were sweating blood. Then he drew near the shop, playfully pretending not to have noticed her; he shook his head over something he was vainly seeking in the window.

There were wigs and long pony-tails of hair on display; hung high up, they thinned out as they descended to the level of the flat surface at the bottom of the shop window where – amidst pyramids of stage make-up and paper-wrapped cosmetics – round little supports bore up theatrical hairdos in historical styles abounding in flowing curls and in long shocks of hair that had been shaped with a hot iron. At the sides, two waxen busts of women – a brunette and a blonde – showed rosy, smiling faces beneath well-starched wigs, while their pale breasts peeped out from beneath a deep sea-blue wax covering.

"So?" asked the coachman, turning to the girl, who stood motionless on the threshold. "I still don't see my white wig. When's it going to be ready?"

"Soon," she replied, blushing.

"Well, I'll wait for it," he said with a mischievous smile; then he bent down and asked her softly: "Don't you want to come any more to see the horses in the stable? You mustn't be afraid."

There was no reply. Embarrassed, he contemplated the two busts.

"And yet," he murmured with comical regret, "there are women as beautiful as these in the world. Some lucky fellow will have them!"

The girl was forced to smile; the man climbed into the box, released the brake, and sent the horses on their way. She remained at the threshold until the carriage – with the monumental, black-clad coachman sitting taller than a funerary sculpture – vanished around the corner of the first cross-street.

"What are you up to?" her sister asked her when she went back into the shop. "You're always talking with that man. I don't like it. Instead, you should get to work; you're late with your wig."

The girl seemed not to have heard her. She opened a drawer and began to make a selection from among a wide range of paper-wrapped samples of glassy, fragile dead hair of varying colors.

The elder sister – short, gray, imprisoned in fat – was busy implanting long hair into a skull-cap whose netting was spread over an armature of flexible little sticks. Working quickly, she attached the blond strands, shaping them and parting them with a little comb.

"Father has gone to take the order from the costumer," she said abruptly, in order to resume her conversation with her sister, whom she realized she had offended. "It'll all be work to be delivered in a hurry for the opera season, but afterwards we'll go to the country for a week." Thinking of the countryside, where she always succeeded in enjoying the air and the restfulness, she sought a smiling assent from her younger sister, who was still bent over her samples.

"Tell me," she went on with a certain harshness. "Who are you making that white wig for, the one I saw in the cupboard? So far as I know, no one's ordered it."

Her sister gave a start.

"It's for him," she answered after a painful pause. "I realized that his outfit isn't complete without a wig, and I thought I'd make him one as a present." Then, as though in self-justification, she held out to her sister a sheet on which were drawn wigs in various styles, along with suits, hats, gloves, and boots in matching styles.

"People are no good at judging these things," she added. "Even that lady yesterday had chosen the wrong head for her outfit. It's a good thing that I..."

She broke off in mid-sentence, aware that, by wandering from the point, she was increasing her own embarrassment and her sister's distrust.

"And what's the coachman supposed to do with your white wig?"

"He'll wear it when his duties call for a really luxurious style," she quickly answered; and she blushed and grew agitated, as though the question had opened an investigation into a secret thought.

"That man doesn't deserve anything from you, nor from anyone," concluded the elder sister, bending over to comb the hair she was using.

The younger girl buried her face in her hands, so as to hide an ill-intentioned, rancorous gaze.

Her sister had been too ready to forget the mutual sympathy and trust of those painful years of waiting: the time when, the day's work being concluded, supper with their father had been a torture for both of them. They had feared that he would understand their suffering, which they endured in silent, modest rage, especially when they suspected the widower – who had raised them with a practically maternal solicitude – of maintaining, quite close to their home, a lover, a girl younger than themselves.

Later on, as a distraction from the endless days in the shop, they had begun to spy together on the coachman in his coach-house. He didn't bother to close the door: not even when, undressed and hairy, he was busy washing himself. An unconscious pleasure led them to say that he was ugly, filthy, bestial; then the elder sister, as if she had suddenly become aware of the dangers of such a pleasure, had abruptly ceased to take up her position behind the green-tinted shop window and had given up making comments, leaving her younger sibling to continue to indulge in solitude her weakness for the game. The peace the elder girl had found in a torpid fatness, accumulated practically from one day to the next, had shielded her from feeling the same torments as her sister. The latter, constrained to silence by her shame at being unable to give up her practices, had remained alone, no longer able to control a desire which, together, they had been capable of turning into disgust, of hiding behind the suffering of wild laughter.

So it was that – condemned through the betrayal of her elder sister, who had been her only help in the daily effort to make the most of her own sterile purity – she had no defense left to her save the repulsion which certain of the coachman's attitudes occasionally aroused in her. But even when she thought of things in this light, she discovered that she was attracted, with no capacity for recovery. It was like when, as a child, lying with her head hanging down over the edge of the mattress so that she could touch the base of the bed with her fingertips, she had experienced an onset of nausea – a sensation insufficient, however, to stop her from completing the experiment, almost as though, having tilted beyond a certain angle, she could sense only useless warnings of danger. Her impotence in this matter led her to envy her sister, who had been so easily cured of a desire that led only to self-contempt.

These were very unhappy days: days during which humanity, fully dressed, prepared itself for the inevitable spectacle of her, the younger sister, naked before the black coachman.

Despite her hostility to the image that had become the focus of all her sexual fantasies, she had once derived from his lower social status a cherished sense of superiority, the certainty that he would like her, a taste for thinking that he would be amazed and almost shy at his own conquest: reflections of her own virtues which, discouraged as she was by all those empty years, she would never have dared to see in other men. Later on, the explicit proposals and attempts of the coachman, with whom she had come to share a risky familiarity – his proud male exhibition of his naked chest, his quick attempt to seize her one evening when she had accepted his invitation to enter the stable for a look at the horses – had robbed her of these illusions. Having saved herself by the skin of her teeth, she had resolved not to yield before finding within herself some quality capable of taming the beast in him and evoking, on his part, a sweet gratitude. This was why, in the indirect manner of one who has been irredeemably humiliated, she was trusting not to her own person, but rather to a gift long meditated upon. Keeping her work hidden from her father and sister, she was making him a white wig to wear beneath his three-cornered hat on those luxurious occasions from which his employers excluded him – more, perhaps, on account of inadequacies in his behavior than in his costume. The white wig was meant to lend a noble tone to this coarse man – just as all the work carried out in her father's workshop, with its stench of the theater, was intended to prepare the heads of beggars who, even if they were only supernumeraries, would have to look like princes.

Her instinctive need to elevate the man from whom she felt that she could not escape was thus invested in an object she could make with her own hands; at the same time, she was creating a talisman that might protect her against the animal crudity of a purely sexual adventure.

The coachman, who had received from her, if anything, too many announcements of the gift, asked her about the wig – without suspecting that he was displaying great acumen – just as he would have done about any object that a woman was using as a delaying tactic: he seemed to be asking her to remove the obstacle as soon as possible. She, thinking of that hairy and provocative flesh, felt confused; as a punishment, she wrapped up the half-finished wig in a cloth, tying it up tightly and hiding it away, as though it were one of those grandiose embroideries that one works at in one's spare time over a period of years.

Now and then, in order to provoke her, he took up a position before the dolls in the shop window and made comments meant to discourage her from aspiring to the possession of his face and body. These were veiled threats, astute, unfailingly effective embroideries: the girl would resume work on the white wig which no one had ordered and which she had to keep hidden.

An imprudence had sufficed to arouse doubts and speculations on the part of her sister; but she no longer reproached herself for that imprudence. During the long silence following the inquiry that had been so painful for her, she had prepared to confess everything, in hopes of taking some of the weight off her back and receiving comfort. She shut her eyes to overcome her shame, moved her lips to speak, and dared not do so. The elder sister, thoughtful and hostile, remained silent; and time passed slowly, as hair after hair was inserted into the pink skull-caps.


A shadow approached the shop-door.

"Someone's here," they said simultaneously, raising their eyes to the person who was entering.

It was a woman dressed in clothes of worn-out, faded sumptuousness; she had a small face beneath a large hat that cast its shadow as far as her nose. To speak and look people in the face, she would have had to tilt her head backwards, but she didn't speak, seemingly seized with shyness. Head down, she hid herself from the mute interrogation of the two sisters, who saw her painted mouth contract in tremulous grimaces of pain.

"Sit down, make yourself comfortable, Signora, and tell us how we can be of assistance to you," begged the elder sister.

"Isn't there a back room?" asked the visitor in a voice

tinged with suffering, looking about in search of one.

"Yes, there is, behind that curtain," replied the younger sister, who immediately regretted having spoken, seized as she was with distrust.

"Well, if you don't mind, I'd like to go back there with just one of you. I ask this because otherwise I'd be ashamed. I have to show you my misfortune, my unhappiness."

"Just as you wish, Signora," said the elder sister; but as she drew back the curtain hiding the back room, she let her sister see that she did not wish to remain alone with this strange customer.

The three women were in a small, dark room where the electric light revealed piles of dusty boxes, a rectangular mirror hanging on the wall above an iron sink, and a small table covered with a gray cloth.

"I ask you to keep a secret," said the woman, imploring them with her gaze. "I've come here the way one goes to the doctor."

Receiving no reply – no gestures, no words – she opened her purse, took out a torn, yellowing photograph that was missing its lower portion.

"This is the way I was," she said, holding it out.

The two sisters bent over to look at it with diffident curiosity.

It was the image of a young woman whose naked breasts were provocatively covered here and there by the fall of her full-flowing tresses. The artificial smile and ostentatiously displayed flesh gave a sense of professional provocation – of the total, obscene nudity of the whole body, cut off halfway down on account of second thoughts or out of a modesty imposed by calculation.

"That's the way I was," sighed the woman, "but here's how I am now." She removed her hat. Her small, bald skull was dotted here and there with a few thin tufts of grayish hair; the nape of her neck bore a wave of longer, curly hair: blond, but so faded as to be almost transparent.

The woman's hand painfully stroked her skull; then she timidly raised her eyes to observe the onlookers' horror. "It's dreadful, isn't it? I'm condemned not to let anyone look at me any more. I understand that I must be revolting. I can see it for myself: I look like a guinea-hen."

Meanwhile, the two sisters were trying to recognize in the woman their first image of her; it was lost, destroyed by that bald skull. The younger sister bent down so as to be able to see the face alone, from a viewpoint below the eyebrows; and then she was able to say to her:

"No, Signora, calm down. After all, these misfortunes befall people."

"Yes, a great misfortune! Poor me! It was an illness that reduced me to this state. At home I wear a bonnet, but in the street…I'm ashamed. Tell me, Signorine, tell me–you who certainly know about these things–whether I can get a wig so well made that it will hide my disgrace? It exists, it must exist – doesn't it?"

She had put her hat back on her head, and was awaiting both the answer and the sense of warmth on her head that would dissipate the cold and the shame of her misery. The elder sister spoke.

"I will tell you, Signora, that a wig, however well made, never looks as natural as real hair. If you don't want others to notice it, you've got to wear it with real flair. Anyway, with your hat, no one can notice anything."

"Thank you," murmured the woman. "Your words are a great consolation."

"Anyway, in such a small size, we have nothing but the two wigs in the window. Do you want to try them on? Which color do you want?"

"My natural color: blond. A beautiful blond, don't you understand? The way I was before my misfortune." She again held out the photograph; almost rudely, the elder sister refused to look at it.

"Go bring me the blonde doll," the elder sister said to the younger.

The bust was removed from the window and placed on the table in the back room.

There was a silence, a long hesitation, almost as though an enviable stranger had taken her place among the three women. In a semicircle, they remained staring, enchanted at that model of feminine beauty, upset at how distant they felt themselves from it.

The elder sister turned the waxen woman around, the better to illuminate her. As the light fell on her, the doll seemed to emerge for a moment from her serene languor and laugh with a strange, vital malice that showed upon her too-red lips and in her glass eyes.

"What a beautiful little lady!" The customer admired her in a regretful tone.

Following these words, the sisters were struck by a resemblance between the mannequin, nude down to her cleavage, and the image in the photograph lying on the table. Having in common a sense of idiotic, lascivious humanity, the photo and the mannequin with its rouged smile displayed the same effort to achieve a generically seductive expression, based solely on the awareness of sex.

"I'd give twenty years of my life to look like that," said the woman. "That's how I was, that's how I was," she repeated, touching the waxen breast and then, lightly, her own. She saw the photograph on the table, placed it close to the doll, and remained lost in contemplation. "Fashions in hairstyling were different back then," she concluded. "Would you mind leaving me alone?" she asked with a gentle smile. "I'm embarrassed to play the monkey before the mirror, but I'd really like to try on this beautiful wig."

The sisters withdrew beyond the curtain; the

younger one hid the photograph in her hand, having furtively seized it.

Having carried out this action, she felt troubled. The customer's demeanor, at once mincing and imploring – and capable, nonetheless, of expressing a carnal horror at her own renunciation of the pleasures of the flesh – had led the younger sister to such an intimate and disconsolate consideration of her own case as to inspire rancor towards the other woman and a desire to find in the image a reason to humiliate her irreparably. But, not yet certain of her sister's thoughts, she hesitated to open her hand, although she kept on sniggering like someone who has got a good grasp on things.

The elder sister took this as a mischievous invitation to return close to the curtain, and she tiptoed over. The younger sister stayed right behind her.

From the small, dark room came the rustling noises produced by a person making little gestures; the sisters thought that the woman must be standing before the mirror, adorning herself.

In the slightly stuffy silence, they could hear the words she was addressing to herself in an excited tone.

"You won't be bald any longer... You'll no longer be the guinea-hen that that horrid Silvio called you. You'll be as beautiful and modern as this little lady."

"But what's wrong with her? She must he mad," murmured the elder sister, pulling the other away, overcome by a sense of fear.

"Leave me be: I want to see her for a moment."

The creaking of a chair told the listeners that the woman was sitting down. They cautiously opened the curtain. The woman was, in fact, sitting: they could see her head, made blond by the wig. The mirror reflected her movements; she was making up her eyes.

She stopped: she was looking for something on the

table. She turned towards the curtain and listened with a worried air.

"I've got it, that photograph," revealed the younger sister in a murmur. Her sibling glanced at her admiringly; and then, together, they moved to a spot where the light was better, so as to study the piece of cardboard.

"A whore," muttered the elder sister. "We should send her away."

The younger sister remained silent and didn't take her eyes off the picture, which the coachman would have liked a great deal.

"Men," she said, "are capable of finding a woman like this beautiful. How revolting! Who on earth was the photographer?" She tossed the piece of cardboard onto the counter. She was suffering, overwhelmed by an unhappy sense of envy for a woman who could strip herself bare and smile in an alarming little room where the gaze of a man – a man bent down beneath a black cloth as he looked through the view-finder – was taking its time over its lustful scrutiny of her defenseless nakedness.

"We must send her away, this shameless woman," said the elder sister with an arrogant smile, drawing near the curtain.

"Look," she murmured. "Just look, now."

Standing before the mirror, the woman was striking vaingloriously beautiful poses.

In constant motion, she smiled at herself, touched up the make-up on her cheek, opened her arms wide and then brought them together over her breast as though eager to cherish herself. It was clear that, once the ugliness of her bald pate had been eliminated, she was finding a renewed pleasure and consolation in her own appearance. There was, however, something unfree in her gestures, all of which had a studied slowness. Every now and then she patted her head with her hand, to make sure that the wig had not moved.

"You have golden hair, just as you once did," she declared with deep emotion.

In the silence that followed, her eyes filled with tears. She suddenly felt that she was being observed from behind. "Signorine, Signorine," she called out without turning around. "Where have you gone? You can come back in now." The two sisters entered the back room with the hard, severe faces of judges. The welcoming smile vanished from the woman's lips and she adopted a standoffish, almost ironic expression when faced with the other two, who carried out their inspection in a sullen, bovine manner. She had changed incredibly. Tall and proud, she displayed the insolent, carnivorous beauty of a woman who, no longer young, is putting herself on display with a provocative intent. As though to humiliate them, she grew happier and happier in their hostile presence. She laughed, sending forth brief looks, lascivious and flashing, like a dancer who has to look in many different directions during her performance; she draped her dress about her, while still maintaining a rigid position of the neck that might have produced pain.

"Isn't it fine, Signorine?" she asked with a throaty laugh. "Tell me it is, because I'm really happy. No one can take this away from me," she added, touching the gold on her head. "It's mine. A secret, I beg you, keep it a secret. I've got to be attractive to a man who's really nice, an absolute dear. If you only knew how I've suffered!"

The two remained silent, incapable of unlocking their lips. At last the younger sister smiled, as though she had finally found a consolation. The woman's deep black eyes made an overly strong contrast with the blond wig, and this little flaw made it possible to rediscover, little by little, the little bald head beneath the felicitous weight of the false hair. "What's the matter?" asked the woman, gritting her teeth. "Come on, tell me."

She didn't wait for the reply; she went into the shop,

followed by the sisters as if by two bloodhounds. There, finding more space around her, she took a few tentative steps. Every now and then she touched her head with a somewhat confused air.

She saw her photograph on the counter.

"I didn't think I'd left it there," she said in a harsh voice, putting it back into her purse. "It's a souvenir I care about. Anyway, you must have noticed that now I look like myself once again. What a joy it is to have hair! You can't understand! Let's be clear about this," she added, "I require secrecy. I've come here the way one goes to the doctor."

She jammed her hat down onto her head.

"I would like to know the price of the wig."

Neither sister replied.

"I asked how much I have to pay," the woman insisted, and then turned around as she heard the door opening.

The girls' father came into the shop. He was a short, withered man, with a hard black moustache that gave him a meditative air, despite the effect's being diluted by his silvery hair and eyebrows. He bowed deeply to the customer, put down a large bundle on the counter, and cast an inquisitive eye at his daughters, who struck him as immobile and remote.

"This lady," said the elder sister effortfully, "wants to know whether you can sell her the blond wig from the bust in the window. She's already got it on her head."

The father stared at his daughter, amazed at such a question.

"But of course," he replied, turning to the woman, who was standing still as she awaited the reply. "It costs three hundred lire. I can't part with it for less, because it's a model." The woman opened her purse, handed him the money, and headed for the shop door.

Having got beyond the threshold, she turned to offer a farewell smile, luminous and scornful.

"What's the matter with you two?" asked the father. "Nothing," answered the younger, who stood at the glass door watching the woman's undulating steps.

He didn't insist, aware that he was never capable of offering them consolation. He sighed, humiliated. Opening his bundle, he began to take out its contents: moth-eaten theatrical wigs in need of refreshment.

"Get to work, girls," he said. "We have to be quick with the delivery."

"Just a moment," replied the younger daughter; detaching herself from the front door, she went into the back room.

Her sister joined her, saying angrily: "If Father hadn't come back, I would have made sure to send that shameless creature away without a wig!"

"No, it's better this way. What do we care about her men and all the filthy stuff she gets up to? She's paid, and that's what matters."

Her elder sister stared at her in amazement: "It seemed to me that you were very angry with her," she observed.

"I was for a moment, but then I realized I was wrong. Sometimes we old maids suffer from jealousy. Now I'm glad that she went off happy and cheerful; three men went by in the street, and all three looked at her. She must have felt as young and beautiful as when that photograph was taken."
As she spoke, she displayed an ill-tempered smile that revealed her gums.

"I thank that woman: she came here to open my eyes to my own stupidity. Why are you looking at me like that? Don't you understand that my hair doesn't come out?" she asked, seizing it at the crown of her head and giving it a powerful tug. "And that nobody has photographed my breasts? But does that mean that people appreciate me more than her?"

She drove her sister away with an angry gesture that simultaneously implored her to remain silent, and then set about rummaging through the boxes to find a new blond wig for the doll who was waiting, bald and smiling, on the gray table.

Having restored the doll's slightly perverse grace, she glanced at herself in the mirror. Above her own colorless face, she saw that her hair was mussed up; but, although she made a grimace of disdain, she did not bother to comb it. She picked up the doll and went into the shop in order to put it back on display.

Across the street the coachman, having returned from his outing, was driving the coach into the coach-house.

She reclosed the back of the display window and, unobserved by her family, slipped out into the street.

The man smiled when he noticed her, but then he turned his attention to the black horses, occupied as he was with taking them out of harness.

She entered the coach-house resolutely and touched his shoulder.

"What is it?" he asked, seeming to smell her.

The girl didn't answer: she threw back her head, as though suffering from some acute pain.

They moved together. He led the horses down a resonant corridor; she kept on looking behind her, as though frightened at the proximity of the animals' warm muzzles. Opening the door of the stall, the coachman — whose eyes were shining a bit — took her by the hand and, in order to remove a mischievous doubt, asked her about the wig. She pursed her lips, shut her eyes, and replied: "It's a present I no longer wish to give you. I've come to understand that you don't need it. I have no time to waste."

The man let go of the halters: freed, the horses bumped up against the wall of the stall, eager to reach the trough. The sound of hooves and a dizzying sense of movement thrust her down upon the green hay heaped up in a corner.

# The Goat

In the diary of the two summer months that I spent in solitude, recovering my bodily health and my spiritual calm up there in my hut in the mountains, you could read about the poor use I made of the instructions I had requested from a local old woman in order to learn how to milk the capricious and ill-tempered nanny goat that provided me with nourishment, and about how I ended up organizing my days to fit those of the animal, having recognized the similarity that linked the two of us in our stance toward vegetative life and the task of sustaining it.

Having lost the diary, and with it the reliable chronicle of the agreeable relationship gradually established between me and the black goat, I now have only my confused and, I would say, contradictory recollections; this is the fault of the eccentric beast which behaved badly at the end, just like many human creatures.

Our common home was the crest of the mountain, with its view of the sky stretching empty as far as the point where it met the sea, which I saw embracing, along the sandy shore, the firm, hard, yellowish land, made green here and there by rushes growing amidst the shining pools of vast swamps. Below us, dry, steep fields; then the thickets of arbutus and hazel; the dense strip of chestnut trees with their light green leaves; and lastly, the burnished silver olive groves and, among the olive trees, the houses and churches, and the bell towers whose clangor sounded near or far off according to the wind.

The goat tended to feed beyond the over-grazed area surrounding the hut; and I consented to go with her to certain steep slopes covered in fragrant bushes, or else, coaxing her away from the tedium of her shed, I would take her with me when I went down to the highest-up of the villages in order to buy food. To tell the truth, she obliged me to go back and forth continually along certain difficult paths; it was impossible to foresee where she would want to stop, or to understand why she would suddenly set off at a good clip to clamber up some previously neglected promontory from which, digging in her hooves at the edge of the precipice, she would proudly admire the landscape, without ever turning around to heed my impatient calls. My imperious voice, the stones I threw in order to get her away from there — none of it served any purpose. I would go on by myself. And suddenly, having taken a shortcut that had struck her fancy, she would be ahead of me, nervously agitating her stumpy tail, bleating from some discontent or regret, the almost anguished resonance of which I had a hard time shaking off.

At other times she would turn up in the middle of the path, truculent and full of menace: this was her invitation to take part in a private game of hers which, I admit, I should not have allowed her. Bounding up to her, I would seize hold of her horns and laughingly prevent her from butting me.

In the village, on account of my always turning up accompanied by the animal, they must have thought I was crazy — or worse. The goat would wait for me outside the shop, crouching on the pebbles in the public space: annoyed, and ready to punish the little dog by butting him, had he dared to approach her too closely with his irritating yapping.

Memories of the crisis of guilt submerged in the opaque veils of illness, of the rights and wrongs of my disdainful distancing of myself from my beloved, and of my obsessive confrontation with her equally disdainful distancing of herself from me: these things no longer tormented me. It seemed to me that I had forgotten everyone and everything in my hermit-like way of life, so favorable to the recovery of my physical strength, and likewise to my faith that I would soon be able to expect fresh fruits from my renewed spiritual energies. But my ecstatic lingering on the mountain was brought to an end by an occurrence that I had not dared to hope for.

One afternoon while out grazing the goat, I was heading down towards the village when I was struck by the sound – uncommon up there above the houses – of a motor being gunned as an automobile proceeded along the steep and ill-maintained stretch where the road ended in a stony path through the fields. I found it disturbing. Next, the unexpected return of silence brought with it an irresistible warning. I felt an impulse to get there before the car, driven in search of a non-existent passageway, might leave again, headed for the valley.

I precipitously clambered down the mountainside. In the end, fearing disappointment, I was going back up the path like any old wanderer, fixing an indifferent expression on my face in preparation for an encounter with strangers, when I saw Matilde. She was sitting on a low stone wall next to her little gray car, watching my arrival, dazed and not believing her own eyes.

"Were you expecting me?" I asked, leaning forward, smiling before her. Matilde took my hand, seeking in it a trustworthy sign of my emotional state, and clutched it to her breast, desirous of comfort for the pang she was feeling. "Now I can say that I was," she murmured. "Isn't this a miracle? But where were you off to?"

"To do the shopping for our house," I replied with cheery readiness; moved, I gazed into her eyes, which were already veiled with tears. "I can't imagine you'll want to carry me off without a look at my hermitage. You must live there for one full day at least."

Her nod of assent was sweet, but we didn't get a

chance to seal that happy repudiation of our misunderstandings with kisses and tender words: laughing in somewhat embarrassed hilarity, some young peasants were approaching in order to admire the cause of this rapid and very evident end to my much-discussed solitary existence.

Nonetheless, the intruders soon rendered us a service. Having pushed the car into an empty stall, they promised to buy for us the best foods in the shop and to bring them to us in the hut, along with Matilde's luggage. I was in a festive mood.

We set off, alone, up the incline. "It's stupendous, it's stupendous," said Matilde, new to the lightness of the silvery shadows in the olive grove, and to the violet-tinted satin spread by the sunset upon certain bare patches of meadow; and she did not yet know of the beauty – open, grandiose – that we were going to encounter at the top of the slope and upon the crest. So as to find an outlet for the anxious need to express ourselves that we both felt, we sat down next to a crumbling hut, in a place where I had often chosen to take my rest. There, before speaking, we kissed. A rustling amidst the grass made my companion break free of the embrace.

"Don't you see it? What does it want?" I heard her cry.

I turned around. It was the goat. It was coming forward, looking at us with lowering hostility. I laughed, but I leapt to my feet to save Matilde from being fiercely butted. In my haste, I took the blow, glancingly and in attenuated fashion, on my legs. Driven off by my kicks, the animal ran rapidly down the slopes, bleating.

I had to explain to my beloved that the goat was mine and that it was given to strange and unpredictable moods; but there is no doubt that this only aggravated her disagreeable impression.

"And now, where can that dreadful beast have got to?" she asked, obviously fearing a fresh clash.

"I don't know. It certainly won't come back here. We'll find it at the hut. It gives exquisite milk; once you've drunk it, you'll make peace."

She quivered in horror. "Its milk? Never! What evil eyes it had. I'd prefer never to see it again, your goat. Did it butt you?"

"It barely touched me," I lied. "Tomorrow," I added, "I'll hand it over to a shepherd, since it seems to me that you two are going to have a hard time getting along. Come on, don't think about it any more." I took it for granted that, since I was joking about it in this way, she would laugh too, consoling me for my unhappiness over their failure to reach an understanding. But Matilde's smile lacked conviction.

As we resumed walking, I realized that she was worried.

When we reached our destination, evening was falling. Having lit the candles and taken her on a tour of the two rooms, I was in ecstasy over her presence and thrilled at the naturalness with which, driving away my memories of solitude, she was preparing the food and setting the table. Suddenly she asked me, as if led to it by a random thought, where the animal that was so dear to me slept.

"Outside there, in her shed," I replied, barely able to repress a deprecatory gesture. "Don't worry. You won't see her again. Let's eat." However, I immediately remembered that it was my habit to eat leaving the goat free to circle the table in eager anticipation of the lettuce leaves that I gave her after sprinkling them with salt. At this point, I started to close the door; but I was forbidden to do so by Matilde, who had no intention of missing, from her place at the table, a marvelous patch of starry sky. A few instants latter, she dropped her fork into her plate and let out a scream. The goat had bounded into the hut. It stood there, indecisively, near the threshold, staring at Matilde with a strange red gleam in its eyes, which were struck by the candlelight. I leapt into action before it charged, and this time I managed to elude the blow, grabbing it by the horns in time. I brutally dragged it outside and pushed it into its shed, furious that it was ruining, for me and for my beloved, the memory of the place where, in beneficial calm, I had stayed until the day of Matilde's arrival.

Back in the hut, it was difficult to restore a shared intimacy, the full abandon required for the coming night. Something was dividing us, keeping us almost fearful of each other. And when, without speaking of it, we realized that we were both thinking about the jealous goat (even allowing for the different images we had of it), the wild laughter that brought us close together once again was certainly not appropriate to the seriousness of our reunion. It's true: love overcomes everything.

The next day I left my hermitage with Matilde; but first, I took the goat to a shepherd. "Take good care of it for me. I may come back one day to reclaim it," I said, startling myself with the idea that this might happen; and I walked off.

The goat, whose new master had already tied it to a stake, leapt up in an effort to join me. It felt the rope pulling at its neck and, straining forward, let out a long and sorrowful bleat that sounded like a reproach to me for having sacrificed it to the god who encourages the gravest sin of forgetfulness.

# The Sleeping Companion

Andrea smiled, displaying from afar the two cigarettes he had bought from a balloon vendor, who was wandering in a melancholy fashion about the pond in the deserted public garden, but Gerolamo gave no sign that he had spotted them. Sitting on the bench where he had been waiting for a few minutes, he was sleeping, heedless of his own desire to smoke and of the companion who had gone off in an attempt to satisfy it.

His companion's arrival did not wake him. Andrea lit a cigarette and sat down beside him, once again suspicious and almost envious of Gerolamo's inexplicable ability to interrupt his self-awareness every now and then and lose himself in short, cheering moments of sleep. Andrea looked at him. He was squat and poorly balanced upon legs that didn't even reach the ground, while the springtime sun revealed every crease of clothing distorted and worn thread-bare by obesity; each breath ended in a raucous noise and his face, shaded by a low-tilted hat, expressed contentedness. Andrea felt afresh the weariness and embarrassment pro-voked by the clinging companionship of a man separated from him by too great a difference in age and way of life.

The old man, with his poverty, his slovenliness, and his somnolence, was a dead weight that he had to drag around for hours and hours, in the intervals between the those wondrous flashes of insight born of a harsh wisdom and a confirmed contempt for the world. For some time, however, even the expectation of such compensations had begun to strike Andrea as hard to bear: a rich man's tolerance of the brilliant poor man in whose nature he was unhappy to recognize his own.

Gerolamo's body slumped forward a bit. Now he was sleeping in a posture of precarious abandonment, with his hands upon his belly and his head lolling limply, so heavy and full of blood that it was on the point of plunging, along with his inert mass, down into the gravel of the avenue.

A humorous glow on his brow – and the distension of his nostrils above the sparse, silvery down that failed to cover his swollen, violet lips – imitated an ironic, self-assured smile that made Andrea want to shake him, so as to get him out of danger. Recognizing, however, that this impulse was the result of a certain revulsion, Andrea waited and – ready to support his companion – bent down to seek the handsome curls of gray hair upon his temple and upon the lofty, clean-cut brow beneath the crooked hat.

By thus examining him, by isolating, amidst so many shapes ruined by physical and moral illness, the few that had kept their nobility, Andrea selfishly dragged Gerolamo to safety.

The latter tried to recover from a fresh, sudden droop of his head, gasped for air, and regained his composure with absent, bleary eyes. Andrea touched his shoulder and offered him a cigarette. The other man, with a smile that requested comprehension for his enjoyment of the warm stone and the sun that brought torpor to the blood, turned it down and dropped off again in a moment, but in a more prudent position.

Yielding to the invitation, Andrea half-closed his eyes, complaining of his own weak submission to his companion's laziness; but the irritation that had been building up in him during their stay in the garden did not allow him to let himself go. He opened his eyes again to impress upon his painter's memory a little tree whose new leaves had a reddish-yellow hue; they were tender and transparent at the ends of the little black branches, like a swarm of butterflies at rest. Lowering his gaze and continuing to look in the same direction, he discovered a dark-clad woman who peeped out every now and then from the shadow of a tree on the far side of the pond in order to look at Gerolamo and himself with a rapid nervousness, as though afraid of being recognized.

Distance made it impossible to make out her features. Her thinness and her movements resembled those of a mechanical figure on a clock. Perhaps she was playing a game with some hidden child; perhaps she intended to steal some flowers, and was on the lookout for an invisible watchman. At last she vanished behind a hedge, and Andrea watched her distractedly as she reappeared in an open part of the avenue that encircled the park like a ring.

Bit by bit, his annoyance boiled off. When Gerolamo awoke, he would tell him of some beautiful dream that he had made up in order to justify his having fallen asleep; and Andrea would laugh, happy to give in to a seemingly point-less bit of clever naughtiness which was, in reality, as potent as a child's. He even tried to guess what the topic of the story might be, basing his speculations upon other amusing chat-ter of Gerolamo's, who had once told him of waiting in a dream for a person who would reveal to him the numbers for winning at lotto. But a glance at the sleeping man, hunched down in the sunshine that brought laughter to his face, convinced him that the subject matter was something happier than anything his own experience of his companion might suggest to him.

He had met him at a dinner for painters made mem-orable by Gerolamo's tears over his own obesity. Afterwards, he had seen him on various occasions, when the older man had been expansive and confidential, perhaps to reward him for being the only one who didn't greet him with a joke. At any rate, the fat man was capable of defending himself when he thought it useful with replies that – had they been made by another man, one less shipwrecked or, simply, thinner –

would never have been forgiven.

Thus it was that, out of an interest in listening to him and understanding him, Andrea had found himself a prisoner of the old man's intimacy and of other concessions he had made to this battered but very able picture dealer. He was not too unhappy about it, because Gerolamo's unexpected friendship served his turn, weary as he was of his colleagues, of amusements and of stimuli.

Gerolamo turned out to be, after his own fashion, an artist, a connoisseur, and a discoverer of delightful things — at least, in the intervals between one doze and another in the course of his day. Once the anxious haste that drove him to want to close a deal at all costs had fallen away, he would resign himself to following the painter on some long walk outside the city.

His tales, drawn from life or invented, not very dramatic and without that obscene side that Andrea had at first expected, were dense with images that repaid study with slow enjoyment on account of their rich concision. They resembled the works of those old painters of illuminated manuscripts: artists capable of constructing within an initial letter, on a small round ground, the same composition found in a great fresco.

From admiration, Andrea had quickly arrived at affection; and yet, he was not ready to decide whether his gluttonous companion, swollen with sensuality, was truly reserved and chaste, or whether he was not, instead, so aware of his own vices as to be marvelously able to hide them.

If Gerolamo had to speak of women, as though to free himself from their weight of flesh and contrary desires, he would compare their physical appearance with that of painted or sculpted women; if he chanced to enter the studio of one of his painter friends while a nude woman was suffering more from weariness than from the embarrassment of posing, Gerolamo would smile at her in festive friendship, as though nakedness were a cheerful joke rather than a stimulating sight.

By chance, Andrea had found out that he was married and a father. He had been married early on to an ugly girl of the Nordic type, the very image of rain, as he said one day, displaying an old photograph of her, together with another picture showing a fat, short little girl.

He never spoke of his wife with his friends. He expressed real tenderness only for his daughter, who was twenty-five years old by now; but he always referred to her ways when she was a child, imitating her by bending his own body into expressive postures so felicitous and graceful as to astonish those who weren't expecting it. One had to love him then, as one loves certain elderly and bulky pianists when they lean over the keyboard, awakening the grace of scores that no one thought suited to them.

At such moments, Andrea reproached himself, seeing his own expectation of some unpleasant revelation as a sign of cruelty towards an ingenuous man who depended upon him completely, forgetful of his family and of the need to steer the leaky boat of his own affairs. Gerolamo, in fact, sought out Andrea's company with a simultaneous joy and resignation, as though he had finally found the interpreter for everything that he had been incapable of expressing in a lasting fashion, hindered as he was by the laziness that was part and parcel of his obese, unhappy body. He admired Andrea above all the other painters of his city and nation, with no regrets or infidelities occasioned by any other rising star. "Come off it, you never make a mistake. You were born a painter," he would say to him in the studio, when faced with a still uncertain new work.

After his outbursts of enthusiasm, he would curl up on the couch and fall asleep. Andrea could work as though he were alone, and the model was no longer shy about undressing in front of that stubby and spirited sleeper.

Gerolamo did not look at young flesh like a lascivious old man: he slept as though life were, by this time, a mere repetition of what he already knew.

Nonetheless, the sleeper's presence created an awkwardness between the painter and his model. They both avoided speaking; both seemed to fear yielding to an impulse for which the third party might judge them. Andrea feigned a total lack of interest in the charms of the model, who was in love with him, and she, immobile, grew sad while Gerolamo snored, indifferent to the idea that the world might or might not procreate.

Only when the light began to fail as the grayness of evening fell through the great window looking out over the roofs did the day's work end. Having dressed behind a screen, the girl would go out silently, seemingly happy to escape from a disturbing place. She would leave Andrea brooding upon his dissatisfaction with the work he had done on his canvas, and upon the gesture which the girl seemed to expect as a reward for the devoted patience for which a coin, accepted irritably, was inadequate compensation.

"Let's get going, too: it's dark."

Touched on the shoulder, Gerolamo shook himself, gesticulated as he gathered up the strength needed to heave himself up from his resting-place, and finally, avoiding looking at the canvas so as not to annoy his tired friend, went first down the dizzying staircase, blocking it.

A bit numbed with cold, he moved with a heavy tread, step by step, as though to the rhythm of a long count. Once out in the street, he ceased to be the victim of Andrea's austerity and got his own back. He would begin to run nimbly, amidst the amused admiration of the passers-by, so as to arrive in time to enjoy a glimmer of sunset on the corner of an old tower. He would buy a packet of pumpkin seeds from the first vendor who happened along; but, unable to open them properly with his teeth, he would nibble at them for a

long time with his gums in order to find, besides the poisonous crust of salt upon the skin, a bit of the tasty greenish soul
of the seed. Andrea stayed far away from him, as though he
did not know him.

In this fashion, they would reach the café. They
would sit down in a discreet corner, occupied, for the most
part, by a group of old men whose health and pocketbooks
were both in bad shape. Sitting beside Gerolamo, who dozed,
soothed by sounds that were perhaps more familiar to him
than those of his own home, Andrea could meditate – sometimes with the intention to break free – upon the chance
that had led him, so young and full of dreams, to live among
such failures.

Later a young man with a shock of prematurely gray
hair, a pointed beard, and sad, watery eyes would come to
their table: he was a poor devil, reduced to penury by his
insistence upon being an artist rather than a workman. He
sometimes worked for Andrea, whether as an errand-boy or
a model; and Andrea often wound up offering him dinner,
although with a detached air which the other did not heed,
convinced that his host was interested in the gossip he
brought of the other painters he hung around with.

At eight o'clock the café emptied out. Andrea and
Gerolamo would go out together with the young man with
the shock of hair, headed for a restaurant where the propri-
etor looked after them with special care.

Often the dinners were cheerful and noisy on
account of the arrival of a slightly crazy German painter and
a compatriot of his who was nearsighted and gifted with a
sonorous and resonant voice. The compatriot, an underem-
ployed searcher after rare books, possessed an enormous and
varied culture, but had little experience of the more com-
monplace aspects of life, so that it was easy to astonish him,
credulous and in good faith as he was. Just seeing him come
in with his pockets stuffed with books, Gerolamo became

animated. He enjoyed confusing him, mystifying him, deceiving him with words, gestures, and also with cards, when they remained seated at the table for a game.

During a game at which Andrea and the shock-headed artist were more spectators than players, Gerolamo would get up from his seat so as to glance at the German's cards; prudently, the German would now and again hold them against his chest, and so, running no risk, Gerolamo would gain an advantage over him, laughing until he cried at seeing him fall victim once again to bad luck. If his adversary, unhappy and suspicious, kept his cards well hidden, Gerolamo would soon grow weary; he would put his cards in his pocket and fall asleep. The German would thrust his head forward to see whether a hostile card was on the table; rolling his bulbous eyes behind his glasses, he would lean forward until he spied Gerolamo's happy, sleeping face. Then, having yelled out an insult, he would beat his fist on the table, while Gerolamo would resume play with a smile of commiseration, punishing him for his failure to understand what a wonderful amusement sleep was for grown-ups.

Sometimes victories and revenges followed upon one another until the inn-keeper, having lost patience, would ask everyone to leave because he wanted to shut up shop.

When the weather was fine, this point would mark the beginning of the group's nocturnal wanderings, while Gerolamo would grow progressively less animated, turning thoughtful and dull, as though returning home was a punishment.

Skillfully, by promising performances and extraordinary appearances in the deserted streets, he would lead everybody to sit down on the steps of some palazzo, proposing that they all remain there until daybreak. After a few minutes, reassured by the tranquil posture of his companions and by the tone of their conversation, he would yield to sleep, leaning on his neighbor, as though he were afraid of being left alone. Just like a drunk, he would have slept in the rain, just so long as he could count on the friendly or complicitous presence of another person: his sleep was restless, troubled by fits and starts and hoarse little cries.

After a while, weariness and irritation at wasting the night in pursuit of Gerolamo's whims made everyone fall silent. Gerolamo would suddenly wake up, but he would be sad and droopy, quite different from the way he was during the daytime; and it was only after having begged them to stay with him for another quarter of an hour that he would once again close his eyes upon some mournful dream that was tormenting him. Groans and moans issued forth from him as though the weary time of night reawakened some inner suffering, bearing its vortex of horrid images.

The shock-haired one laughed, pointing out Gerolamo to his companions; the big German shook his head, expressing some bitterness, some not-entirely-clear compassion, and spoke in his own tongue to his compatriot, so as to keep him quiet, since the latter was always on the point of making some brutal joke. Then the trio would depart with a cautious tread, leaving Andrea with the sleeping man. Andrea was incapable of abandoning him, ever since he had seen him awaken alone in the shadow of a door where, feeling deeply humiliated, he had burst into tears.

"But what are you doing? What's happening to you? Don't you see that I'm here?"

"You... you... where are you? My dear, dear boy." Gerolamo had clasped and embraced him with the frenzy of a dog that has found its missing master. "Forgive me. I'm acting this way because you're a good person." He had dragged him along with him, asking: "Who said that the innkeeper's wine is too strong? Don't you remember? Whoever said so was right. You see? It's done me harm. I felt lost." He had insisted upon blaming his disorientation on the powerful wine. As they made their way down the street, he had told –

as though freed from a nightmare – of a garden from back when he was a child. He used to go down into it in his underpants in order to boast, with his well-fed appearance, of the way his parents used to stuff him with food: they thought it necessary if he was to grow up sturdy.

"That was a different period, my dear boy. Back then, fat was a sign of health. Don't ring; I've got the key. Good night, and thanks once again for your kindness."

The memory of that painful awakening was strong in Andrea; and now, as he thought of abandoning Gerolamo on the bench in the sunshine, he felt indecisive, bound by that "you're a good person" which spoke straight to his weakness: his claim to be more human than everyone else.

He smiled in resignation and lit the second cigarette, the one intended for his companion. In reality, Gerolamo's sleep and his immobility were beginning to trouble him in the empty garden; everything was so tender and new with springtime, suspended in the wind, that it seemed to him that they had come there by flying, rather than along the flat, dusty city streets.

The spray from the fountain, bent into a capricious rain by the breeze that relentlessly played with the feeble stream, marked the direction of the sky, which sailed along amidst waves of air and the reflections of clouds. The wings of the bronze swan in the same fountain were covered with a coat of moss; but from their edges, and in the open beak from which the water flowed forth into the light, golden gleams shone forth; at times they were dazzling, as in something that palpitates and floats on the water.

Andrea stood up. He felt like walking.

The balloon vendor, wandering about the basin, came up to him against the white gravel. The wind lifted the balloons as high as the strings would let them go, caused them to collide, and mixed the colors over the head of the man, who came to a halt as though struggling to remain with his feet on the ground.

Andrea thought of speaking to him in order to console him for his having waited in vain. This man had deprived himself of cigarettes for Andrea's sake: he had pulled them, skinny and crumpled, from his pocket, reluctantly yielding them in order to be of assistance, rather than for profit. But perhaps the reward he deserved was the purchase of some of his aerial merchandise, to be tied to the buttons of Gerolamo's jacket, so as to keep him better balanced.

The man abruptly changed direction and vanished down a pathway where the wind was less threatening to his crown. When he got to the balustrade, Andrea stopped short. He was waiting for Gerolamo to sense the void next to him on the bench, for him to wake up, feeling the absence of protective warmth next to him; but he didn't hear the alarmed and emotional voice of his companion. He bent over to look for goldfish in the water. He saw none against the somber background. They were farther off, at the borders of the tangle of water lilies where the spray, falling back into the pool, made joyous flashes as it fell into the darkness before returning calmly into play.

It seemed to him that a long time had gone by in this manner; he turned to observe Gerolamo, who was still immobile in sleep, and at the curve of the avenue he saw the approach of the woman who had earlier been hiding behind the tree-trunk: a middle-aged woman with a pallid face and eyes made red by weeping. Seeing Andrea's gaze, she halted as though intimidated.

Her threadbare hat and faded clothes led him to think that she must be one of those begging ladies with a weepy and lugubrious voice; he sought in his pocket for a coin that might shorten their encounter and compensate her for her painful boldness. Standing still, she summoned him with a gesture. Andrea looked behind him to avoid any error. There was no doubt about it: the woman had meant that gesture for him, and now she was waiting. Slowly, resigned to both her poverty and her impudence, he drew near her. It seemed to him that he had already seen her, but he couldn't remember when or where.

The woman was trembling a little; her tight mouth seemed ready to give vent to some sort of rage.

"Do you know me?" she asked aggressively. "I'm his wife," she added, pointing to Gerolamo, "and I need to speak with you for a moment."

"It's my pleasure," Andrea said, removing his hat. "Tell me everything."

"First come over this way a bit more, please. Do you understand why?" She smiled bitterly, inviting him to join in her subterfuge. He followed her beyond the curve in the avenue, to where Gerolamo – should he awaken – would be unable to see them.

"Tell me everything," Andrea repeated, with a sense of painful embarrassment. He felt the hostility of her stinging gaze, and guessed at a rancor that could not be healed by any explanations.

"You are the painter, my husband's dear friend, if I am not mistaken."

Her voice was low and a bit hoarse from emotion. He assented, and she remained silent, as though gathering up her forces for some mighty invective.

"Oh! You mustn't think that I watch over you, that I follow you in the street. I spotted you by chance as I passed by; and since he was sleeping, I decided that it was a good moment to speak with you face to face."

"I wasn't thinking anything of the kind," protested Andrea in a firm voice.

"So much the better, but now, pay close attention. Does it strike you as right to ruin the life of a man so much older than yourself? Yes, let me say it, because it's you – yes, you – who took him away from me in order to ruin him completely."

"I don't see... Signora..." Andrea began, feeling an irritation that got the better of his pity.

"It's the truth, the truth. Ever since he met you, Gerolamo no longer wants to live with me and with his daughter. He pays no more attention to his business. He no longer adapts himself to us; he says that he has finally found someone who understands him, because you let him sleep when he wants to and you amuse yourself by letting him drink. Is this what your friendship is about? Don't say it isn't so; I know what I'm saying. Does it seem right to you for a father and husband to leave his family to pass the whole day with young people? What good do you think can come of it? Gambling, drinking, doing filthy things..."

She had grown vehement; in her yellowish face, the reddened eyes were mean and hurtful.

Andrea managed to keep his self-control, pained by the bit of truth that he recognized in the accusations.

"Believe me, Signora, neither I nor my friends would ever wish to lead astray a man who might be our father. To the contrary, I have tried to check his excesses, but I don't care whether you believe me or not. Anyway, I can make you happy right now, and say goodbye to Gerolamo forever."

The woman seized his arm in order to hold him back.

"No, not that," she begged him, looking about her with frightened eyes. "I asked to speak with you confidentially, not in front of him. What a good friend you are to this unfortunate man! You're ready to ditch him right away. For you, he's just a drinking companion."

"You're wrong, Signora, I care a great deal for Gerolamo. It's just that I don't want to get involved in issues that don't concern me."

Disoriented and powerless, she bit her own hand.

"Is it true that you're supposed to set off together on

a journey?" she asked, shutting her eyes as though faced with something monstrous.

"We've talked about it, but nothing's been decided. Perhaps we'll never set off," he added, more for himself than for her.

"That would be a good thing," screamed the woman. "You think you know Gerolamo through and through; you think you know all about him, because you always see him cheerful and smiling. If you only knew... if you only knew... You, too, will get to know him better, and then you'll be the first to bring him back home to me, you, his dear friend; but then I won't open the door, not even if he needs me in order to torture me as he always does. You've taken him away from me, and you're going to keep him. I'm tired of suffering. I'm going away with my daughter... but you'll see... you'll see..."

She made a threatening gesture to lend weight to her words; rolled her eyes, reddened by weeping, in order to show an inner strength that surpassed that of her fragile body; and left, jumping as though a painful twinge in her back were interrupting every step she took.

Andrea did not try to call her back or to catch up with her. He felt weary and humiliated by the weight of a situation that had come into being without his knowing anything about it.

"Am I supposed to do something?" he asked himself angrily. "I'm going to abandon Gerolamo forever, so that this witch will understand that she has no right to take out her rage as a neglected, perhaps hated, wife on me."

But, given his desire to find out the truth, it immediately struck him as a better idea to ask Gerolamo himself for an explanation of those obscure threats and prophecies.

"You don't know him yet," she had said. "You'll see... you'll see..." In a state of torment, he asked himself, "What's hidden beneath all this?" Now he was held back by the suspicion that the tale of the woman's attempt would make

Gerolamo furious with him – a fury unknown to his friends, yet terrible, if his wife had shown herself so fearful of being discovered.

After this thought occurred to him, he felt the need to see his companion once again, to confront him with what he knew about him, to hear his somewhat frail voice, with its harsh inflections, which had surprised him during their first encounters.

With cautious steps, he headed back to the bench. While he examined the huddled body of the sleeper, it struck him as possible that those short, stubby arms were capable of delivering hard blows against the two women who waited at home for the artists' ever-smiling friend.

Andrea remembered certain smiles of Gerolamo's while speaking of his wife and certain phrases that seemed to portray her as an inoffensive creature, one who had been rendered innocuous. The more he thought about it, the more the image of a secret, atrocious brutality instead attached itself insidiously to the older man's physical appearance. In order to distract himself from such ideas, Andrea recalled instances in which Gerolamo had displayed kindliness of soul and innate good nature. There were many cases in point, but they were all restricted to the narrow area of aesthetic enjoyment, and Gerolamo's dealings with his artist friends hardly constituted an absolute proof. If the sleeping man's life seemed devoid of any known infamous deeds, it was also too profoundly desperate for there not to be something obscure and ambiguous lurking at the bottom of it all.

The artist had stopped a few steps from the bench in order to take a hard look at Gerolamo.

He saw his back, as round as a sack, contained within the threadbare, shiny fabric; the backwards-leaning neck, reddened by the congestion of the blood vessels; beneath the hat, the ears, small in comparison with the cheeks; the beautiful hands, trembling slightly as they rested upon the knees.

This man was so alone and defenseless, trusting in the world as he slept out of doors with no fear that the gaze of others might fall upon his ugliness, that Andrea mourned his own inability to consider him gentle and sweet, like one of those old men whom one sees being led by a child to the bench where they are going to take their rest.

Two nasty creases and an opaque veil over the eye were enough to render Gerolamo's fat face atrocious. Now the sun, beneath the shadow cast by the hat, lit up his half-open mouth in which, as he breathed, there swelled up like a bubble a little web of saliva: it was the monstrous mouth of a murderer.

With a sudden, brutal gesture, Andrea awoke his companion: he wanted to free himself from an anguish of repugnance.

"What's the matter? What's the matter?" Gerolamo whimpered, frightened and dulled with sleep.

"I'm tired of watching you sleep," said Andrea, without succeeding in controlling his anger.

"Good God, calm down a bit. There's no reason you shouldn't be tired of it," Gerolamo conceded. "I'm ready to come along with you, wherever you like. I've enjoyed the sunshine." He stretched so enthusiastically that he almost lost his balance. Then somnolence overcame him anew and his head drooped forward. He was staring at the gravel at his feet, as though astonished to find it so near, or as though it seemed to him that it was in motion. He was awaiting a more complete awakening from his torpor, a clearer vision of things, and he sighed continuously, as though breathing through a bellows.

"My cigarette?" he asked.

Andrea didn't reply.

"Ah! You've smoked it yourself, you wretch. Good for you!" He laughed – a high-pitched, childish sound. "Let's get going, I'm ready; it's just that my feet are still asleep."

Andrea had already moved away. This was perhaps the moment to leave him there and never see him again as a friend; it would appear to be one of those contemptuous whims which are too cruelly offensive for the victim ever to ask for an explanation. But Gerolamo, as though sensing danger, leapt to his feet and joined him.

"Is it the effect of springtime, or are you feeling ill?" he asked affectionately, taking him by the arm. He looked into Andrea's face and eyes. Gerolamo's smile turned to a half-smile, a pained grimace meant to disguise the alarm that pervaded him. "Springtime, right..." he repeated, so as to prevent Andrea from speaking, and his grasp on the latter's arm was loose and cautious.

"Maybe that's it," admitted Andrea, without finding the courage to drive away a man whom he sensed he had wounded. "I don't feel like working, and I'm sorry to be wasting time in this way."

"Work!" exclaimed Gerolamo, in a tone that he did not succeed in making cheery. "But you already work too hard! You're always in that studio, brooding over your pictures. It's a good thing we've decided to go away. You'll see what kind of trip I'll take you on! When do you want to leave? I'm ready. This evening? Tomorrow morning?"

"I'm not coming," Andrea replied in a hard voice.

Gerolamo swallowed hard; then, as if afraid to seek a clownish way out, he held his companion back and forced him to show his angry, contemptuous face.

"We'll talk about it another time," said Gerolamo, lowering his gaze in discouragement. "Just now, you're in a bad humor, and I don't know why. If I didn't know you well, I'd be ashamed of the favors I've asked you for. He went on, shaking his head; perhaps he already regretted his proud answer.

"Don't say stupid things," Andrea responded. "I hope I have the right to feel any way I want to."

They walked in silence to a street corner where trams, headed for the center of the city, passed by.

"Farewell, I'm off to the studio," said Andrea; without waiting for a reply, he leapt onto a tram that was already in motion.

Standing on the sidewalk, Gerolamo gestured at him and called out something that Andrea could not hear. Through the window, the painter saw him staring disconsolately at the ground, humiliated; even though he was excited to be free at last, he felt remorse.

He entered his studio full of good intentions regarding a new way of life. He realized immediately that work called for a disinterested, calm attitude towards that which had just transpired, but instead, the big room seemed empty, and the unfinished canvases on the easels struck him as images of a happier and more selfish time. He realized that he was going to be unable to paint. If he distanced himself for a moment from the things around him, it was as though he had been touched on some painful bruise; he saw Gerolamo gesticulating on the sidewalk, and he thought of the words he might have spoken to him instead of fleeing.

In order to distract himself, he let more light into the studio and leafed through the illustrated catalogue of an auction of pictures. He looked for a sheet bearing notes regarding the number of hours of posing for which he would have to pay the model. He wanted someone – the model – to come calling now that the awkward sleeper had been banished; but at this late hour, such a visit was highly improbable. By an act of will, he sat down at his table to draw a landscape that he thought he remembered clearly. He crumpled up the first two sheets and threw them away. They were the products of effortful, mannered labor. Then he yielded to the image of Gerolamo and started to draw him asleep on the bench. The image went, crisp and very accurate, right onto the paper, and this cheered Andrea up: the thought that he, like other artists, did not fear, when motivated by high ambition, to prefer the work of art to human scruples of but little worth.

With a sort of cruel insistence, he did not fail to jot down Gerolamo's deformity, but when he tried to depict the ambiguous smile that illuminated the latter's sleep, he couldn't manage it: there was something ill in the figure of the solitary, defenseless sleeper. Drawing upon the artifices of his technique, he tried insistently to convey something roguish about the figure; and as he worked, there burst forth from him, word for word, the aggressive speech with which he should have explained to Gerolamo the need for a separation. He spoke the words out loud, in a voice broken by unhappiness; suddenly realizing that he was doing so, he felt ashamed and perplexed.

Looking at the sheet where he saw his companion so cruelly depicted in his heavy sleep, he was moved to pity, and understood that it had been an act of weakness to abandon him on the basis of suspicions that an obscure speech had aroused with the help of his own imagination.

"Spring makes me nervous," he told himself. "I want to see Gerolamo and speak with him."

He tossed the drawing into a drawer full of souvenirs that he never looked at and left the studio, which was rather gloomy in the evening, and too far removed from any sound save the hum of the electric wires that were hung from one roof to another.

Having calmed down, he reached the trattoria, where his friends must be waiting for him before beginning their game of cards. He longed for that scene, and he yearned to see Gerolamo once again in that atmosphere of safe masculine friendship, to watch him trying his sly tricks as a card-player, only to abandon them when sleep – almost like some moral scruple – overcame him. Andrea entered with a smiling face.

In the back room he found the two Germans and the shock-headed youth, but not Gerolamo. They were sitting at a bare table without playing, saddened by the older man's absence.

"Well? What's happened? Where's Gerolamo?"

"You're asking me?" Andrea burst forth angrily. "I'm not his nursemaid. I left him at three o'clock. I haven't seen him since."

The German said, "There are four of us: we can play. Gerolamo will turn up. Sometimes he goes off in pursuit of some deal or other."

Andrea sat down. "Let me eat something. Then I'll be right with you."

During the meal, the others watched him curiously. They seemed to suspect that he was keeping some secret. Every now and then they exchanged glances, disappointed that Andrea was saying nothing.

"The owner here saw Gerolamo pass by in the afternoon, rather distraught."

This bit of news, told him by the shock-headed youth, gave Andrea a start.

"There's no point in your adopting an air of mystery," he said defensively, but in a firm voice. "I don't know anything at all about Gerolamo.

"So shall we begin play?" proposed the German. "Gerolamo will turn up later." But Andrea wasn't listening. He was watching the door to see if Gerolamo would appear, fat, smiling, ready to mock his young friend with some joke about spring.

The shock-headed youth, who was shuffling the cards, showed them to the painter as a repetition of the invitation.

"No. Forgive me. This evening, I don't feel like staying shut up in here. See you tomorrow." He went out, annoyed at having yielded to an impulse that might reveal to the three others that something had really happened.

"Let them think whatever they want," he said to himself once he was out in the street. But he was worried, and would have shouted from joy had he encountered Gerolamo.

He wandered aimlessly for a while; then he returned to his studio, where he counted on his books to distract him. He had already been there for a while, and had attained a certain calm by reading, when he heard someone coming up the stairs, along that last stretch that led only to his studio. The length of time between one step and another led him to hope that it was indeed Gerolamo. He leapt up to open the door. "Is it you?" he asked in an anxious voice.

"Yes, Andrea. I've come to see whether you were ill. You were acting so strangely today. So how are you? Are you feeling any better, or aren't you?"

"We'll talk about it later. Come on in."

Gerolamo appeared from out of the darkness, bent and panting. "These stairs!" he murmured. "Let me rest for a moment."

Feeling compassion, Andrea was only able to make a gesture inviting him in; having climbed the last steps, Gerolamo entered the studio and threw himself down on the couch.

"Let's have a look at you," he said once he had gotten his breath back. "That's right, stand in the light."

"No, let it go," said Andrea, defensively. "I'm fine. It's just that I'm unhappy with myself. I would like to change my way of living: to live a healthier, happier life. That's all there is to it."

"That's just what I've been thinking, too, for a long time. What do you need in order to change? If you really intend to start right away, why don't you leave tomorrow with me? A little journey, just four days... We won't spend much..."

Andrea made a gesture of refusal.

"I mean to work a lot between now and the summer, and I need calm and solitude."

Alarmed by these words, Gerolamo bent his head forward.

"You don't even want to see me. I understand. I waste your time, I bore you. You want to be free, and I'm always here."

Andrea felt pity. "I wasn't referring to you. I was speaking in general. I feel that I should think more about my own life and work. The fact that you've come gives me nothing but pleasure."

"I looked for you everywhere," said Gerolamo, encouraged by these last words. "I spent a long time listening in the stairwell. I really thought you were ill. I'm glad to see it isn't so." He started to arise from the couch.

"No. Stay where you are. I'm really happy to see you. I've got nothing against you, don't you understand? Stay where you are. Take a rest. Would you like to smoke?"

"Yes, thanks."

Having lit his cigarette, Gerolamo remained silent; it was as though he were disoriented by something he couldn't understand.

"Do you often find me boring?" he suddenly asked.

"Don't make a big deal of these stupid questions," answered Andrea after a pause, trying to keep his face in the shadows.

Once again, there was a long silence.

"Maybe it's better if we don't set out tomorrow," Gerolamo said at last. "My wife is torturing me because I'm not looking after my business. Tomorrow I really mean to see the people I need to see. Everything will work out; if not, it's all the same to me."

"Maybe your wife is right," Andrea suggested insidiously. "Does she ever help you with your business?"

"Never. She doesn't understand anything about it. The only thing she knows how to do is to torture me. She's aging badly and taking it out on me. In her own way, she's jealous," he laughed.

In the meantime, he had lain down on the couch. From there, he gave slow answers to Andrea's further questions. Andrea was intent upon his investigtation.

"Yes, she's a good woman... She's known my defects for years, and she always reproves me for them, as though she had just discovered them. She's stubborn... Yes, you're right: she never wants me to see a soul. She's always afraid that people will do me harm... But let's let my wife be! It's true that I'm angry with her. But she played a trick on me..."

He fell silent, as if saddened or frightened by some thought; his cigarette went on burning by itself in his hand, while Andrea felt remorse at having pursued a mistaken course during his wild imaginings of that afternoon. He stood up to free his sleepy companion from his cigarette. "Go on," he said, laughing.

Gerolamo leaned back on the couch, but waved his hands, as is to keep himself awake or remind himself of something.

"Do you want to take a snooze?"

"Listen," said the other, heaving himself into a sitting position. "Let me sleep here tonight. Grant me this favor. My wife is out until tomorrow morning with my daughter. There's nobody home, and as you know, I'm afraid of sleeping alone. All right?"

Andrea took his time before answering.

"So where has your wife gone?"

"To the devil, I hope," yelled Gerolamo. "I mean," he added, calming down, "that I don't know. She's left home out of spite. We argued about my business. So can I stay here?"

"Certainly, you can stay here," agreed Andrea, thinking all the while about the woman's obscure threats.

"Early tomorrow morning, I'll wake you up and you'll leave."

"Fine – early tomorrow morning," murmured Gerolamo happily, bending down to unlace his shoes. Then he took off his trousers, unbuttoned his shirt collar, and removed his tie.

"I haven't got any sheets," Andrea warned him. "All I can give you is a blanket."

"Thanks. Don't worry about it." He gathered up the blanket Andrea tossed him, wrapped himself up in it, and lay down on the couch.

"How do you do it, always sleeping alone? Aren't you scared?"

"Scared of what?" asked Andrea, smiling.

"I don't know. Of being alone, of falling ill. Don't you ever wake up in the middle of the night?"

"Yes, sometimes."

"And how does it make you feel?"

"Not very well, if I don't succeed in falling back asleep. At any rate, it happens to me only very infrequently."

"To live alone... It takes a lot of courage... But one day or another, you'll get married..."

"Maybe," Andrea broke off. "Good night." He opened the door of an adjacent room where his bed was located.

"Leave the door open," Gerolamo begged him.

Having made up his mind to put up with Gerolamo's obscure fears, Andrea did not oppose this desire.

"But turn out the light," he added. "Otherwise I can't sleep."

Gerolamo turned out the light, and Andrea turned out his own once he was undressed and in bed.

"Are you sleeping?" he asked, hearing no movement.

"Not yet," replied Gerolamo. "I'm thinking how lucky you are to be unafraid. I can see that you don't suffer from nightmares. I dream every night that I'm dying in a different way, and I fight against my spider." As though these words had chilled him with terror, he let out a little scream.

Andrea waited for further words, but heard only the creaking of the couch and the somewhat strenuous breath of his guest, which gradually quieted down into the rhythm of calm sleep. This was his last clear memory prior to the confused horror that awakened him in the middle of the night. He dreamed that he was descending into the darkness of a cavern to help someone who was crying out, there at the bottom, amidst a resounding echo.

When he had regained consciousness, a cry — sometimes raucous, sometimes high and shrill — and the breathing of a throat choked by anguish were coming from the other room.

"Gerolamo is ill," he thought, trying to overcome his own alarm. He jumped out of bed and went to the threshold. By the feeble light that the reflection of a street lamp above a white wall cast in the studio through an open panel of the skylight, he glimpsed Gerolamo moving in agitated convulsions on the bed.

"Gerolamo," he called. "Are you ill? What's wrong?" There was no answer.

Hesitant, he remained at the threshold. "He's having bad dreams; he's talked to me about them," he said to himself. But he didn't dare approach the bed to wake him. It struck him as indiscreet to disturb a man who was prey to an unconscious terror. So he slammed the door loudly, and then reopened it, listening. It seemed to him that Gerolamo, his dream interrupted by the loud noise, was calming down, murmuring ever more quietly. He went back to bed and, beneath the covers, tried not to listen and to fall back asleep. But the incomprehensible, terrifying anguish besieging Gerolamo's bed reached his own; and now he, too, was waiting for something monstrous to befall him. He preferred to remove the covers and wait, listening. Now Gerolamo was gurgling ceaselessly, like a fountain; then he began to struggle silently; and from that struggle Andrea heard the blows, the sound of the springs of the couch, the rubbing of the blanket.

"Gerolamo," he called once again, unable to bear the other's silence. Gerolamo did not answer. He was writhing less, but panting harder. At last, in the frightful void of his nightmare, he let out a cry: "Go away! Go away! Go away!" This cry, high and white, sailed up into the infernal darkness. Then, once again, there was absolute silence. Gerolamo seemed to have disappeared, defeated in his desperate resistance.

Andrea hastily leapt out of bed and returned to the threshold. Yes, Gerolamo was still breathing; but he was panting, holding his breath, like a man oppressed by an immense, crushing weight. At last, against the darkness, there emerged in the vague light his legs entangled in the blanket; they fell back twice against the couch, accompanied by a long, feeble lament. Then there returned the horror of his  convulsed struggle with the imaginary monster.

"Watch it! Watch it! Watch it!" cried Gerolamo in a spasmodic crescendo. He panted, twisted about, sat up in bed and dropped back on the pillow.

Trembling, Andrea drew near him with caution, because he was afraid that the obsessed man would seize him in the darkness.

"Gerolamo," he begged. "Gerolamo, I'm here." But an invincible fear kept him from raising his voice. He pushed forward. Gerolamo's dark mass gave a lurch, as though he had become aware of a danger. One of his thick, stubby legs brushed against Andrea, who cautiously drew back.

By now Gerolamo was lying there, exhausted, and his lamentations were feeble, like those of a child.

"Now is the moment," decided Andrea, bending

down over the bed. Holding out his hands, he said, "It's me, it's me, Gerolamo."

He heard a great, strangled cry; he felt the man's body moving brusquely beneath his own. Then he received a very hard blow in the face, which made him yell out in pain.

He threw himself onto his companion in order to hold him down, and without realizing he was doing so, he struck him a hard series of blows in order to break the spell. The result was a blind, furious struggle. Andrea's terror matched that of Gerolamo, who was now caught between dream and reality. His strength as he writhed about was frightening; he was even weeping and begging for mercy.

"Leave me alone, you monster, leave me alone. Don't hurt me."

"But I'm Andrea," cried out the other, holding on to him as powerfully as he could.

At a certain point, Andrea found himself with his neck imprisoned in Gerolamo's armpit: the short, strong arm had an inexorable hold on his nape. His ears were buzzing. Out of an instinct for self-defense, he dug his fingernails into that tenacious flesh. The grip relaxed, allowing him to escape. He drew back, filled with disgust and horror. Escaping from the bed, Gerolamo rolled onto the floor with a dull thud. He stood up with a cry and rushed to the window. Seeking a way out, he ran and leapt about, a stocky, swollen shadow. The sounds filled the room, and the floorboards trembled and shook.

Andrea, who was near the light, finally found the courage to turn it on. As though struck by lightening, the other dropped to the ground, covering his eyes with his hands.

At first, Andrea could not speak a word. He saw that his hands were torn and covered with blood.

"Don't act crazy, Gerolamo. It's me."

Without removing his hands from his eyes, Gerolamo

whimpered, "I'm dying. I'm dying." With a sort of brutal strength infused into him by fear, Andrea forced him to stand up. Then he pushed him over to the couch.

"Look at me," he ordered, "and stop acting crazy. Hold still, but look at me."

Gerolamo didn't open his eyes, but he lay down and allowed the blanket to be drawn over him. Andrea sat at the far end of the couch. He felt a desperate need for forgiveness. He remembered Gerolamo's whimpering, and the swollen, elastic body at which he had struck so hard.

"Are you getting over it?" he asked. "Did I hurt you?"

Gerolamo opened an opaque, glassy eye and moaned something; but it was incomprehensible. With a fumbling, feeble hand he tried to undo his shirt. Andrea helped him to remove it. Thus were revealed his reddened chest and the arms bearing the marks of Andrea's fingernails, with some drops of coagulating blood.

Andrea could bear it no longer. He fled, washed his hands, and then remained sitting for a long time on his own bed, listening to the other's breath as it grew progressively calmer. At last, he heard Gerolamo calling him in a weak voice.

"What happened?" he asked. "What have we done?"

Andrea ran in and found him calm; his eyes had regained their transparency.

"It's all my fault," said Andrea in a heartfelt tone. "I came in to awaken you and save you from your nightmare. You got frightened and hit me first. I had to defend myself. You seemed crazy."

Gerolamo once again covered his eyes in shame. "You saw, eh?" he murmured. "Just think, almost every night I have these terrible nightmare and think death is near. It's my wife who protects me. She knows how to wake me up and speak to me until I get my mind off it and fall quietly asleep. She was right, today: I can't leave her and go off with somebody else. She managed things so that I gave it a try. Forgive me. I've caused you a lot of disturbance," he ended, almost weeping. "I was struggling with an enormous spider."

"Don't think about it any more. Tell me what I can do for you."

"Thank you. Don't leave me alone. I would like to get some sleep." He smiled gratefully at his friend.

Andrea sat at the far end of the couch, wrapped in a cloak; Gerolamo turned out the light. In the darkness, they spoke no more. Every now and then, beneath the blanket, a foot touched Andrea's body; then this, too, ceased. Gerolamo was asleep.

It seemed to Andrea that he owed it to him to watch over him patiently, after all the doubts of the day and the revelation of the night. If he heard a movement, a creaking of the springs, he grew desperate, fearing that Gerolamo's sleep would once again be disturbed by this sinister phantoms that his friend wished to keep at bay.

Little by little, the dawn light grew brighter in the studio, revealing the sleeping man to the scrutiny of his guardian.

Gerolamo had one hand outside the blanket, and it was trembling slightly, as if his sleep led to vertigo. When his chest swelled up as he breathed in, his mouth hinted at a smile; as he breathed out, he lost his happy expression and seemed, instead, to be suffering. It was as though he were sleeping on a window sill, and an unconscious force were warning him of the painful, constant danger.

When the dawn light had grown more intense, Gerolamo displayed the signs of an overwhelming and sickly fatigue; his fat face appeared livid where his cheek rested against the pillow.

Tired and chilled, Andrea felt his own powerlessness to help him; he thought that, in the final analysis, it was not up to him to challenge the jealousy of a wife who believed herself necessary to Gerolamo's care and comfort. Nonetheless, in order to continue the task he had begun with his vigil, he went cautiously into a little room where he had a stove for boiling coffee and warming milk.

The whole time, he kept looking into the studio, which was ever brighter and more filled with light. He felt a strong desire to see the sleeping man there no longer – to banish, along with his presence, the sense of nightmare that hung in the air, poisoning it. In order to increase the brightness, he opened the highest panel of the big window. There were already some pinkish reflections in the white morning sky.

Turning toward the couch, he saw Gerolamo looking at him in confusion.

"Let's drink our coffee," he said. "I've also got some milk, if you want it. But stay where you are. I'll bring it to you."

"Thanks, my dear fellow." With Andrea's help, Gerolamo drank first the coffee, then the hot milk.

His pallor had disappeared; but, above the blanket, every one of his gestures was feeble, as though he had reached the limits of his strength.

"Do you think your wife will be at home by now?" Andrea asked.

"Perhaps," admitted the other, with a voice suffused with pain. "She had threatened to leave me on my own, but she must have gone home afterwards. Today is going to be a nice day: look outside," he added, trying to change the subject.

"Yes, I've already noticed; soon it will be time for us to get going."

"Let's go," repeated Gerolamo, timorously trying to meet his friend's gaze. Reading nothing in Andrea's calm expression, he went on: "My wife will be worried," throwing his legs down onto the floor. Having put on his trousers and shoes, he stopped, as though he were too tired. Andrea caught him in this pose, but Gerolamo kept on looking at him, as though he wanted to ask him something about the night but didn't dare to do so. At last he said: "Once again, forgive me. I'll swear to my wife that I gave myself these scratches. She would never forgive you." He laughed, passing a finger bathed in saliva over his wounds.

This gesture provoked in Andrea a great desire to push Gerolamo out of the studio. With rather brusque gestures, he helped him into his shirt.

"And now finish dressing on your own; I'm going in there to get dressed myself."

"Go right ahead," was the reply, accompanied by the creaking of the couch on which the other was sitting as he waited.

Andrea was in his room, and as he got dressed he thought: "I'll help him downstairs. At the far end of the piazza, near the fountain, there must be a cab. I'll awaken the coachman. During the ride, I'll say nothing to Gerolamo. When we get to his house, I'll ring the bell. I'm sure that that woman is at home and that she'll stick her head out. Perhaps, in front of him, she won't have the nerve to say anything to me, to rant and rage. I'll help Gerolamo climb the stairs. She'll be on the landing, rumpled and half-dressed, and maybe her daughter will be there are well. I won't say a word, and I'll let her point at me in triumph. Gerolamo will enter his home with his head bowed. I'll go down the stairs without turning back, even if the woman yells something after me. I'm too young to be the guardian angel of a man who does battle every night with the angel of death."

He shivered at the memory, lifting his eyes to take in his studio, filled with clear morning light. Gerolamo was lying on the couch. There was a glimmer of early-morning sunshine on his face, and he was sleeping – healed and crafty – in the protective light of day.

# The Sick Hotelkeeper

I am the owner of a big hotel in the mountains which I bought and rebuilt all by myself, with my own money.

My hotel – as I can state here – has the best location in the valley, and the view from its windows and terraces is enchanting, whether in summer or winter.

At one time I also ran the firm, with help from my son, a secretary, and a good concierge. So I got to know the clientele personally and, in a certain sense, to cultivate friendships.

Unfortunately, for over a year now I've had constant health problems, and so I'm rarely to be seen conversing with our most prestigious guests. Should this chance to occur, however, I still speak of the investment of capital, of age-related illnesses, and of how, heedless of expense, I am improving the bathrooms and the furnishings of the rooms. When we get to this last topic, my important guests insist on the same flattering comparisons: they only stay at luxury hotels like my own, and they want me to take note of the fact.

I should tell you that the hotel stays open all year round, except for a short period in the autumn when we straighten it up from top to bottom. This means that I have to consider it my true home which, in a word, consists of four rooms on the ground floor, in a section devoted to service facilities and to private use. I enter from a little inner courtyard and not through the door, now bolted shut, that – corresponding with the office – would otherwise let in the constant hum of noise from the entry hall.

For myself and my family, whenever they grow nostalgic for the old table at which we all used to share our meals, there's a small kitchen where the chef's most skilful assistant prepares my food the way I like it: intensely flavorful and rustic. But, more often, he makes the light soups that the doctor recommends for my diet.

As for my son, I see him in the course of the day, if I wait for him in the office. He doesn't care for these little rooms, in which I have tried to maintain the intimacy of family life; he's always in the hotel, supervising, collecting money, and courting every woman whom he thinks might accept him. My wife, who has given up being so jealous since I fell ill and who feels very young by comparison with me, seeks her companionship among the guests and comes to bed late, after playing cards. She's so passionate about gambling that she no longer pays any attention to me, the most solitary guest in the hotel.

In the morning, while I'm shaving and getting dressed, I catch her spying on me from the bed to in order to make sure that I perform these tasks properly, and that I won't show up in public dirty or slovenly. But I've been accustomed to ironing and polishing myself up for too many years now to neglect the tiniest detail, even if my hands tremble a bit and my eye, staring into the mirror, quickly grows tired.

Contrary to popular belief, I'm not rich. The hotel is all I have. Restorations, improvements, the extension of a wing, the swimming pool – little by little, all this has eaten up the money I had set aside. My son, who really does intend to become wealthy, has become greedy through thinking about it all.

"Let them pay, if they want to enjoy these luxuries! Do they think that none of it costs anything?"

Now, I must admit it: few hotels are as handsome as mine. The year I built the big terrace, I had to go into debt, but I was the first to have – following models already common abroad – an outdoor space where we could serve coffee with milk in the morning and tea in the afternoon beneath big, colorful umbrellas.

Insofar as the service goes, I am convinced that my guests, except for a few old-fashioned members of the upper class, do not enjoy such choice food at home, nor such excellent bed linen, dishes, and silverware. I am pleased to add that our clients are faithful to us, even though the greater part is made up of individuals and families of various nationalities. Our secretary, who has been in half the world's countries and who speaks five languages – none of them from the heart! – tells me every now and then that here he feels like a passenger on an ocean liner; and he smiles at me, this husky blond mountain-climber, with a self-satisfied air, unaware that I would happily go back to live where I was born, far from the mountains and the foreigners, and far, too, from the sound of the little orchestra that, without my being able to do anything about it, drifts into my room, where I am right now.

Perhaps, rebuilding a couple of walls with costly new materials, I could succeed in insulating myself in total silence, but this is an expense that my son keeps putting off. The music hardly bothers him at all. When there's dancing in the hotel, he never fails to go down into the ballroom, dressed better than many of my guests, in order to offer his gallant services to some lady about whom he is very well informed.

It's a shame that, between work and amusement, he can't find a little time to devote to me! By now he thinks of me as an elderly partner who has run out of ideas, and he feels that decisions should be made behind my back.

Having grown up among so many servants as would make a nabob jealous, he's rather tyrannical: he almost never forgives a failing, and he fires and replaces people as resolutely as a general. His victims used to come to me to protest and entreat; nowadays, they don't even stick their heads in. It must be very clear, even to newly hired employees, that I've been dethroned, and that I'm so abased and weary that, in order to avoid family arguments, I prefer to remain shut up in my four rooms.

As a matter of fact, it's been a while since I stopped making my usual boss's visits to the upper stories of the hotel, even though I've got two elevators that could take me there. My son takes care of it: he even carries out his inspections at night, as I have found out from the conversations among the personnel in the courtyard, who think that I'm asleep behind my windows. In reality, I sleep very little, and I've got too much experience of sounds and noises not to understand, from one moment to the next, what's going on around me.

I sleep very little, as I've said, but in the last few months I've given up wandering mysteriously about the house while my wife is up late playing cards. Under the weight of the years, and even more on account of my bad health, I'm forgetting about the sexual instinct; and my last accomplice in fleshly delights remembers me as a poor devil who was so afraid of everything that I wasn't even capable of defending her against a treacherous accusation.

Sick as I am, I feel neither restraint nor shame about declaring my sin and my physical and moral failings. I have the relaxed attitude of one who is used to showing himself naked to doctors, and besides, I maintain that full confession earns one a little indulgence. Anyway, here's the story.

A beautiful girl from Lombardy, chosen by the chief of the service staff, did a brief stint as chambermaid in our private apartment. She attracted me right away. She didn't sing or laugh more than the others; but, new to the mechanical discipline that we required of our domestics, she had the gift of moving about with the liveliness and sureness of a woman in her own home. When she turned over blankets and mattresses with careless energy, without those hasty and calculated gestures that I always see around me, I forgot about the hotel and enjoyed miraculously resuscitated images from my adolescence: my good-looking cousins, intent on making the beds, the neighbor's young wife kneading dough, the washerwomen beating and wringing out garments on the rocks by the river.

In her attentiveness to me, there was a good deal of timidity and, at the same time, something benign and protective, as though I were a willful child who, unfortunately, had to be excused because of the poor state he was in. On account of these enchantments, so rare in my den, and because of my desire, which grew sharper from day to day, for the whiteness and warmth of her body, in the end I gave up on my good intentions and on the austerity of a man who means to be wise. Given my sedentary existence (I hardly ever left my rooms) and Giovanna's shyness (she was afraid to say no to the owner of such an imposing joint), it took just two weeks of blandishments for me to make her my lover.

This relationship, born, on my side, in a vulgar and almost tyrannical way, subsequently became a source of sweetness for me and, I have reason to believe, also for Giovanna, who, having begun on her first hotel job, found herself uncomfortable among the bellhops and her too-knowing and experienced coworkers.

Today, I feel remorse at having obliged her, out of certain scruples arising from prudence and, at bottom, from meanness, to reply to my intimate *tu* form with the respectful *lei* form of address, except at certain moments of special intimacy. What does it matter if my friendship allowed her to avoid the heaviest tasks and to make some extra deposits to her savings account? How could she have failed to accept gifts that came from the boss – she not being free to see me in any other way? If I think back on my selfishness, having lost her strikes me as a well-deserved punishment.

In order to go to her in the basement room – far from other people – that I had succeeded in having assigned to her, I had to descend a narrow staircase and pass through the kitchens. I never turned on a light: I was helped in finding my way among the tables and still-warm stoves by the gleam of a few lamps out in the piazza. Sometimes the cooking odors were so powerful that I felt faint and clutched hold of a still-hot pipe or a chair left out in the middle of the floor. In the course of that journey, my handsome, enormous kitchens were filled with traps and fears. At last, at the end of a corridor beyond the icebox, I saw a little light coming from beneath a barely open door; and, thanks to this sign that I was awaited, my breathing lost the anxious rhythm it had taken on in the darkness. As soon as I rapped two warning blows on the wall, Giovanna would look out to greet me with a joyous gesture and then would draw back, as though seized by shame.

Her room was small, but with a good double bed and pieces of cloth hanging from the walls to hide the peeling and the damp patches that awakened my rheumatism. I spent many lovely hours in that room; especially towards the end when, having achieved with Giovanna that true, trusting intimacy which is so rare between lovers, I went to her – even after it was all over – out of a need for company. She understood me. She was the first person who, upon discovering my heavy drinking, found a gentle and touching manner of pointing out that it was ruining my health. I even remember weeping as I told her of certain dire prophecies of the doctor in which, with the sun and the mountains limpid before me, I had found it impossible to believe. Touched by her warmth, I felt, at the idea of dying and disappearing, shivers of tenderness towards myself such as I had never experienced since childhood.

The way back from her room to mine was riskier, given the suspicious time of night and the absence of any other noises which might cover my rather heavy and dragging footsteps.

Someone must have seen me: perhaps my own son, ever awake and alert – because, at a certain point, I became aware that he knew about Giovanna. He was furious, even though he remained silent. I, his father, the great hotelkeeper, had become the lover of a humble chambermaid! What an offense against his concepts of his own superior authority, of iron discipline – and of social distances, which I was fundamentally endangering!

Having endured this revelation, he maintained towards me a cold and distracted reserve that made me suffer and led me to fear, rightly, that he might take some sort of revenge against poor Giovanna. Filled with guilty thoughts and anxieties, I anticipated what was, indeed, eventually going to happen, but in the meantime, my son didn't take action. His awareness of our affair, which humiliated him even more than my bad habit of getting drunk alone in my bedroom, deprived him of his usual energy.

Sometimes, in the office, he would stare at me for a moment with the cold, light-blue eyes he had inherited from his mother, almost as if he were asking me to justify my wretched way of life. How could I have explained to him Giovanna's value, the sense of being reborn that I had when I was with her? Was I supposed to accuse my wife, the mother he adored? And of what wrongs, even if it wouldn't have been base to shield myself by revealing the secrets of our conjugal intimacy? No: ours was one of those cases in which the bond between father and son prevents understanding and reciprocal consolation.

It was winter, I remember, and I knew that he was in love with a very beautiful blonde who had been staying at the hotel for quite a while – without paying, I believe. She used to go out early in the morning to make skiing excursions with our secretary, who is half-German, an expert mountain climber, and the darling of our guests, on account of his skill and his scientific way of giving lessons to novices and experienced mountaineers alike. A serious rival, he used to take advantage of the daily search (in the blonde's company) for snow suitable for advanced skiing exercises, while my son, eaten up with jealousy, calculated the damage that would be inflicted on our firm were he to fire the secretary on the spot.

On certain days, the meeting between the three of us, in the restricted space of the office, turned into a scene worthy of the stage. Nervous and ill-tempered, my son would discover deficiencies and disorder in more than one account book; the other man, ever courteous and obsequious, would win him over with the weapon of reason, showing him that the accounts balanced even where there had been fortuitous errors; while I, thinking about Giovanna, felt myself a youthful third party, the most fortunate of the three, because I had a love. I had to hold myself back from confiding in the other two in a good-natured and lofty attempt to make peace, the kind of impulse one feels at happy moments when everything seems easy.

But as soon as the secretary had stepped out the door, the risk of a hostile speech from my son struck me as intolerable, and so, without delay, I fled to put in an appearance at the bar, which was full of cheerful young people.

As soon as I arrived, the bartender would prepare my usual cocktail beneath the counter. I would gulp it in a hurry, make my adieux, smile to left and right; then, calmer and with a firmer step, I would return to the entry hall to interrogate the concierge about the most recent events in the hotel.

Later in the day, I would resume drinking in my room, where I have a cupboard full of various bottles and of glasses which, if I don't remember to wash them, remain dirty and caked with a film of old liqueurs. Once I'd stretched out on the bed, the alcohol would help me to provide the setting – a series of confused and enchanting landscapes–for a recurring fantasy: a seaside sojourn in the company of Giovanna who, dressed like a fine lady, was waited on assiduously by two servant girls.... Such were the generous rewards for her goodness that I invented when drunk.

Now that I've lost her, now that I know and feel that I'm ill beyond any remedy, drink has a sad way of setting me dreaming. I almost always see myself as a boy, many years before my marriage and the hotel, and if I close my eyes, I can feel once again my lightness as I ran downhill in the country, almost flying. This is lovely, but immediately afterwards, I am seized by a growing dizziness until, falling down from a measureless height, I find myself in bed once again, with the weight and body I have today. I try to make a deep impression in the mattress, which stops my fall; I grab hold of the pillow and no longer dare to make a move, for fear of my dizziness. Little by little, lost in the darkness which grows up all around me, I no longer remember where I am. It's a state of utter disorientation, and I would like it to last a long time. Instead, my sick mind transports me to an entrance hall, and I recognize it, even if it's different every time. I know that there's an exit, painted to blend into the wall. Groping my way, I seek it by touch; I open it, yielding to the temptation to go into the corridor that I see before me. Here and there are large mirrors, dim and greenish; but, still out of my terror of vertigo, I avoid seeing how they reflect my image from one to another. At a certain point, a strong cooking odor grabs me by the throat. One more step, and I'm in Giovanna's room; but she's not there, and I look for her behind a screen and behind the curtain that hides the storage space. I would like her real presence, not the nightmare of discovering that she's far away, entirely naked and with a sad face, in the mirror over her sink. I call her, raising my arms in a waiting gesture which the mirror repeats above a surface enormously close to me. Alarmed, I move away and stare fixedly from a position where I can't see my own reflection. The little figure doesn't move. I cry: "Giovanna! Giovanna!" in an anguished voice. There is no reply. Then her features, her form, and her color vanish, as though the mirror had been fogged over by a breath.

When I awaken from this dream, every movement costs me an immense effort. More than an hour goes by before I'm able to get out of bed, overcoming the aches and stabbing pains that torment my legs, my back, my stomach, my liver. Once out of bed, I drink some more liquor in order to regain my equilibrium and drive away the anguish of my awakening, an anguish that makes me want to weep at feeling myself so dirty, sick, and incapable of action. It takes two healthy doses to give me back even a moderate bit of strength. Then I wash myself, comb my few gray hairs, and go into the hotel to take a turn about the public rooms. But I'm careful: I don't stop to talk with anyone. I greet them and make my escape, because I'm afraid of saying incoherent things to strangers to whom I must display every sign of respect, which also means not making them sad.

This year, the "marquise" – a lady from a great family, but old and lamed by an accident – is not here, so I no longer have the person who welcomed and even provoked my indiscretions regarding my clients and myself. I realize that I used to take shelter under her restless and bossy little shadow, thus protecting my own shadow: that of a sick man who is always wandering about, alone and aimless.

The marquise used to come up here at the beginning of the season together with an elderly woman to was, so to speak, her cane, and she was the last to leave. "I'm going to come here to live," she used to say, escaping from the boredom she suffered for months on end while residing on her own lands; and "living," for her, meant passing her time in uncovering the intrigues of various couples and in seeking out the appearance of a vice or hidden flaw in those above suspicion.

Her extreme and malign desire to know everyone's worst side seemed to keep alive the fire in the too-black eyes in her waxen face, compensating her – in a room where there were other people – for the steps she was unable to take without assistance. Bad weather made her happy; limping from room to room on the arm of her companion, she managed to grasp hold of the threads of events that had occurred far away from her, of new relationships between individuals on whom she had already turned her aim.

When, seeking confirmation, she would reveal to me the results of her extraordinary penetration, I felt uncomfortable at tittering and pretending to be interested. It was as though she were obliging me to enter into a curiosity so morbid that it even exercised itself in a vacuum, with no precise goal, and yet, I resigned myself, almost out of friendship, to being interrogated and investigated. In all those years, I never had the courage to tell her to go to hell or to evade her insidious little questions by means of some pretext or other.

My son was likewise intimidated by her, and for this reason detested her so much that, the last year she was here, he would have insulted her by refusing her a room, had I not intervened in time. It was a superstition that lent me the energy to do combat with him; I felt that the marquise was as strongly connected with the hotel as I was myself, the owner of the place. Now that she's dead, I miss her presence, and think that she has preceded me by just a short while.

Poor marquise! She addressed everybody as "my son" or "my daughter," and she amused herself by letting it be understood that she knew things, thus revealing that touch of madness which, together with her age and the great name she bore, won for her the meek indulgence of her victims.

I myself had to put up with her; I fell victim to her on account of the final, ill-concealed chapter of my career as an aging lover.

I remember that Giovanna, who was then assigned, along with some other maids, to the ground-floor guests, often had cause to complain of the ever-more-indiscreet questions that the marquise asked her in a brusque and authoritarian manner. But, seeing that I abased myself and was unable to rid Giovanna of this embarrassment, from fear that any interference on my part in the assignment of tasks might put an end to the tacit truce granted me by my son, the girl wound up laughing it all off, giving vent, at the same time, to a certain instinctive revolt by telling me – while she herself lay there in all her splendid nudity – about the bony, yellow, contorted  body of the implacable investigator. Because she behaved with such restraint, it didn't even cross my mind that the poor naive creature – frightened by skilful speeches and by threats of a religious nature regarding the sins she was continually committing in the basement, where it was not for nothing that someone in the management had contrived to send her to sleep apart from her companions – as I was saying, it did not even occur to me that the poor girl might have reached the point of confessing our relationship to the marquise.

One evening, I was wandering through a maze of corridors, hoping to run into Giovanna, to whom I wanted to give a minuscule gold watch concealed in a box of sweets, so as to enjoy, later that night, the fruits of her gratitude. I was unpleasantly surprised by the sound of a series of dull, muffled blows behind my back. It was the marquise who, leaning on a radiator, was attracting my attention by pounding on the floor with her crutch. When we were close together, she looked at me with a sharp face lit up with malice.

"My son, my son, you're already too old for certain things, don't you think?"

She said nothing more, and I, stunned, was unable to utter a word. The marquise was laughing, holding out her arm to her companion who had just come out of her room, laden with shawls and capes; as if driven by her own hilarity, she limped along with a sort of ridiculous, triumphant lightness towards the lamp at the foot of the stairs.

"You sneaky spy, you old witch!" I was on the point of calling after her; but I managed to contain myself and to respect the client in her.

A few days later, I saw her taking tea by herself. She invited me to sit down at her table and immediately began speaking about Giovanna – such a good girl, and so capable of devotion.

"My son, you're very selfish, to say the least. It's time to get that girl settled. Don't you see? I can find her a good man who suits her well, where I come from."

"But I don't understand... I don't see..."

"Cut it out. It seems to me that the time has come for you – it comes for everybody – to repent of your sins, not to commit more of them."

I was upset, although I wasn't angry. I should have taken her advice, instead of waiting for my son to force my hand. I am well aware that this is a sad regret.

In reminiscing about the marquise, I had an intention which I've lost track of somewhere along the way. In a word, I wanted to state clearly that her presence kept the guests from noticing my own presence over-much. Now, I myself have become the strange and disturbing presence – the phantom – in the hotel.

They've even found a way of saying it to my face. I'm referring to an unpleasant day last summer. In the evening, I was sprawled in an armchair near a group of people who had seen me pass through the room without returning, and I was on the point of shutting my eyes and yielding to fatigue when I heard them talking about me. They were saying: "Old M."... and they meant me, since to the guests my son – they usually ignore our Christian names – is "young M."

"He's a more interesting character than you might

think," said a writer of around thirty years of age, thin and nervous, the very archetype of the restless client who books a room for a month and leaves after three days, because he can't stand staying still and hasn't found the adventure he was dreaming of.

"He's interesting? Tell us why," said a woman.

At this point, I cautiously tried to catch a glimpse of my judges' faces.

"I would call him the phantom of the hotel," replied the writer in a professorial tone. "He's not old, but he's tired and very ill. He drags himself out here among us, because he has no home, no refuge..."

I felt hatred for this presumptuous person who, besides offering a horrifying definition of me, was allowing himself to introduce me into some novel of his own without my consent: I was a model he had caught on the wing. Although every one of his words stung me, I kept on listening.

"However," interjected another lady, "I don't know what one could write about such a boring character. The poor thing must have very little to tell about."

At this point, the writer sprang to my defense, with a touch of irony meant for the imprudent woman who had dared to speak.

"Don't you see?" he said. "It's just that which interests us modern people: the problem of a man who's all alone, with a frightful lack of faith, with no real family, with no traditions to keep alive..."

"Certainly," added the first woman, "art is discovering new horizons precisely in a world which may, at first glance, strike us as flat and gray." She sent little smiles in the direction of the writer, considering herself, like him, far above her fellow guests, who struck her as anything but choice.

"At any rate," concluded the master, "it's relatively

easy to attribute to such a man certain elements that make his psychology more explicit. All it would take would be to put him face to face with a love affair, a failed ambition, a vice…"

I wanted to yell, so much did his words strike home. It was all too easy for the young gentleman, with his stock phrases, to guess at my life! I felt a hatred such as I had never felt before for this inventor of sad stories stolen from people who, like me, had no place to hide, and I stood up to leave.

The group only recognized me when I had already reached the door. Silent and fearful lest I had heard them, they exchanged glances and nudged one another with their elbows; and then the writer, whom I could see very well in a mirror in the other room, examined my back, my stiff legs, while the ladies observed him at work – or at least in his filthy pretense of working.

Anyway, I've never been able to forget the sense of that indiscreet chatter overheard last summer; and when my son succeeded in sending Giovanna away, accusing her of a theft committed in one of the rooms to which she was assigned, I felt like writing to the author to tell him, despite the deep resentment I felt towards him, that he should go ahead and make use of the circumstances of my life which he had guessed when he saw me in the hotel, on condition that he should also make public the infamous stratagem by which two defenseless people had been separated. But then my courage failed me, and I couldn't turn to a man whom I remembered – and whom I still remember – for the horrible sense of nakedness his words had provoked in me. At bottom, I was desperately seeking someone to defend Giovanna better than I had been able to do with my cries and spasms of solitary rebellion.

I wept along with her, explaining the reasons for which I did not dare oppose my son and begging her forgiveness, with my hands full of gifts: showy and futile counterpoises to the meanness of my soul.

The next morning, while the poor thing was leaving, I was in bed with chattering teeth, as though her departure had pierced the walls of my room, letting in a freezing wind.

Without Giovanna, without anyone to whom I can open up, I think of myself day and night, continually. I have finally arrived at the conviction and the illusion that I am an interesting person for the very same reason for which everyone around my den believes me to be a burned-out survivor. That's why I've picked up these pages and started writing: in order to give the lie, through the truth, to the false and disagreeable tale that the writer might eventually invent about me.

At the outset, I intended to set down a fine and orderly story of my life, to be printed at my expense and distributed to friends and customers along with the prospectus of the hotel. Afterwards, I gave up on that idea: first, because my son would never have forgiven me for such a serious error vis-à-vis our clients; and second, because I soon came to understand that I lacked both the energy and, I believe, the material for such an undertaking. In fact, I wouldn't be able to say anything about the many years I've passed here. I have the impression that I've only discovered myself since I've been ill, and that I see the things I touch with trembling hands, as though I had to carry their images with me over the threshold that I must cross before long.

So everything boils down to a few notes on recent times.

I occupy the most melancholy hours of the winter afternoons by writing these pages.

The little courtyard is full of soot – begrimed snow. Its still – white reflection lends an unusual, almost unreal brightness to my isolated rooms. The season reaches me by way of light and silence, but at least in here, it is as though I were within a fortress where the many water-pipes that pierce the walls maintain such a warm temperature that I can shed my clothes at my leisure.

My wife can't stand seeing me in my undershirt and underpants; she doesn't understand that, sick as I am, I feel more comfortable when wearing little clothing. I feel closer to the safety of the bed, where I lie down every now and then to wait for a pang to pass, while the hours go by slowly and the banks of snow in the courtyard grow black, as though all the soot from the machinery of my hotel had fallen on them.

I turn on a table lamp and pick up some letter paper to write to the nun who helped me last autumn when, after so many years, I fled from my hotel to shut myself up in rest home on the shore of a lake.

The nun already knows about my gratitude, but I still feel that I must apologize for the profanity and lack of decorum and modesty that I sometimes displayed in order to offend her.

I would like to write: "Dear Sister, I still haven't taken your advice and I never go to church. However, I'd be happy to go if I knew that I would find you kneeling at the altar like that morning when I negotiated my visit, on condition that you would greet me with a smile." But can I remind a nun of these things? What will they think of her, if the letter falls into the wrong hands? How hard it is to write to a nun with the proper respect! And yet, I'd like to tell her to come here to look after me with all her sweetness, and to give me those tranquilizing injections, with no more fear of my coarse sinner's provocations.

"I hope you've forgotten them, Sister. In any case, I ask your forgiveness."

It would be a sincere letter. Some nights I feel so much remorse and shame that I weep and wish that the nun — always calm and seraphic — would console me by saying that, after all, my sins are not important sins but, rather, just jokes in bad taste. Instead, my wife comes into the room and becomes sad at the sight of me, without uttering the single kind word I would expect from her.

And I would wind up this way: "I look forward to seeing you soon, dear Sister. Write to me and tell me whether you've had to quarrel in the kitchen in defense of some embittered, crude sick person like me."

Rereading the few sentences I've set down on paper, I realize that I can't manage to write to the nun in the style I judge appropriate to her. I'm too afraid of wronging her. So instead, I'll resume the thread of these notes, although it's an effort, since I don't know what scruple or hope is holding me back from speaking about what I feel in my solitude – a solitude from which I observe others' lives only because they serve as clocks for the prisoner.

All the courtyard windows are lighting up, from down at the bottom all the way up to the snowy, threatening sky. Tired skiers are coming back in time to wash up before dinner. Within the walls, all the pipes are singing of water rising and water running down. As soon as I turn off the lamp, as I frequently do in order to rest my eyes, a reddish light from the courtyard reveals, through the fogged windows, the heaps of snow, and if I open up a crack to refresh the dry, burnt air, I can smell a gelid stench that strikes at my very heart.

Over there, my wife is getting dressed. The winter is long for her, too. The hotel is full of young men and women who are rarely willing to make up her evening game of cards. She gets dressed, because she's always hoping that, by smiling enough, she'll succeed in finding the three companions she needs in order to entertain herself. She never decides to stay with me in order to comfort me and free me from the anguish that assails me in the dark. She says goodbye, tells me that she's ordered my light soups, and goes out to dine in the bright lights and confusion. This happens every evening.

As for my son, it's enough for him to have acknowledged me at some moment during the day. I would almost say that he's avoiding me; but as for me, there's something I've got to talk to him about. Oh, he needn't fear, the subject of Giovanna won't come up! What I've got to say to him is far more important even than my will. They tell me that he's started drinking, too. Twice already the waiters in the bar have had to carry him to bed in a pitiable state, as often happens to the other elegant young men by whose company he seems to feel so honored. I would like to implore him to stop in time, showing him how drink has ruined me; but I fear his cold and contemptuous gaze – or even worse, I'm afraid he may answer me with the same excuses I've always offered for myself. He wants to be the master of his own life, to use it badly, following my example, and once again, this is a situation where I have to look on powerlessly. Right at this very moment, up in the dining room, he'll be eating at the table of some adventuress whose expenses he is paying. He, too, likes to play his little games.

And meanwhile I'm here on my own, at the heart of this fortress which is insufficient to protect me from my fears. I'm the only one who's afraid of these mountains, to which I wasn't born and which I hate, which make me dizzy, which make my blood run cold with their precipices and with the chunks of rock that roll down their sides when the crumbing glaciers detach them from the unstable peaks. When fog invades them, the mountains look like gloomy shadows looming up in the mists, and I'm terrified that they'll collapse. To me, the scenery that others enjoy is a source of suffering, like this winter snow that goes on forever, like this roaring and gurgling that I hear all around me as the waters undermine the little patch of land on which the hotel stands. One day, the corroded stratum will slide along the rocks down into the valley, and we'll all be swept away.

To go on writing and to give myself courage, I've had to light a candle. We're in the midst of a snowstorm. The electricity has failed; the whole hotel keeps going by candle-light, and everything is strangely calm and silent, while out-side the very heavy snow swirls as though it wanted to fill up the entire valley and come up here to bury us. In the dark-ness, one can no longer tell where the mountains are, with their sheer drops and their avalanches. I tremble at the thought that we're right below the most unstable, rockiest peak in the whole chain, and that the snow is building up on its slopes and bringing it nearer; but at least I'm sure that, tonight, everyone here will be keeping me company in my fear of death.

The second obituary by Eugenio Montale published in
*Nazione:*


A Man and a City


I speak of the friend: there will always be time to
speak of the important writer he was.

Yesterday—rather, today, after midnight—I had just
left the office of my newspaper [*Corriere*] when I had to
return urgently in order to write the few lines about Loria
restrictions of time and space permitted. I wrote very little,
and some of what I did say was cut; but I wrote with a certain calm, because the unexpected news of Arturo's death
had about it something unreal. It was part of a dream from
which, sooner or later, I was going to awaken. This morning,
however, Gavazzeni [probably the musician and conductor]
rang me, and they brought me the *Corriere* containing my
few lines in the final edition; and so now I know that it's really true.

I live in an attic that gives me a beautiful view over
the roofs of Milan, but the space is so minimal that I can't
keep books or periodicals there. So tonight, as I wrote about
Arturo, I had neither his books nor any word about him. I
had only a date of birth—whether correct or not... I had
only my memory and the attenuated pain typical of fresh
bruises. (The worst will come later.) I say all this—that I live
overlooking a vast expanse of roofs—in order to explain
what a man like Loria represented for me, now that I have
left Florence. To me he represented not just the whole city,
but also the archetype of the stable man, as opposed to a man
unstable, rootless—myself. To me, Loria meant not just
Florence, but also the possibility that I might return to
Florence. I spent twenty years in Florence and loved the irre-
placeable city very much; but perhaps I might not have loved

it at all had there not existed men like Loria. For me, he was an indispensable corrective to everything I held alien to myself: the stereotype of the "Florentine eating beans," the old saying that "guests are like fish...", ceramics from Montelupo, contorted masks, cave restaurants in the style of *Sem Benelli*, all the arrogant trappings of "Florentineness." Although more gifted than his predecessor, Loria was for me what Piacci, in other times had been for others: a man in whom elegance and even, in certain instances, worldliness, the love of society, became a moral style, a rule of life which was also spiritual. A man such as Loria (and, some years ago, he was not the only man of his type in Florence) is not just the product of a city: he is also its curator and, in a certain sense, its creator. It may be an illusion; but when one returns to a city specifically to see a particular man once again, the man and the city become identified with each other, taking on a single face. I'll tell the truth: had I one day been able to lead a life, a supplementary life, *du côté de chez Swann*, I could only have done so with the help and guidance of a master: Loria. Now this illusion, too, is over and done with.